inVisible

Book 5
Crocodile Dreaming Series

Graham Wilson

BOOKS IN CROCODILE DREAMING SERIES

Prequel – Vengeance
Part 1 – Vertigo
Part 2 – Vortex

Crocodile Dreaming Series
Book 1 – Visitor
Book 2 – Victim
Book 3 – Void
Book 4 – Vanished
Book 5 – inVisible

Reader Reviews

Great Five Stars - Great end to an outstanding series. But don't begin here. Begin with the first book, 'Visitor' and see if you can guess where the story goes.

Highly recommend series; if you enjoy suspense novels or reading about Australia and especially both, you'll be glad you got hold of this.

Exceptional story. Just loved it. The sense of place and aboriginal culture is great too

You must read this series ….. the content is excellent

It's superb... So sorry to finish it!

I read this series one volume at a time, over the last two years. It's very entertaining, well-written and really makes you feel like you're there with the characters. I can't praise it highly enough!

What a good series, so many stories, so many lives, growing darker with a thread of hope

A compelling story, told with sincerity. It would make a good plot for a television mini-series!

I thoroughly enjoyed this combined series. It is a nicely composed, thrilling script with essentially a fairy tale goodness. With this book I had my virtual tour through Australia.

Contents

Author Note

This is a new, substantially revised version of book 5 of the Crocodile Dreaming Series, based on reader feedback and editorial review.

The ongoing writing and refining of this book series has been a labor of love, assisted by many people along the way. You are too many to name and some do not want to be named, but you know who you are. I thank you all. Telling this story has been a long journey, both for me as for the story. It is both satisfying and sad to be at the end.

For readers who have enjoyed the series, thus far, I appreciate the time you spent in reading. I have gained both pleasure and insight from those who told me of enjoyment through reviews and other means. I hope this final part lives up to your expectations. For those who have not found this book or series to their liking, and said so, I thank you for this too, both for your time to read and for your effort to let me know. In revising these books all this feedback, both good and bad, is valuable.

Particular thanks to my editor, Candra Hodge, and cover designer, Nada Backovic. You both did great work in your respective roles.

Thanks to many people from across Australia's Northern Territory. You, and its vast landscapes in their ever-changing hues, have given me the ideas which grew in my mind to become this story.

Special thanks to an unnamed English backpacker I met briefly in Cairns and who then came to the Northern Territory for a short stopover to see its remote places. She spent two days trav2elling with me in Kakadu and Arnhem Land, seeing places similar to those in these books.

None of the awful things of this story happened to her. However, for a brief period, she was a delightful travelling companion and her English mannerisms and joie de vie remain burnt brightly in my memory.

From this memory came the idea of the character at the centre of this story, Susan. She now lives on in the minds of thousands of readers, having gained her immortality through the medium of this book. It is likely her memory will continue long after we are all gone. But, without a real person to inspire the idea, she never would have been. So, to the real English visitor I say a profound thank you. I am in your debt for giving me a series of great memories as the foundation for this story.

Prologue

It was a small hour of the morning, its number around three or four. Her mind was sharply awake in an instant- but she did not know where her body was, except that it was in a bed and the bed was unfamiliar.

There was the sound of another human drawing breath, in and out, regular but not too loud. She moved her arms around to explore the bed space. There was another body lying not far away, the source of the breath sounds. It was a hard and angular shaped body, a body of elbows and bony protuberances. It must be a man. She had no idea of this man's name or face. She knew only that she was here and he was here too: sharing this time, space and place.

Who and where was she? Who was he? Her mind held no image of an identity: hers, his or any other. It held no image of any future or any past; she knew only that the present was an unfamiliar place.

At the farthest edge of her mind, she glimpsed a vision of another place. It was a desert landscape of late, bright sunlight reflecting off glowing hills. Within this fading light, sunlit shadows were dancing. These shadows were in part familiar and part unknown- as if she should know them, but still did not. Faint music came from where they were. It seemed the shadows called out to her. Yet she could discern no specific voices or words, only that they seemed to be calling to her to come and join them. The calling was with yearning and sadness, both mixed together into what became a bitter sweetness. She knew them not, yet their kinship reached into the very edges of her soul.

She willed a return to sleep so as not have to discover this present reality. She felt hope she would awake to a new morning reality in which memory and perspective were clear again. A reality in which knowing was returned.

Chapter 1 - Daybreak

It was early morning when she woke again. She knew where she was and her name was Jane- Jane Bennet. This was the name she was holding in her hand when she had first discovered herself some months ago, a person without a past. The name was on a baggage label written in crude marker pen writing. It was attached to the small overnight bag she had been grasping in her hand. The bag had held a dress, a pair of loose track pants and matching top, some underwear and a pair of light shoes. It also held an envelope filled with cash, Australian money, with a value of around seven hundred dollars. Her person had no other label on it anywhere. Her memory held no other identity and the name Jane seemed to fit. Jane rhymed with plain. She was plain Jane- an ordinary person. As such, she took the name and used it.

The first morning of her remembered life, she had awoken in a roadside shelter, lying on the bench seat. The shelter was built from four timber posts with corrugated iron on three sides and a roof. The fourth side was open to an empty dirt road which had seen no traffic since she awoke. It looked like a place built by a local farmer to shelter his children from sun and rain while waiting for a school bus to come. Its furniture was two planks of rough-hewn timber, bolted into a seat shape. The bench seat stood on four timber legs which rested directly on the bare, red dirt. This described her temporary home. It had been a place to sleep, but it was not a place to stay.

Somehow, she knew she was in outback Australia. It was not cold, so it was probably somewhere in the northern half. It was also not desert as she could see good-sized trees growing nearby her shelter. At the same time, though, the ground was dry and the grass was a dead brown color. This was as far as her knowledge and memory could take her, beyond having her own written name in her hand. It was a name she was determined to hold onto. It was the one thing that that had felt solid to her at that time.

She had looked at herself. There was no mirror around, so she could not see her face. What she could see was she had thin, pasty arms and legs- objects which had been long hidden from the sun. Her hands were soft and free of calluses, so they must have done little manual work of late. Her hair was shoulder length and, when she pulled to the front of her face, it appeared to have a dark brown or black color. It smelt unwashed, too. A loose-fitting smock, which looked like any other cheap dress, covered her body in a shapeless manner. It had a pale floral design and was otherwise indistinct. It gave her no clues. As she ran her eyes over her dress, she saw her belly protruded greatly out in front of the rest of her. She smoothed her hands over it. The realisation came suddenly: she was well and truly pregnant. Not only was she expecting a baby, but the baby was not far off from the look of her belly.

As she'd contemplated this new fact and what it signified, she'd heard a distant sound. A plume of dust was coming towards her slowly. It appeared to be a sedan car. As it came closer, she saw its occupants were an aboriginal woman driver and another similar passenger. She'd waved to the car. It pulled to an immediate stop.

These people showed little surprise in seeing her They gave her no greeting of recognition, but a casual welcome. It seemed this was a place where people came and went often. She was but one more to them.

They spoke to her in a broken English, "You want ride?"

She nodded. Then she held out her hand to both the passenger and driver, saying, "Hello, I am Jane."

The driver nodded, pointed to herself, and said, "Me, Rebecca. That one Suzie." They took her proffered hand in each of their own in turn. Suzie opened the back door and pushed a dog off the seat to give her a place to sit. After perhaps an hour, they came to a place where other black people lived. It had a shop, a petrol station and signs which indicated it also had a hospital and school nearby. The ladies let her off at the petrol station and waved goodbye to her before driving on through the town.

Now, she had to decide what to do. She did not feel lost, scared or as if she was running away from something. She just did not know how she came to be here. She had no memories of a life before today. She felt reluctant to tell anyone that she did not know why she was here or where she came from- it sounded too weird to talk that way in broad daylight.

She decided to open her bag to retrieve some money. She took out a twenty dollar note from inside it and walked into the petrol station checkout. She purchased a coke and a bag of crisps, then asked for directions to the toilet. In the bathroom, she washed her face and tidied herself up in front of the mirror. Sure enough, she had dark brown-black hair with a wavy, Mediterranean look. She could also see she had blue eyes in a bland, not unattractive, face. Her face did not trigger recognition in her memory. It was a face which could have belonged to a hundred people walking along any given city street. It was a plain Jane face.

She wondered if she'd actually been on her way here, after being offered a job. Maybe she'd just bumped her head during her trip and lost her memory. If that was the case, perhaps it would return in a day or two. She decided this was the most likely explanation for being in the middle of nowhere, on her own, while also having no clue as to who she was or why she was there. Perhaps, she should ask the man behind the counter at the petrol station about any jobs available in the town. She could, say she'd been told they were looking for someone to work in the community and had made her way here in the hope a job was available. She asked the attendant if he knew of any jobs around here.

He looked up at her, showing little surprise and stated, in a friendly tone, "Well, we're not looking for anyone here right now, but I hear tell the shop across the road is. They were expecting someone to come from the town the day before yesterday, to do bookwork and ordering, along with stacking shelves, but the lady never showed. Perhaps they got their days mixed up? It may be the job you heard about. Why don't you head over there and ask about it? The lady in charge's name is Matilda. Maybe she is expecting you."

She walked across the road carrying her overnight bag. An aboriginal lady was serving at the checkout. Jane asked her if she was Matilda. Instead of answering, she was directed to a small office at the side. An older aboriginal woman was sitting at a desk inside the office. She looked up at Jane with a smile as she came to the doorway, saying, "Hello?"

Jane introduced herself and said she understood they were looking for someone to work here. She'd heard the job included doing bookwork and ordering, along with other work, and she hoped they might give it to her.

Matilda explained how the local employment service in the main town had been seeking a bookkeeper-type person for her for a while now. The last one had fallen through unexpectedly, so the job was hers if she wanted it. It seemed straightforward. There was a detached building, a one-bedroom cottage, behind the shop. It went with the position. The salary was $40,000 for working five days a week as a shop assistant bookkeeper. She agreed and the job was hers.

"We'll sort out the paperwork later," Matilda said, adding, "I am glad to have engaged the services of Miss Jane Bennet." She was shown to a second desk in the office. This one had a computer on it. It was hers to use along with the contained set of files to maintain.

Matilda suggested Jane go to the cottage, have a shower, then go for a walk around the town to get familiar with her way around it. After lunch she could come back to be taken through their systems for an hour or two. She would begin her proper work tomorrow.

Matilda called out in an unfamiliar language to the checkout lady. This woman brought in a set of keys to the cottage which she handed to Jane.

Since that day, almost a year had passed. People called her by the name of Jane Bennet. She had found out she lived on a small aboriginal community in a place called Cape York in far north Queensland. She had two children now who were almost a year old. They had been delivered in the local hospital with a minimum of fuss. She had given them the official names of Anne and David Bennet, children of Jane Bennet, father unknown. She knew Anne and David were their right names, for some reason she couldn't explain. She had yet to choose middle names. She thought she should know what they were supposed to be but couldn't remember what these extra names were.

A year on, her new life was beginning to create its own memories and joys. She was planning a birthday party for her two babies in a month's time. It would be a time when her extended friends from the community would come and celebrate this landmark with her.

Only occasionally, like last night, did she wake up with fragments of another life somehow running through her mind and body- seeking release from the fog in her mind. But, as always, with the new day dawning, her current and simple reality returned.

It was a reality where hers was the only body in the bed, except at times when her children cuddled with her. It was a reality where she felt almost no curiosity about what had been before. It was a reality where, if someone had asked her if she was happy, she would have said, undoubtedly, yes. She could think of nothing else she wanted or of any other place she wanted to be.

Chapter 2- A Gulf Muster

Vic had spent a week mustering on Vanrook Station- a place way up towards Cape York on the eastern corner of Gulf of Carpentaria in North Queensland. It was a huge block; several adjoining stations were under the same management running to nearly ten million acres, with somewhere around a hundred thousand cattle. They'd had a few dry years, but last year had been wet. This had been good for the station. It was now putting together lots of export steers to go out of Karumba for the South-East Asian markets- Indonesia, mainly.

It was further east than he knew or had ever worked before, but beggars could not be choosers. Vic had a big loan to pay back for his new helicopter. Due to this, he grabbed at the offer of this block of work, ferrying across from Borroloola, after just having worked two days for the Macarthur River Mine where he had been paid to survey prospective new mineral sites alongside the NT border. Next week, he was booked to head south to work in the Barkly Tablelands. The week after, Buck booked him to work out west in the VRD.

This meant he had two solid weeks of mustering, after this, before he could take a week off to go up to Darwin. There he would meet with Anne and Alan to see how the investigations into Susan, and the other missing girls, were proceeding.

Three months before, Vic had flown in his helicopter to Darwin for a week, to be in the town for the memorial ceremony dedicated to the five Lost Girls. The memorial was located on a harbor headland looking out over Darwin. It was a peaceful place with a beautiful view, but he'd found the day of the ceremony to be absolutely gut-wrenching.

Five sets of parents and various friends crying over their lost girls, along with other families searching for missing sons and daughters, too. Everyone had their own story of loss. Every story told of devastation for those concerned. He felt for them all, pain piled on top of pain, although his heart really only had space for one missing person.

It was now nearly eighteen months since Susan had disappeared. He still felt a raw ache in his chest every time he thought of her. One day she was there with him and it was wonderful, the next day- gone. Just utterly and totally vanished! It felt like a huge piece had been torn from his heart.

In his wildest dreams, he could not imagine what had happened to her since the day when she had never come to the hospital. Vic remember first ringing Alan to ask him to go and check his flat for her. He had been thinking she would be fine, but he was just being extra safe since he hadn't heard from her since his surgery. But the flat had been empty. Her few things were still there, but not her. It was like the movie "Gone Girl."

Then, a month later, they had found the pair of flat shoes, borrowed from Anne, that Susan had been wearing when last seen. They were beside the Mary River billabong: a bare half mile from where Mark was eaten by that huge crocodile. Anne was sure, or at least as near as she could be to being sure, that these shoes were her own. If this was right, it could only mean one thing: Susan had gone back to the billabong where she killed Mark, a place which was full of lots of huge crocodiles.

After this discovery, other people said Susan had deliberately gone there to return to Mark. They thought her body, if any of it remained, was somewhere there in the billabong. Some thought she had swum out to meet him. Others believed she had been pulled off the bank by a vicious crocodile. But there had been no other trace found. No footprints, no scuff or drag marks- just two shoes in a plastic bag, lying in the dirt about ten meters from the water's edge. Some said they should shoot all the big local crocodiles and open them up, lest her body was inside. Others said they should search the bottom of the billabong in the same way they did to find bits of Mark. But, as the shoes were found more than a month after she vanished and there had been no other evidence of her at the billabong before or after the shoes were discovered, it seemed a pointless search and never happened.

Instead, Alan brought the old man, Charlie, to the billabong. He was the one who had first found Mark and now, more recently, found the sandals. Because of that Alan brought Charlie back to the place and asked him what he thought- whether he felt her body was here, too?

Charlie had sat by the water for a while. He'd sat there with Alan. Sandy, Anne, himself and some others, all watching on. After a few minutes, Charlie stood up and shook his head. "Maybe, maybe not. I be sure she not here now. No crocodile spirit here," was all he said. When they tried to question him further about what he meant, he just shook his head emphatically.

Vic did not know what to think. He felt kinship with this old man. A small part of him felt relief that Charlie could find no trace of her presence here. On the other hand, he felt unsure what was true. He was uncertain if Susan really returned there, despite the shoes, even though others seemed sure.

He knew she'd been messed up from all that happened to her. But, in his heart of hearts, he refused to believe she did give herself up to the crocodiles and to give up the hope that he might one day see her again.

Vic did not really know what love was supposed to feel like, but he had spent four nights holding her body next to his. The wonder of this memory was burnt into his brain. Now, there was just a great big empty hole in his heart. He had been with plenty of girls over the years- but it had never been like this. It was both her dependency on him and how her being had gone deep inside him: mind to mind and spirit to spirit. It had made him feel whole. It was as if, in the same way their bodies were joined together, so, too, were their souls. It was like they had become a fused person. He had loved her totally: her body, even filled with another man's children, her face with the laughing blue eyes and her smile that could charm angels.

Now, sometimes, he would dream of her: but she was fading. Each day it was getting harder to remember some details of his love. Because of this, he mostly worked non-stop. Often, Vic would have an extra beer of two to try to sleep and forget everything. When he got the chance, he would go to Darwin and meet with Sandy and Alan to see if there were any new leads or if there was anything else he could do to help them find her. He would not admit to her being dead. He had rescued her once- he would do it again. But, first, he had to find her, and he had no idea where to begin to look.

No one else had any ideas either. All they received were endless dead-end sightings. At first, all of them had felt hope when these sightings started to come in. Soon, however, they realized reports of people seeing a girl in her twenties with dark hair and an English accent, which were each reported immediately as a new 'maybe Susan' sighting, were never right. Too many people who looked vaguely like her were walking around the towns and cities of Australia. So, while these reports were not instantly dismissed, it was easier not to keep hoping through all these false alarms.

At the same time, if Susan was alive, she must be somewhere! Vic's mind refused to contemplate the alternative. Therefore, he must keep trying to find her. Because of this, he was looking forward to getting to Darwin- even though it was still over two weeks away. The idea of this trip gave him hope and that kept him going with all the hours and days of flying. He planned to finish here this afternoon and ferry home to Borroloola tomorrow. The day after that, he would be going down to Anthony Lagoon for a daylight start and the beginning of his week of Barkly work.

At this moment he was fuelling up and getting ready to leave Vanrook to fly onto Normanton for the night. As he was about to leave, a telephone call came in asking him to do a job further up the Cape tomorrow: nothing too big. It was an aboriginal station, out along the Staaten River somewhere. It had a few hundred cattle in a back paddock for him to put together and then bring to the yards for their yearly branding muster. There would be some steers, as well, to muster to be exported on a boat.

Vic was tempted to say no. If he took the job, he'd miss a day back home and have to ferry straight to Anthony from here. But it was hard to keep up with the bills for his new chopper when, most months, he spent a week in Darwin, continuing a hunt for Susan. He couldn't afford to lose the chopper. It was hard to get a loan for this machine when the insurance came up short from the crash in the Fitzmaurice. On top of that, flying this chopper was the one thing that kept him sane since Susan went missing.

For those few hours each day, when working his machine hard, he was too busy to think- living only on his reflexes. Then, and only then, it was like the bad stuff got pushed away and he could feel passion and joy return to his life again for a little while.

With this thought in mind Vic decided to take the extra day's work and money which went with it- although it meant a whole month when he never got to go home. There was nothing at his home for him, anyway. It was just a bush timber shanty at the edge of Borroloola with a view down to the river.

Vic accepted on the phone, booked the job and, as they did not seem in a great rush to get started, he told them he would ferry over first thing in the morning to be on-site, ready to start, at about eight o'clock. Perhaps he would make a stop over there tomorrow night. This way he could see what the community, a former mission, offered, before he did a long day of ferrying across the Gulf and across endless miles of black soil to Anthony Lagoon for the next day. The station manager, who had just booked him, told him they were having a barbeque tomorrow night. He promised the job came with a bed for him, that is if he wanted to stay on in town tomorrow night.

As Vic put the phone back on the hook, one of the ringers came and tapped him on the arm to give him the drink sign- beers in the station mess hall. He followed the ringer across and ripped the top off his preferred beer, a yellow stubby bottle called Four X, commonly known to locals as barbed wire. He savoured the sharp flavour as beer washed the dust out of his throat.

The next morning, with the edge of a headache, he walked over to his new machine. His leg was paining him today. It always hurt at the same place where the steel plate was bolted in, following from the surgery when they had cut and re-joined the crooked, broken bone.

He felt niggling resentment at this metal plate. In hindsight, he'd rather have been hobbled with a half-crippled leg than have gone to hospital for the operation: since he had woken up only to find Susan gone. He knew if he had only stayed with her that night, then she would still be here now. Something bad had happened when he was not there to mind her. She had run off to God knows where. Now, his leg was acting up today. It had not done that for a few days. He hoped it did not signify further trouble: it seemed to have a mind of its own and had acted something like a barometer of change.

As Vic roared into the air, his helicopter blowing a huge dust eddy that the south-eastern wind picked up, he felt his mood lift. Today was a chance to see a new part of the country. *This country is spectacular,* he thought, seeing vast grass plains rise into hills of the Cape. It gave him a happy buzz.

An hour's ferry later saw him at the station. The half-white manager, a man similar to his skin color, greeted Vic telling him his name was Rick. With Rick there were six aboriginal stockmen. They had their horses saddled up ready.

They all sat together around a table with a map and, in five minutes, a mustering plan was agreed upon. Then stockmen rode off, heading towards the back half of the paddock, the place where Vic would start working to put the mob together for the stockmen to walk back towards the yards.

Vic talked to Rick for a few minutes as he topped off his fuel before they both headed out. The manager would be driving a bull catcher.

Vic then flew to the south-east corner which was about ten kilometres away. The paddock was pretty big and the manager reckoned there should be six or seven hundred cows with calves in it, along with their yearling steers. They both reckoned they'd have these cattle yarded by about 11 AM. Then, there were another couple hours work after lunch, mustering the bullock paddock which had a couple hundred biggish-sized steers. These would join the Vanrook steers on the next cattle boat to Indonesia.

It after three before the boat steers were yarded. When it was done, Vic knew he had time to return to Normanton before dusk. He was restless and was tempted to thank Rick for his offer of hospitality but decline it and head away. If he did this, he could have a night in the pub at Normanton. However, there had been too many of those pub nights lately and they gave little joy to Vic. The hole in his heart and life always remained after a night of drinking. It would just be joined with a new hangover.

There seemed something kind about these people here, in this little place. It was like they had a sense of family and belonging. It reminded him of Alice Springs, the place where his aunts, uncles and kids were hanging around with time to chat. He felt their absence deeply. Plus, he loved the kids here. They chattered as they gathered around the helicopter, asking endless questions, with bright eyes. They made him feel good.

So, what the hell, he'd stop here tonight- even if he thought the barbeque would be a very tame affair. Plus, with it being tame, he could get up early and head off to his next job in the morning.

Now decided, Vic walked over to the yards to watch the activity going on there. They were drafting up the cattle into different groups. He climbed onto the top rail, sitting alongside ten or more school children. The excited screams and chatter, as they watched the cattle work, lifted his mood. Vic felt a wave of nostalgia for similar happy times of his own childhood and, with it, an even stronger desire to go back to Alice again. He could see his mother and favourite sister and play with her children.

One of the children, sitting next to him, turned around and shouted out, "Miss Bennet, Miss Bennet! Come and see the cattle!"

He assumed Miss Bennet was a school teacher, as school was just ending for the day. He turned to see who this person was. There was a lady in her mid-twenties, with dark hair tied back, walking towards them along a dusty road. Two toddlers were walking beside her, each holding one of her hands.

He felt his heart stop. Her eyes were blank as she looked towards him, but the sight of her was so achingly familiar.

Several of the children jumped down from the rail and ran towards her. Two of the bigger ones immediately took up the two toddlers in their arms. She patted their black heads affectionately as her own children laughed with excitement at their newfound playmates.

Chapter 3 - A Mirage

It looked like Susan. The children looked like they could be Susan's children. But- her eyes were empty. She looked at him as if he was nobody she knew or had ever known. Perhaps her eyes showed the vaguely curious appraisal which a new visitor to the town would expect, but he saw no flash of recognition or even any significant curiosity.

Vic's eyes bored into her- desperately seeking something more! But nothing came back. Well, maybe a trace of annoyance at why this stranger was staring so intently at her- as if an invasion of her own being.

His feet compelled him to move. He climbed down off the rail and walked towards her. He tried for a smile, but he knew it came out all wrong. In return, she sent back something else- a half smiling and half frowning puzzlement at his interest. It was not quite unfriendly, but it was guarded. Yet the eyes were oh so blue and they looked just like Susan's eyes- except their sparkle in the light and a bubbling vitality was missing from them. Was it really Susan?! Or was it a mirage, one in his desperation to find her, he had created? Was his own mind playing tricks on him?

Vic walked towards her with his hand outstretched, seeking to touch her- if merely by way of a handshake. As he drew closer, she raised her own small hand which he took in his. "Vic Campbell, helicopter pilot," he said, then held his breathe to await her reply.

A trace of a smile edged her eyes as she surveyed him, appraisingly, "Yes, I knew you were the pilot. I did not know your name, though. Hello Vic. Welcome to our small community."

Vic thought it sounded like her voice but, at the same time, it was wrong in some way. The intonation was English but curiously flat- missing her Susan's vibrant sibilance and confident projection. It was like her……but not her. Vic waited for something more. Nothing came. He still held her hand and she had not attempted to withdraw it. It even felt like her hand. He searched her eyes again for some fragment of recognition- still nothing. He finally found his voice again, the words tumbling out of his mouth, "And you are?"

It was like his second statement roused her to life. She quickly withdrew her hand, glanced at her children to check they were 'okay, and then replied, "Jane. I am pleased to meet you, Vic."

Now, she turned to the other children who were gathered around her and spoke to them, "So, today is cattle mustering day and you are all here, watching. Would you like me to come over to the yard for a little while and watch with you? I can do it before I take my children for a bath?"

"Yes, Miss Bennet! Come, watch!" they chanted in sing-song voices.

Jane walked towards the rails at the edge of the yards, taking care to keep hold of her two children in each hand. The other children all gathered around her at the rails, chattering excitedly- half to her, half to each other.

Vic walked along with them, a couple steps to the side. He was not part of the invited group but was there anyway. He wanted to talk to her. He wanted to ask so many questions, but did not know how to begin.

As Jane came close to the yards, she looked indecisive. Her face seemed to say that holding the two toddlers up to look, together, was going to be difficult. Perhaps, she was looking to find one of the older children to come and pick one of her toddlers up- but they had all deserted her for being on the top rail and getting a better view.

Vic saw this was his chance. "You look like you have your arms full, with two little ones. How about I lift one up to give them a view. Then you will only have one to worry about?"

She nodded with a grateful half-smile.

Vic picked up the closest child, a boy, who looked at him with a curious, slightly cheeky grin. As he looked at Vic, a smile crinkling at the edges of his eyes, there was something which was so like Mark that Vic felt a jolt pass through him. It was as if he had been taken back in time to when Mark was barely more than a baby and Vic had just seen him for the first ever time.

He realized this was a time more than twenty years before he'd first met Mark as a grown man. But that look held something distinctive- as if this small boy would later become the man he had once known. It was just a simple look. Yet it was a smile which screamed out his dead friend's name.

Almost involuntarily, he spoke, "God! You look like Mark."

The kid stared back, uncertain now, as if he may begin to cry. Vic realized, at the same time, this Jane-person was staring at him, intently.

Now, Vic felt awkward. He shrugged an apology, saying, sheepishly, "Sorry. Your boy looks really like someone I once knew. The similarity startled me for a second. I hope I didn't frighten him."

Before she could reply, Vic hoisted the boy onto his shoulders. This action brought the boy's head to the same level as the other children who were on the top rail. The boy now had a full view of the yard. Immediately, the kid chortled with delight and patted his small hands on Vic's head.

Now, this Jane-person smiled at him again, this time a full and genuine smile. Then, she turned back to look at the cattle.

Vic found himself tongue-tied. It was hard to think of anything useful to say. Making polite conversation seemed inadequate. So, he simply stood beside her, drinking in this person's presence. It was like the scent of a long-lost fragrance. He thought he knew her. Everything fitted: the age, the looks, the kids, even the mannerisms and voice sort of fitted. She must know him! He could not shake this huge conviction that it really was her!

Yet, she did not seem to know him. Not even the name of 'Mark' had triggered any slight recognition. He did not think she was trying to hide it- there was no trace of anything evasive like that. But she looked at him like he was a total stranger she had only first met a bare five minutes ago.

They stayed like that for five or ten minutes, not talking, just watching the action unfold as cattle were drafted this way and that. Soon, the yard nearest them was filled with cows bellowing to be re-united to recently separated calves. Vic found himself transfixed by unspoken communication with the little person who sat behind his head. He was a small boy who was captivated by the scene before him and who expressed his enthusiasm with whoops, pats on Vic's head and kicks of his little feet.

For a minute, Vic forgot about the woman beside him as he shared this child's infectious delight. Then, he realized this woman had laid her hand on his forearm and was talking to him.

"I am sorry. I will have to head away now. I must bathe my children early. I have promised the others to help them set up things for the barbeque. So, if you don't mind, I will have to retrieve him from you now," she said, pointing to the child on his shoulders.

Vic grinned, "Of course. Let me carry him along for you as you walk home for a little way. I think he is enjoying the ride up there."

Now, the lady gave him a genuine smile, "I think you are right about that. Well, if you don't mind, I live about 300 yards down there- behind the shop. Your place for the night is half-way there. I will point it out when we get to it. So, why don't you walk along with me- until then. After that, I will take them both on home from there."

They walked along, side-by-side, kicking little clouds of dust up from the dirt street as they walked.

Vic asked politely, "What are your children's names?"

"Oh," she said, apologetically, "they are David and Anne. Sorry, I should have introduced them as well."

All too soon, they reached the front of the bunk house where Vic was staying. She reached for David as Vic handed him down.

David shook his head as Vic went to hand him back, "No, not go!" he pouted. He grabbed onto Vic's arm tightly and tried to stay with him.

Jane raised her eyes and said, "Well, that is unusual. He will almost never let a strange man pick him up at all. Yet, here he is, him not wanting to come back to me. That really is a change! He must really like you."

"Just the view," said Vic, patting his head with a self-deprecating smile. Turning to the boy, he said, "Well, you can ride up there anytime you like. If you want to get a really good view- you must get your mother to bring you for a ride in my helicopter."

Jane laughed in return, "I think he has to grow up a bit before then."

Vic responded, "I was inviting you, too- along with little Annie."

She replied, seriously, seeming to let the humour pass her by, "Well, thank you. Not today. Perhaps another time. I have things to do now."

With that, Jane walked off down the street with her two children toddling beside her, each holding one of her hands.

He watched, unmoving, as she went all the way to where the road turned a corner and disappeared out of sight. As she passed from view, she turned back to smile at him. She gave him a wave before she vanished.

Vic fought down an overwhelming urge to run after her. The urge came to call out the name, "Susan" and see if she turned back. But he could not do that. She surely would not have ignored him before if she already knew him. If she knew him, when they first met again, she would have come running to him. She would have run to him with a bright smile on her face, flung herself at him and hugged herself to him. He knew that was how his Susan would have reacted.

So, who was she? Was she the wife of another man who lived here and who just happened to be a dead ringer for Susan? Was she just a look-alike who Vic had imagined was Susan in his desperation to find her? Or was she the real Susan, with all her memories and former life turned to dust somehow? Could she be a mirage that he had imagined out of nothing, a figment created in his mind? A mirage like those seen far out on the black soil plains and, once he came to where he had first seen her, she would vanish into the air, become invisible and never be seen again?

Vic found himself unwilling to leave this place: lest he break the spell, find out it was but a daydream of a person who no longer walked on solid ground. He suddenly felt great dread that she had returned to the crocodile spirits, that just a faint essence of her still walked in the world of people. He could not bear it to be so, but felt no other certainty in his mind at this time.

Vic could not ask her who she was, he must not tear at her broken memory strings if this was her. But he must find out more. Tonight, at the barbeque, he would try and discover from others who she was.

It was still too early to go inside, so he turned and walked back to his helicopter. He had a photo of the real Susan in his briefcase. He would get it out and look at it. He could at least see if there were any tell-tale clues that either linked this Jane to that picture or made it clear she was someone else.

As Vic came back to the yards, the manager, Rick, was there. He was standing near his helicopter with some papers to sign- receipts for fuel used. In Vic's captivation, he had almost forgotten about his regular business He wrote out an invoice for five hours of hire for mustering and two hours for ferrying- with the fuel taken from here deducted from his bill. They both countersigned and the bill payment was promised within two weeks.

Then, he asked Rick, "Who is that lass with the dark hair and the two small children? She was here at the yards for a bit."

"Oh, that's Jane," Rick replied. "She is an odd fish, isn't she? She is the bookkeeper at the shop. She has worked here for around a year and a half now. She doesn't seem to have any other family or friends from outside town. She keeps to herself mostly- apart from going to church and singing in the choir. She is a looker and a few blokes around here fancied to try it on with her. Yet, she never takes any notice of them. She never seems properly interested in anything or anyone- except her two little kids and, maybe, God. All the rest of the world passes by and she barely seems to notice it. It is like some part is missing inside her head. Still, she is sweet and nice in every other way. We have just gotten used to her now and stopped asking questions."

Vic went to the helicopter and found the photo of Susan. He showed it to Rick. "Do you think that looks like her?" he asked.

Rick looked at Vic curiously. Then he looked hard at the photo and frowned. "Well, yes and no," he said, "Looks-wise: she is almost a dead ringer even though her hair is cut differently. But the girl in this photo looks so alive. This Jane here, when you look hard at her, it is like she is not really alive at all. It's like you can look straight through her and she is not really there. So, it could be her, but it is more like two identical sisters. One who is alive and normal and the other was born without a soul, as if someone took it away at birth. So, all I can say is: maybe, but I don't really know for sure.

"But I know you know more about this one," Rick said, pointing to the photo. "So, if you tell me the whole story, maybe I can help you figure it out."

Vic looked at him, serious and intent, as if considering, "I would love to tell you. But, as yet, I don't begin to know what the answer is myself. Once I work it out a bit more, I will let you know."

Chapter 4 - Barbeque

The sun was now falling low in the sky. Vic was suddenly conscious of his need to spruce himself up if he wanted to make a good impression tonight. After all, this was a big social event of the town, this barbeque.

He pulled out his overnight bag from behind the helicopter seat. He was hoping he had something clean amongst the pile of dirty clothes he had been intending to wash once home at Borroloola. He suspected the pickings would be slim, but he wanted to make a good entrance to his next meeting with this girl, Jane- whoever she really was.

Vic whistled as he walked back to his room. At least she was real- that was what he had got from his conversation with Rick. Now, he needed to turn on the charm and find a way to get inside her head, in order to see what secrets were hidden inside: even if they were buried deep.

He showered, shaved, found his cleanest shirt, and gave it an iron so it looked almost neat. He checked himself in the mirror. Not perfect, but it would do. At least it would be nothing to short-circuit his charm offensive. Vic saw a monogrammed hanky that his mother had given him. It was sitting inside his bag, the only article not yet in the dirty clothes pile. *That may come in handy if I spill some food or drink*, he thought. He tucked it into a pocket.

Someone had said that the barbeque was in the church hall alongside the church. He had seen the church with the cross on the roof as he made a circuit of the town when he first landed. It was at the other end of the town, past the shop and petrol station. He stepped out- feeling a lightness in his step that had been missing for the last year or more.

Vic came alongside a grey-haired couple walking along the street. He hailed them as he passed. They returned his greeting, smiled broadly, introducing themselves: the church pastor, Doug, and his wife, Ruth. They were out for an evening stroll before they, too, went to the barbeque.

Vic fell into step with them. As he joined their conversation, a sense of courtly manners and wise kindness radiated from them. He found himself telling how he came to be here, almost by accident, and how he had to dig deep into his limited clothes to find something suitable to wear. They had a presence like some of the missionaries he had known as a child: simple, good people. He felt at ease chatting with them.

They told him that, as of today, he was a minor celebrity in the town: the aboriginal helicopter pilot. Now, he had half the school children wanting to follow in his career. They told him how their good friend, Jane, had told them how he had made a big hit with her toddler, David. They spoke both names with obvious affection and they continued to explain how David, who up until then, had not let any other men come near him, seemed to have taken to him. They all shared a laugh at this. They asked him how long he was staying.

Vic said he must fly back to the Northern Territory in the morning, as he had a distance of 800 kilometres to cover before daylight Monday.

The pastor asked, "Would you have time to come to church in the morning before you head away?"

He shrugged and grimaced, slightly, "Well, you know Pastor, it's not really my cup of tea, better not to make promises. Plus, I plan to go early. I won't say 'yes,' but stranger things have happened. You never know."

Doug and Ruth both smiled and nodded knowingly as the conversation moved on. Vic found himself wondering at his even half-agreement. It had been more than he had intended, but he felt in the current of something much bigger and just had to go with the flow.

Soon, they came to the church hall. Vic was introduced to all there, about 50 people, a quarter white, three-quarters black and a few in-between shades, like himself. They were standing in loose groups, conversations drifting here and there. A big gang of children, maybe twenty, ranging from toddlers to ten plus, ran between the adults, grabbing handfuls of nibbles while the grown-ups chatted and drank fruit punch. It was friendly and welcoming. Vic found himself looking for Jane.

Suddenly, she was at his elbow, carrying a platter of savoury pastries which she was offering around. She treated him to her brightest-yet smile: not quite Susan-like, but now seeming more familiar and welcoming than before. He thanked her and she moved away, continuing her rounds.

She was dressed simply and plainly- no glamourous make-up or hairstyle. Her clothes were probably thrift shop hand-me-downs, neat but without any concession to fashion. Yet she looked lovely. He felt a huge compulsion to talk to her. Vic needed to get to know this reincarnation that looked so like Susan, even if the light at her core was missing.

However, that was easier said than done in this busy social gathering. She continued to take a lead in the service of food, and he had many people who wanted to talk to him. They wanted to ask his advice about the cattle work, find out about how he came to be a successful helicopter pilot and trade stories with him of the bush. He enjoyed it and found it engaging- yet part of him, wished for a quiet place where there were just two people, a place where they could talk alone.

However, Vic participated with good heart, knowing he must be patient for a chance to arrive. He found himself seated with a big plate of food, surrounded by several stockman and Rick, all telling stories of cattle work. Jane was seated at another table talking to the Pastor and his wife. Her two children were like unguided missiles: shooting amongst the floating mass of others, running here and there, sometimes eating but mostly laughing.

He felt something grab his leg. It was David. He hoisted him to his lap and directed pieces of food his way as the conversation continued. David seemed content for a minute just to sit there and gaze around this crowd of men's faces. After a few minutes, he wriggled back down and ran off.

Vic watched him as he hurtled back towards the place where his mother sat. Suddenly, a small foot caught a chair leg. Vic watched as he crashed face- first into the wooden floor. Vic was up and over to him in a bare second, lifting him up before he could start to cry. He did not begin to understand how his reflexes had moved him so fast.

David had a cut on his lip and looked to be about to burst into a crying fit-- but then he saw this man's face holding him. He took a deep breath as he calmed himself and controlled the tears. There was something so 'Susan-like' in that little gesture. It shook Vic to the core- that ability for self-control.

He took the hanky from his pocket and dabbed it on the cut. There was just a smudge of blood. He gently held it there for a minute while the boy remained quiet. He removed the hanky and the lip seemed OK. Though, no doubt, the lip would be swollen in the morning. He returned the boy to the floor, giving him a pat on the head and saying, "You are a brave little fella."

David toddled off- minor injury forgotten. Vic looked up to see Jane's eyes on him. They were serious, not smiling, but seeking- as if trying to find some tiny fragment of another self. As he caught her eyes, she looked away.

It seemed all too soon when the night was ending. There was no late-night revelry here. He had found no chance to talk to her in anything approaching a private setting. Now, Vic saw her walking towards him while bringing her two little children, one holding each of her hands.

She stood before him, in a simple and unassuming manner, saying, "I am sorry. I need to take my children home to bed now, for they are both tired. I wanted to say thank you for minding David- particularly when he fell over.

"I am not sure if you can manage it in the morning, before you leave, but if you can, it would be really nice if you could come along to church. Service starts at nine o'clock and our choir has been practicing some songs to sing. I would really like it if you came."

He wanted to jump up and escort her home, but something restrained him. He had a sixth sense he had to take it slowly: allow trust to grow and give her time to open up when she was more comfortable. He still did not know if this lady was Susan, or someone else, but it no longer mattered so desperately. He just wanted to know her more: the face of the enigma. So, he stilled his impatience and watched her walk out the door, knowing he was destined to be at church in the morning.

He looked up to see Rick looking at him in an appraising manner, "I don't pretend to know what is going on inside your head, but there is something happening there. And not just for you. Our Jane has shown more animation tonight than in the year and a half she has been here."

Vic nodded, "You could be right. I promise I will tell you, soon. I need to do more work around here and have a reason to make more visits. Make sure my name gets to the top of the list if you hear of helicopter jobs going. Hell, I can even drive a bull catcher if it comes to that."

Rick nodded, saying, "I get it: jobs north, south, east and west of here with ferry stops and overnights here. I might need a commission to act as your local agent, but I will see what I can do."

Chapter 5 - Monochrome

Jane dreamt of lying in bed, without a memory and with the unknown man there again, that night.

It was a broken night of sleep. David was restless and irritable with his cut lip. In the end, she brought him into bed with her to help him settle. Of course, Anne would not stay alone without her inseparable brother in the crib next to hers. So, they both ended up sleeping in her bed. Fortunately, it was a big double bed, so they all had space to stretch out. She put them on the inside where the mattress was hard against the wall. That way, she knew they would not fall out of bed and wake up screaming.

For a couple hours after she came to bed, she lay there in a restless state while soothing her children until they finally settled. Even after that, she found her own mind was wide-awake and active as it relived her remembered life: the almost eighteen months since her memories had begun in April last year, just at the end of the rainy season, with her children born in early May. It was now late September and the nights were getting hot. She could feel sweat on her skin from places where her children were touching her despite the ceiling fan whirring away. The covers, which her children needed to settle under, seemed too heavy on her skin and made her hot.

She found herself wondering about David and why he had taken to this strange new man. the man who looked at her with such piercing eyes, as if she should know him, though she had no idea of why he thought that.

He was just another stranger who she had seen for the first time earlier today. The funny thing was, he had begun to have a color in her imagination this night: a nut-brown color, not all of him, but the bare skin on his arms. The strong arms which had effortlessly picked David up and hoisted him into the air, sitting David on his shoulders. She found herself smiling as she remembered the way David had chortled as he sat on top: loving the view and patting this man's head like a pet dog.

Every past time another man had reached for David, to pick him up or restrain him, he had cried out in fear and she needed to comfort him. Even now, after well over a year, he would barely allow Pastor Doug to touch him- although he went happily to his wife Ruth and to other children. Yet, he'd gone straight to this man, without hesitation. When he offered, she'd intended to give Anne to Vic to hold, knowing she would be fine with this. Instead, he'd picked up David before she'd a chance to suggest anything.

Jane felt a small bit of worry about David. Anne was resilient and outgoing, but David was shy and dependent on Jane and his twin sister. She'd have liked him to be more confident. When she was out with other people, he mostly clung to her skirts. Maybe it was a stage he was going through. She had no one else to compare him to. While she loved her importance to him, she wanted him to become braver and less dependent. So yesterday had been a big step forward. She really hoped this man would come to church to see and listen to her sing. Singing was the one time she felt complete, as if she had something of value to give to others.

It was funny, but when she'd first come to this place, she had no real sense of a missing past: just an empty place before her memory started and a new reality began. However, she knew there must have been a past somewhere: a man to father her children, a mother and father of her own. She did not really miss not knowing them, but she did feel a vague curiosity about who these people were- most particularly, her mother.

It had come to her clearly one day, when she wanted to know when her babies would be able to walk. People had told her that most children learnt to walk at about one year of age, but some learnt as early as nine months. Some even took up to a year and a half to learn to walk. She found herself wondering how old she was when she took her first steps. Then, the thought occurred to her, if she had a mother nearby, then she could just ask her. This led her to wondering what had happened to her own mother so that she did not know her.

Now, as she lay tossing and turning in bed, her mind wandered to another place. She began thinking affectionately of her best friends, the church pastor and his wife, who seemed to have adopted her. She first remembered them coming to the hospital the day after her babies were born, introducing themselves, and offering to make a prayer for her babies' health and happiness. She had accepted- thinking this must be the normal thing that people did with babies. It had been nice to hear them say kind words for her and her children.

When Pastor Doug suggested she have her babies baptized, soon after, she assumed this was also part of what one did, so said, 'Yes,' again. He asked her if she wanted to invite anyone like parents or family. She said she did not know where her parents or family were. He suggested an aboriginal man and woman from the church as godparents. She accepted that, too, as they seemed like nice people and were also her friends.

As she looked back on her remembered life, she thought about another thing she'd discovered which was peculiar. Her life had no colors.

People often talked about the color of things: the green of trees, the blue of the sky and the brown of the earth. She saw shades which she thought were those colors. Then, a few months ago, she had been having a cup of tea at Ruth's house while her babies played. She was looking at two books on the coffee table there. They both had pictures of people and places. To her, the pictures in both books looked pretty much the same- nice, but nothing special.

Ruth had come and sat alongside, looking with her. Pointing to one picture, Ruth said, "Isn't that sky the most beautiful blue color?"

She had replied, "It looks the same to me as that other picture," pointing to a picture with the sky in the other book.

Ruth said, puzzled, "But that is just a black and white picture. How can you say they look the same?"

Jane said, "They both look the same to me."

They had turned a few pages of both books together and Ruth had pointed out different colors- which all looked the same shade to Jane. Gradually, they had both come to realize that Ruth was seeing something that Jane could not: a thing she called colors.

Jane had thought, before, she was seeing colors, too. Since then, she realized that what she was seeing were shades of grey. It did not seem a big deal to her: she could see fine and work out what things were from the shades she saw. Ruth, on the other hand, seemed a bit concerned.

Soon after that, she started to go to church each weekend. At first, it was only to keep Ruth and Doug happy. But she realized it was nice. Pastor Doug mostly told happy stories which she liked.

However, what she discovered which she most liked at the church was the music. The church had a choir and she really liked listening to the choir. One day, the choir sang a new song which she had never heard before. It was an aboriginal song by a blind man called Gurrumul. He lived at a place called Gove: somewhere towards Darwin in the part of Australia called the Northern Territory. This day, someone played a new song which Gurrumul sung on the CD player. The church choir sang along.

"I was born blind, I don't know why.
God made me blind, because he loves me so."

As they all started to sing, this beautiful blue color suddenly started to come out of their mouths. She had sat there crying- it was so beautiful. The music was really beautiful. It had the most exquisite notes and melody. The words were also really beautiful: as if they had been written just for her.

Jane realized that, like this man Gurrumul, she had a part of her that could not see, both were invisible to her. She could not see the past and she could not see the colors of the world. But now, she knew it really did not matter because God had made it so and he loved her anyway. What had made it so special was that, as Gurrumul sang and the choir sang along, as the words and music came out together: she could see a color, too. It was just one color, but it was the most beautiful blue. Because it was so, so very beautiful- it made her cry.

That day Jane joined the choir. She loved to sing all the songs but, most particularly, this song. When she sung other songs, she felt she could almost see some color. It was like the sun trying to break through a thick cloud, when it was raining heavily, and she would see tiny glimpses of colors flash. But, when she sang or heard this song, the purest and most beautiful blue color came out. She could see it so clearly even if other people did not seem to. Knowing this made her feel really happy, all over.

Yesterday, not when she first met Vic, but when he picked up David, and put him on his shoulders, then again after David cut his lip, Vic suddenly had a color, too. It was not an all-over color, but it was a color on his arms- where they were wrapped around her baby. It was a rich brown color. She called it nut-brown in her mind. It was so real and warm.

If Jane could see this colour on him, perhaps Vic would see the blue color she saw when she sang. She really hoped so. And so she had invited him to come and hear the singing.

It was not something she had ever done before- to invite anyone to anything. Ruth had been the one to organize and invite people to a couple things for her, like the baptism and the birthday party of her children. This time, it was she who had wanted him to come and the invitation had just popped out of her mouth. Now, she was glad it had. She hoped he would come and hear the singing. She also hoped he would like it because his opinion mattered to her, for some reason she couldn't explain.

She was feeling comfortable and happy thinking about this as she finally drifted off to sleep late into the night, with her children's bodies pressed into her. Then, she woke with the dream. It was just like the ones she had before: where there was another body in the bed, and she did not know it or anything else. She had felt the shape. I was a hard and angular shaped body- a body of elbows and bony protuberances. It must be a man.

This time, she really wanted to see it. To be able to see a face and to know who it was. Yet, she was so afraid at the same time. Afraid to know this person and the story that went with him: lest it tear her apart and destroy her. Therefore, like before, her fear stopped her. Instead, she buried her face in the pillow and tried to hide it from her mind. But, in forcing herself to pull away, she began to feel so lonely, so utterly alone. This loneliness was to the point where her insides even felt desolate.

As she woke in the morning these new memories came flooding back. She knew it was only a dream, yet a sense of a great loss of something remained in her heart. It was a thing she knew she must find. But, at the same time she knew she could only reach it through this dream, a dream which filled her with pure terror.

Her children were now stirring. Jane washed and fed them then dressed them all for church. As she was getting ready to leave her house, she heard a roar of something which was flying overhead. David rushed to the window, pointing, and making a sound for some unintelligible word. She realized he was trying to say, "helicopter, helicopter!" She glimpsed it flying away.

She felt sharp disappointment. She had invited the pilot, Vic, to church to hear her music. She thought he would come. He had not said he would come, but his demeanour had suggested it.

Yet, he was already taking off and leaving. This meant he would not be there. The color in her mind faded back to grey.

Chapter 6 - The Choir

Vic went for an early morning walk in the dawn to still his impatience to see Jane again. He found his mind had given a new identity to this person- the name she wore. Perhaps she was Susan still, but his mind had begun to call her Jane. As he walked, he found the surrounding bush with its screeching parrots and the thump of kangaroos, which hopped nervously away as he came into shooting range, helped soothe his jangling nerves. This was like how he felt at the outset of a new romance. He thought of this woman as a blank canvas waiting for the painting to be drawn.

As Vic walked past the petrol station and shop on his way back to town, he could see a light on in her cottage and hear little children's noises. It gave him an inner glow of anticipation. He went back to his room and packed up his things. He found some breakfast which he preceded to eat. As he had nothing more to do, he decided to go to his helicopter and do the pre-flight checks. He worked his way through the list. As he did, he noticed a small gathering of black bodies- first three, then four and soon, there were eight. They were watching him with bright eyes filled with questions.

He found pleasure in their enthusiasm. It was like when he, too, was a child at stations around Alice Springs, remembering how these magic machines would come and go. With this walk down memory lane came the memory of his first ever helicopter ride as a child of eight- just around the age of this little gang. He remembered the way the world below had unfolded before him. It was as if he was seeing through the eyes of a bird- a new picture seen from the helicopter that took him into the sky.

He looked at his watch. He had full fuel- more than enough to get to Normanton, where he would top up. He had half an hour free before it was time to go to the church. He would treat these kids to the same treat he had been given all those years ago.

"Anyone want to go for a ride?" he asked the crowd, grinning.

All nodded furiously. He separated them into three groups: two groups of three smaller children and one group of two larger ones. He told them they all had to stay together where he could see them at all times- only those coming for a ride could come closer than where they were right now. He loaded the first three and started up, going skywards with a cloud of dust. Five minutes a trip gave him time to fly over the houses, sweep down along the creek for a mile before coming around over a small hill behind the yards and setting down again. He swapped children and did it twice more. He checked his watch and saw he would have to hurry to get to the other end of the town in time for church.

He remembered there was a clear area just next to the church. It would be faster to fly there and would speed up his departure. As he came flying over, he saw the figure of a woman with two small children walking along the road, coming towards him, about a hundred yards away. He landed and walked to meet them. The greeting was a big smile each from one big and two little faces.

Jane looked at him, seriously, and said, "When I heard your helicopter take off before, I thought you decided not to wait. I'm glad you are still here."

He shook his head, "No, I just took a few of my local admirers for a joy flight. If you have time, I hoped you might come for a quick helicopter trip, too, before church begins."

Her face came alive as she nodded. He brought them over and showed them their seats. He strapped David in tight with a belt in the middle while Jane held Annie on her lap. Then, he looked across to her asking if she was set. Her face was tense, but she gave him a mouthed, "Yes."

He pulled a straight-up climb until they reached a couple hundred feet, the helicopter effortlessly soaring in the cool morning air. He looked across at Jane. She was wide-eyed with enthusiasm, so like that day more than two years ago when he had soared skywards with Susan and Mark. Just for this instant, he had an unshakeable belief that it really was her. He looked at them all questioningly asking, "Ready?"

"For what?" she asked.

"For the thrill of your life," he said.

She nodded- eyes serious.

With a flick of his hand, he turned the helicopter sideways and plunged towards the ground like a falcon diving. As the ground rushed towards them, he dialled on the power, using all his mustering trick skill to zoom amongst the trees as if chasing a bull. As he raced forward, skimming the ground, he pulled the stick up and used the power and speed to pull hard into the sky. He felt the weight in his stomach. Then, down amongst the trees again as he wove his way along the creek, before breaking skyward to come back around over the town and land smoothly alongside the church.

She was breathless and flushed. The children were clapping their hands. He worried he may have scared her. She turned him, eyes glisteningly bright and oh, so blue. Her smile was radiant. "I think that was the most exciting thing in my life. Thank you so much."

Vic took a deep breath to calm his own breathlessness. "When you look at me and smile like that, I think that look in your eyes is far more exciting than a helicopter ride."

Jane blushed and looked away, uncertain.

Then, she looked at the watch on his wrist. "I must fly, the choir needs to do a quick practice before the church service begins."

Vic walked to the church once he had finished his machine shutdown. The pastor's wife was waiting for him, minding the two children. She brought him to sit next to her near the front of the church, introducing him as she went and making polite conversation with the others. They sung an introductory hymn. Then, the pastor talked and led some prayers. Next, the choir came forward for its performance with Jane standing in the midst of a group of aboriginal women and the men standing behind them.

The first song sounded like a negro spiritual. He did not know it- but it was lovely with blending voices, although he could not distinguish any one voice in particular. Then, came a song with a familiar sound. He realized it was one of Gurrumul's songs. Vic sometimes listened to this lovely voice when he was feeling a bit low. He looked up and realized it was not Gurrumul, but Jane, singing as the other women hummed.

"I was born blind, I don't know why.
God made me blind, because he loves me so."

As she sung, he was transfixed by her loveliness. She was glowing, as if with a shimmering light. She was so very beautiful. He wondered if she was an angel. She was singing about him and singing about her. He knew, with certainty, it really was her: his own lost Susan. She'd become lost and blind. Without her, he was lost, too. But now, it was okay. It did not matter if she knew or remembered him. In her blindness, she had found peace and escape and that was enough. It was a complete goodness in its own strange way.

He found her eyes with his and saw they had tears in them. He realized his own eyes had tears, too. He did not want the song to end. He just wanted to keep looking at her.

The rest of the service passed in a blur. Soon it was time to go. She was walking with him back to the helicopter, her hand resting lightly on his arm. She asked, "Will I see you again?"

He said, "I hope so. I will make it so."

Suddenly, he wanted to know- he needed to know. He took the photo of his Susan, the one taken from before, and showed it to her. He asked her if she knew this person.

She looked at it intently and shook her head. "It looks like me- but it is not me. She had a different life spirit inside her to what is inside me. I think that person has gone now and cannot come back. Are you looking for her?"

Vic nodded, mutely silent.

She said, "I hope you find her. I don't know if you can ever bring her back. It is like she has become invisible."

She paused, silent for a minute. It was as if she were searching for words of comfort, perhaps looking for something buried deep inside herself.

She said, "I think she would want you to look for her. To try to find her- even if she does not know it and may not be able to return. So, good luck."

Suddenly, Vic was unsure. Half an hour ago, he was sure he had found his Susan and would find a way to bring her back. Now, he was unsure on two fronts: whether it was really her and, even if it was, whether he could ever reach her again to bring her back to him and the others who loved her.

In the end Vic simply said, "Goodbye."

In return she touched a finger to her lips, then to his lips. It felt and tasted of an inexpressibly precious life essence.

He took off and flew away- looking back at her as her form dwindled into a miniscule dot and finally vanished into the horizon.

Chapter 7 - Revelation Dilemma

As the tiny person on the horizon faded from view, Vic's thoughts returned to what to do about his discovery of this person: Jane. His gut reaction said she was Susan- but his logical mind just did not know. Even if it was her, he had a whole lot of conflicting things to resolve.

He did not feel he had the right to drag her back into the awful situation she had been in before she vanished. She had fought so hard to hide the other side of Mark to protect her children and, also, to protect her own sanity- which had started to come apart at the seams as it all unfolded. In one of their nights of loving, she had told him she was but seconds away from ending it all when he had arrived in court.

That thought had chilled him to the bone then. It scared him even more now that he had seen her and her children again. He thought this new apparent demeanour of calm vacancy was not real. It was like that thin layer of ice which forms on frozen water in an Alice Springs winter dawn- but where one knock shatters it into fragments which never reform.

It was not her fault that she had ended up in such an impossible situation. However, the thought that it had almost driven her to take her own life and, but for an almost miraculous intervention, she would have actually succeeded- was horrific to him. He did not think anyone else knew just how close it had come, although, she may have told Anne. But fate, God, or something had intervened to keep her alive then. If it had intervened, yet again, to bring her to safety in this place, he would allow nothing to threaten this safety.

Alongside this her vanishing had torn a hole through the lives of a whole lot of other people. They all had a raw vein of grief running through them, too. It was particularly her family and Anne, but others who knew her, too, were also in that place. This group included Alan and Sandy who had a great sense of guilt for their own role in bringing her to this point. All of them deserved some light to come from this, if real light there was.

His initial inclination, as her saw her face fade from view, was to just find a way to come back here to work- day after day, month after month. As Vic saw her, time after time, he would slowly befriend her. Then, he would win her confidence- maybe even win her heart anew.

He needed so much to have her back in his life. The thought of trying to woo her and win her, when she knew him not, was hugely appealing.

He felt he had been given a chance to start all over again with her- as if they were each discovering the other for the first time. In this vision, she was for him, alone, to know and find.

But now, as these thoughts rolled around, he realized it was highly unfair to deny others the knowledge he held if it could ease their own pain. At the same time, balanced against easing their pain, and even more important, was the imperative of protecting her from the hostile outside world which had almost destroyed her once before. Even if that meant he could see her no more, he would choose protecting her so as not to let something bad like that happen again. In the end, he just did not know what to do.

As these thoughts kept circling around and around inside his head, he realized he was approaching Normanton where he had to fuel up for his next leg. He decided to would ring Buck and seek his wise counsel. After all, Buck was the best friend he had left. He should be at home today at lunch time since it was Sunday after all. So, once he had fuelled up, Vic pulled out his mobile phone. It had reception at the airport.

Julie, Buck's wife, picked up on the third ring. Vic heard her holler out for Buck to come to the phone after they exchanged a few pleasantries. At first, Buck was his usual blunt self, "Why are you ringing me on a Sunday, at lunch, just when I have gone for a siesta? Barely shut my eyes. Can't it wait till you see me next week?"

Vic gave him back, "Now, you are turning into a pussy- a big fat pussycat who needs a midday sleep in the sun? Some boss, you!"

Then, it all came babbling out in a rush, "Buck, I think I have found her! Susan! Up at a blackfella place on Cape York. It looks like her, it sounds like her, but she does not know who I am, and I feel like I am just imagining it all. But it fits: she had two kids the right age, named David and Anne. She has taken the name Jane Bennet. I could have sworn it was her until I saw the blank look in her eyes. Now, I really don't know."

Buck said, "Whoa there, slow down. Too much information all at once. Start again from the beginning."

So, slowly and carefully, he told the full story. This time, all Buck could say was, "Jesus! Well, I be fucked!"

Then, Buck's rational brain took over. "Where are you and what are your movements? I think you and I need to get to Darwin pronto and talk to Alan and Sandy. I know they won't spill the beans and we'll all need our thinking caps on for this one."

Vic filled him in on the rest of the details.

Buck told him to standby in Normanton while he sorted out arrangements. Soon, Buck had it all organized, along with cover for Vic's job tomorrow at Anthony's Lagoon Station.

As he arranged this part, with another chopper to ferry across from his station to Anthony Lagoon this afternoon, he had Julie on the computer looking up a flight for Vic from Cairns to Darwin. On a second phone, Buck confirmed with Alan that he and Sandy were available tonight.

Vic could hear Buck talking on the other line. Buck did not tell Alan the content Vic had relayed. He simply said that something of critical importance about Susan had come up and they all needed to talk tonight.

Soon Vic was on his way for a five-hour helicopter flight back to Cairns, from where he was booked on a late plane flight to Darwin this evening. Buck and Julie would take the station plane to Darwin this afternoon. Vic's flight arrived at nine in the evening. They would all meet soon after at Alan's flat.

It was after 9:30 PM when Vic arrived. The others were already seated out on the veranda around a big table. He was surprised to see three extra people and felt apprehensive at seeing them: Susan's mother, father and Anne. Alan broached it directly with Vic.

"Mate, I am sorry to put you on the spot like this, but these others are flying out in the morning- returning to the UK after meetings over the last week with the police and coroner. We promised each other to immediately share any leads we get, no matter how small or inconsequential. Plus, we all have exactly the same interest: to find Susan and help her anyway we can.

"Buck has been tight-lipped about what you know, but I can read between the lines. I know it has to be significant. You would not have flown halfway across the country and Buck and Julie would not have come up from VRD at the drop of a hat- not unless it was really important.

"I don't want to have to relay what you say, so it seemed the best solution was for you to tell your story to us all at once. We have already agreed, in advance, that nothing you say will leave this room and none of us will take any action on it without your agreement."

Vic felt pressured. He'd really only wanted a frank one-on-one chat with Alan and Buck in order to toss around what it all meant and what should be done. But he took on board what Alan had said- they all had the same right to know. He could not bear the idea that someone else would have held back from him news this significant.

He nodded and took a deep breath. Buck and Julie were nodding, too.

"I think I saw Susan yesterday and again this morning. But she did not show any sign of knowing me and I really am not sure about it," he began.

Vic saw the shocked and dazed looks on people's faces, struggling to take in this naked fact and make sense of it.

Buck put his hand on Vic's shoulder. "Mate, you should just start at very beginning and tell it as you saw it- not what you think now."

Vic nodded and the others nodded, too. Vic began, again. He told the story of his week- deciding to leave out the exact location. He told of mustering in Queensland, then about the booking to muster the aboriginal station. He told them about him standing by the yards, thinking he might head away, but how he enjoyed chatting to the local kids. Then, how they called out, 'Miss Bennet, come and see the cattle.'

Vic told how he looked around to see who this Miss Bennet was and how his heart almost stopped when he looked up to see someone who looked just like Susan walking towards him. This person was holding a toddler with each hand, a boy and girl who walked at each side of her.

He told of the excruciating moment when he searched her eyes for a sign of recognition and found none. Then he told of the barbeque and the singing in the church. Finally, he told them about how he showed her the photo of Susan and how she said it looked like her but it was someone else who was no longer there, someone invisible. He told them how he asked others about her and found out she had first come there around the time Susan vanished. He said how her children were the right age, sex and names. Also, her name was Jane Bennet- fitting the Mark identity.

He finished by saying, "My mind says it is Susan. My heart so wants it to be Susan. And yet, I really don't know.

"When I asked Rick, the station manager, about her, he said she seemed like someone who was nobody. A person you could look through and see no one there, a person without a soul. I don't think that is right, but if it is her, she is not the person she used to be. I don't think she remembers anything from when we knew her before. The minister's wife, who is her best friend, said that once Jane asked her how old her own children were when they first walked. She said she would have asked her mother how old she was when she first walked, but she did not know who or where her mother was.

"My best guess is that it is Susan. But, if you go there expecting to find the person you once knew, she is no longer there. The best way I can describe her now is she has a calm, flat surface: as if she is happy and at peace.

"It is like the surface of a frozen pond- a thin shiny layer which covers something else underneath which she cannot see. And, if you look hard, you start to see cracks running through everywhere, located just below the surface. It is like someone broke the ice on a pond, smashed it into a hundred pieces. Then the bits of ice refroze and made a new surface- but underneath are all the broken bits still. With the cracks running all through it, you can no longer see anything reflected in it properly- just mixed-up bits. It has shapes that look familiar, but with most bits from before jumbled and gone.

"So now there is this person who looks like Susan and who sounds like Susan, but it isn't really the Susan that any of us knew. And this new Susan is like a piece of ice that is really thin. One tiny knock could break it all apart and then there would be nothing left that we know.

"Before I tell you where she was when I found her, I need you to promise you won't rush off to see her and make her try to remember. Not only that but you will not let anyone else know where she is unless we all agree."

Vic looked at the stunned faces, one by one, all struggling to come to grips with this new information, hope and heartbreak in equal parts. One by one they met his eyes and nodded.

So, he continued on and finished the story with the 'where.'

When Vic stopped talking, Susan's mother came over and sat by him, taking his hand. Her shoulders were shaking with emotion as she said, "Thank you so much for rushing back to tell us all. It means so much to me that there is hope my daughter is still alive, no matter how broken she may be inside. And not only that, but perhaps we have grandchildren- a double blessing. I will trust you to tell us when you think it is safe for us to go and see her. When you next see her, could you please take a picture of her with her children so that we will have that to remember her by?"

Vic had never really talked to Susan's mother before- apart from odd cursory greetings. But now, as she talked earnestly, he could see Susan's mannerisms and personality in her reflection. He felt a flood of warmth for this woman. He started to tell her about the children: of the boy who had sat on his shoulders, patting his head like a dog. How this person, Jane, told him, "David has never willingly gone to another man before." He said how David had fallen and cut his lip at the barbeque, how he picked the boy up and took out his hanky to dab the blood from his cut. Then, once he'd cleaned off the blood, the boy had pushed away his tears and gone back to play. He said how this seemed to have happened in another life now. It was hard for him to believe it was only last night.

Sandy was sitting next to Susan's mother, talking quietly to Anne. She must have caught the edge of their conversation. She turned to Vic and said, "Did you say you have a hanky with the boy, David's, blood on it?"

Vic frowned, needing to think what he had done with it. All his dirty clothes had been put in his bag in his helicopter. He had left them at a laundry in Cairns to collect on his return. The only exception was the clothes he was wearing right now- the very same ones he had worn last night. He'd figured on buying another set or two of clothes in Darwin tomorrow before he returned to Cairns. He felt in his pockets. Sure enough, the hanky was there with a small dark spot of dried blood in one corner.

Sandy reached over and took it, looking closely at the spot. "That's more than enough for what we need," she said.

Others looked at her, puzzled. They asked, "For what?"

"To know who she is," Sandy answered. "David's DNA is on there. We have both Susan's and Mark's on file. We have Mark's uncle's DNA on file, too. And we could even get yours as well if we needed," she said, indicating to Susan's mother and father.

"We can match this DNA to any of those other people's. Once we test this blood, we will know whether this boy is related to them. It appears there is no dispute concerning him being this woman's child. So, if his DNA matches our record for Susan, or matches any of the other people related to her, it is confirmation of the identity of the mother as being Susan. If it doesn't, we will know it is not her. I am assuming we all really want to know, right?"

Sandy looked from person to person.

All thought for a minute and then nodded.

Only Alan shook his head, saying, "We need to think carefully before we go there. If we submit an official sample and it comes back positive- what do we do then? Can we withhold the information? Both Sandy and I are officers of the crown. We will be obliged to report our findings and act on them. Not to mention, these samples will have to be logged in our database when we seek to match them to Susan's identity. There are others who also will have access to the same database. So once this information is in there, I am far from sure we can keep this to ourselves.

"If it is Susan, I am not sure if it is in her best interests for it to come out so quickly. For now, we only have Vic's information saying this person may be her. It gives me a basis for further investigation, but doesn't oblige me to release information suggesting it's her. A positive result will change all that.

"If it comes through the NT laboratory system, I am far from confident I could keep it hidden- even if I wanted to and had agreement to do so from my superiors. There have already been several leaks of what was supposed to be 'confidential information' about Susan.

"I, for one, don't want to know until it is decided what to do with this information. Don't forget there is still a warrant for Susan's arrest from when she disappeared on bail. It was never revoked. It never seemed to matter before, but now I need to work out what to do about the warrant before this knowledge gets outside this room.

"So, at a minimum, I need to talk to the judge and crown prosecutor before we contemplate doing this DNA test. We need to ensure some gung-ho officer does not go flying over there to arrest her- or worse, for someone to leak it to the media and have a pack of journalists descend upon her.

"I think Vic should keep this hanky as his own property for the time being. If there is to be DNA testing, for now, I think it would be better if it was to match the hanky to a sample from Susan's parents. This should only done through a private laboratory and preferably overseas. By doing this, they cannot match it to Susan's sample in our database.

"If it really is her, we can soon get an official sample for testing. If it is needed, we can get it directly from her."

Vic took the hanky back and went to put is in his pocket. Then, as an afterthought, he handed it to Susan's mother. "Perhaps I can leave this with you for safe keeping," he said.

She nodded, "Of course. I will ring you and tell you once I know a result. I understand what Alan is saying: some people are better off not knowing right now. But I, and her father, need to know. I think you also need to know. Even though, at the same time, you must keep seeing this lady- whoever she is."

At first, Sandy looked chagrined. After a bit, she nodded her agreement.

"I hate to admit to a smarter mind, but, actually, Alan is right. So doing the testing overseas is a good idea.

"Now, before we go further, I have a big pot of dinner in the oven. I think we should all have a plate and a drink to take hope in this momentous occasion. It is the first time I have felt real hope in a year and a half. I don't want to get in front of myself, but somehow it all fits," Sandy said.

Chapter 8 - Impossible Legal Guarantee

Vic slept on the sofa in Alan and Sandy's flat, while Buck and Julie slept in the spare bedroom. Sandy had wanted him to take their bed, but he would not hear of it. They were all so keyed up from the news that they slept poorly.

In the early morning, about an hour before dawn, Vic rose and walked the kilometre to Nightcliff beach. He found walking out amongst the shallows and wavelets of a far-out tide soothed his jangling nerves. He was bursting with impatience to get back to Cairns and find a way to do more work in the Cape, as he really wanted the chance to see Jane again.

Vic was determined to call her Jane in his mind, and in that way to create a new identity for this person within himself and thus not get drawn into any old identity problems of the past. He believed there was a continuity between this person and Susan. But as of now, for him, she was Jane- not Susan. He would help her build a new life. But first, he'd promised to go with Alan and seek an urgent appointment with the police commissioner, a senior lawyer for the crown and the trial judge, to see if they could find an official way to maintain secrecy. Alan's story would be that Vic had come to him for advice, indicating he had information about where Susan was currently living. At the same time, Vic was determined not to reveal this information unless he could get an ironclad guarantee, from all concerned, that this information would not be disclosed to anyone else without his consent.

Alan would state he was seeking to establish a legal basis of how to maintain confidentiality, by this to give Vic the certainty needed to share this knowledge. This would allow the information to be passed to others who needed to know- such as her extended family and also allow Alan to make progress with his long-standing investigation of where Susan had gone.

Vic talked to himself as he walked along the beach, feeling ideas form in his brain. He felt steel hardening inside him. He would not give a millimetre- not without a watertight guarantee. It must be a guarantee an independent lawyer could check and confirm: all other promises were worthless to him.

If not, he would simply walk away. By tomorrow, he and Jane, if he could get her to come, would have vanished a second time. He was not going to tell Alan or anyone else this, though. After that point, the only person he would communicate with- apart from his own mother, sister and Buck- would be Susan's mother, as he trusted her.

Vic hoped it would not come to that. Even so, in his mind, he was clear that he would do it if it was necessary. He had learnt from Mark how to hide in plain view: now he made his own plan to disappear. He was confident he could pull it off, if he must.

He returned just as the sun was rising and showered. He borrowed some clean clothes from Alan which were near enough to his size. Alan was about to head to work, but he said he would ring him with the arrangements to meet the lawyers and others as soon as he could put it together. In the meantime, Buck, Vic and Julie shared a leisurely breakfast with Sandy to pass the time.

While Julie and Sandy were chatting away, Vic brought Buck onto the veranda to have a private chat with him. Vic found his mind was much clearer now, after his walk. He wanted to put Buck in the picture. It was not that he did not trust the others, but he did not want them involved. It would be putting them in a bad place- particularly Alan and Sandy with their jobs.

Vic had a powerful sense it fully rested with him to ensure this person's safety: Susan or Jane. He must not rely on others for such an important thing.

He knew these others meant well. Yet, he did not trust their ability to keep the lid on this. So, despite whatever promises might be made, his sense was: now he had found her, it would be too easy for others to find her through him. His flights last week could readily be tracked by the police as he had logged them with flight control. That meant any half-smart journalist could do it, too. He knew any leak could be a disaster.

No matter what promises of secrecy were given, he reasoned that too many officials would get to know for her location to stay secret for long. Even if people did not know exactly where to look, there were not that many communities in Cape York. It would not take long to check them all out.

While Vic had said he would go to the meetings that Alan arranged this morning, he had now decided he would be on the lunchtime flight to Cairns, instead. By tonight, he would be back in the community. He knew he could not return in his helicopter for it was too traceable. It would have to stay in Cairns. Instead, he would get a cheap set of wheels.

By getting a vehicle, he could drive back there tonight. If he could convince Jane to come away, they would be gone by morning. Together, along with the children, they would vanish into the big population spread out along the full length of the east coast of Australia.

What he needed was a bit of help with the arrangements, someone to look after the chopper once he disappeared, someone who could buy him a cheap set of wheels in another name and also a person he could trust as a relay contact. Buck seemed like his best option on all accounts.

Vic also had a plan to throw out a false trail. He knew that, despite his care, someone might hear a rumour that Susan had reappeared and try to follow Vic to her. One of his Alice Springs mates, another half- aboriginal bloke with a dash of Indian, was almost a dead ringer for him.

Vic had left his passport with his mother in Alice. He had it from when he had done his one and only overseas trip to Bali with this same mate. He would ask his mother to get Ravi to go overseas using Vic's passport and return on his own one. He had even talked to his friends about getting away to Canada to start a new life- so it made a plausible destination. His mate should enjoy a couple weeks there, on a holiday, at Vic's expense. Then, the "Vic" identity would vanish, and Ravi could return to Australia under his own name. It seemed pretty straight-forward. If it was not quite legal, who was to know? His mother could arrange it on the quiet.

Vic started to explain his logic to Buck. He explained how he would need to arrange for Jane and him to both disappear for a while. This would give Alan and the others time to sort out the legal issues. He hoped they would be able to get a new legal identity for Jane and clear up any arrest warrant or bail issues. In doing so, the police and media would hopefully lose interest and let them quietly get on with their lives.

If they had time alone, he thought Jane would come to trust him and he could, thereby, better protect her. Maybe in time, it would not matter if her identity became known. But, right now, it needed to stay buried- anything else was like a fuse burning on dynamite.

Buck nodded, "Yes, I can see that now. Perhaps we should never have come to Darwin- it was my first instinct but, perhaps, it was wrong."

Vic said, "No, you were right. It was good we came- particularly before Susan's parents left. They needed to know. Alan and Sandy needed to know, too. I am glad they all know now.

"But, at the same time, it was always silly of me to think she could stay hidden for long in such a small place. The safest place for now is where there are lots of other people. After all, it is much easier to hide in a crowd.

So that is what I am going to do. I don't know where yet- but I need you to be my contact to the rest of the world. At this moment, there are three things I need. The first is for someone to take over my helicopter and pay its running costs- hopefully, it can make enough to cover the mortgage. Perhaps one of the big stations around here can make use of it and make the loan payments as the price for having the machine."

Buck nodded, "Yep, that should not be too hard. We can do that at VRD, if needed. You just send me the account details for the payments."

Vic continued, "Then, I need a set of cheap wheels. Nothing fancy. I just need a reliable old sedan from a car yard in Cairns which I can collect this evening. Best if it's not in my name- as that will make it harder to trace me. Can you sort that out if I arrange to give you the cash?"

Buck nodded again.

"And, lastly, I need an ongoing way to access money without going to an ATM or bank. My mother has an account which I put twenty thousand in, to keep safe for a rainy day. If I ring through instructions of where I am each month, can you get her to start drawing out the money and sending it to me?

"I think a couple thousand for the car and another couple thousand a month should be enough. I might need more, from time to time- like to rent somewhere, for instance. Once I get a steady cash job, I should not need it anymore. I also need someone to keep track of what is happening up here: any court cases or other things like that. You can tell Alan and Sandy, in general terms, what I have done. Not any of the specifics, mind you, but enough so they don't worry. I also need Susan's family's address in England, so that I can get in contact with them if I need to."

Buck nodded, saying, "Sounds like you will owe me one whopping commission by the end of all that- but it does not sound too hard, all in all. So, leave it with me. I will text your mobile this afternoon with the car and her parents' contact details. You should buy a new SIM today and send me the number- just in case the old number is used to track you."

Vic said, "Oh, and one more thing, for your and my mother's ears only right now: I want to fake my departure to Canada from Cairns. I have a mate that could do it, since he looks just like me. He could depart on my passport and come back on his own. That way, any serious journalists who hears a rumour about Susan and tries to get to her through me will find I'm officially out of the country. My mother can organize the trip part. What I need is for you to put the word out in a couple weeks, that this is what I' done. It will give a reason for why I have off-loaded my helicopter and gone away."

Buck said, "God! You have it all planned out; Vic. Mark would be proud of your brilliance. It is seriously sneaky and, no doubt, illegal. Though, that fact never stopped Mark in any of his schemes.

"While you are on a roll, why don't you just hit the road and get on your way back to Cairns? I think there is a half-ten flight you can catch. I will go with Alan to any needed meetings. I can relay the information, nice and general, about what we know. That will put another layer to separate you and slowdown any traces. After all, Mark made us jointly responsible for this girl's welfare. If you take care of her, I can look after the rest."

With that said, they shook hands. Vic made his brief goodbyes to others and was on his way. He knew he could trust his friends to let nothing slip.

He first went to Casuarina where he had a super short haircut and bought some new sets of clothes along with a new phone. Then, he withdrew all the available cash in his bank account.

By eleven, he was winging his way back to Cairns.

Chapter 9 - Trust

Sure enough, Buck had a car waiting for him in Cairns by the time he landed. The details had been texted to him on his new mobile number. It was an older model Ford Falcon with a big six-cylinder engine which ran sweetly. The car had a couple minor dents in the body work, but they were trivial. The upholstery had seen better days. Regardless, it was sound and as good as expected for $1900. Cash was king and Buck had negotiated down from the asking price of $3000.

It was registered in Queensland in Buck's name, at his family's farm address near Rockhampton. The story Buck had given was Vic was driving it down there as a favour to him. Buck explained he intended it to serve as a second farm car and made it very clear: if the car was a lemon, he would pay the salesman a visit on his next trip to Cairns to get a refund. Buck told the salesman he had a persuasive manner about him when needed.

It was a slow drive over unfamiliar roads to reach the isolated aboriginal community where Jane lived. Vic felt anxious about how Jane would react to him turning up late at night, unannounced. But he was driven to keep going, no matter how he was received. Most of all he wanted to see her again.

It was after nine o'clock that night when Vic reached this place. Fatigue washed over him as the town lights came into view, but he was driven on by a surge of nervous anticipation.

He would have to play this encounter by ear. It seemed a huge ask to say to any girl to come away with him, out of the blue. This woman barely knew him, he felt a little foolish proposing it to her. At the same time, his mind and emotions joined together in telling him this was what he needed to do.

Vic knew her mental safety was a terribly precarious thing- particularly if she suddenly became the centre of attention over something she had no prior knowledge of. It would be a huge disaster if they returned her to jail and took her children away from her.

His emotions for Jane were a complex mix of a hundred things, which all blended together. First and foremost, he felt hugely protective of both her and her children. He was very conscious of the risk that his contact with her and his telling others about it, could bring about her undoing.

He felt glad, when he pulled up outside her cottage, to see a light was still on. He hoped this meant she was still awake. He sat in the car for a few seconds, composing himself. Then, realising that planning was pointless at this stage, he opened the car door and walked towards the house. He was pleased there were no other houses nearby- just the bulk of the back of the shop 50 meters away. He was also glad there were no dogs barking.

He knocked on the door and another light came on, lighting the outside. Jane stood there with the light behind her, illuminated in silhouette. She was wearing a light slip. It was not quite a nightie, but something similar. It illuminated the outline of her body within the gown. He felt a huge rush of affection for her- this new Jane who seemed to have occupied his Susan's body. He wanted to take her to him, hold her body close, caress her and give her reassurance. She stood there looking uncertainly into the outside night, seeking to make an identification of her late-night visitor.

His voice came out a bit croaky, "Jane, I needed to see you, again."

Now, recognition came to her. In a tone showing she was part puzzled, part welcoming and another part apprehensive., she whispered, "Vic?"

Vic continued without directly responding to her question, "I am sorry I did not get here until it was so late. I hope I have not frightened you."

As he spoke, Jane seemed to relax. She opened the door to invite him in. They stood facing each other about a meter apart. He knew he needed to connect with her in a way which went beyond words.

Vic put out his hands to greet her and she responded in kind like a mirror. He walked forward a step and took her small hands in his. They felt so delicate, even though they were now hardened by manual labor. She gave him a tentative smile on such an open and trusting face.

All his rehearsed words fell away from his thoughts. He looked at her and she looked back at him with a curious intensity- as if she was seeing him for the first time. He released one of her hands and put his hand to her cheek to stroke it. She brought her hand to the hand now on her cheek and softly squeezed it. Almost unconsciously, she stepped forward to move towards him. Their bodies were almost touching now.

Vic put his arms around her shoulders and pulled her through the small gap, until all the space was gone between them. As he felt her body come against him, he knew it was still her- made anew, but still her. He cradled her in his arms and stroked her head. She was the most precious thing he had ever touched. He lifted her face to his, as if to kiss her.

She looked at him intensely. Her serious, trusting eyes locked on his eyes. Without knowing, she was open to his soul.

He said, "You are all I have thought of since I left you yesterday. I just needed to see you, again. More than anything, I needed to look at you, I needed to touch you, to feel your breath and hold you close, to know you were not just a dream, but a living breathing person."

She nodded, "I am really glad you came. I have wanted to see you, again, too. It has a feeling of rightness to see you…. though I do not know why. I think partly it is because David trusted you. I trust you, too."

Vic said, "Will you come away with me? Leave here and come with me? Just you and your children?"

She said, "If that is what you want, then I will come with you. How soon shall we go?"

He asked, "Can we leave tonight? I would like to leave before the night is over. Perhaps we could rest for a while and go an hour before the daylight comes- at a time when others in this place are still sleeping."

She said, "Yes, we will come with you. We can leave then."

She went to the fridge and found some bread. She toasted it and served it to him with a mug of tea.

As she sat beside him at the table, she picked up a pen and paper, saying. "I must write a note to tell Matilda at the shop, along with Pastor Doug and Ruth, that I have gone away and will get in touch with them again as soon as I can. They will be worried about me if I don't leave a note."

When it was done, she folded the note and left it on the table.

Then, she said, "We should rest now."

Vic looked around and saw some cushions on the sofa which he could lay on the floor for a bed. He said, "I will use those cushions to lie on tonight."

She said, "There is space to lie beside me on my bed."

So, they lay there on the bed, side-by-side. Jane turned her body to face Vic. She took his left arm and placed it over her shoulders. Then, she closed the space until she was fully alongside him and pushed her face into the hollow of his neck. This was the way they slept, bodies touching. It felt so good to him and she said it felt right to her.

She awoke in a small hour of the morning, around three or four AM. Her mind was sharply awake in an instant. She did not know where her body was: except it was in a bed and the bed had become familiar.

A sound came of another human drawing breath, in and out, regular but not loud. She moved her arms around to explore the bed space. There was another body lying next to hers- the source of breath sounds. It was a hard and angular shaped body, a body of elbows and bony protuberances. It must be a man. Now, she knew who this man was. The man had a name and a face. He had no history in her mind, but his name was Vic. He was with her, right beside her with his arms around her and she was so very glad.

She could remember no other past, and her future was an unknown place to her, but he was here, and he was known. That was enough to make her trust her life to him. She went to sleep again.

He woke her in the early dawn, and she knew him still.

As the first light tinged the eastern sky, washing it with touches of pink, they each carried a sleeping child to the car, to begin their drive together to another unknown place.

Chapter 10 - Making a Family

Almost two months had passed since the day when Jane and Vic had driven away from the first place she had memories of. Vic could not think of any time before this when his life had been better or more fulfilling. Not that there weren't a lot of little speed-bumps or frustrations along the way- including the inability to satisfy his sexual desire for this beautiful woman whose body pressed to his every night.

These were, at most, minor frustrations. They did not detract from all the goodness which now filled his life. In his earlier life, when he visited his sister in Alice Springs, one of the things which gave him the greatest pleasure was her three children. They were always coming and going, talking to Uncle Vic, sitting on his knee, showing him their books and drawings and sometimes telling him their stories of the days. At times, they played little games which involved him. At other times, he just sat and watched them play.

Now, Vic had a family and it felt like it was his own: his Janie, his Annie and his Davie. He had given them all pet names of affection. Janie was his wife- in all but name. Apart from that full sexual union it felt just like being married. They did everything together: talked, shared, worked side-by-side and held each other in the night. He felt so comfortable with her and knew it went both ways. And he loved their children. Even though they were really hers, not his, he felt the same level of kinship and protectiveness he would have if he was their biological father. At first, they mostly called him Vic. Now, he was just Daddy. He had filled up their memories in this space of their mind. He rarely disciplined them. A couple times, he had given Annie a small slap when she was mean to other kids at the playground and, a couple times, something similar to Davie when he did something dangerous which could have injured him. He told Janie each time and she had said, "Of course, you are their father now- like I am their mother."

As he walked off to work this morning, he rolled through the events of the months in his mind: *that long drive across the Cape to find her again. Her uncertainty in the doorway and then, as they touched each other, their bodies and minds had connected in a safe place.*

In that second Vic had committed himself totally to care for Jane and her children. She trusted him to do so in whatever form it took. It was this total trust which was so compelling to him. It drove him to be better than he otherwise could have been. In a way, he felt he was minding three children- not two- except one of them had the body of an adult. He sensed he was entrusted to rediscover this adult, carefully and gently, beneath the child in Jane. This trust was the best thing life had required of him at any time.

He believed that, in giving her this space and safety, she would slowly rediscover herself: an grown adult made anew from the child he now held. He felt and thought that she could never be the Susan of before, again. Too much had been broken inside her- parts which could not be remade anymore. Instead, she had the chance to create a new self- one who already was and would become his Janie. This woman was the one he knew and loved. The woman who, in return, loved him.

Vic knew he must hasten slowly and let her rebuild her life piece-by-piece. He knew he could take and love her body at any time he chose. She would trust him with this, too. But, to do so now, would be to take a part of her innocence and to make the choice for her before she could make the conscious choice for herself. He most wanted her to regain her sense of womanhood and choose him. He did not want to seduce the trusting, child-like adult who would then become his bonded woman in an unchosen way.

He did not know why this seemed so important to him- but it was. For now, he must just push away his sexual desire for her. He must pretend, when she cuddled her body into him and pressed her thighs against his maleness, that he was doing no more than cuddling a sleeping child.

His mind stepped through the weeks which had passed. Week One: they had crossed the peninsula to the east coast and followed it south to a small town south of Townsville.

There they had found a caravan park with an empty van and stayed there for five nights. Days were spent watching their children play on the beach and going for walks through the sand dunes. Nights were simple meals and storytelling. Jane seemed to have no interest in watching television and he preferred it this way. He feared the stories of the missing Susan, Mark, Anne or the other 'Lost Girls' would appear and shake her mental stability.

While he was not sure what was the best way for her to regain her past knowledge, his sense was that any memories or desire for knowledge of the old had to come from inside her. It must not be pushed onto her by telling the stories of who she had been, by others she had once known.

Instead, they both told other stories. First were stories for the children. Then, stories of her life in the mission since her babies came and stories of his helicopter mustering, the people he had met and places he had been, slowly entered into their tales. As they talked, they linked their eyes together and shared their imaginations. In that place, he felt totally joined to her.

In Week Two, they had drifted further south, still following the coast. More little villages drifted past, places with holiday accommodation or budget rooms where they stayed- each for only a night or two. One day, they treated themselves to the ferry to Great Keppel Island. They stayed out there for three days: swimming and snorkelling in the clear water while watching their children play in the shallows. In Week Three, the family came towards Brisbane. They were stopping in towns like Bundaberg and Gympie- finding the city, as they approached it, to be too confronting for an unfamiliar family with two small children. By Week Four, they had come back to the coast. This time, however, they came to the Sunshine Coast.

Here, they finally found this place which felt right: a holiday and caravan park just a short distance from the town of Caloundra. The ocean beaches were beautiful. There were sheltered inlets on the bayside which were safe for small children. The people were friendly and incurious. They had been given a free mobile home to live in, along with a modest wage for Vic. It was paid in cash in return for him doing a few hours of caretaker and handyman duties each day for the caravan park community. He also did a bit of casual laboring in places nearby. The jobs came in by word of mouth.

There was plenty of work around. It was easy work for someone with his mechanical skills: ground maintenance, welding, fabrication, fixing small machines like lawnmowers and maintaining the pool complex and gardens. It was not a job for life, but the pay was enough to cover their daily living expenses. It also gave them both a sense of stability and security.

He used the name Vic Bennet- giving the impression of being married to keep life simple. At the same time, he avoided pieces of paper which could be traced by anyone. The money he was paid funded a day-to-day existence, meeting their basic living costs without the need for a verified identity.

For Janie, this was a place to put down new roots. Her best friend had become Thea, a single parent who lived in the cabin two doors down. She had two children, aged two and four, and supported herself by making the beds and cleaning the units in the park.

Janie now had a part-time job doing this, too. She mainly covered days when Thea was extra busy or not available. When neither was working, they would meet for a slice of cake and a cup of tea. This was mostly done at Thea's unit. During work, when required, they could share the child minding. Usually, though, Thea's children came from unit to unit as she tidied them. Jane had started to do the same with her two, when Vic was not at home.

Vic liked Thea but he was wary of her becoming too curious about their life. He tried to skirt around the occasional questions she asked: things like where they were from or where they had lived and worked before. He just said he came from Alice Springs and they were both living and working up in the Cape before they got together. On the other hand, Thea was a keen magazine reader and TV watcher. This gave Vic bouts of anxiety- lest she make the connection to such a well-covered media story.

Vic found his mind returning to their trip down the coast. Along the way, as they travelled, he had made a weekly phone call to Buck to get news of what was happening with the legal case in Darwin. At the same time, he would pass on news of Jane for her parents and friends. Wherever possible, he used payphones to avoid using his cell phone- lest it be traced.

His concern was about a mole in the NT police or court system. His first suspicions had been well-founded. Within a week of them leaving, a vague rumour was aired about sightings of Susan, still alive, in a town in north Queensland. Fortunately for them, no location was specified. Still this story seemed to have more of a ring of truth than previous "Susan sightings."

At least there were no new names and no current photos. His Janie now had her hair cut in a short bob and her face had plumped out some. The ability to link her to the Susan released from jail in Darwin nearly two years before was fading. The pasty-faced, heavily pregnant girl of the old media photos was very much changed into his Janie.

In his first telephone conversation with Buck, Vic identified himself and told Buck they were together. He told Buck all was fine but avoided more specific news. Buck, himself, had two pieces of news. One was that Susan's parents had tested the DNA from the handkerchief it confirmed David was indeed their grandson- though Vic's doubts of this were already gone without an official confirmation. The second news was about a rat in the ranks of NT government, someone who was feeding information to the press, fuelling speculation which was now gaining cover, as evidenced by the Queensland sighting. So, as Buck said, they both had to be really careful about any communications and particularly about not giving any locations or names.

On the inside of the NT government, Alan and Sandy were informally aware of the DNA result. Alan had been talking to people, unofficially, in legal circles about how to proceed: whether to seek to reopen the court case and seek a change to the conviction or, alternatively, to try and have the sentencing concluded to a level where Susan was free to lead her life. At the very least they needed to find some way of removing the legal requirement for her to return to custody for having broken her bail.

There had been speculation about Vic having a role in her disappearance. Some called for an arrest warrant to be issued for him, based on the suspicion that he had in some way aided a convicted prisoner. However, the story Buck let slip of his going to Canada was accepted for the most part. After all, he no longer flew his helicopter.

Alan had done a good job of calming the horses from inside the police, so no one had formally attempted to locate Vic for questioning or to pursue more serious matters.

The other conversation Vic had recently was with Anne. This call happened when they were staying in Yeppoon, one night, when they had checked into a motel. They had just spent the three glorious days on Great Keppel Island where they stayed in a small, basic bunkhouse which was a short walk back from a pristine, white sandy beach. The beach was dotted with corral atolls spread throughout the deeper water. Another couple, with small children, were staying nearby. They all became instant friends: sharing meals and drinks while their children played together. They had taken turns to babysit the combined children while the other couple went for a swim together, alone, out amongst the coral.

It was not something Vic had done before, but Janie knew all about it. She even knew the names of many of the fish and pointed them out to Vic, glowing with enthusiasm as they explored. She was delighted this part of her knowledge had carried over from a former life. She even was able to have intensive discussions with the husband of the other couple, Eric, who was a marine biologist. Vic loved seeing this part of Jane's adult personality and memory return.

That night, after having returned from the island and with all the activity of the last three days, Janie and the babies were completely exhausted. They all fell asleep together in a tangle on the large bed. Since he had talked to Buck, Vic had been reluctant to use his own cell phone too much- lest the police try and trace him through this. It did have a new number, but still, he was not positive he could not be traced.

He eyed the room phone and decided to chance it. Buck did not pick up, so he thought who else to try. Alan and Sandy were a bit risky. Also, he did not want them to have knowledge they might have to deny later on.

That only left Anne or David, neither of whom he knew well, or perhaps Susan's parents. He was not yet ready to talk to her parents, although he had recently taken a picture of Janie and the children to send to them on his phone camera.

He thought about waiting for another day, but chances were not easy to come by. In trying to understand this person he was with, he really needed to know more about her. After all, Anne was Susan's best friend. She had been Susan's best friend since school, so who better to fill him in on her early life? These little snippets could be something he may be able to use to see if they triggered any of her memories.

After thinking this through carefully, Vic called Anne and she picked up on the first ring. "Anne here," she answered in a more businesslike manner than he was used to.

However, after a minute of making polite conversation, he found himself comfortable talking to her. He explained, "I felt like I needed to touch base with one of her friends. She and the children are fine. They are asleep on the bed next to me as they are very tired from the last few days of fun.

"Now that we know for certain it is her, I am trying to think of ways to help her remember. At the moment, she has no memories of anything from before being here in Queensland with her babies. The amazing thing is, that she has full knowledge of some things- like working with computers. Today, she was talking to a marine biologist about Barrier Reef fish, as if she were as much of an expert as he was. At the same time, she does not know where she was born or grew up, she does not know how to cook a meal except for eggs and sausages, or of any of those other things which would come from her past memories. So, I am trying to find out things that she might know about. I believe it will help us to have things to talk about and it may also lead to other memories which she can't reach now."

In the end, they talked for over half an hour, and he got lots of details of Susan's early life. He also promised to text her the picture with Janie and the babies so Anne could pass it on to Susan's parents.

After that, as they travelled on, Vic used his newfound knowledge to try and open up more of Susan's past knowledge and memories. He found her knowledge of what she studied at university was remarkably good, though she had no knowledge of the courses of study or the people she knew at the University. Now, they could talk about archaeology or medical technology- even though these fields were not Vic's strong points. But, in this, Janie was a great teacher. She seemed to be able to retrieve vast stores of knowledge of her technical background to build Vic's interest in these unknown fields.

He really liked seeing this side of his companion. In these things, she was the master and he was the apprentice. It brought more balance into their relationship. It also seemed to satisfy a need in her to have more meaningful things to think about and discover. Now, she would collect inexpensive books on these topics in second-hand bookshops and devour them voraciously.

However, in other things, she stayed a child. Mostly she seemed unaware of her childish state. She had no sense of what clothing suited her, how she should cut her hair or apply makeup. Her food and cooking knowledge was basic. Her knowledge of normal children's development was abysmal.

One day, Janie told Vic she could not see colors. The way she had recently identified and told him the names of the fish on the reef by describing their patterns and shapes, it had not occurred to him she could not see what she was describing. It came out as she told him more about singing in the church and how it let her see the color blue, when before that, the world she saw around her was only ever shades of grey. She told him how she now could see the brown color of the skin on his arms when he held her children, but only in that place and at that time. She said, one day, she hoped she would be able to see some other colors- but, for now, she was happy that she could see these two colors as they were so beautiful.

The thing he most loved and marvelled about in this new woman was her positivity. She had lost almost everything she had ever known. And yet, in the things she did have: her children, him, and the two colors she saw, she conveyed irrepressible joy. The eyes that looked at him, her blue eyes, gave him total attention and were for him alone. She looked at and played with her children the same way. They both basked in this joy, just as did he.

Chapter 11 - The Girl and the Woman

In the months that had passed since Jane had come away with Vic, she did not understand what caused her to trust him so much, so that, when he asked her to come with him, she had said yes without any hesitation.

Her life before, on Cape York, had been simple and she was contented. Yet, when Vic came into her life, he brought his color to it and David trusted him. So, she trusted him, too. Now, she was overwhelmingly glad to be with him. However, she was starting to sense that their life together was missing something that other couples had.

As she thought about the life she had now, her principal emotion was one of profound happiness. The words her mind held to describe emotions, based on past memories, were very limited things. So, she struggled to verbalise what she felt towards this nut-brown man who shared her life. In books, she read about a concept called 'love.'

She felt this 'love' thing must be something more spiritual, akin to her emotions when listening to singing in church. Her feelings towards this man were earthy. She smiled as she thought of the smell of the sweat of his body when he worked in the hot sun. She liked how the muscles in his brown arms corded and stood out when he strained to move something heavy. Most of all, she smiled inside when she thought of how he played with and held her children. They looked at him with simple adoration. He was always good and kind. He always had time for them. He cared for them in an easy and uncomplicated way- the same as he cared for her.

All in all, it made her feel warm inside when she thought of him. She, Janie, felt trust and affection for Vic. She felt many more things besides these emotions, but for most of her feelings- she could find no words to fit. She knew, though, the sum of it all was happiness.

Yet she knew there was more. She had minute glimpses of another life where she knew him, too. These were like the tiniest reflections of light sliding through gaps in a fog which covered all the surfaces of her past. These flashes had slivers of anxiety attached to them. They did not spoil her happiness, but they were always there, and she knew them for what they were- warnings to leave well alone whatever had been before.

Sometimes, Jane thought she should ask Vic to tell her what he knew about her from before. Was she the girl in the photo that he had shown her when they first met, the one he was searching for on that first day? Or was she someone who looked like that girl and who had taken over her place in his life? These were little puzzles which her mind glimpsed. She trusted he would tell her when the time was right. Buried deep was also a fear to know what had come before. She did not want a shadow cast over her life now.

There was something else about him that she could not define. It was part of the happiness- but, different somehow. It was something to do with him being a man. She had glimpsed his naked form, as he had hers, and it stirred other emotions which she did not understand. She had felt hardness at his middle, where his belly muscles joined his legs, and it stirred similar emotions in her as had his naked form- but again, she did not understand.

Sometimes, when he slept in the night and his body was touching hers, he had pressed this part of his body against the place where her legs joined her body. Then, she had wanted this feeling to go on and become more- but she did not know what followed from here. So, each time it had occurred, after a minute of enjoying the sensation, she would turn away. At the same time, she felt regret in the undoing of this contact.

Sometimes, when she could feel him wound up and tense, she had this vague sense of wanting to do something more with her body to relax and pleasure him, in order to help relieve his tension. But, again, she did not know what exactly to do.

It was not a big thing. It did not spoil her happiness. However, sometimes, she wished she had a sister she could ask what else she could do with her body to give this man more comfort and pleasure.

She was also slightly uncomfortable about them living in the same house and sharing the same bed when they were not really married. The minister, at the church where she went each Sunday, talked about living in sin. He did not say it to her, as he thought she was married. He would speak about it to the young, grown-up boys and girls who came to the church. She did not understand what this really meant, but gathered it had to do with a man and woman living in the same house or sleeping in the same bed before they were married.

Jane had seen weddings at their local church. She knew that she and Vic had not done this wedding thing, for it was something she was sure she would have remembered. Even though Vic told her to say to people they did not know that they were married, and she had agreed, it could not be true. She understood it was said to explain the children and stop any questions.

Now, as she thought of the men and women she saw going to church to get married, she thought this would be a nice thing to do with Vic. However, she did not know how one decided to do it: what arrangements were needed, whether it was something a woman asked a man to do it or the other way around, or whether it just happened when the time was right.

Anyway, now it was time to stop thinking about these complicated things. Her friend in a nearby caravan, Thea, had given her a cooking book. She wanted to try the recipes from it. In her mind she knew, from when she first remembered anything, how to make toast, tea and cook eggs, sausages and other simple things like that. But she did not know how people made fancy food. Now she had been given this recipe book, she realized she could learn to do this. It was time to move beyond things out of tins and toast. It appeared that cooking nice food was a thing which a woman did, apart from minding her babies, when the man went to work.

Vic was due home from work in an hour He was working some days as a laborer for a local builder a few miles away. She wanted to have this recipe, a dish called Lasagne, that Thea had told her about, ready and waiting for him when he came home. The thought of his smile and the praise that would come when she served it, made her feel warm inside. She set to work- feeling upwelling excitement as she waited for him to come home.

Tomorrow, she would ask Thea what other things she could do to please a man- apart from cooking him nice food and stroking his hair as he lay beside her. She knew Vic really liked those two things but there must be something more. She needed someone to tell her what else there was and, as Thea was her best friend in this place, she would ask her.

Just after she finished preparing the dinner and setting it in the oven, Vic was home. She ran to him and wrapped her arms around him, to convey her joy at being in his presence.

He looked at her and grinned, "Well, I loved that! Give me more, more!"

At that moment, David and Anne came running towards them and he picked one up in each arm. Both giggled with delight. Then, he smelt the dinner cooking and looked at her inquiringly.

"It is a dish called 'Lasagne'. I got the recipe from the book Thea lent me. I hope you like it!"

Dinner was a great success and the toddlers shared it, too- smearing as much over themselves as went in their mouths. After this, Vic helped her bathe them. Then, they all sat and played together for a while before they went for a walk along the beach in the fading light. After ten minutes, they were each carrying a sleeping child. They returned to their cabin and lay together on the bed, quiet for a moment.

It came to Jane, in a flash of clarity: they needed to move beyond this point to something closer. Maybe Vic could help her, instead of asking Thea.

She took his hand and touched it to her face, saying, "Vic, I need to begin to know who I am. I have tiny fragments of memories, but not enough to put together by myself. I also need to know about so many other things, such as why you and I call ourselves married and are not? Why the church tells me it is sinful for a man and woman to live together when they are not married, but we live together, and it feels so right? I also need to know how a man and woman should behave when they are together alone.

"There are so many things I should know but do not know. As I watch other people, I start to see how many holes there are in my life- things I should know but do not. For instance, when I met you, I only knew how to cook toast, sausages and eggs. I still have no memory of meals from before: of what things I liked or even how to make them.

"The things I don't know are the ordinary things of life. I know how to work a computer, how to do figures and ordering, nobody needed to show me that. But that stuff is just there in my head- I don't have to think about it to know it. Whereas, when I try to think about the ordinary things, like what to wear or how to do my hair, I just do not know.

"Where I lived, before I met you, I was lucky because Ruth was my friend and she showed me many things. Whenever I did not know something, I would just ask her. She never seemed to mind. Because of this, I thought it was normal not to know things and to have to ask her to show me.

"It is only since I have come with you, that I have started to realize all the things that I don't know- but need to. At first, when we came away together, I was so happy just to be with you. I did not think about needing to know these things. It was like something that happened to another person I do not know. But, even if I cannot remember a life before, I know there was one. It must be full of things I did and of people I knew. And I think you know some parts of it.

"So, even though thinking about these things scares me a lot, deep down inside, I think it is time for me to begin to know who I was- in part, to know how to behave better towards you. I feel there are things I need to do for you to make you happier and I do not know what they are.

"Tomorrow, I was going to ask Thea to tell me about the things a woman should know and do to please a man. I would do them for you if I only knew. I think they would please you like the dinner did. That is why I must discover them by asking others.

"But then I thought, *'You are my best friend. You are the one I trust the most. So, before I ask others, first I should ask you to tell me about who I have been, about how I should be with you.* Please tell me these things?"

Now, Vic put a finger to her lips. "You are so perfect the way you are. I could not imagine how you could be better for me and make me happier than being the way you are now. I would rather be with you, the way you are, than be with anyone else I have ever known. If there were a thousand people in a room, I would pick only you.

"If it would make you happy to be married then, of course, I want to be married to you the way other people are. But it would make little difference to how our life is together- our taking joy in being with each other and being together with your children.

"I have not been married before but I think what being married is about is making a promise to the person you marry that you will love them and care for them always, in any way you can. When I asked you to come away with me, I was making such a promise to you.

"When you said you would come with me- you trusted me to keep my promise. So, you were making your own promise to me as well.

"Getting married in church is a way of making these promises while your friends, family and God are looking on- so everyone knows they are true.

"But, as to telling you what I know about you, you are right. There are things from the past that you need to know. There are simple things like about your mother, father, brother and old friends. There are also things that it may be better if you do not know. Things that hurt you before and could hurt you again. These are the things that caused your memory to go away in the first place.

"It is too much for me to tell you all I know at once. There are also many more things you will want to know that I do not know and so I cannot tell you- even if I wanted to.

"As for how to please me, you please me so much already. The other things you want to know are things that only a woman can know. So, perhaps, those are things that Thea can tell you.

"Right now, I want to hold you close, to feel your breath on my cheek, to feel your body touching mine, to feel you inside the circle of my arms. This is the way it is meant to be between us now."

As they lay together in a still place, Vic said, "Perhaps I should start by telling you about how I first met you- the girl in the picture."

She said, "Yes, tell me, but not tonight. Tonight, I want to first tell you something. That is: I want to be married to you. This is what I most want to do. Tonight, I want you to show me and teach me how it is to really be married to you. I want to behave with each other in the same way other married people do.

"It is, like you say, if there was a room with thousands of other men in it- all rich and handsome and nice and I could take my pick- the only one I would choose is you. I cannot imagine wanting to be married to anyone else, but it is what I most want with you.

"It seems to me that when people get married, they make a promise to try and be the best they can for the other person. I want to make that promise to you- like the way you made it to me when we came away.

"It feels right that I should do it in a church where I know God is listening. But that part can wait. For now, I want to know what it feels like to be fully married you- not just where you have made a promise to me, and I have trusted you- but where I have made the same promise to you and given all I can of me to you. I know I can give more, but I don't know what. So now, I need you to tell me and show me."

"After that I want to know about my family. I did not know I had a brother and I most want to know of him."

"But to begin with, before you tell me or show me other things, I want you to first tell me about you. I need to know about you to know best how to please you. So, please, tell me about you. You must have a family, too. I want to know where they live, what are their names and the things you remember from when you are little. Perhaps we can go to the place where your family lives and get married there. Then, I will start to feel like I have a new family which is your family. Once I have discovered who you are, from you telling me about you, I think I will start to know better how to please you. Once I know that, I will be ready for you to begin telling me about myself."

So, as they lay together in the night, he told her about his mother, sister and himself. He told her about everything, except for Mark- up until just before the time when he first met her. She had barely moved as he talked, just asked occasional questions along the way.

Now, she looked intensely into his face with a dreamy smile which quickly transformed into a wicked grin. Very slowly and deliberately, she kissed him on the lips- a long and lingering kiss- which went on and on. His body felt on fire with the intimacy of her touch.

At last, she broke away and asked, eyes crinkled in a smile, "Did you like that? I have seen married people do that after they get married. I wanted to try it and see how it felt with you. It was so much better than I imagined. Now I want to do it again and again."

Vic answered, "For someone who doesn't know what to do to please a man, you seem to be working it out pretty fast. My whole body feels on fire with desire for you. Soon, we really will be living in sin if you keep doing that. I won't be able to stop myself from having all the rest."

Jane gazed intently at him in a puzzled way, "If you liked it, why do you want to stop doing it? If you desire me this way, why stop? I don't want to stop you from doing anything with me or having any part of me. I don't care what the man in the church is talking about."

Vic felt himself drowning in the sea of her eyes. He wanted to keep kissing her. He really wanted to do much more- to fully join his body to hers. *And yet, and yet…..* he did not want to abuse her child-like trust by taking her this way without her understanding what this act was or meant. He must find a way to give her understanding of what she was offering, to let her choose whether this was what she still wanted when she knew what it fully signified.

He willed himself to block out his awareness of her closeness and to only focus on what he thought was best for her. She needed to know who she was, and from whence she came, so she could make a real choice about whether to go to this next place with him, or not.

That was what they had started to do before the distraction of her mouth joining to his had intervened. He did the only thing he could think of: he put his finger back on her lips to break the spell and stop her from going back to this place of intimacy.

He said, "I don't want to stop this anymore than you do. But I think we first need to talk some more about who you are. Then, you can decide if this 'being really married' is still what you want."

An uncharacteristic look of annoyance and hurt came over her face, as if she felt rejected as a woman by his not taking her fully right now.

Vic felt torn. He wanted her so much! He both desired to have her body and did not want to hurt her self-esteem- yet it still did not feel right to consummate their togetherness without her full understanding.

He felt her pull away as if to leave the bed. He put his hands firmly on her shoulders to stop her from going. He looked at her with all the intensity that was burning inside him.

"I have loved you since the day I first saw you. Tonight, I want so much to keep doing what we were just doing together: kissing and more. But please, trust me. Don't pull away or leave me. Just let me hold you and tomorrow we will start the telling of your other life.

"When enough parts are told for you to know from where you came, then you can decide where you want to go from here and if you want me there with you. Once you have chosen with real knowledge, I will go with you wherever you want, as far as you want, without limit.

"You are the most beautiful and precious thing I have ever known. I want you so much- in every way that a man can want a woman. Now, seeing your sad face, I cannot bear to see you hurt.

"But I have been entrusted with my own knowledge of what came before which I must honour, too. So I must find a way to bring those two things back together before we go further from here."

As Vic spoke, he could feel her begin to relax and see the hurt wash out of her face. It was replaced by an intensity of her own. She nodded. For both of them further words seemed inadequate to match their feelings.

Vic drew Jane back in close. They lay very still together and barely touching. After a few minutes, her breathing slowed to an even, regular pattern. He knew she had fallen asleep while still trusting and touching him. He felt so blessed. Soon, he slept, too.

Chapter 12 - Once

The next day, after breakfast, Jane found herself making beds with Thea. She wanted to broach the subject with Thea about how a man and woman should be when together, but she did not know how to begin.

It seemed too unbelievable to admit that she, a woman with two children, did not know about intimate things between a man and a woman- but it was true. Thea was her friend and she needed to find these things out, yet she could not find a way to broach the subject.

She must have seemed distracted because, suddenly, she realized that Thea was talking to her and she had not been listening. Thea snapped her fingers in front of her face, "Hey, you, Jane, wake up. You seem to be off with the fairies this morning. I was asking you something. Well, really, I was making an offer. But if you are too busy to listen, I will stop talking and save it for another day."

Jane brought her attention back to the now, "Sorry, I was trying to think of how to ask a complicated question. What were you saying?"

Thea said, "I suggested I pay you back for the times when you minded my children when I had to go out. I thought, maybe, I could mind David and Annie for the night, so you and Vic could have a night out together. Perhaps you could go to some kind of movie or something. What do you think?"

This idea sounded really exciting to Jane. She said, "That sounds great! I will say it to Vic. What night is good for you?"

Thea said, "Why not tonight?"

Jane said she would check with Vic at lunchtime as he was working around the park today and would be back then.

So, when he came home for lunch, she said it to him.

Vic agreed with a wide grin. She suspected it was as much to please her as for himself, but he had told her before how he had loved going to the pictures with his friends when he lived in Alice Springs.

Tonight, they decided they would go to the picture theatre in Caloundra- just the two of them. She felt thrilled. She said to Vic that, even though they had been together for months, it felt like their first date.

When Vic went back to work, she told Thea they would go and asked her for any suggestions about what to see. So, over a cup of tea, they sat down and looked at the paper together which listed the movies.

Thea pointed to a movie called "Once", saying she had seen it a couple years ago and loved it. It was a sweet romance about an Irish busker and a European immigrant. Now, the musical of it was coming to Melbourne and the movie was being re-shown as part of the publicity. Thea said she thought, perhaps, that Jane would like it. Then, Thea pointed to a couple of other movies and said Vic might prefer them as they were more action movies.

They each went their own way once they had confirmed arrangements. Tonight, once Vic got home around half past five, Jane and he would get ready to go out. Thea would come to their unit at six o'clock to mind David and Anne in their own place. She would feed them and put them to bed once they were tired. Then, Thea would bunk her children down on the lounge next to her while she watched TV until they got home.

Jane dressed up, washing her hair, putting on lipstick and perfume the way Thea had shown her. She felt happy anticipation bubbling within her.

Then, Vic was home and in fifteen minutes he was ready, too. They sat and enjoyed a beer until Thea came. Jane felt the excitement- it was her first remembered date. She would make sure tonight would be special.

As they were finishing their drinks, there was a knock on the door. Thea, with children in tow, came in. The children settled in front of the TV to play while the three adults sat and chatted for a few minutes.

Then, Thea stood up and shooed them out, saying, "Go off and enjoy your night. Don't hurry back. Go out for some supper after. I will just fall asleep on the couch if I get tired."

As they walked out to his car, Vic took Jane's hand- which she really liked. He told her how beautiful she looked. She liked hearing this even more. He asked, 'Do you know what you want to see?"

Jane said, "Thea had suggested a movie called 'Once' which is on at seven o'clock, but I am happy if you want to choose something else."

Vic said, "Once sounds great to me."

They parked the car in the town and walked up the road to the theatre. Other people were gathering in the foyer and creating an excited buzz. Vic went to the sign called 'Box Office', bought tickets, and handed one to her.

She read, "Once – Cinema 3". They walked into the dim room and she chose a seat towards the front, just off to the side. It was as if her mind had unconsciously known where she wanted to sit.

Jane felt a thrill as the lights dimmed and she watched with fascination as the advertisements for local businesses and a series of what turned out to be previews to other movies came on- all looked really exciting. Unconsciously, she slipped her hand into Vic's and snuggled into him while her head rested in the space under his neck.

Then, their movie came on and she settled into the story. There was a man sitting on the pavement playing music and this girl came along. She was drawn to him and fascinated by his talent. They went to a place to make music. Now, they had started singing a song together.

Jane was entranced and, as she listened to the words, she felt tears running down her cheeks. It seemed the song had been written specially for her and Vic:

"I don't know you
But I want you
All the more for that."

When it finished, she looked at Vic through tears, "That was a song about you and me, especially about me and how I feel with you.
It is burnt into my brain and inside I am singing it just for you."
She sang quietly in a voice that only he could hear.

"Falling slowly, eyes that know me
And I can't go back.
You have suffered enough
And warred with yourself
It's time that you won
Raise your hopeful voice you have a choice
You'll make it now"

She continued speaking, softly, "This song says what is important to do. Even though my mind does not know you from before- I want you all the more for that. Your eyes look at me and know me and I can't go back. We have both suffered enough, we will not war with ourselves. It is time that we win and have what we want. I will raise my hopeful voice and make a choice to have you and only you from now.

"It means we must have our full life together from now. I choose to give you all of myself. I know you want to tell me who I am before I decide about us. But, as the song says, *'I don't know you, but I want you all the more for that.'* I don't need to know anything that came before. It is sufficient to know where I am now. Being in this place, with you, is the only thing I want. I know that it is more than enough to have this.

"So, from tonight, let there be no more talk of needing to know the past to decide. I know you now. I want you now. That is all that matters. That is enough for me."

Vic felt overcome by emotion. This beautiful girl, with no knowledge of her past, had chosen him now. It was more than enough for him, too.

They sat and shared the movie in solitude together. Others were there in the theatre, too, but their world had only space enough for two.

They went out for supper together. It was a crowded place. For Jane, however, it was a place only with space for two, again. She sat snuggled into Vic, feeling total trust. She knew tonight she would discover the woman within herself with this man. She told him as much.

He said he was totally happy to just live in this place with her. To just let the past take care of the past.

They came home to a quiet house with five people asleep. Thea woke up and stumbled off back to her own house. Vic carried one child and Thea the other, asleep in their arms, to her home.

Now it was just the two of them. They went to stroke and cuddle their children, both asleep in their own room.

Then, Jane said, "It is time. Now show me how to become the person who really is married to you. You have chosen me and I have chosen you."

Vic brought Jane to their bedroom. He lifted off her dress. She stood there in the half-light, wearing only her underwear.

He said, "God! You look beautiful. Take off the rest of your clothes, too. I want to fill my eyes with you."

She nodded, self-conscious under his eyes, her entire body was tingling with an unknown feeling of aching desire. She turned her back to him so he could unclip her bra. Then, she slid off her panties and turned to face him.

He led her to the bed and she lay there while he took off his own clothes. Now, they lay naked, side-by-side. Then, he gave her a long and lingering kiss before he took her breast in his mouth. He stroked and caressed all over her body until finally, when she could wait no longer, he came inside her.

Slowly, Vic moved and brought her to a place where her body was rising and falling with his, like waves in a sea. As he did, she hugged him tight and kept her eyes, brimming with tears, locked onto his. In that moment of pure adoration, she felt him let himself go. His whole body shuddered in time with hers and as it did, she was in a place of ecstasy, too. It was like the first time for both of them. The physical pleasure was almost unbearable. The most wonderful thing, though, was the joy she felt as their joining went on and on. She was riding on the crest of a wave in the ocean that went on forever.

After, as she lay dreamy in his arms, she said, "Now, I understand what a man and a woman do to give pleasure to each other. What we did was far more wonderful than anything I could ever have imagined or dreamt. Can we do it again and again, lots more times, and soon?

"I am glad you showed me. It would have been difficult to ask Thea about it. If this is part of being married to you, then I want this part most of all."

Vic did not answer with any words. Instead, he just kissed her and made love to her, again.

After that they slept until sunlight and children's chatter woke them. It was good to be a complete family. Lying together, with their children, Jane said, "I would like to know my parents- just as my children know theirs."

Chapter 13 - A Legal Minefield

Alan had spent two months going round and round in circles with the lawyers and the police, trying to figure out a way to get somewhere with this case, so Susan could re-emerge without her whole world imploding.

The judge who had heard the original murder trial was sympathetic. The police commissioner was sympathetic, as he knew there was lots of public sympathy for Susan following Anne's programs on TV. But the prosecution was playing hard-ball. A legal minefield in dealing with Susan's conviction for murder, then vanishing while on bail, needed to be overturned.

Alan felt his life was more and more caught up in endless meetings with lawyers who all had opinions for sale and big egos about how their view of the world was correct. But none had a way forward to get this mess of legal process resolved- other than something like a new hearing and a retrial.

Alan did not want to go there- even if he could get Susan's or her family's cooperation. Without her having memory of what had gone on before, the whole thing seemed futile. This was without even considering the further damage it may cause to her if a trial reopened all those wounds again.

Anne, using David's money, had retained the best lawyer money could buy. He seemed to have the best ideas about how to unscramble this omelette, but even he seemed to have no concrete way forward.

Then there were the ever-present leaks which kept coming out. There was a mole in a key place, either inside the Police and or the Attorney General's department. It was not someone with access to everything, but with enough to keep stoking the fires of a campaign against this girl. It seemed to centre on one English tabloid or web-news service where a black journalist, by-line Jake SS, seemed to keep digging up juicy morsels. Some of them included: this girl had run away and gone into hiding to escape the consequences of her actions and that she was still the evil, conniving bitch as portrayed in the papers of a year and a half ago, when she first had disappeared. This journalist was based in England, but he clearly had an NT source who was feeding him information.

The one thing Alan was pleased about was that he had been able to calm requests for a full-scale search for Susan led by the Queensland

Police, as it was believed she was living there. He stuck to the line, which was true, that he had no direct knowledge of Susan's location. He had just been advised by an intermediate source of her existence and must secure a legal guarantee, one saying she would not have to return to jail, before she or her family would agree to her return or to giving any further assistance with inquiries.

While she was technically guilty of murder and out on bail, with the conclusion of the inquest, it was clear she had no direct role in any murder other than that of Mark. In his case, the finding was she acted on the basis of a real fear for her life. Therefore, a retrial would almost certainly find she acted in 'self-defence' now that all the facts were known. But there could be no retrial without her, and no useful purpose would be served by having one after everything else which had passed.

It seemed the best legal option was to seek some form of pardon. It would let the conviction stands but, in view of the circumstances, no sentence would be imposed and she would be free to resume her life in whatever form she chose. However, there were plenty of problems with this option: including her authorising this request, which would require her having knowledge and understanding of what had gone on before. At some stage, it needed formal communication to occur between her and the parties of government, to arrange this. A pardon was also normally only exercized after an appeal had failed.

In this case, Susan had pled guilty of the crime, thereby agreeing with the verdict. This made it hard to see what basis there was for an appeal. It also would be even harder when she now did not know what her crime had been, or about her first decision to plead guilty.

Due to all this, it went on and on, round and round. This afternoon, Alan thought he might go and see Rebecca, the personal assistant to the Attorney General. She seemed a bright young thing, quick and smart. She was also vivacious, in a slightly boyish way, not exactly beautiful but with cute charm.

She was a lawyer in her own right and seemed to have the ear of the big boss. The big boss was the one who needed to cut a deal in the political world. And, after all, she saw Mr. AG every day. She also seemed sympathetic to Susan's plight. Both Alan and Sandy had past casual conversations with her about the case, in the earlier stages of proceedings, when they had both attended meetings there.

She was someone he thought he could trust. And, working in a high position in which she was privy to all her boss's confidential papers, she could have real influence. Therefore, he should seek to talk to her off the record, just to see if she was willing to use her legal brain and some influence to try and get some new ideas on the table.

Alan wondered if he should go off to university and study law to figure out all this complicated legal manoeuvring properly. However, that would take years and would not help him now.

He felt like the meat in the sandwich as he was the go-between separating his own friends from the government. He had to walk carefully on both sides of the fence. He liked his job as a policeman, with the freedom it gave him to run cases and investigations. He did not want to throw that away through this event. Yet, his strongest loyalty lay to this girl and to trying to find a way out for her, one that left her free to quietly get on with her life.

Well, he decided he would just have to chance it. He would see if Rebecca would meet him for a drink after work so they could have an 'off the record' chat about where to go from here. He knew it should be handled by the barrister David had retained, but Alan thought his own non-legal background might allow him to be more pragmatic in finding creative solutions. Solutions which would pass a reasonable level of legal scrutiny but, most of all, would work in the real world.

Alan decided that, in half an hour when he had finished the report he was writing about a minor burglary, he would take an early mark and head into the city and call to see Rebecca on chance. It would be around four o'clock when he got there, nearly knock-off time on a regular day. He would see if he could get a chance to talk to her and hope it was quiet in her office. Alan knew her boss was away in Melbourne at a conference about something legal. With a bit of luck, she would be on her own without much to do.

Alan would ask Rebecca if he could have an 'off the record' chat about this case, just to try and nut it out. Perhaps she would have time for a coffee break or an 'after work' drink. While they were not exactly friends, they knew each other well enough for a conversation.

He arrived and found himself the only person in the office, apart from Rebecca. He was not sure quite how to broach the topic.

She smiled at him brightly, saying, "So, my favourite police officer has come to pay me a visit on a quiet afternoon- with my boss away and nothing else happening. Perhaps he will offer to buy me a drink in the local in a few minutes once I have logged off my computer."

As they walked outside from her office, she asked Alan to call her Beck-saying 'Rebecca' was too formal. He found she was easy to chat to as they walked. She had a manner which set strangers at ease- not flirtatious, but earnest and interested.

Alan bought them both a drink. They found a secluded corner in the bar which gave them some privacy. They exchanged pleasantries for a minute as they sipped their drinks.

Beck struck Alan as a person with lots of intelligence who was used to thinking outside the box. He had some inklings of reservation about giving too much away. However, she would hardly be in her current job if she was unreliable. He had high-level security clearance and hers must be even higher considering all the sensitive 'cabinet in confidence' documents she dealt with.

Beck opened the door to a more serious conversation with, "I am sure you did not come to visit me to flirt or pass the time- you are too focused for that. And I know that Sandy would cut your balls off if you made a pass. So, I suppose you should tell me what it is you want to talk about."

He gave an outline of his problem, "I have been told by a friend of a friend that a person has discovered where Susan is. But she seems to have lost her memory and apparently, she does not know or remember anything from before she vanished. And she still has a murder conviction, with her bail revoked when she disappeared. It is clear from all that followed, including the coroner's findings, that what she did was in self-defence. However, if she surrenders herself, she will be returned to custody in the NT.

"It is unclear how this can be resolved. Her time for an appeal has long since passed and, if she cannot remember what happened, how can an appeal be made? Even if she is willing to make one, it would be on the grounds of events she doesn't remember. I am told, when she disappeared she was in an extremely fragile emotional state- even suicidal. Her current memory loss seems to be the result of some sort of nervous breakdown.

"So, it seems unlikely she is in a fit state to stand trial. Yet, without a retrial, it is hard to see how she can have her guilty plea undone. To put her back in jail and let her conviction stand, or even for the judge to resume the case for sentencing and then release her, would mean she would have to return to Darwin. If this happened, she'd become a huge sensation again, overnight. The centre of enormous media scrutiny. I'm told it would be very damaging in her current mental state. The people I have been talking to refuse to agree to any return by her to Darwin at this stage, due to her mental health. As we do not know where she is, we do not want to damage the current cooperation we have with these parties by acting in a way which appears to threaten her. If we do so, we may lose our connection with her.

"While we could seek to locate her independently, to arrest her or have her extradited if she is interstate, I am advised this is likely to be both harmful for her well-being and to cause extensive sensational publicity. Thus, forcing her to return is expected to arouse very strong sympathy for her plight- along with a bad public reaction to the actions done to bring her in. This public response would be even greater if any harm comes to her.

"One or two people have floated the idea of a pardon. But I don't quite see how it could be done. And, of course, anything which happens would need the OK of your boss. So, rather than have lawyers talking to lawyers and going in endless circles, I thought I should just try and get your ideas. Perhaps if we can think of something that makes sense, you could tell me how best to make it work through all the official channels.

"What I am really asking is for you to use your legal brain, and perhaps to also use your contacts through your office and your boss, to try and help me figure out a solution to this whole mess."

They talked for almost an hour. Beck was as smart as a whip. She knew about both the politics and the two sides of public opinion: those who saw 'Saint Susan' and those who saw only the murdering witch. Her legal brain quickly explored the various options and dismissed them in much the same manner that others had. The retrial was fraught with problems. The media sensation which would accompany it would be even worse than last time- not to mention the futility of conducting a trial when the defendant had no memory of the events.

Some sort of commission on inquiry was also possible which would lead to a recommendation from a judge to the Attorney General for release. Asking the judge to convene a private hearing for sentencing was also possible. But they were all full of risks, loopholes and problems. In all cases, it seemed that Susan needed to return to the NT.

Her ability to give any useful evidence remained an even bigger problem. It was not as if she was mentally incompetent and needed to be put into mandatory psychiatric care- just that she had no knowledge of anything which had happened from this previous part of her life. This fact had no bearing on her guilt or innocence, only a bearing on her ability to testify.

The option of having her psychologically evaluated was considered, but it came with a high-risk of disclosing her location. Therefore, it was doubtful that an agreement could be gained by the other party for it. If it confirmed she had no memory, it took them nowhere. Whereas, if it was considered she was scamming, then that created a whole new set of problems.

The only thing which seemed to have some merit was the pardon option. However, the Administrator, who was the official with this power, had to act on government's advice. That meant the government needed a good basis for recommending it. Beck agreed she would commission advice on this option. At the same time, Alan agreed he would float the idea to the other side.

As they talked, Alan grew more comfortable with Beck. She seemed to be on his side. She had sharp intelligence and could see all the angles. After they finished their legal discussion, Beck asked him about himself and Sandy. She said she had heard a rumour they had first met on this job, and she asked if it was true. She also asked him what it was like to be living with another serious professional who lived and breathed their job. She wanted to know whether they planned to marry and have children.

He found himself telling her of how he first met Sandy: him thinking she was a bloke and being at first dismayed that a wet city girl was on the job. Then how she caught him out about the fish, which Charlie had caught and hidden and how it led to his friendship with Charlie. Then, he told her of the huge and freaky crocodile who watched their every move.

He thought Beck would laugh at this and tell him it was superstitious nonsense. But she said she was a Territory girl, born and bred, and she had seen too much strange stuff out there to laugh at these things. She even got the 'spirits of the land' thing as it made a strange sense to her.

He found himself telling Beck of his romance with Sandy- leading up to their planned wedding last Christmas and how they had ended up postponing it with all the mess over Susan. He told of the strange mind-link which had seemed to exist between Sandy and Susan. A mind-link which had revealed Susan's terror on the day the murder had happened.

He told how, at first, almost to outdo each other, he and Sandy had been determined to turn this case into a murder. They'd worked together to unearth the clues that made it so: the timber fragments in the skull, the tyre track that linked the vehicle to the site, Susan's DNA in the vehicle and the CCTV footage of Susan. Back then all they knew was she was an unknown person who had been together with the murder victim at Uluru. Then he found the girl at the roadhouse who remembered Susan telling how she had met this man while diving on the Barrier Reef which led to the discovery of her identity in Cairns.

But then, once they had discovered the person responsible for the murder was an English tourist visitor and was someone who had never done anything remotely like this before, it had stopped making sense. This was the point at which they knew there must be more to the story.

Alan told of the weeks he had spent in England trying to get the story from this girl as they went through the extradition process. He told how strongly she had reacted when she felt she had been tricked into giving something away. Then he told of her voluntary decision to return to Australia for the murder trial and of her seemingly inexplicable decision to plead guilty while still telling nothing of what caused the events to happen.

He told Beck how both he and Sandy felt responsible for what followed, because, without their continued digging into it, to make it into a murder case, it never would have begun. Yet, once they found the girl, they knew it did not make sense for her to deliberately kill this man.

He told Beck of his race against time to find out about the texts before Susan was convicted and sentenced to spend her life in jail. He even told her about Anne and Sandy's premonition that Susan would try and commit suicide rather than have the truth come out.

Alan felt as if, in telling this story, he would make Beck into an ally who understood what had led to this bizarre set of events. In doing so, he hoped she would feel sympathy for the situation which followed where Susan was convicted of a murder, but the most reasonable understanding of the events was that she had acted in self-defence. She had only pled guilty to stop damaging information about the man she killed coming out. She had done this out of a strange sense of misplaced loyalty or, perhaps, to protect her children from this future knowledge.

Beck was a good listener. Alan felt she was in Susan's corner as she was showing sympathy for her plight. However, as the conversation progressed, he began to become just a tiny bit uncomfortable. It was nothing specific that he could put his finger on, it was just that her curiosity seemed to make her want to burrow deeper into this girl. Why was Beck asking questions like: where she was living now? Was she now living with someone or on her own?

They were all perfectly reasonable questions which someone in her position could want to know. Yet, he still felt unease with this direction of questions. As this suspicion grew in him, he became evasive in his answers by saying he did not know- even when he did.

Alan knew Beck could read this in him. At first, she did not let on that she knew he was hiding something. It became like a cat and mouse game.

She ended the game by saying, finally, "I know you know more about where she is and how she was found, than you are letting on. Let's leave it that way, for now. I can see why you want to keep this information secret."

As they went their separate ways, he felt he had another ally in Susan's corner. Beck understood what was at stake and she told him she would use her influence to try and untangle all these mixed up threads.

Chapter 14 – Finding Family

It was now December and getting close to Christmas time. Vic thought about Jane's request to know her parents. He also remembered her mother's plea to see her daughter, again, and meet her grandchildren. It seemed time to do something, although he was not sure what.

His occasional talks to Buck and Anne had not revealed any new threats, but he was still nervous about disclosing their location to other people. For now, public interest in Susan was fading. But he knew it would not stay that way for long if there was any real information to go on. Vic knew he must keep being really careful. He did not use any credit cards or go to banks. He got paid in cash for work. He also usually rang the others on a public phone. He did all of this to reduce the risk of their location being found out.

Vic hated to think what effect it might have on Jane if she was tied to 'Susan' and her past life. Jane had made no more requests for information about her parents and seemed to have no desire to know about other parts of her past life. Since the night of them becoming lovers, he felt they had made a pact not to try and reopen the past anymore.

Yet, for the sake of Jane and her parents, Vic wanted to allow this connection with them to happen. He did not know whether it may trigger old memories, but he felt it was time for them to meet, regardless.

The challenge was to work out how to do it without this becoming a way to trace him or her. In the end, he rang Anne to ask her how she thought they could do this, since she seemed to be the source of the best ideas about things such as this. She was also the most logical link to Jane's parents, being the childhood friend who was still keeping in touch with them.

Anne said at once, "How about a Christmas reunion? David and I are going to his family property for Christmas. It is over the Blue Mountains at the back of Sydney. His parents know Susan's parents as well, as a result of their engagement and the trial. They have stayed in touch since then. Plus, there are other cousins in Sydney who Susan's parents may want to visit. So, I am almost sure that, if we invited them to come out for a visit, they would.

"I talked to both Susan's parents on the phone last week. I try to ring at least once a fortnight. They both said how much they wished to see their daughter and their grandchildren before they grow up too much. They did not seem to have anything important planned for Christmas.

"Perhaps, while we at the farm over Christmas and New Years, David could arrange for you to visit us. He could tell the farm staff that you are a friend we met in the NT. He'd say you are bringing your girlfriend with her two children and will all come and stay for a few days. At the same time, David's parents could invite out Susan's Mum, Dad, and her brother Tim. They can stay at the main house. There are plenty of spare rooms.

"There is an empty cottage about two hundred yards from the main house where you could all stay. It is down near the creek and is surrounded by bush, so it will be very private.

"That way, when you come to visit as David's friends, they will be there, too. There will be no obvious connection for workers to notice- not that I don't trust them, but it is still best if they do not know, just in case.

"As it is a property in the country, there will be no snooping journalists or other people who will gossip. It will be a visit of my good friend, Vic, who happens to bring his girlfriend, Jane, and her children. You will be staying in a farm cottage, while Susan's parents are there as guests of David's parents. No one will know they are really Jane's parents. I think that will work.

"For your travel, it is best if you drive down. That's, assuming the old banger of a car that Buck bought you, is still reliable," Anne laughed. If you fly, your movements will be readily traceable. And when you drive, stay in cheap motels or caravan parks along the way and don't use credit cards. With that, I think there will be very little risk of anyone working out who you are.

"And, to be even safer, I think Jane should dye her hair a different color. Strawberry blonde would look good with her blue eyes. That would make it even harder for anyone else to guess her identity.

"So, let's make it happen. I know her parents will jump at the chance to see her again and meet their grandkids. As for me, I can't wait to see my friend, again…. even if she does not remember me.

"I will call next week, once I've had a chance to get it organized."

That night, when they were in bed together, he asked Jane, "Remember how you said you wanted to know your parents? Would you like to meet them at Christmas time?"

Jane hugged him extra tight and said, smiling, "I would love that."

Next morning, she had a pensive look on her face.

Vic asked, "What's the matter?"

"I feel scared I won't know who they are when I see them. Or, what if they don't want to see me?"

Vic said, "I promise you they do really want to see you and they also really want to meet David and Anne since they have never met them. They are their first grandchildren. I will ask them to post a photo of themselves, so you know what they look like."

With that, it was agreed. The next day, they told David and Anne they were going to a place near Sydney to visit their grandparents. They were immediately wild with excitement, too.

Slowly, the days ticked by. It was coming ever closer towards Christmas. Vic had his car serviced. He told the mechanic to give it an extra careful check-up, ensure everything was working well and it was safe for a long trip.

At times, Vic saw Jane looking pensive, again. When he did, he'd ask why.

She always smiled brightly and said, "It's nothing really. I'm just scared about whether I want any of my old life back. I am so happy here. I could not bear for anything to spoil what we have now."

A week before Christmas, a photo arrived in the mail with an England address. It was a picture of Jane's parents and her brother, Tim. On the back was written: "We all can't wait to see you, again."

For a minute, Jane looked at it intensely. Then, she put it down, saying, "I wish I could remember them- but I can't. I do think I want to meet them. But at the same time, I am so very scared- what if our good life comes apart?!

Part of me feels like there is a bad monster hiding in the shadows, one wanting to break loose and smash all the good things we have together."

Chapter 15 - I Beg Your Pardon

Two weeks went by before Alan heard from Beck, again. This time, she rang him saying, "I think I have worked it out. I think I found a way forward. I have spoken to the Attorney General. He, in turn, has talked to the sentencing judge and to the coroner who investigated all the girls who disappeared.

"All are of the opinion that we are in uncharted water here. It is nothing like any case they have encountered before. Their general view is that the nearest thing to correct legal procedure would be to hold a re-trial in which fresh evidence is brought forward to justify Susan's actions. This could be done with or without her consent.

"They also agree, based on what you told me about her current mental state and lack of memory, that such a retrial would be of little value and pose a serious risk to her wellbeing. They all agree it could be a great risk to her of sustaining more mental harm or having a new breakdown.

"And apart from harm to her, should the government seek to force a re-trial, they believe it would play very badly in the court of public opinion. Many people have sympathy for her plight, since the TV program telling her story went to air. To them, she is guilty of nothing other than having bad luck. Of course, at the same time as they come to her defence, all the nuts on the other side will seek to vilify her, too.

"An alternate option discussed was for the trial judge to resume his sentencing hearing following the coronial. He would do this based on the evidence that has since been revealed- including the tape in which Susan told Anne how she killed this man only after he tied her up and she believed he intended to kill her by feeding her to the crocodiles. However, it would be difficult to treat this as formal testimony if Susan is not able to be cross-examined on it. Without that evidence being admitted, it would be hard for the judge to order 'no sentence' be imposed.

"Also, continuing the sentencing hearing, even if done in private, would be impossible to keep secret. With this happening it would become clear to the general public that Susan is alive somewhere, whereas, for now, it is only a vague rumour. With the level of media scrutiny that would follow this revelation, it would become extremely difficult for her to stay hidden, even if she did not return to Darwin for the hearing.

"Having regard to all this, my boss, the coroner and the trial judge want to do two things. The first is for a court-appointed psychologist to evaluate Susan and confirm her absence of memory appears genuine. This examination could be done in a confidential manner- without disclosing when or where it occurred. It could occur in a major centre, like Brisbane or Sydney, to assist in the secrecy.

"The second thing is they will seek advice from a former judge of the High Court about the option for a pardon- if her memory loss is confirmed as genuine. All are assured, at this point, that there is a good basis for her conviction to be set aside and her not to have to serve out any prison term.

"This is based on the phone text evidence from the sentencing hearing and the account of what happened by her friend, Anne, given at the inquest. At the same time, they need to find a way to do this legally. Their current opinion is a pardon appears to be the best option."

"But they want eminent legal advice, given in confidence, to confirm this. Today, I will prepare a brief to seek this advice by mid-January. If the advice confirms that a pardon is legally sound, then the Attorney General will seek the confidential agreement of the other members of the NT Executive Government before proceeding.

"With this being done, I expect we will have a definite answer in the New Year. Meanwhile, I thought you should know now. Officially, my lips are sealed. As yours should be. But it would be good to know if there is agreement to this by the other party. I would not want to have this formally announced without it.

"I have even found a legal precedent that it does not require the consent of the guilty party to seek a pardon on their behalf. It seems this could be done 'in absentia.' Once granted, she would be free to get on with her own life. While the pardon would have to be disclosed, her location would not have to be. This means it will be possible for her to continue her life in whatever way she is now doing. It does not mean that nobody will track her down- but it does gives her a chance to stay hidden if she wants to.

"The Attorney General could announce that, following the inquest and representations from her family, he has sought and granted a pardon for one 'Susan Emily McDonald' to her murder conviction.

"If it is to go ahead, we need to arrange a psychological assessment. In addition, we would need a letter of request for a pardon from her parents, as they are her next of kin."

Next day, Alan rang Buck and asked him to pass the information to Vic and others, but only as required on a strict need to know basis. Buck rang Anne and told her. In return, she told him of the just arranged meeting of Susan and her parents, happening in a fortnight, at Christmas. Vic and Susan's parents could discuss it then. To Anne, it sounded like a good way forward, but it would be for others to decide.

Chapter 16 - Farm in the Mountains

Vic and Jane set off the weekend before Christmas. The car was packed with their camping gear as they had decided to find places along the way, in their drive through the mountains, to camp. They planned to treat this trip as their own holiday, done in easy stages, before they came to the farm.

Last night, Vic called Anne, again. He told her of their approximate plans: three easy days of driving, coming around the back of the mountains and avoiding the big cities of Sydney and Brisbane. The first night, they would be camping in the New England, in a national park at the back of Armidale. The second night, he planned for them to stay somewhere between the Hunter Valley and Mudgee, at the back of the Blue Mountains. He expected them arrive at the farm in the middle of the third day. He had an address and directions to follow from Lithgow to David's family's farm.

They were three wonderful days of swimming in crystal clear mountain pools, giving the children swimming lessons, teaching them to dog paddle and stay afloat without help. They climbed hillsides and plunged under waterfalls with panoramic views, cooked on an open fire and enjoyed the music of birds, along with occasional glimpses of wildlife. They went walking in the night with a torch to pick out forest animal eyes: possums and sugar gliders in the trees, wallabies and native cats on the ground and the frogs which croaked in the creeks. Vic and Jane made love each night under star-filled skies and in the dawn as the first birds called.

Part of both of them wanted to keep driving. With just themselves' for company, forever, it felt as if they could endlessly postpone the day of the meeting. However, they knew it must happen. It was the only way forward for all of them. Vic hoped it was the start of a return to a life in the open- an end to all the hiding. At the same time, he understood and shared Jane's terror of it all coming apart.

Jane had her hair cut short and died a strawberry blond color. It made her look almost boyish and a bit like a hippy. Thea had helped with it, getting into the spirit of the game of a 'new Jane.' Part of Vic hated to lose his familiar partner, but knew it was for the best. She looked great, either way.

Each new version of her was like a new woman emerging from the old. Vic told her it was really sexy, getting to make love to a different-looking her. Jane was happy he found her alluring and exciting. The children complained at first, but within a day, they were used to their 'new look Mum.'

Two days before Christmas, at lunchtime, they drove up the road towards a grand farmhouse which was nestled into a hollow in the hills. There were high mountains rising behind it and an elegant, formal garden in front. The road wound through lush green fields with cows, sheep and horses grazing. A sign on the farm gate told Vic they had arrived.

With no one in sight, as they pulled up, Vic tooted the horn. Then, he reached over and squeezed Jane's hand to feed reassurance to her clearly anxious state. Anne came bounding out and saw her friend sitting in the front seat. Without pause, Anne ran over to Jane, pulled open the door and pulled her out. As she did, a light went on in Jane's eyes. She knew one person from before! She hugged her friend as tears streamed down her face.

She said, "I don't know how I know you- but I do! It is so good to see someone that I know I know- even if I can't remember from when. I think, maybe, you were my friend when I was little at school. Though, that seems like such a long time ago."

Anne nodded, tears in her eyes, too, "Yes! We first became friends at the start of High School. We were both twelve when we met. It does seem like a long time since then."

Following, a few steps behind Anne, were three other people: Susan's mother, father and brother. Again, Jane did not know how she knew them, she did not remember them, but she knew them in some way, all the same. It was not from the picture they sent her. It was something more primal. She knew, without understanding why, knowing they were her family, they were of her, and she was of them.

Jane ran to them and hugged them, "Mum, Dad, Tim!" she cried as she wrapped her arms round them.

They hugged her back. "Em! Our own dearest daughter, our Susan Emily"

She pulled back and looked puzzled, "I must be mistaken. I thought I knew you, but my name is Jane. I don't know an Emily or Susan."

Suddenly, she looked like she might run away in fear, at having made a terrible mistake.

"Of course, dear. Our daughter's name is Jane. Susan and Emily are her pet names from another life," her father said, quickly. "You are our daughter, Jane. You have that impish smile you did, from when you were a little girl."

Jane still looked uncertain, but the fear on her face receded.

Her father continued, "I remember you when you used to ride on my shoulders- when you were the same size as these two little monkeys here," as he looked to where two small children and a man still sat seated in the car.

She nodded and walked back to the car. She started to lift out the two children and paused to look for Vic to come with her. He picked up David and she picked up Anne. They carried them to where the others were standing.

Now, the circle was joined by David, his parents and a farm worker.

David took over and did the formal introductions, saying, "Mr and Mrs McDonald- I would like you to meet my good friend, Vic Campbell, and his partner, Jane Bennet. She is here with her two children, David and Anne. They are visiting for a few days and staying in the cottage down by the creek."

Everyone shook hands and exchanged formal greetings.

David's father followed on, "Actually, we were about to sit down for lunch. We set extra places in the hope you might arrive soon. Why don't you come inside and join us? After lunch, David will show you to the cottage where you are staying."

As they walked inside, Tim came alongside Jane and linked his arm to hers. He whispered in her ear, "You may not remember us properly, but I sure as hell remember you. Wait until I start telling all the others of all the things we used to get up to when we were little together, Sis."

Jane found herself grinning back at him and said, "If you tell on me, I will tell on you, Bro. I don't remember lots, but I do remember some things I am sure you don't want told." *If not quite true- it would soon be,* she thought.

A wonderful week passed. They swam in the dams and creeks. They walked in fields and forests. The children had unlimited attention from so many others who were always willing to play a game or listen to them.

Despite initial intentions of secrecy from the staff who worked on the property, it was clear this could not be sustained. There was too much unconscious behaviour and affection between Jane, Anne, Jane's parents and her children, for this to work. For one thing, Little David and Anne were shouting out 'Grandma' and 'Grandpa' each time they saw them.

David talked to the cook, gardener and the general station hand- the only ones who were working while they were staying over. He explained the situation to them and the need for 'no talk of this' to leave here.

They all readily agreed, and David knew he could trust them. They had all worked here for years and were close, family friends as much as they were employees. After this, they really could be a family together, again. From then on, they spent most of their time in each other's company.

Jane and Vic went riding across the farm to help move the sheep and cattle from paddock to paddock. Jane particularly loved this. She found she had a natural affinity for horses and balance in riding. Even though she could not remember her lessons as a child, the knowledge had stuck. Typical riding parties were David, Vic, Anne, Jane, Tim and the station hand. While they were doing so, the children would do things with their grandparents.

David joked they had so many horsemen, they could easily muster a thousand head of cattle- not just the tens and hundreds in their paddocks. In reality, the riding gave them time and outdoor space to discover the world along with each other. It was broken up by bursts of wild galloping up and down mountain trails, the wind whipping their faces.

Jane confided in Vic on the second night, "I don't know why I was so scared. It is really wonderful to be back with my family again and also with Anne. I only have occasional memories of being a little girl with my Mum, Dad and brother and only remember odd things with Anne in High School. But it is enough. I feel like I have a past and belong somewhere, again."

Chapter 17 - A Family Meeting

All too soon, the last day came before Vic and Jane began to drive home. The others were leaving the next day, too. David needed to return to Sydney for work. Jane's parents' flight back to England went the day after tomorrow so they would drive back to Sydney with David and Anne.

It was a very poignant day. They all wanted to slow it down. However, it seemed like trying to make the clock run slower, only made it run faster.

Anne was conscious of a big elephant in the room. She needed to talk to Vic and Janes' parents about the news from Alan of a possible pardon and tell them of the steps involved. So far, she'd made no mention of it, except to David, as she did not want to spoil the wonderful holiday mood. Now she must do it today or lose her chance. But it was difficult for her to get these others on their own without Jane being there.

It was funny how, in the space of ten days, Susan or Emily had become Jane in her mind- along with everyone else's, it seemed. Perhaps it had been that almost-disaster on the first day- when Jane's Dad had used the wrong name in an unconscious display of affection. Then he had expertly retrieved the situation, turning Susan and Emily into childhood pet names. After that, everyone was very careful with the name they used- but it had only taken a couple days until the difficulty passed.

Anne wondered how she could get the others together without Jane. It seemed rude to deliberately exclude Jane from a family meeting which was about her. But they could not discuss the legal options with her present- not without telling her the truth that her 'Jane mind' was hiding from her.

Then, it came to her. Jane had been talking about learning new recipes to cook for Vic and the cook had offered to teach her a couple. That would be the excuse! Anne would ask the cook to spend an hour or two this afternoon, teaching Jane, as part of preparing their final night family dinner. It promised to be a special occasion, fitting such a goodbye: a roast leg of lamb, salmon entrees and a selection of wonderful deserts. She went and asked the cook, a lady in her middle years, if she would take Jane under her wing for a couple hours this afternoon and get her to help with the dinner. Anne suggested the cook teach Jane some new dishes along the way. Once Jane was occupied, she would ask David's Mum and

Dad to take little Davie and Annie out for a walk to occupy them while the rest gathered in the living room.

Five minutes later, Jane came bubbling excitedly up. "Cook asked me to help her in the kitchen and she is going to teach me some new dishes. I have left the children with Vic. I am really looking forward to this."

Anne asked David to run down to the cottage to gather Vic and the children while she went and found Jane's parents- who were currently chatting over a cup of tea with David's parents. She quickly explained to them all what she needed to do: to talk with Vic and the others about the options to get the murder conviction removed from Jane. David's parents gladly agreed to take the children for a walk in the garden.

David kept watch to ensure Jane stayed in the kitchen while Anne spent five minutes repeating what Alan had told her. The pardon option appeared to be the most promising but, with it came the need for Jane to have a psychological assessment to confirm her lack of memory.

Anne could feel resistance in Vic. He was the one who had given up his other life to be with and care for this girl, and he had already lost her once before. He said he did not want to take any chances with her wellbeing when he felt she was making good progress in her life with him. Vic added that they had decided to get married, and it was mainly because Jane had decided this. It was what he had always wanted, but he had wanted it to be a deliberate choice on her part- which it now was.

Jane's parents had said little up until this point. Now, they said the marriage was wonderful news. They said they had no words to adequately express their gratitude to Vic for all he had done for Jane and knew he would make a wonderful husband for their daughter. While they wanted to get the legal situation resolved, they said they would trust Vic's judgement about what was best for Jane.

It was at this point that David, who had been silently watching from the door, finally spoke, "Vic- for Jane to get married, you will need to resolve her identity. To issue a marriage certificate, the registrar or church will need to confirm her identity. As she is an English citizen, the UK government will have to have a role in it. I am not saying that you should tell her what her real name is, but you need identity documents which match her name on a passport or birth certificate, in order to get married.

"If she can get a pardon, then at the same time, her parents could seek for her name to be changed to match the name she knows herself by.

But, to do this without her requesting it, you need some form of authority for her parents to act on her behalf. It sounds to me like this will need an evaluation which confirms that she believes she is Jane Bennet and does not know her other identity. This would lead to the natural conclusion that her name should be changed accordingly.

"It is a job for a lawyer in England to figure out how to do this name change. But, at a minimum, I think it will need a parental request along with a medical document which confirms her lack of memory.

"So, to get married, as you both want, you need a way to do this. I can see no way without something like the psychological assessment that Anne is talking about. However, at the same time, we must ensure this examination does not cause further damage.

"I have a lot of contacts in the medical field from my work. How about I start by inquiring who has the best expertise in this area? Then, I can arrange for you to have a private meeting with whomever seems best. They can then inform you about how such an examination is done. When you understand this, you can make an informed decision as to whether it is worth the risk.

"The risk of trying to maintain the life you have now is also great. If the children or Jane get seriously ill, people will seek an identity for her. It will be the same in another year or two when, it is time for the children to go to school. So, we need to find a way forward and this is the best way I can see."

Vic nodded, reluctantly, adding "OK. I see that. I hate it- but I could not bear to get into the situation you are talking about where her identity comes out anyway and she is arrested and taken to jail. So, I agree to you trying to find a good medical person to do this and meeting with them."

After this, they worked out details for another half hour, before they all agreed this day was too precious to waste sitting around and talking.

Instead, they had an afternoon picnic in a hollow in the hills, sitting amongst screeching parrots and kangaroos. Then, they had a wonderful evening dinner. The two children took place of pride, this party particularly was for them, the family birthday party they had never had before.

As the stars came out into the clear air of a mountain summer evening, they sat on the veranda in little groups sharing company and tales. For a while, Jane's parents sat with Vic. They were telling him how much they appreciated all he had done for their daughter and that he was part of their family now. They added they hoped to meet his own family, shortly, too. Then, the groups rearranged. Now, it was Vic and Jane talking to David's parents while Anne and David talked to Jane's parents. Then, Jane and Tim were locked in close conversation while the rest sat apart. Finally, the whole group joined together to share a glass of port while two sleepy children slept on their grandparents' laps.

It was a difficult goodbye the next day. They had all become so close, like one huge family, over the last ten days. Jane said she wanted to see all her newfound family and friends again, soon. She also said she wanted to get on with arrangements for her and Vic's wedding. She wanted to go to Alice Springs, meet Vic's family and get married there. And she wanted this new family of hers to all come, too.

Everyone agreed it was a good idea and said they would all come once it could be arranged. It was too hard to tell Jane of all the obstacles which had to be overcome before it could happen. However, as Anne and Vic said their own goodbyes, both had a sense they had opened the Pandora's Box in bringing Jane back into the world of others who knew her. It was as if they had started a runaway freight train, with no one at the controls. Stopping it from here without a train wreck may be easier said than done.

Vic felt pleasure in the happiness he had brought to this delightful girl who sat beside him, cuddled into his arm, as they drove away. At the same time, he felt a great fear that it could all go horribly wrong and control could slip through his fingers.

His mind's eye saw Jane as an exquisite crystal: flawless perfection outside, but cracks running through the core. One big knock could shatter this crystal into a million fragments- never able to be made whole again.

An old nursery rhyme ran through his mind:

"Humpty Dumpty sat on the wall.

Humpty Dumpty had a big fall.

All the King's horses and all the King's Men.

Never could put Humpty back together again."

Chapter 18 – Divided Loyalty

The next week, after updating Alan about the holiday visit, David arranged a teleconference with his barrister and the NT Attorney General's office. On the other end of the line was the NT Minister and his executive assistant, Rebecca Singleton- the 'Beck' of Alan's conversation.

His barrister spoke on his behalf, "My client's representative may be willing to agree to the psychological assessment you are proposing, to show she has lost all memory of the events which occurred. This is on the basis that, if we do so, you will seek a pardon for my client from the murder conviction, without the need for a retrial or a resumed sentencing hearing.

"Such agreement must be on the basis that all events which have occurred prior to a pardon being granted must remain absolutely in confidence. Both the medical examination and all future dealings with her or her representatives must be done in a way which does not reveal my client's current location and allows her to continue her current undisturbed life."

The Attorney General answered, "That is very much what I had in mind-with the examination to confirm her mental state being the first step.

"I have sought expert advice from a former justice of the High Court to confirm a pardon is legally appropriate in this situation. I expect to receive this by the end of the month. If this supports our proposed course of action, I will then give an undertaking to seek a pardon on behalf of my government. In the meantime, I am happy to give an undertaking of confidentiality on behalf of my department for any of the other steps which need to occur.

"The only caveat is that the psychological assessment needs to be done by a person who is acceptable to my office, both on the basis of their expertise and their independence. This party may be required to give, in person, private evidence to NT legal authorities of their findings. I will leave it to Rebecca to confirm the suitability of such a person directly with you."

The barrister replied, "Have you identified any such people you consider to be suitable to do this examination at this stage?"

Rebecca replied, "As you are aware, most of the leading psychologists are based in cities such as Sydney, Melbourne and Brisbane. I have a list of names which may be suitable. I have yet to meet with any of them or to discuss what is required of them. Because of the sensitivity of this issue, I wish to meet in person with only a small number of relevant specialists, to determine who has the most appropriate skills and, at the same time, ensure this person fully understands the absolute confidentiality of this task. I am happy to fly to one or more major Australian cities to meet these people- if we can agree on a shortlist with requisite qualifications and expertise."

The barrister replied, "Do your list include Dr. Ross Sangster of Brisbane?'"

"Indeed, it does," Rebecca replied. "He and 'Dr. Pamela Hunt, in Sydney,' are top of my list. In Melbourne, 'Dr. Veronica Ritchie' is also high on my list."

"Is Dr Sangster acceptable to your client?"

The barrister replied, "I believe he is likely to be. I would want to have the opportunity to interview him, in person, before confirming this."

Just like that, it was agreed. They would meet in Dr Sangster's Brisbane examination rooms the following week to work out the details and confirm he was satisfactory to all. They would only arrange to interview other doctors if either of them had reservations about the suitability of this man.

Beck flew to Brisbane on the next Tuesday evening for a Wednesday meeting with the psychologist and the barrister from the other side. She could have flown on the red-eye flight which left at two o'clock in the morning, getting in at breakfast time. However, she really hated spending nights on an aeroplane when she could sleep in a comfortable bed. Not that there was anyone to share this bed with at either end right now, but it still a bed sure beat an aeroplane seat.

As she sat into her seat that afternoon and banked over Darwin before heading south, Beck thought about how drab her life had become over the last two years. She was an up-and-coming lawyer with a prestigious job, although the pay was only mediocre.

She should be living the high life in her own apartment. Instead, she lived at home and cared for her Mum who had Motor Neurone Disease. Her Mum was going downhill fast. Not that she begrudged her Mum the care, for they were close. There was no other family still living in Darwin. Her brother and sister were long gone- one to Kiwi Land and one in Perth. Her father had been dead now for five years, although she still greatly missed him.

It was the least she could do. But, still, it was nice to be away for a night and know this night was her own. It had been hard keeping the money up for her Mum's treatment. Sure, the public health system paid a fair bit. However, the extra new treatment, which promised some hope of stopping the disease's awful progression, was paid for out of her own pocket.

While it had been a struggle thus far, she had managed to raise this extra cash. But there was nothing left for a life of her own. Thus, her social life had almost vanished over the last two years. Despite this, she kept a bright smile on her face and tried to act as if she was a party girl.

Her outgoing demeanour had really come in handy when she had met that journalist, in town, the year before last. It was six months after her mother's diagnosis. It just after she had moved back home, but before it had got too bad. It had been one of her few nights out. This man was in town for the trial and sentencing of the notorious 'Crocodile Man killer,' the English witch-bitch dubbed 'Crocodile Girl.'

At the time, Beck had largely bought negative gossip doing the rounds that this girl, Susan, was a cold-calculating killer. She was flattered when a guy, Jacob, had come up to her in the bar and told her how hot she looked. After buying her a few drinks, he suggested they go back to his hotel room to finish the night.

It had been one of the last and best lays she had. Good sex was hard to find when you lived with a Mum who depended on you. In the pillow talk after, when it emerged that she worked for the Attorney General and had the inside info on the case, and she had also told him about the struggle to pay for her Mum's treatment, he had offered to help.

He said, if she could provide some inside information about the case, he could arrange for his media outlet, an online news service in London which syndicated to many papers across the world, to make generous donations to help cover her mother's medical expenses.

With this offer, she told him what she knew, from the inside, about this case, back then. She'd not known about the last-minute defence pitch which got Susan out on bail until it had happened. However, Beck had known that, after Susan's release, she was staying with her new boyfriend Vic, the helicopter pilot. She also knew this girl had taken up use of her middle name, 'Emily' instead of 'Susan.' This fact had been part of the bail related information that had come to her boss.

With those bits, plus Jacob's existing knowledge about this girl whose life he had been digging into for months now, it had become the article he entitled 'The Two Faces of Susan Emily McDonald. It had been a big splash in the paper just before Susan had gone missing. Beck also knew it had been a huge story across Australia and England for days. Susan's disappearance had then made it even bigger and more sensational.

The ten thousand dollars which had turned up in her account a few days later, labelled 'bet winnings,' had been very welcome. She had thought the article Jacob wrote had been a bit over the top, but hell, the girl was no saint. She was an uppity Pommie bitch. At least that was how Susan had struck her, on the one day she had seen her in court for her trial. It was the way she smiled from the witness box as they asked her about the murder. All said and done, Beck did not feel bad that a big part of the story had come from her.

She remembered the next time she saw Jacob. In town for the inquest, he had looked her up to ask for any more insights. Another good night of sex had followed- the last one she'd had. He had asked her if she had any more inside info. She did not have much at that stage, just a bit more about the police investigation which had never quite got out before. It was only minor details, but it added local color. Jacob paid another $5000 for this. He promised Beck that any more bits would also be paid for similarly.

When the rumour of the girl turning up again got going, she fed this too him, too. It had earned her another ten thousand. It seemed harmless enough. She had never walked in the shoes of this girl, but Beck thought she was an English tramp who had been caught and had run away from facing the music. That money really helped with her Mum's latest treatment.

But, as fast as she spent money on her Mum, new sets of needs and costs appeared. A better wheelchair was the latest on the list. It was another cool ten thousand of which the state would pay near zero. They said the old one was 'good enough,' even if her Mum was no longer strong enough to push it up even the gentlest hills on her own. Now, Beck needed another ten big ones for this motorized wheelchair. She knew Jacob would pay.

However, Jacob was getting antsy. He was saying it was past time for more juicy inside info, suggesting she needed to try harder to find some. He went as far as to say how he would 'hate it if the deposit slip for the money he had paid her was to turn up in her boss's mail.' Jacob was chasing where this Susan girl was holed up and figured it was probably in Queensland somewhere. Yet, he was getting nowhere. Now, he suggested Beck was not trying hard enough to find out.

She knew she would lose her job instantly, along with her career, if the payments ever came out. She hated the way that what she had done was being used against her. But the money for her Mum had made such a difference. Therefore, she had told Jacob she would try harder to find out where Susan was, and she had meant it.

Then, the real story had been dropped in her lap by that copper, Alan. Trouble was, she liked the guy. She liked Sandy, too. She was not jealous of their relationship in any way. There was also something honest and good about the way he was putting his job on the line to protect and help this girl. Alan had told her about the guilt he felt for his role in convicting her. As she saw his decency this way, she started to feel ashamed about her own role in the public sensationalism of the crime. It was too easy to wriggle out of any blame by saying the information she had given had made no real difference and Susan got what was coming to her.

However, as Alan told his tale about Susan to Beck that day they had sat in the corner of the pub, Beck had started to walk in Susan's shoes. She was seeing how it must have felt from the inside: so desperate and so alone that she was even suicidal. There was something honourable about the way in which Susan was refusing to disclose the true nature of the man she had killed, even though it had come out later in the police investigation. The idea of Susan protecting her own unborn children from 'guilt by association' with their biological father also did seem well intended.

Knowing all this, it was no longer easy to be the inside source when the information would be used to damage this girl. Though, God knew, she really needed that money! The next ten grand would buy the wheelchair.

For now, Beck tried to block out her dual-role and focus, instead, on the here and now. The fact that she was doing something now which may help this girl- maybe that could even undo some of the harm she had caused. It was a nice thought, although it would not pay the bills.

As well, living this dual-life gave her empathy for this other girl, Susan. Beck now understood how it was to be trapped by bad decisions and their consequences, even if a decision was well meant. She was pleased that what she was doing now may help this girl. She was hoping it would tip the balance back a bit against the bad she had done before. However, now, she had a big moral dilemma to deal with: whether to pass on this new stuff to Jacob in return for more cash or not. That decision could wait.

Chapter 19 – Mind Jigsaw Maker

The next day, Beck went early to the doctor's waiting room. She hoped to meet him before his day's work began and form her own view of him and the case before the barrister for the other side arrived.

A receptionist showed her in. Beck said she was early for an appointment with Doctor Sangster. As she had some reading to do, she said she would sit and wait until the due start time arrived. The lady nodded, then ignored her. She obviously serviced a range of consultants, each with their name on their own room door, although no other patients or activity were evident.

While Beck waited, she studied the dossier she had compiled on this doctor. He must only be in his mid-thirties, based on the date of his initial graduation. Despite this, after his primary degree, he'd moved quickly to specialise in psychiatric illness associated with memory loss of traumatic origin, and particularly long running cases.

After doing his Master's Degree in memory associated disorders, he had worked as a consultant psychologist in a highly regarded Sydney practice. Within three years, he enrolled to do his doctorate on a fellowship to study at John Hopkins University in the US. He had worked there for a further five years in a post-doctoral role before returning to establish his own specialist practice in central Brisbane.

It was clear Dr. Sangster could have made a bigger mark in Sydney or Melbourne, but his choice was Brisbane. Now, he was generally considered the leading expert in traumatic memory loss in Australia and saw patients from all over the country. This brief was a bit different, though. He was not being asked to treat a person, but simply to assess whether the memory loss seemed real and could be explained by these types of circumstances. He would also be asked to give an opinion on the risk of harm if the person was forced confront the events of which the memory was suppressed or lost.

As Beck sat reading about his career and rapid rise, she lost track of the external environment. She was absorbed in reading through the list of the abstracts of his key publications. They seemed highly relevant to this circumstance. Most were about the impacts of physical injury, but some about other emotional triggers.

She became aware of someone standing near, looking down at her.

This person was tall with straggly dark hair which was a bit dishevelled, as if personal grooming was not a big focus for him. In contrast, he was well- dressed. He looked as if someone else chose good clothes for him, but he then selected and dressed in them with minimal effort and care.

She would not have said he was handsome, but there was something attractive about him. She looked up and asked, "Yes?"

"I was wondering if you were waiting for me. As far as I know, none of the other consultants are in this morning. I don't have my first appointment for another half an hour. You seem to be here waiting for someone- though, you do not look like a patient," he responded.

Beck looked at him properly now, "Are you Dr. Sangster?"

"Last time I looked at my face in the mirror, it seemed to answer to that name," he answered, giving a self-deprecating shrug and a cautious smile.

She stood up now and held out her hand, "Beck Singleton, from the Northern Territory," she said.

Now, he raised an inquiring eyebrow. Dr. Sangster really did have a curious and expressive face, "A singular origin and a singular name," he said, then added, "Pardon the pun. Too many singles, all in one place."

Beck gave him a searching look, "Way too cryptic for me, Doctor. But, yes, I am here waiting for an appointment with you. Though, I am still rather early. I decided to sit here, to read about you, rather than wait down in a coffee shop. Your biography is impressive, but I would have not joined it to your face if I had run into you in the street. Perhaps, in the same way that my life is full of singularities, yours is full of little discordances."

Now, he genuinely smiled, "Ah! Someone to rise to the challenge of the mind. I do like that! My work with memory and the mind is like riddles within riddles. I fear it has affected both my speech and manner.

"But, seeing you are not waiting for me in a coffee shop, and I am yet to have a morning coffee, please come inside and join me in having one. I have yet to brew a coffee- which I need to fire up my memory and mental faculties in preparation for my formal meeting with you and the other lawyer, a Senior Counsel his clerk said- who, I presume, is yet to arrive. So, rather than me drinking my caffeine dose alone, perhaps you will share it with me?"

He showed her through to an anteroom at the back of his examination room. It held a computer with a large screen on one side. A mini kitchen with a gleaming coffee machine along with a large jar of chocolate cookies next to a sink was on the other side. Between the two places, there was a large window which looked out onto the river. In front of the window, there were two comfortable chairs with a small table between them.

Dr. Sangster indicated to Beck to have a seat while he filled and pushed a button on the coffee machine. Then, he set two cups and plates, each with a cookie, on the table. He sat silently in the opposite chair while the coffee bubbled away and filled the room with a delightful aroma.

In a couple minutes the coffee was made. He poured them both a small cup and offered Beck cream and sugar, saying, "This is one of my American acquired indulgences- to sit and sip my coffee with a dollop of cream and sugar, along with an American cookie, before I start on my day's work. I work on the task of trying to understand how the mind works and, when it stops working properly, how to put it back together.

"I think my days of work are like making complex jigsaw patterns, trying to find shapes amongst many mixed-up bits. The mind is like that: it holds vast stores of information and, remarkably, manages to keep them organized and retrievable. It's not unlike a massive filing system. What's surprising about memory is not when it malfunctions or fails, but how, when a part of it does fail, the rest of it still works so superbly in all the millions of everyday tasks. Understanding how and why it works, and the reasons when it does not, is my life's great challenge.

"But we should leave business until its time has come. For now, tell me about you- the singular girl from the singular NT?"

Despite the bizarre introduction, she found this man easy to talk to. She told him about her study to become a lawyer and her job in the NT. She even told him a little of her difficult life with her mother. She did not want to get stuck on this topic with expressions of sympathy, so she quickly moved the conversation on by asking about him and what had brought him to Brisbane- especially when a glittering career in the US seemed on offer to him.

"Well, like you in the NT, this country is my home. After years in the US, I found I was homesick for Australia- particularly for its tropical places. Yet, at the same time, I needed a big city to pursue my work. Brisbane seemed most desirable. Now that I have moved here, I find myself content. Neither of my parents is alive and I do not have any other family. Sometimes, I think of moving further north. However, it would be hard to sustain my practice and expertise in a smaller town. Here seems to offer the best of both worlds."

There was a tap on the door and the receptionist indicated the other barrister, Michael Roberts, had now arrived. Dr. Sangster went out to meet him and bring him in, saying Beck should finish her biscuit and coffee before she joined them in the examination room.

Dr Sangster poured Michael his own cup of coffee and went into the examination room to wait for everyone in there. Full introductions were given before they proceeded with their meeting. Beck and Michael explained what they needed: for Michael, the most critical requirement was for absolute privacy in relation to his client and for Beck, it was the need to have an objective examination which would stand up to legal scrutiny.

They both agreed that they wanted the examination to not add any further injury to an already damaged person.

After this, both of them gave a sketchy outline of the situation from their point of view: the claim of loss of memory by a person accused of a very serious crime in the NT, the need to evaluate if it was a real memory loss, and to provide a confidential report on this for legal consideration. This was all said with only generalities given of the situation.

Dr. Sangster put up his hands, saying, "I need to stop you both there. My rooms are private and soundproof. The other consultants all are away doing hospital work this morning. The receptionist is the only other person on the premises as of now. She is paid to answer the phone and I have told her not to disturb us.

"Therefore, I feel we are going in circles and not getting to the point. I am happy to give an undertaking for total confidentiality in relation to this meeting. But, if I am to examine this person in any capacity, I need an accurate history of what has happened, so as to give you my best and most accurate advice. This history is needed regardless of whether I give you a report on her memory loss in general or I try and treat her memory loss.

"Every person is different. Every examination is different. It is something I need to plan carefully before I meet the client. I need to be as open as possible about my knowledge once I know them. I cannot do this if both of you keep talking in circles. Perhaps, we can begin by you both deciding on whether you are willing to give me full information about this matter.

Then, once you have considered and hopefully agreed on that that, we can decide on the next steps from there. I will go out and talk to the receptionist about my patients for the afternoon. While I am there, you can talk between yourselves and decide whether you can be sufficiently frank for us to proceed. There is no point going any further unless I understand what has happened. If I do not know what happened, I risk causing much more harm in the process. I will not do that."

With that said, Dr. Sangster walked out of the room. Now, they had to rapidly strike up an agreement about how to deal with the unknown Susan. They also had to decide how much to share with each other and how much each of them could then tell Dr. Sangster.

Beck and Michael quickly agreed they were both happy to engage this man, he was the best in his field and, despite some quirky mannerisms, there was no doubt about his skill. Therefore, they would jointly tell him about the murder trial, Susan's disappearance and the inquest.

When they got to that point, Michael informed Beck that the information he held about Susan's current situation could only be disclosed privately and without Beck present. This was because there had been previous internal leaks from the NT government about this case.

She winced internally at this, realising she was on thin ice, and agreed she would leave the meeting while this information was provided. Then, once it was done, she would return to confirm arrangements from there.

With all this decided, they called Doctor Sangster back in. When he was seated, they began the story each taking turns.

Beck started off saying, "The person of interest is 'Susan McDonald.' I am not sure if you have heard of her, she is the person sensationally labelled by the press as 'Crocodile Woman.'- if this name is more familiar to you."

Beck watched an expressive eyebrow go up as the name was said and a small nod to indicate that he knew exactly who she was.

Over the next few minutes, she gave a quick summary of the 'agreed publicly-known events' from: Susan first coming to Australia, travelling in the company of a man with the alias of Mark Bennet, discovering his role in the disappearance of other backpackers and, then, killing him. She told of the discovery of the head and forearm, the evidence linking his death to Susan, of her extradition to stand trial and of her guilty plea to murder- along with her refusal to describe what happened and why.

Beck told of sentencing day, with an expectation of a twenty-plus year sentence, then of sensational evidence given on the day of the texts linking Susan's action to her belief this man had killed the other backpackers which gave grounds for self-defence. Then, she told how the judge had ruled that, while the texts were being investigated, Susan MacDonald would be released on bail. Last, Beck told how Susan had vanished less than a week later.

Beck told of information suggesting she had become suicidal, evidence suggesting her return to the waterhole of the murder and of the failure of all further inquiries to determine her fate. Beck said there had been a widespread view that she was dead- but with lots of doubters who thought she had fled justice. Beck told how the inquest had returned an 'open finding' about her fate while also making a finding that, despite her guilty plea, there was good evidence to believe she had acted in self-defence.

Beck then told of recent contact by parties claiming to represent her, indicating she was alive but had a total memory loss of these events and they were refusing to disclose her location. She also told him that the desire of those she represented was to resolve her legal situation, with the idea of a pardon, based on the inquest evidence along with her inability to testify.

But, for this to occur, they needed an assessment of her mental state to determine if her memory loss appeared genuine. They also sought advice on the risk of further harm should she become aware of what had happened before she disappeared, as well as the risks to her if she was returned to jail or subjected to any further legal processes.

When Beck finished her recitation, Ross Sangster leaned back, flexing his fingers and looking at her intently. "Well, you have certainly described a situation which captures my interest. Of course, you are asking me to 'play God' and tell you the consequences of finding out unremembered events- which is unknowable. But I can at least evaluate her current psychiatric state and point out what the key risks are. These are likely to be great."

Beck returned his ironic tone, "Well, I had not quite mistaken you for 'God,' but as I read your biography- it appears that you are generally regarded as the nearest thing to his surrogate in your field in Australia. So, I can settle for an expert opinion from God's deputy."

He nodded and smiled back, almost warmly, "Well, I think you have given me all you can for now about the events up to the disappearance. Now, I need to talk to your colleague in private to find out what he can tell me about what has happened since then.

"There is an excellent coffee shop just around the corner from my office. I suggest you allow an hour before you return for us to have a full and frank discussion about the next part. Then, after that, hopefully we can wrap it up fairly quickly and agree on what we need to do from here on."

Beck went and sat in the coffee shop but she drank tea this time. She found herself thinking about this strange man who had burst into her life. He was not particularly physically attractive, though he could improve this fact with more attention to his grooming. However, he had a mind full of sharp edges. They drew her in, challenged and intrigued her own mind. He was a few years older than her- perhaps eight or ten years. He had probably got to a stage in his life where his peculiarities were no longer as well held in check, and he did not socialize enough outside of his work to knock off his rough edges. But, meeting this man with a razor-sharp intelligence which probed and tested her own was enjoyable. She had an ill-defined desire to see more of whatever was hidden below that veneer.

When her phone rang and jolted her back into reality, she realized she had been musing for nearly an hour. It was time to return to the meeting.

Quickly, they finalized the contractual arrangements for the fees, the examination and the report preparation- along with the need for the doctor to be available to be present for legal examination in the NT, if required. They then agreed on how the client visit was to be managed. Beck agreed to document all of this and email it out. Then, each side would come back with their own confirmation within a week.

One thing she asked for was to have the examination recorded, and an edited version be provided to her to accompany the report. Surprisingly, the other two agreed to this suggestion. The video was to include shots of both the doctor and patient, with Susan's face obscured, if required. It would cover several questions and the answers which were made in response.

Beck knew this would convey a much stronger impression of a real person than any report could. She thought it may help garner support from the Executive Government to seek a pardon. She also had to admit that she felt a burning curiosity to see this girl: to see how she looked and how she acted since after her memory loss, as well as how she had changed after another two years from when Beck had last seen her in the witness box.

Chapter 20 – Real Mind Games

It was the middle of February before the examination with Dr Sangster could be scheduled. By now, the NT Attorney General had the advice sought from the former High Court judge. While less fulsome than Beck would have liked, it supported the view that a pardon could be used in this situation.

They also had a letter from Susan's parents seeking the pardon for their daughter. It emphasized her cooperation in giving her testimony after she was released from jail. It also pointed out this testimony was supported by the inquest findings. This further added weight to the legal advice. From the point of view of her boss, the Attorney General, it was a sufficient basis to take the request to the NT Government, once the assessment of Susan's mental state was made.

In Brisbane, Vic now sat in the waiting room while Jane waited at the motel minding the children. He had insisted on a 'pre-meeting' with the doctor, Ross Sangster, before Jane came in. She was scheduled to see the doctor first thing tomorrow morning.

Her examination was scheduled from 7 am to 8am to ensure it occurred before anyone else was on the premises. A pre-positioned video camera was to be placed behind and to the side of where she was sitting. This camera, along with a microphone in front of them, would record what occurred. Vic had the right to see the video tape with the barrister and remove any sensitive parts before a copy was provided for others to view.

Vic had asked to be able to attend the meeting with Susan, but this been had declined by Dr. Sangster. He said it may interfere with how she acted and responded to his questions. If this happened, it would compromise his own independent evaluation.

Instead, Dr Sangster suggested this 'pre-meeting' this afternoon. He said it would allow him to gather further information about Susan- the only name he knew her by. It would also provide Vic with an opportunity to ask his own questions about what was to occur.

Now, Vic was just waiting for this meeting. He was full of anticipation and trepidation at how it could go wrong. He realized he was jumping at shadows but, still, it found him on the edge of the chair with anxiety as he sat there.

Vic decided he must clear his mind and focus on the now and how to best protect his Jane. To do this, he pictured her smiling face while she played with David and Anne. He found this picturing of her helped him to be calm.

A tall, lanky man walked into the room. He had an over-grown beanpole look to him: straggly dark hair, mismatched clothes and a slightly weird demeanour. He looked a bit like a mental patient.

Vic felt annoyed at another person being here. Dr Sangster, when they had talked yesterday, promised he would be here by himself. Vic asked for this precaution to be extra safe- so no-one else could identify him here.

What was another person doing being here? Vic was on the edge of getting up and walking out when he realised this strange-looking man was talking to him. "Vic Campbell, I presume," he said, as he held out a big hand.

Vic realized he had mistaken the doctor for a patient. He felt less than reassured by this fact. He was just about to say something cutting when the doctor beat him to it.

As Dr. Sangster spoke, Vic realized- despite his weird look, this guy was seriously sharp! "I know I could be mistaken. But, despite your sceptical look, I'm not a madhouse inmate come to visit. Ross Sangster, at your service."

Vic found himself laughing, "Well, I guess my face gave me away, Doc. I have to admit that you sure had me fooled!"

The doctor led him out the back. He offered Vic coffee and a chocolate cookie biscuit while they sat and chatted.

When the coffees were finished, this man looked at Vic intently, again, and said, "First, you can stop calling me Doctor. My name is Ross, so please call me that. Second, I need to know about this person, Susan. I understand she currently lives with you, along with her two children.

"I know you are very concerned to keep her location hidden. I don't need to know where you live. However, I need to know about her life: anything at all that she remembers, what she does each day, about any friends, where she goes, her interests, what she knows and what she does not know?

"When I talk to her, I must be very careful. I need to ask questions that demonstrate her knowledge, or lack thereof, of the past. But, in doing so, I must not undermine her sense of who she is and cause more damage."

Vic said, "Well, you need to start by calling her Jane. I did know a Susan once. They tell me the tests show this is the same person- the same DNA or whatever you call it. But the person who lives in this body now- is no longer Susan. She knows herself only as Jane. She remembers none other.

"Any suggestion she is not Jane will distress her greatly. It is the only piece of identity she had to hold onto. So, you must not suggest that she is another person whose name is Susan.

"It seems to me as if more than just her memory has gone. It is as if the part of her, the part once called Susan in another life, has been ripped out of her body and mind. Into that vacuum, a new person has moved in and taken up residence. That person is Jane.

"She is the warmest and loveliest person I have ever met. But she is like a person held together by bits of sticky tape. The bits could easily come apart if something else bad was to happen. Then, I don't know what would be left; if there would still be any person there? But just the thought it could happen, scares the Bejesus out of me. You need to be careful, really careful."

Dr Sangster did not reply at once. At first, he nodded but said nothing. Then, he remained looking intently at Vic, as if deep in contemplation. Finally, he spoke, "What do you think? Where have all the memories gone? Are they still sitting somewhere deep inside her? Buried to stop the pain? Or have they really vanished? Have they been torn out and got lost, so they can never be recovered? Does she need that part of her back?"

Vic shrugged, uncertain what to say.

The doctor continued, "I know you don't know the answers, but they are things you must think about. Today and tomorrow, only a small bit of what I need to do is to confirm this girl has lost her past- and along with it her memories. I don't need to see her to know that. It is abundantly clear from all I have been told. It fits as the only way for her to escape an impossible situation- that is short of her own death. I think suicide must have come very close to her: feeling like a best friend, a way to take control of her life, the only way to let the pain end.

"Still, I must make it appear to others, specifically the lawyers, that my main purpose is to assess her memory. I must go through the motions.

But, in truth, it is not my main reason to see her. Any half-competent doctor or psychologist could do that part."

Vic asked, "Why then?"

"My first concern is to be gentle. She has clearly suffered enough. I think denying her past was her only way through the pain without destroying herself. Neither of us needs to be Einstein to know that.

"The real question I put to you, as the person who holds care for this damaged person to the deepest extent, is: What should we do about it? Do we need to try and join the old and the new? Does she need to reconnect to her old self to live a full and happy life? Or is she better left to begin again? To have a new life with the old one left completely behind, as if it were the baggage of another person?

"That is the real question. That is the thing you need to think on before I meet with her. It will help shape what I do at the meeting and afterwards.

"Do I try to find the pieces of her old life and help her mind to connect them to her new life? Or do I help her to bury them in an unfindable place? A place where they can never bring back the pain again?"

Now, it was Vic's turn for silence. It was such a great responsibility, such a distressing choice. He thought of the girl he knew. She was utterly beautiful, bewitching, kind, good. Yet, with no past, she was an emotional child.

He loved this child. Yet, when remembering the adult he'd known before, he realized the loss and incompleteness of this child. It was like the colors she was unable to see. Her life was missing dimensions of existence that others had. It felt safer to leave her this way, but it was not enough.

In his heart of hearts, he knew it was not really a safe place for her. The bright smile that covered the taped pieces, parts still broken but held together, was inherently unstable. Without real joins between the old Susan and the new Jane, there was no resilience in this person. Without finding the old person, the new one could never be much more than a shell.

Yes, he loved her. She loved him and it was good. However, it was nowhere near enough. There was so very much more needed to make her complete. Ultimately, his own completeness was inextricably linked to hers. She needed her to re-know herself too, in order to truly know him.

The "I don't know you, but I want you" song from 'Once' was true- but it sold them both short. He wanted far more than that for both of them.

As these thoughts swirled through his mind, he remained silent. Vic was only half-aware of the other's intense eyes, watching him. Now that he had these facts clear in his mind, he could answer.

"You are right. I've thought it through and now I know. We must try and find a way to build a bridge between the old Susan and the new Jane. They are both wonderful people, but both need to know and value the other to form one complete whole. Frightened as I am by what this all means, we must try to find a way to bring them back together. It is for the sake of the many people who know and love her, but mostly, for her own sake."

Ross Sangster nodded, agreeing, "I hoped you'd see that. My intuition told me the same. Yet, not knowing her, it is not something I could know with certainty. I feel much better if we are both agreed on that.

"My real responsibility is, of course, to her. She is my patient- assuming you and she agree to such. However, I still need your help and support. What we must try to do is part-exorcism, part-healing. It will be hard and painful for us all, so I really need your belief in this for when the dark days come.

"As we open the cracks to allow the healing to begin so, too, the pain will come back. It will be hard for her. And, in many ways, it will be harder for you as you will be watching the bringing of pain to someone you love."

"You must tell me all you know of this person- from before and after. I particularly need to know about the after. Although neither of us sees them now, in the new person are clues to direct our way back to the old."

The sun had fully set. The room was only lit by light reflected from the river by the time talking was done. Vic returned to the hotel to find this woman sitting on the floor with her children on her lap. It was both beautiful and touching: a child with her children. He loved her with all he knew. Yet, he was sure he wanted all of the old to come back along with the new.

Chapter 21 – Memory Flashes

Ross Sangster brought two comfortable chairs into his examination room, separated by a low coffee table, in preparation for his early morning meeting before he and Vic parted last night. Then, he set up the camera.

At the end of their meeting, they had decided to tell Jane the reason for the visit was that Doctor Sangster was going to try and help her remember things from her past. If she agreed, he would begin with trying to help her remember more of her childhood before she came to Australia. Regardless of his agreement to do this assessment of her, he would only go beyond an initial introduction if she agreed to this.

Vic had only told Jane thus far that he would like her to come to Brisbane with him to meet a doctor friend of his who had some ideas on how to help people get back their memory. He had said he hoped she would be happy to talk to this doctor.

Jane had answered that she would meet him, although she did not feel she needed to remember her past now that she and Vic were fully together and happy. Yet, she would do it for him if it pleased him.

So, this morning, Vic helped Jane feed and dress the children. Then, he said he would take the children for a walk in the park for an hour while she met the doctor. After that was done, they would meet at a nearby café for a delicious cooked breakfast of bacon and eggs for him along with coffee and pastries for her. They would also get treats for the kids.

Vic and Jane were staying in a hotel just two blocks away from the doctor's rooms. He and the children walked with her to the meeting place.

As they approached, they saw Dr Sangster was waiting at the entrance to the office building where his rooms were. As they parted, little David and Anne smothered her in hugs before running off excitedly with Vic to play in the park alongside the river. She followed the doctor inside.

Ross Sangster had first thought of bringing in the receptionist early so that she could put a formal face on the process and could also operate the recording equipment. But, after meeting Vic yesterday, he decided it was better if it was only him there. He would have a meeting transcript from both the audio and video recordings anyways. The machines were simple. He only had to turn them on, before he started, and they would run in the background. He was not a techno whiz kid, but it was simple stuff. All he had to do was press two "Power On" and "Record" buttons and let them run.

Now, Ross looked carefully at this lady who stood before him. Her hair had auburn-blond tresses with darker roots beginning to show. She wore good quality clothes, but with no intrinsic sense of style or how they worked to best effect on her. Her hair was loosely tied, without obvious care. It seemed she looked at her image in the mirror without real recognition and with no sense of how to use her natural beauty to best advantage.

What struck him most strongly was the almost childlike innocence in her face. It was open and trusting without the counter-play of those typical more complex emotions of an adult. She looked slightly nervous at the new and unfamiliar place- but that was the only discernible emotion.

He brought her to the anteroom and began with his coffee and biscuits routine. He had stumbled on this as a great way to relax uncomfortable people and build trust. It seemed to work now, as her manner softened.

Jane is lovely, he thought, as he watched her in the morning light. *Ethereal and vulnerable* were first thoughts but, alongside them, *damaged*.

He explained to her what he wanted to do. "Vic has probably told you I am a doctor who tries to help people who can't remember things properly.

"Vic is hoping I can help you remember things from when you were little, not bad stuff, but memories of growing up in England. He thought it would be nice if you could tell your children your own stories from these memories as they grow up. It will help them to them to know more about their mother.

"I thought the way to start is to sit and chat for half an hour in the other room. You can tell me whether you want to do this or not. If you don't, that is fine. However, I promised Vic I would meet with you and talk about it."

She nodded at him thoughtfully, her face looking unconvinced.

Coffee finished, he brought her to the examination room and showed her to a chair, saying, "I use a camera and microphone to record my meetings, so I remember what happened later. Do you mind if I turn them on now?"

She replied in a small voice, "Yes, that is OK."

After Ross turned on both recording machines, he sat down opposite her on the other side of the table. He expected it would be up to him to open up the conversation but, instead, it was her who began.

"Doctor Sangster, I know this is important for others, so I am doing it for them. But, you see, even though it seems important for these people to know about me from before, it is not important to me. I know I was someone else once, but I am not that person anymore. I don't need to know that person anymore to live a good and happy life now.

"For a little while, when I first met Vic and I wanted to know how to behave as a woman with him, it seemed important. Now, I understand about that part- what a man and woman should do together after they are married. So, it is not important to me anymore. All the other things I need to know for my life now I can learn through watching TV or reading books. These things slowly fill my mind with new memories and make me happy.

"I can see it may seem to be important to the others for me to remember from before- but it is not important to me. I am happy to talk to you, but I don't feel broken and in need of fixing. If it makes Vic happy, I will try to find memories from when I was little- but it is only to please him."

Ross Sangster nodded and said, "Okay, let us just talk about what it is you do remember. Why don't you tell me about when you met Vic? What do you remember from then? Tell me the story about you and your children, how you met Vic, what made you decide to come away with him?"

Jane recounted the story of the meeting of the helicopter pilot to Ross. She told of her son's instant trust in him and how she wanted to sing for him in the church. It was a simple story, simply told, with a gentle loveliness. At the same time, it had an unreal feel to it. It felt like a story from a picture book: full of bright light but without any complex emotions.

Then, Ross said, "What can you tell me about coming and living in that place from before you met Vic?'

Jane described finding herself by the side of a road, with the bag with her name on it and nothing else. She told how the aboriginal ladies had given her a lift into the town and she had gone to ask the lady in the shop for a job. She told how she had lived and worked there for a while. She continued on, telling how her babies were born soon after her arrival and how she became friends with the people of the town- particularly the pastor and his wife.

Ross asked Jane if she had remembered anything about her life before that day when she found herself on the bench beside the road.

She said, "No. I thought I must have banged my head and got amnesia somehow. I figured the memories would soon return. But they never did."

He asked her, "Does this worry you?"

She said, "No, it is just the way it is. My life has been good with my children. The only time I wanted to know more about what came before was when I wondered about things like 'how soon my children would walk.' Then, I thought it would be nice to ask my mother how old I was when I walked. Instead, I asked the Pastors wife, my friend, Ruth. She answered my questions about things like: how old are children when they usually walk."

Ross found these simple, unemotional descriptions were clear, but felt unsatisfying. It was as if Jane accepted she would never know about her other life and had no desire to look any further. It was a tale without color.

Ross asked Jane about the things she did know, like how to do the accounts at the shop. He asked her whether it seemed strange that she knew how to do these kind of things, but had no idea of how she learnt them.

Again, Jane simply replied, "It is just how it is."

Ross asked Jane how she felt when Vic came back and asked her to come away with him. For the first time, he felt there was real emotion involved in her words. Jane told how Vic had arrived in the middle of the night, that she had been so happy to see him and trusted him completely. She told of how they had shared the bed that night with Vic just holding her.

She explained how, as she lay in the circle of his arms, she had dreamt again a dream she had dreamt before. It was a dream of an 'unknown man' that she knew she needed to know. This night, however, she had realized this 'unknown man' was really Vic and it made her feel very happy. Because of this, she'd trusted Vic and had come with him. Now she was happy to be with him and to share her children with him. The time since then had been wonderful- even better than she could have ever imagined. At first, the only strange part was not remembering how a woman should be with a man. Now, this was no longer a problem.

Right from the start she'd known she loved him and that he loved her- although she did not have the right words to express her feelings. Then, once she realized that people like them got married, she wanted to marry him. When Jane said it to Vic, he told her he wanted to be married to her, too. She explained to Ross how this was the moment she became Vic's lover, as well as his friend. Jane finished the story by saying, "Meeting Vic in my little town was the most wonderful thing that has ever happened to me."

Now, her emotion was real and vibrant- although the rest of the story had remained without color. But, as Jane told of starting her relationship with Vic, Ross was filled with a strong sense of her simple goodness and joy. For the first time, Ross experienced real doubt as to whether he should help Jane to remember her life from before.

Ross then asked Jane about the visit to meet her parents. Once again, she recounted the tale in the simplest fashion: her happiness at meeting them and also in meeting her friend Anne again. The way she just knew, even without remembering, who they were to her.

Jane told of the tiny memories she now had of parts of her childhood with her parents. They were mainly memories of her brother and Anne. Even though they were just a fragment here and there, it seemed to be enough for her and it gave her a connection to a distant past.

It seemed to Ross that, for all the intervening years, her memories had ceased to be important. Instead, it felt as if she was fully happy to ignore this huge, empty space in her life.

Ross asked Jane what she most wanted to do with her life from here. Without a moment's hesitation, she answered, "I want to get married to the man I love. That is what I spend most of my time thinking about when I am not busy. Now he has agreed, I want it to happen as soon as possible."

As Jane said this, she spoke with a dreamy and beatific smile which overflowed with happiness and melted Ross. There was no sign of pain at memories repressed. It felt like a part of her life had been washed clean- as if it had never been to begin with. Part of him thought he should just leave it there, that there was no need to dig further.

At the same time, a sense of huge unreality gripped him. Jane said it was enough, she acted like it was enough and she was clearly happy now.

However, as she talked of her life now, her emotions were like the emotions of a child. She experienced real joy, sorrow, happiness and sadness, but it seemed all the complexity was missing from each one. What had happened to the negative emotions that were a normal part of a person's life?

Ross asked himself, in his mind, *Where have all the shadows gone? Where are the mixed emotions of love and hate? Where is the envy, jealousy and anger? Where are the disappointments in anything? These are all the things which make a 'real human being' real.*

Jane said she did not want the memories and did not miss them in her life. Yet, without them, Ross felt that only half a person was sitting in front of him. Ross asked himself, *Do I have the right to try and open cracks between the old and new if she says she is happy to only have the new?* His ethics said he must not. Yet, his deepest self and part of his intuition, told him he must.

Ross decided to explore the edges of memories from before she vanished. Those early childhood memories seemed like a safe starting place. He would take her back to them. Then he would see if he could get her to step forward- even a tiny bit- to find out more of her childhood and of her life as a teenager in England.

Ross asked Jane to tell him the last thing she could remember from when she was a little girl. It ended up being her first year in High School, when she had met Anne and the two of them had become friends. She said she could only remember the day she first met Anne. They were two gawky twelve- year-olds in their first week at High School. They had desks side-by-side and used to talk when the teacher was not looking. Ross asked Jane to try and put herself back into that place now. He wanted her to try to remember the school holidays before that year: to remember where she had been and what she had done.

Ross watched as Jane's mind drifted into this space. He saw little flashes of light enter her eyes as memories came to her. Then, she began to speak:

"I do remember those school holidays. They were summer holidays. We went to a farm up in Scotland. It was the farm where my dad had grown up, in a valley between big green hills. His parents lived in one house. His sister, who was married also, lived in another house nearby. Her husband did farm work. My Dad loved to help, and I did, too. So, he would bring me out on the farm with him. My brother, Tim, did not like farm work much. He had a cousin his age and the two of them spent hours playing together. There was another cousin, but she was younger than Tim. I felt too grown-up to play with her. I liked her and talked to her, but did not play with her much.

"I also remember my Aunt Em, my dad's youngest sister. She still lived at home with her parents as she had just finished school. She was the baby of the family- that's what Dad used to call her. I was twelve and she was eighteen. She was to go off to college after summer. She was really pretty and a bit wild. I would sit with her and talk for hours about boys, going out and things like that. I can't really remember exactly what we talked about, but I do remember how much I liked being with her. She was so excited to be going off to a big city to live and study. It all sounded really exciting to me, too. She would talk to me like I was as grown-up as she was.

"I remember how she, me and Dad would sometimes talk, all sitting around the fire in the evening. Em and Dad both loved wild animals. They particularly loved big animals from other countries: lions, tigers, elephants, giraffes, monkeys, chimpanzees and gorillas.

"We all wanted to go to Africa and see them. We wanted to see the lions, leopards and cheetahs hunting in the national parks. I don't know if we ever did, but we dreamt and talked so much about it. We would talk about being camped by a waterhole and watching all the animals coming into drink. And about how a lion pack would try and ambush them, while we watched from a hidden hide."

"What were your favourite animals?" Ross asked.

Jane thought for a minute and then answered, "I am not sure. I thought the apes were so amazing, they are so like us- their behaviours and the way they interact. But I loved the predators, too. The way a cat would stalk up or silently wait in ambush until something came along."

Ross asked, "Did you ever see any that you remember? Perhaps at a zoo or something like that?"

Jane thought hard and then replied, "I think the year before those holidays, my dad took me to a zoo called 'Whipsnade Zoo.' He also took me to 'London Zoo' in Regents Park. I can remember watching a cheetah stalking someone who was walking along the outside of its enclosure at Whipsnade Zoo. I remember feeling sorry for the lions at Regents Park

Zoo. They were lying out in the sun and their enclosure was concrete. I thought of them out in Africa: in the long grass, hunting animals. I thought, *What a pity. They have nothing to chase and nowhere to hunt in here."*

Ross did not know why, but the image of a crocodile lying in ambush suddenly came into his mind. Perhaps it was all the media speculation about the Crocodile Girl. Perhaps it was that freaky story Vic told him last night of a huge crocodile swimming alongside him as he escaped from the wilderness after crashing his helicopter. Or perhaps it came from a simple association with the predators in her story. The words popped into his mind and were on his tongue before he could think to take them back.

"Have you ever seen a crocodile?"
Ross watched Jane's face as he spoke, wishing he could take the words back.

First, Jane screwed up her face as if she were thinking. Then, her face transformed into blank dread from which, like a slow-motion picture, it morphed into abject horror and overwhelming fear. As it did, a noise began somewhere deep inside her. Her mouth took a rictus shape. A thin, banshee wail flowed from it. It rose in tone and volume until it became a screech of unrelenting terror. Suddenly, the noise was gone as suddenly as it had begun. It was bitten off into even more ominous silence. However, the terror in her eyes was undiminished. Her body began to shake before giving way to heartbroken, convulsive sobbing of the words, "No. No. No. Not My Babies."

Ross was first paralysed into inactivity by the noise, but as it transformed into sobbing words, he rushed around the table to put his arms around her shoulders. He pulled her to him and talked to her as he would to a small child, "It is OK. No one is hurting your children. They are safe. They are with Vic."

Slowly, her sobbing and shaking abated. Her eyes returned to where they were focused on him, but with an accusatory look, "Why did you say that? That thing about the crocodiles? It is evil. I saw my babies swimming in a pool full of crocodiles. Lots of big crocodiles. They were swimming towards them with their mouths open. My babies needed help and I could not reach them. I was stuck here in the wrong body. I knew the crocodiles would take them, tear them apart and eat them. I knew my babies would be torn into little pieces. I could not reach them or help them. I could not bear to watch it happen. It was so real.

"I wish you had never said those words. I don't want to talk about any memories. I don't want to try and remember, ever. It is all too terrible. I never want to see that awful thing, again. I just want to be left alone."

Ross tried to calm her by telling her they would go out and see her babies now. They were perfectly safe with Vic and it was all something she had imagined. It was not real. Her wild--eyed terror remained though, gradually, the self-control came back and the accusation faded from her eyes.

Ross suggested Jane wash her face, go outside and see the others. She complied immediately, but in the manner of a rag doll. It was as if she were moving without purpose.

Ross brought Jane out to Vic and her children. She hugged her children tightly to her- as if fearful they were a mirage and would vanish.

As she held her children, Ross explained to Vic what he'd done. Ross told Vic about his foolish words and how frightened she was by them.

Vic had an instant flash of annoyance on his face, but he seemed less perturbed than Ross expected, responding, "As you said, Doc, there is a whole world of pain trapped inside her. I am not sure that I am glad about what you did- but it needs to find a way out. So, thank you for trying to help. I will talk to you tomorrow- after she calms down."

Vic walked over and enfolded Jane in his arms. He stroked her hair like that of a small child as he murmured soothing words.

Soon, her children grew impatient at being ignored, whining, "Mummy, mummy. Come and see the boats on the river."

Chapter 22 - The Reporter

Jacob was pissed off. He knew that lawyer tart in Darwin, Beck, was jerking him around. Once upon a time, she had been only too happy to take his good money for scraps of information. He had made it big time-largely because of her. Now, he was the journalist everyone was talking about.

However, now she seemed to have got cold feet. When he rang her work receptionist, asking to talk to her, she was always busy and never returned his calls. When Jacob tried to ring Beck's mobile, it went to straight to voicemail. When he emailed her private email, she never replied. He knew he could not use her government work email – way too dangerous for him and for her, if it was shown he was trying to de-rail the course of justice.

Jacob thought of upping the ante by doing something more direct with her work, in order to scare the pants of her. Perhaps he could leave a message with her secretary that 'Jacob Shoesmith, a journalist from the London's Fleet Street, needed to talk to her urgently about the Susan MacDonald case.'

That would really put a scare into her! He also thought about his threat to send the bank deposit slip, for the most recent sum he had paid her bank, through to her boss in the mail with a 'please explain,' note. It would be anonymous, of course. However, that was just a threat. She would lose her job if anyone followed that trail. Then, the 'goose laying golden eggs' in the Susan story would stop laying.

Plus, Jacob had enjoyed his nights with Beck when he visited Darwin. She was only a mediocre sort to look at: a good body, but a face a bit too angular for his taste. However, he had found she was really hungry for sex when he got her between the sheets. Her other recent hook ups must have been limited, with a sick mother. He recalled the two nights spent with her as memorably good. They had turned each other on big time. Perhaps his black body made her horny. Her milky-white thighs certainly had that effect on him, just thinking of them was a turn on. It would be nice to do it, again, at least one more time.

For now, though, she needed to deliver something. He had money waiting to send her. She needed to use inside information to reopen the trail on the 'Crocodile Girl'- which had gone cold. He licked his lips, savoring the thought of finding that 'Susan tart.' He would be sticking a camera in her face as they brought her back to jail.

It had been far and away the biggest story Jacob had ever broken. He had followed it from the start- from when they unearthed those clues saying the crocodile was not the real killer. The crocodile had only come along after the bloke was dead. It had finished the murderer's work. Instead, it came out that someone with a girl-sized footprint had finished off the Australian Outback dude, Vincent Mark Bassingham. She had done it by whacking him on the side of the head with a big lump of wood and dragging him to the water. This person obviously expected the crocodiles to do the rest and leave no trace. Jacob knew from the start that the woman was as guilty as hell, due to the way she had deliberately tried to hide the evidence. No 'lovers tiff' but a cold and calculated murder. A murder that was committed by a clever, but thoroughly nasty, little bitch.

Jacob had to give it to Susan. She was a great actress. She deserved an Academy Award for her 'Saint Susan' role in the murder trial. She had barely spoken. Silence and beauty were such effective weapons when put together. She was playing the martyr image. But he had cracked that wide open- with a bit of help from the Darwin girl, Beck. He'd also found how Susan spread herself around among the men. That was her past history. Now, she must have moved on to a newbie. Pity she and Vic had not stuck together. Jacob was sure he could have found Susan through Vic- if he knew where she was. However, Jacob had seen Vic's plane ticket for Canada. It had been bought about 18 months, or so, after Susan vanished. Jacob's sources had told him the word was that Vic was all broken up about her disappearance.

A bit after Vic's going abroad, rumors had surfaced about Susan having been found in Queensland. Beck had fed this rumor to Jacob- back when she was still talking to him. She told of a vague story of a person who looked just like Susan working in a town up north. Jacob had jumped on a plane to there and spent a month looking around for any real evidence. He checked out the obvious places: Cairns, Townsville, and went to the smaller places and resorts. He checked out all the shops, bars and businesses, flashing her photo, along with some cash, around. Jacob told them he would pay well if anyone knew where she was. He had been pretty well everywhere- except for a few of those out of the way aboriginal places. They were places where no one in their right mind would go. Despite this, he had found zip.

Still, the rumors bubbled around. When Susan vanished, she was too pregnant for an abortion. A nurse at the hospital told him it was twins. He imagined her, now, with two small children. She should be easy to find.

Jacob remembered the adrenaline rush from almost two years ago when his piece, 'The Two Faces of Susan Emily MacDonald', had been far and away the highest rating story of the English tabloids. Then, Beck had told him about Susan going by her middle name, Emily. He thought that was both weird, and a bit silly. As if, by taking a different name, she could just vanish.

Back then, Jacob got part of his story from an earlier boyfriend of Susan's, Edward. He was definitely still a bit smitten by her and told Jacob the story of how she had dumped him. He told Jacob how she was a party girl and was always willing to try it on with new men. To add to that, Jacob had the story of her shagging both the outback bloke, Vincent, Mark B or whatever, and, at the same time, the rich dude, David. Then, the instant she was out of jail on bail, Beck told Jacob Susan was shagging the helicopter pilot. At that point, he knew he had gold. She was a true English tart- giving plenty on her back, but quick to put the knife in when she no longer wanted it.

Not to mention, the way she proudly carried that belly full of arms and legs from her contest, twins a nurse had told him. Who knows whose it really was? Perhaps, it was one each to two fathers. The nurse had also told Jacob the babies were a girl and boy- which meant they were not identical. The brats in her belly did not come from being a good girl who only went to church. When the pregnancy was added to the 'crocodile killer,' it was a story of sensation made in heaven. It had pushed Jacob right to the top. He loved being in this place where his name was on everyone's lips. Then, it slowly slid away. As it did, he slowly slid down the ratings and pay scales.

Now Jacob had to make the story come alive, again. It would be even bigger if he could find her now- particularly after all the 'Saint Susan' TV publicity her red-headed friend had done last year. He knew, if he could find a way to get the Beck bitch to fill him in on what she knew, he could crack the case. Perhaps, he should double the offer to twenty big ones. He thought about it for a minute. *Yes, I am sure that would bring her round.*

He knew Beck needed a lot more cash for her mother's treatment. Beck may not want to talk to him- but her mother's part-time nurse had no such scruples. She had told Jacob about the need for a new wheelchair for ten big ones. It stood to reason, if Beck needed the usual amount of cash just for one thing- then, she would need more cash for other things as well.

Beck must be playing hard to get to put up the price. He needed to get out there and get in her face. Nothing like more pillow talk, following on after a good fuck, to bring her around. Being there in person would make it very hard for her to refuse him- either the money or the sex.

Having decided how to move it along, Jacob booked his flight to Darwin for next week. It was a small town and Beck would be easy to catch up to. *Who knows? Maybe after he shagged her, paid her and got what she knew- he could spend a couple more weeks working all those Queensland towns again, himself.* If he talked to enough people and threw plenty of cash around, he would surely dig something up.

That afternoon, he got an "OK" from his boss for a ten thousand pound cash advance to pay his source along with another five for his own expenses for the trip he had booked. His boss was as hungry as him for a new big splash- but his patience was starting to wear thin.

"I don't mind paying for results- and you certainly delivered in spades, a year or two ago, on this one. But you have nothing to show for the money we have laid out since then. It is time to move on if this does not pan out. Plenty of local stories in our part of the world that you need to put a bit more effort into or your pay packet will take a haircut at your next performance review.

"So, I am cutting you slack for a month to go and run this to ground. But, if it does not happen, you better find some other big stories while you are out there. Or, perhaps, only a job at half-pay or a new job will be in your future."

Jacob could feel his ears burning as he walked outside. With all the trouble that Rupert M and other big boys were having over the last couple years, it was getting harder and harder to use underground sources to crack the 'big ones' in England. He was done with piss-poor jobs where a thousand hopefuls were looking over his shoulder and waiting for him to trip and fall.

That was why Jacob had decided for cash this time. If it blew up, he wanted there to be no money trail back to him for an inquiry. With a month in Australia, if he could live sensibly, this big wad of expenses would leave enough to pay Beck well and still leave him free to chase down other stories. His boss was right. He needed to find other things to pursue- even if this panned out. No one could live forever on one story. He needed to dig into the other girls who were part of this drama. Perhaps there were some new trails and sensations there.

The coverage on TV of this story had been very soft and lovey-dovey. It had been the making of a new bunch of martyrs. That was fine and all, but what the public most hungered for was a raunchy, out there story. They wanted the requisite mix of sex, violence, horror and tragedy. This was his staple fare: sweet stories about goodies got boring.

As Jacob walked home, he thought how he had risen from his own humble beginnings: a black kid with a Jamaican mum and mixed-up north African bits on the other side- it was muddled whether Egyptian, Moroccan or Ethiopian was dominant. Regardless, he got a bit of it all.

With his origins, Jacob's overall rise had been a big deal in his family. He had gone from a promising school student to a cadetship with a tabloid daily. Then, he had become a journalist in his own right When he had risen to the top of the pool, the year before last, that had been a really big deal for them. Jacob had spent his large income freely to impress his family and friends. Now, it was hard to think about taking a drop back to being another mid-level journalist. One who only just made a living.

The funny thing was, when he had dug deeply into the bloke Vic's background, he had felt a sort of brotherhood for the black kid from a town camp made good as a helicopter pilot who was now running his own show. When Vic seemed desperate to shack up with the Susan witch-bitch after his miraculous survival, Jacob felt protective of him. Perhaps this had a small bit to do with the hard-ball way he had decided to play this girl's story. It left no room in his mind for any sympathy for her. Jacob could not let such things as his kindness get in the way. He had to look after himself to stay at the top, as the 'number one super-trash-digger' in the tough journo game.

Chapter 23 – Beck

Beck had talked to Ross Sangster on the phone several times since their meeting in Brisbane. Most recently, she had talked to him twice since his meeting with Susan. She spoke with him first on the day following the meeting, when Ross told her how the meeting went and mostly about Susan's distress when he asked about her memories of crocodiles. He promised Beck his report and video would be sent next week. This would be after he had agreement from the other side about the video's contents.

Ross then rang Beck earlier today to say he had posted the video express mail. She should have it within two days. Once she viewed it, he asked her to call him so they could talk about what to do from here.

Their telephone conversations had become remarkably friendly and frank. Beck found herself very comfortable talking to this odd man. His cryptic sense of humor gelled well with hers. They had subtle mind contests with words and phrases which were both friendly and challenging. She was unsure if she thought he was attractive, but she liked him and his company.

Ross seemed to enjoy talking to her as much as she enjoyed talking to him. Sometimes, he gave too much away about this case and the meeting- as if he inherently trusted her not to abuse privileged information. This made Beck squirm inside when she thought of what she had already done.

Ross let slip that this girl had two children, a boy and girl, who stayed with a man outside his rooms while the girl was in the memory assessment meeting with Ross. It was obvious, from the way Ross talked about the man, that this woman and he were in a relationship- not just friends. It came out when he told Beck about her reaction to the crocodile words. Ross followed this story by saying that, once she calmed down, he brought her back outside to the man who minding their children. The man had put his arms her and comforted her. Ross also told Beck that, when he asked this girl what she most wanted to do in her life from here, she said she wanted to get married. Odds were that the person she wanted to marry was to the same person minding her children.

Ross had also used the name 'Jane' once instead of 'Susan'- without even realising he had said it. Beck suspected this was the name she used now. Added to this, he said they had driven down to Brisbane from where she lived the afternoon before he met her. This indicated she was staying within a few hours, likely north of Brisbane. Ross also spoke of her taking the children for regular walks along the beach, which suggested she lived in a seaside place.

Each bit alone was not much. But, when Beck put these bits together, it was a lot more than she was supposed to know. It told a story about who this girl was now and gave a much narrower circle around where she lived. She knew it was information which was worth a lot of money.

As Beck walked out of the building to go home, she was torn. She did not want to betray this girl yet again. But her Mum was getting steadily worse while becoming more and more housebound as she lost the strength in her arms to push the wheelchair. Beck really wanted to get her the new motor assisted wheelchair. It would only take one phone call. She promised herself that if she did it one more time, afterwards, she would call it quits. She could feel the balance in her mind tipping towards this, but she had to put some protection in as well. She must make sure, if she gave him this story, Jacob would do two things.

The first thing was that he would never come back to her again and ask for more. All contact with her from here on out was at an end. The second condition she would require was that Jacob not publish any story which could lead others back to Beck. With this requirement, he could not do a piece in the paper which just used the information she told him. Instead, he had to use her information to find out the rest of the story himself, the true story of who Susan was and where she was living now. He could only go public if he got that part of the story by himself.

In the meantime, he must not leak this information in a way where it could be linked back to her. It was not just for her own sake- Beck could not bear for Ross to ever find out that she had used the privileged information he had let slip in their conversations to harm his client.

In the end, Beck decided she would do nothing until the weekend which was still three days away. After viewing the tape, if it did not change her mind, she would ring Jacob in London on Sunday. She would do it when her mother was taken to church by a neighbor. She would not tell him the story right away. Rather, she would get a clear agreement to all her conditions before she revealed anything more.

Beck was locked in her own world, thinking this out, as she walked to where her car was parked. A man was standing in her way, blocking the pavement in front of her. She stepped to the side to go around him. He stepped that way, too. She stepped back the other way and he followed.

She felt annoyed and was about to dish out a caustic, "If You Don't Mind- Get The Fuck Out Of My Way, PLEASE!!!" when she looked up. Beck was vaguely aware of the dark skin, thinking, *Drunk Aborigine.*

It was Jacob. He did not look exactly like an aborigine- but his skin was halfway to that color. She was at a loss for words. Jacob was the one person she did not want, or expect, to see. She thought she had made up her mind, just before, to talk to him. However, now he was here in person, she realized her mind was still in a state of flux. She needed a couple more days to think this through and compose herself before she was ready to talk to him.

Jacob gave her a half grin, saying, "I know you have been doing your best to avoid me- so I decided I had to see you in person. Now that I have got to see you, you had better come with me for a drink and a talk. We have important stuff we need to discuss- lots of important stuff."

Beck could not mobilize the will to fight him, so she meekly followed after him. He led her along the street to a familiar bar. Then, she followed him as he went into a corner booth where she now sat facing him.

Jacob could feel his sexual magnetism grabbing at her. Beck knew he was going to proposition her both for more information and a night in bed. She felt powerless to say 'no' to either.

Jacob went and bought them both a drink. He remembered her usual gin and tonic from last time. He clinked his glass to hers, he said, "Here's to renewing our friendship in all the best fun ways, like before." He took a mouthful of his drink as he looked at her thoughtfully.

Beck lifted her glass in return and took a sip- it did taste good. She took a proper swallow, then thought, *"What the hell!? My body wants another night with him, and I want the money. What's the harm?"*

Three drinks and an hour later, she felt fully mellow. With each swallow, Jacob looked sexier and sexier. In a dreamy state, she let him take her hand and lead her out along the street to his hotel. Once there they went into the lift and up to his room.

As Jacob undressed Beck, she felt incredibly horny. This instantly pushed the little voice of caution out of her mind. Then, he was on top of her on the bed, thrusting into her. While her body was loving it, her mind suddenly snapped back. *Why am I doing this? Why am I letting him fuck me?*

Beck shook her head violently and pushed him away, exclaiming, "This is all wrong! I just want this to be over! I will tell you what you want to know, what I know right now, but only on the condition it ends today. No more sex. No more pestering. No threats of telling anyone anything about me.

"You can take what I give you to see if you can find the girl and that way get your story. In return, you give me the ten thousand dollars I need for the improved wheelchair for my mother. At least that will be something good to come from the bad thing I have done.

"I don't know much about this girl, but she is better than either of us. She deserves a new life after all the bad that has happened to her. Remember that if you do find her. What I know now convinces me you are the asshole in this- not her. Before you smear her name across the tabloids, think, '*What harm has she ever done to you that entitles you to treat her like this?*'"

Beck turned her face, and then her body, away from Jacob. She found herself crying, quietly. How had she let herself come to this place? She wished it was over now. Except for her mother's need of her and her income, she would quit her job, catch a plane and vanish. She would try to do the same thing as this girl was doing- find a new life without a past. She felt anger driving her. She would keep her bad bargain, but only if he agreed to her terms. Then, she would end it today.

Beck grabbed at the sheet and pulled it up over her body. Then, she turned to Jacob with the anger glistening through the tears, "Well?! What is it to be? Do you want what I have to tell you, at my price, or shall I just get dressed and leave now?"

Beck watched the emotions swirl across the dark face before her. Jacob looked shocked and hurt, too, at her stinging rebuke. Despite her mental slap, there was still hunger in his eyes. It was not hunger for her body, that never had meaning beyond the sex act, but hunger for her knowledge. Hunger for the power and status it would bring him if he could find the girl Susan and write another chapter of her story. It was the hunger of a poor boy who had risen to the top and felt it slipping away. A no-longer poor boy who could not bear the thought of becoming a nobody again. Despite her anger, a part of her felt sorrow and sympathy for his degradation, happening alongside hers.

Jacob went to his briefcase and pulled out a thick envelope. saying, "There are 100 fifty-pound notes, in there. They are yours, right now, no strings attached. And there is another envelope with the same again once you tell me what you know. Then, I will leave you alone. I promise I will let you alone after today- whether I find the girl or not."

Beck dressed and then sat in a chair facing him. She was wanting this to be over fast. "What I know is this: She has been found, but we do not know where she is. She has two children. The name she uses now is Jane. I do not know where she lives now, except I think it is somewhere in a coastal town. It is not too far from Brisbane, perhaps somewhere like the Gold Coast, where she can hide amongst other people. She lives with a man whose name I don't know. She wants to get married to him as soon as it can be arranged. He treats the children as if he is their father and she loves him. That is the whole of what I know. Perhaps it is enough to find her- if you are as good as you say.

"The only thing I ask is that, if you find her, you treat her better than you have before. You could still write a good story which would sell and remake your name without harming her. this time, you could try to be a little kinder. She deserves decency and a new life."

For a minute, Beck thought about saying something about Jane's memory loss. She also thought of telling him about the plan to seek a pardon. However, the first thing was only the girl's business and the second was only the law's business. He did not need either for his story. She felt better not to have surrendered these two small things. It was as if a tiny corner of her soul had retained something of value of its own.

Jacob passed her the second envelope with a nod of thanks.

Beck took it and walked out the door without looking back. Her hand holding the money felt like it was on fire- as if she was holding a burning devil. But, having already sold her soul, she would not let the devil go.

Chapter 24 – Secret Pardon

In the days which followed, Beck tried to forget what she had done. She told herself, over and over, that she had done no real harm. The money was for a good cause. The girl was away, free, and would soon be married. She would be living a new life where the past could not touch her.

Her lack of memory was her greatest salvation. It made her untouchable. Even if this man found her and asked questions- all she could say to him was she did not know, she did not remember. That was no story at all and with it interest would soon fade.

Beck walked miles along Nightcliff and Casuarina beaches as she repeated this mantra in her mind. As she tried to walk away the memory, scuffing sand and kicking little waves, she tried to make herself believe it would all work out okay.

On the Monday morning after her chance meeting with Jacob, the mailman brought a package to her work. It was a slim, square package with a note from Ross saying this was the agreed DVD of the interview. She closed her office door, loaded the DVD into her computer and clicked on it. She watched as the icon came up showing it was loading and then, when that finished, she pressed play.

The video was a good quality though, mostly, it showed Ross's face to the camera. The other person was sitting with only her side profile in view from behind. It took Beck long seconds to connect this image with her mind image of Susan. Dark hair was replaced by something auburn to blond. It was tied loosely in a haphazard fashion and conveyed a person who cared little about how they looked. Her face was unseen- but the profile conveyed a sense of unreality, a non-person filling the space. A part of this was due to the strange view, but more was due to a demeanor. A demeanor which was more absent than present. Ross had once mentioned something about this girl seeming to be missing a part of her soul, an empty shell sensation. Until she saw this video, these were just words to her.

Now, Beck understood what he meant. The person sitting there brought to her mind a beautiful, but lifeless, piece of porcelain. It was hard to believe this person had anything linking herself to the girl she had last seen sitting in the dock. That woman who had been smiling brightly, but still incredibly controlled. The one with a will of steel inside a pretty face and an incredibly vital lifeforce emanating from her. It was easier to believe that 'here was a different person.' No wonder Susan was so hard to find.

Beck half wondered if it was really her. Maybe it was really some clever charade of a different person, role playing, who was out for fame and glory. The change in the life essence was too hard to take in.

A few seconds later, this girl began to speak. In that instant, all the uncertainty resolved. It was so her- the voice, the English accent- it was unmistakable.

"Doctor Sangster, I know this is important for others. I am doing it for them. But, you see, even though it seems important for these people to know about me from before- it is not important to me. I know I was someone else once- but I am not that person anymore. I don't need to know that person any more than I already do, in order to live a good and happy life now."

At that point, there was a clear discontinuity as if a part had been edited from the tape.

It then jumped to a place where Ross asked her to tell of her earliest memories saying, "Tell me what is the last thing you remember from when you were a little girl, living in England?"

She replied, "It was my first year in High School, when I met Anne and we became friends. I can remember the first day I met Anne. She was a gawky twelve-year-old with flaming red hair and a big, cheeky smile. We had desks side-by-side. We used to talk when the teacher was not looking."

Ross said, "Put yourself back into that place now. Try to remember the last school holidays before then- where you went and what you did."

A few seconds of silence ensued, then the voice continued, "I remember those school holidays. They were summer holidays. We went to a farm up in Scotland. It was the farm where my dad had grown up, in a valley between big green hills. His parents lived in one house and his married sister lived in another house, nearby. Her husband did the farm work. My Dad loved to help on the farm and I did, too. My Dad would bring me out on the farm with him.

"My brother, Tim, did not like farm work much. He had a cousin about his age and the two of them would spend hours playing together. There was also another cousin, but she was younger than Tim. I felt too grown-up to play with her. I liked her and talked to her- but I did not play with her much.

"I also remember my Aunt Em, my dad's youngest sister. She still lived at home with her parents as she had just finished school. She was the baby of the family- that's what Dad used to call her. I was twelve and she was eighteen. She was to go off to college after the summer. She was really pretty and a bit wild. I would sit with her and talk for hours about boys, going out and things like that. I can't really remember exactly what we talked about, but I just remember how much I liked being with her. She was so excited to be going off to a big city to live and study. It all sounded exciting to me, and she would talk to me like I was as grown-up as she was.

"I remember how she, me and Dad would sometimes talk while all sitting around the fire in the evening. Em and Dad both loved animals, particularly the big wild animals in other countries: the lions, tigers, elephants, giraffes, monkeys, chimpanzees and gorillas.

"We all wanted to go to Africa and see them- particularly the lions, leopards and cheetahs hunting in the national parks. I don't know if we ever did, but we dreamt and talked so much about it: being camped by a waterhole, watching all the animals coming in to drink, how a lion pack would try and ambush them all while we watched from a hidden hide.

"What were your favourite animals?" Ross asked.

There was another pause, as if she was thinking. Then, she answered, "I'm not sure. I thought the apes were amazing. They are so like us with their behaviours and the way they interact. But I loved the predators, too. The way a cat would stalk up or silently wait in ambush until something came along."

Ross asked, "Did you ever see any wild animals that you remember? Perhaps at a zoo or something like that?"

Another pause and then, she said. "I think the year before those holidays my dad took me to a zoo called 'Whipsnade Zoo.' He also took me to 'London Zoo' in Regents Park. I can remember watching a cheetah stalking someone who was walking along the outside of its enclosure at Whipsnade Zoo. I also remember feeling a bit sorry for the lions at Regents Park Zoo. They were lying out in the sun and their enclosure was mostly concrete. I thought of them out in Africa, instead, in the long grass while hunting animals. I thought, *What a pity. They have nothing to chase and nowhere to hunt in there."*

Ross asked, "Have you ever seen a crocodile?"

At first, she said nothing- though a flinching movement passed over her body. Beck could see the side face of the girl's face taking a hard and squeezed-up look. This look was washed away as her mouth opened into what looked like a grimace.

As her face became this grimace, a noise began to emerge, coming from somewhere deep inside her. It started as a thin wail. It kept rising in tone and volume until it became a screech of terror. Then, the noise was gone, suddenly, as if she had bitten it off. Now, her body began to shake. This soon turned into huge sobbing movements, with the words, "No. No. Not My Babies," said over and over and over again.

Beck watched as Ross stumbled to his feet and ran to her. He put his arms around to comfort her. She turned to the side towards him- bringing her full face into view. It was a mask of pure, unadulterated terror. Suddenly, the screen was blank- with the image still burned deep into Beck's retinas.

Then, the face image returned. She was there, again. She was facing Ross, saying with accusing eyes, "Why did you say that?! That thing about the crocodiles? It is evil. I saw my babies swimming in a pool full of crocodiles. Lots of big crocodiles were swimming towards them with their mouths open. My babies needed help and I could not reach them. I was stuck here in the wrong body. I knew the crocodiles would take them, tear them apart and then eat them. I knew my babies would be torn into little pieces. I could not reach them or help them. I could not bear to watch it happen. It was so real!

"I wish you never said those words. I don't want to talk about any more memories. I don't want to try and remember. It is all too terrible! I never want to see that awful thing again. I just want to be left alone."

Beck knew, in that instant, it had been a terrible mistake for her to pretend this girl was alright. To believe she could simply retreat behind a 'no memory' mask. She knew it was not true. Already, this girl's past had destroyed one life.

Now she saw clearly that even though this woman had built something new, which had cut all links with the past and left her with little more than a shell of her past existence, this was a fractured place. Deep cracks ran between the new and the old. The wrong words could tear this fragile edifice apart and smash it to bits. If that happened, Beck would be culpable.

The video was finished now and showed only a blank screen. Beck looked at it with her blank eyes. The only remaining image in her mind was the overwhelming terror in this poor girl's eyes. Shame rose at her own part in all of this and was reflected from this image.

There was a knock on the door. She called out, "Yes?"

Her receptionist came in, saying, "I have a Dr. Ross Sangster on the line. He would like to talk to you, urgently. He says he has to fly to Darwin at the end of the week and thought he could perhaps schedule a meeting to discuss the video and his report on the case. He just needs to know if you can arrange to do that before he confirms his bookings."

She picked up the call which was a welcome distraction from her thoughts. "Hello, Ross. Can I expect to see you in Darwin?"

"Yes, I have been asked to meet with and review the treatment plan for an aboriginal man in Darwin Hospital who has a traumatic and alcohol-related brain injury with severe memory impairment. They have asked me to fly up for the day on Thursday. I wondered, before I locked in flights, whether there was value in me discussing my report either with you or your other legal colleagues. I could do either Wednesday or Friday. To be honest, though, Friday works better for me. If I came then, I would stay for the weekend for a bit of sightseeing as well. I have never been to Darwin before."

She answered, "Can you give me ten minutes? I just need to check the Attorney General's schedule. I also need to see if at least one of the two others, the coroner or sentencing judge, would also be available to fit in a meeting with you."

Beck walked out to her receptionist, saying, "Jenny? Could you get a hold of Judge Davis's assistant, to see if she can squeeze us into his schedule, for an hour, sometime on Friday? It is about the Susan MacDonald case.

"Also, ring Coroner Edwards' personal assistant and check his availability- ideally for the same meeting, though it can always be for different meetings, if needed. I will go and check with his lordship the AG."

She knocked at the door even though she knew her boss had been in for at least half an hour. She also knew he liked to be left alone to catch up on reading the daily pile of briefs for his first hour of the day.

A grumpy sounding, "Come In," came back. Beck walked in, putting on her calm and determined face, as he looked up.

"Oh, it is you, Beck," he said, giving her a much more pleasant smile than his voice belied.

"You sound frazzled," she replied.

"Just these endless crappy cabinet papers for Thursday's meeting. Some people need to learn how to write simple English. They say lawyer English is bad. Yet, we have got nothing on these highfaluting civil servants. Bloody, jumped- up office clerks who think we want to read endlessly about strategic plans, key performance indicators and milestones of success. It is enough to give me a headache and make my beard go grey. Why can't they just say what they mean and put it in short, simple words?"

He paused for a second to draw breath, "Sorry for the rant. I am sure you did not need to know that. How can I help?"

"Friday is a clear day, right?"

"Well, unless I can bugger off for the day after Cabinet and go fishing. But I suppose I can make myself available, if needed- especially seeing as you ask with such charm," he said, winking.

"Dr. Ross Sangster has just called and I said I would call him back in a minute. He sent me his report and the DVD of our own 'Lost Girl,' Susan. I was looking at it before he called. He has to come to Darwin on Thursday to meet with an aboriginal patient. He asked if he could schedule a meeting with us to discuss his report, preferably on Friday. I am good for Friday. Your schedule says the same. Jenny is checking regarding Judge Davis and Coroner Edwards. It would be best if we are all there, together, to hear what he has to say. I wanted to double-check with you before I said 'Yes' on your behalf. I will try to keep most of your day free for that fishing trip afterwards- but no promises."

He grimaced, "That's what I both love and hate about you- your bloody efficiency. The answer is 'Yes', if I must. I will even admit to having a tiny twinge of curiosity about this one. What does the video show?"

"Well, it is definitely her. She looks much different, now, but I know her voice. She looks both genuine and scared. She sounds bright, but brittle, at first. Then …" She grimaced, "Best that you see for yourself. It shook me."

Jenny had found time in both the judge and coroner's schedules between eight and ten o'clock on Friday morning. Any time after that, they were both booked solid.

Beck replied, "OK, put them both in for eight. We will meet here. Make sure to tell them both to block out two hours of time. It may take less, but it is a complicated story and you never know. Tell them both I will hand-deliver a DVD and report this afternoon- for their eyes only."

She went back in and closed the door before calling Ross. It was not that she did not trust Jen, but she decided that one leaker in her organization was more than enough.

By the time the call was over, Ross had gotten Beck to agree to have dinner with him on Friday night and do some sightseeing with him over the weekend. He was booked from eight to nine o'clock Friday for the meeting on his report only. Then, he would have to go off and amuse himself for the day while she and the others decided where to go with this. Then, she would prepare all the required documents to action whatever they decided.

Beck really hoped they all would agree on a pardon- with it to happen as soon as possible. She really wanted to give this girl a chance to disappear totally. The sooner she disappeared, the better, lest Jacob run her to ground. She must find a way to warn her that a bloodhound was on her trail. Perhaps she could get Alan to do that.

Friday came before she had time to think. Beck was at work early to make sure Jen was on her duty of keeping everyone else away. She set up a big screen in the conference room to allow them to all view the video together. On the table, in front of each man's chair, sat a copy of the report alongside a preliminary position paper. This paper included a summary of the report and recommendations on the steps from here.

The others were seated, perusing their documents, when Ross arrived. She escorted him in and did the introductions. Then she passed Ross the remote control, saying, "Before we go through your report, which seems pretty straightforward, could you walk us through the video? Please give us your impressions; both of the patient and of what happened on the day."

Ross nodded and started the video. He began by explaining the first sequence: where Susan spoke to him, unasked, before he had asked her any questions. He said, from after that section, he had blanked out the name of her partner at the request of the barrister for the other side. Otherwise, the video was unchanged.

He then explained the gap in the sequence, saying, "Next, I asked her to tell me about what she first remembered from her life now. She described arriving, heavily pregnant, in a location in Queensland. She said she had no understanding of how she came to be there. She only remembered that, one morning, she was sitting on a bench beside a road while holding a bag with a name written on it. She decided this must be her name and, since then, she has gone by that name.

"She found a job working in the town and, soon after, gave birth to two babies. They are a boy and a girl who are now nearly two years old. Since that time, she has moved onto various other locations. I am unable to disclose her current name or any of the locations where she has been. This fact is why that section of the tape is missing."

Ross then moved onto the next part of the DVD sequence, saying, "Next, I tried to see if any memories existed of her life before. It turned out, she had just a few early ones which end when she lived in England around the age of twelve. Significantly, her last clear memory is of meeting her friend Anne- the person you have no doubt seen on the television documentaries which are titled, 'Searching for the Lost Girls'.

I do not know, for certain, but I assume she is now in touch again with both Anne and her parents. They were all, for a long time, desperately searching for her, with no idea of what had become of her. If so, it is good for her to have a little bit of stability and reconnection after what must have been an extremely difficult and traumatic part of her life."

The DVD started playing again. They all watched, rapt, as she told about her memories of her friend, her holiday on the farm and of her love for the wildlife of Africa. It had a dreamy, almost otherworldly, feel to it. They had all seen it before and knew what was coming. Despite this, all had an intense look of anxiety of their faces as the crocodile question came out.

Ross let it run to the end without a word spoken. Then, he turned it off and faced them, saying,"

"My final question was very foolish. I don't know why I asked it. After that happened, I wished I had not. At first, the other side wanted me to take that part out. I persuaded them not to. This picture speaks far louder than any words ever could.

"We can all see, despite the new life she has made, there is a connection to the old. I do not doubt, for one minute, that she is totally genuine in saying she remembers nothing. Her own mind must have walled off that part of her memories as a last resort of self-protection. Therefore, I would hate to put her in the witness box and start questioning her about that time. I would equally hate for it to happen from a journalist or third party.

"I think the best thing we can do is to allow her to quietly disappear and get on with her new life. To simply respect the wish that she clearly stated at the start of this video- not to know about her past.

"I am troubled that, even then, her past may return to haunt her. I would not like it on my hands to cause it. I really fear it may not end well.

"It is a strange thing. In many ways, she is a delightful and lovely person. She has great warmness and kindness. It comes through very strongly- as if all her bad parts of her character have been taken away and locked out of reach. Now, all that remains, is a kind and gentle shell.

"Yet, the box of horrors is still there, buried somewhere deep. I would not wish to open it. When I spoke those words, the terror on her face was something I would never wish to see again. You only glimpse it in this video. But that is enough to understand what a bad place it must be for her.

"Perhaps, with time, she will find a way to deal with it. Perhaps her family can help. However, for us gathered here today, the kindest thing- in fact, the only decent thing we can do- is not to harm her further. I leave it in your hands to find a legal way to let her get on with her new life. In effect, that's what my report says, even if it uses more long words. While you have already read it, there's nothing in it that you cannot see with your own eyes.

"Her memory loss is genuine. It exists to protect her mind from something at the furthest edge of terror. It would be most foolish, far more than foolish, to force her to confront that place. I advise you, in the strongest possible way, *Do not do that*!

"Now, any questions, gentlemen?"

There were none. Dr. Ross Sangster excused himself and left the room.

The remainder of the meeting took but a few minutes.

All present agreed to recommend to the NT Executive Government that a pardon be granted to one 'Susan Emily MacDonald' for her conviction to the murder of Vincent Marco Bassingham.

Beck was left alone to put the government wheels in motion. By the end of the day, it was all prepared for a meeting between the Attorney General, the Chief Minister and his key advisors on Monday. No problems were expected and the formal process was expected to take about a month.

She took a deep breath and said a silent prayer as she walked out of the office later on that night. She prayed it would go smoothly so this person, now named Jane, could be left to get on with her life. Beck hoped this girl would never be found again by those who would do her harm.

Chapter 25 – Confession

Beck was full of trepidation at the thought of meeting Ross for dinner. With the advance notice, she had arranged for a neighbor to sleep over with her Mum, so she did not need to be back at any particular time.

But, since seeing the video, she had a sense of betrayal of Ross's trust in what she had told Jacob. Beck did not think his or her name would ever come out from Jacob. At the same time, she had used the 'in confidence' information Ross gave her to send Jacob off on his hunt for Susan. Jacob was exactly the type of bloodhound who would succeed.

As a first step, this afternoon, she rang Alan and told him about the agreement for the pardon. She also asked him to warn Susan's friends to be very careful about her location. She suggested to Alan it might be a good idea for Susan to move to another part of Australia as, with documents floating around in senior government circles, which referenced her examination by Ross Sangster in Brisbane, the chance of a leak was much greater. With this came the risk of journalists searching for her in that part of the state.

Alan agreed she was right and said he would pass it on "Immediately."

Hopefully, that would be enough to protect Susan, although Beck did not feel sure. What most ate at her was: she had betrayed the trust of a man she really liked. She hated facing him with this between them. After meeting Jacob, she buried the money deep in a drawer with her clothes. Since seeing the video, she could not bear to bring it out and touch it. This money now had such a tainted feel to it.

As Beck dressed to go out, she looked at her over-strong jaw and nose. She wished she had been born softer and prettier. Not that Ross was a drop-dead gorgeous type either, but she wanted him to look at her with 'liking' on this night out together. She thought that, perhaps, she was as nervous of him and how he looked at her, as she was about whether the secret she held would stay secret. Looking in the mirror, yet again, she decided not to cover her face with a layer of make-up. He would have to take her as he found her.

They met in the lobby of the hotel he was staying in. An excellent restaurant with a mixed Asian cuisine, which she loved, was next door. For ease, she had suggested it. He was already at the bar when she walked in, and he looked as nervous as she felt. That relieved her. Maybe he cared what she thought of him, too. He looked really good in black pants and a white shirt with his dark hair neatly brushed back. He seemed much taller than her when she came up to him. Impromptu, she leaned up on her toes and lightly kissed his cheek in greeting.

In return, Ross took Beck's hands and looked at her saying, in a quaint, old-worldly way, "You look quite lovely."

She blushed with pleasure in response.

They fell into a casual conversation. She started to talk about the case, at first, but he pressed a finger to her lips saying, "It is not so often I get to have dinner with a beautiful girl. How about you begin by telling me about yourself and how you come to be living here, working in such an important position?"

This moved the conversation to her. She found she did not want to pretend with this man. She told him of her mother, again. This time she told him the details: how she lived with her mother, took care of her and how it left little time for other things. She said, "Really, I don't have much time for going out now, I lead a fairly boring life. My days of being an 'out-there party girl' are long gone. It is strange how my work has become my sanity outlet."

He nodded with sympathy, but more than that, as if he understood her. Ross added, saying, "My life is not too dissimilar to yours. Not that I have the reason you have of caring for another. Rather, I am not easy in most people's company. I find small talk does not come easily for me outside work. I often say silly, inappropriate things. So, like you, my work has become my passion and my main outlet. It is where I feel most comfortable. I sometimes wish I was a naturally social person. It is nice to find a kindred soul."

After that, they followed other lines of conversation as they ate their dinner. He liked listening to classical music and they shared this interest. He had dabbled in photography, as had she. The meal drifted by with a pleasant, meandering feel. After the meal was done, they moved to a lounge chair in a small alcove, sitting side-by-side, not touching, and sharing a glass of port.

Finally, Ross asked Beck about the case. She quickly updated him on it.

Ross looked both relieved and pleased when Beck told him about the agreement on the pardon, saying, "I am very fearful for this girl- lest she be discovered. I only hope my own foolish mistake, that question about the crocodile, has not really harmed her. In the second after I said it, even before she had registered it, I wished I could have taken the words back. I think it was my ego- wanting to be clever and play God, the great fixer- rather than just waiting for her own self-discovery. I have damaged her trust. I hope I have not damaged more. The thought gives me sleepless nights.

"Have you ever deeply wished you could undo something?"

As Ross spoke, he looked into her eyes with a searching intensity, as if seeking to discover kindness in her soul.

Beck felt shame well up inside her. His mistake seemed such a small thing compared to what she had done- but for him, she could tell the pain was real. She knew she must take this chance to unburden herself, too. She took his hand, which rested on the couch beside her, squeezed it with her own and turned her face back to his. She was searching his eyes as she gathered courage. "Thank you for telling me. It must be hard to speak of this. In time, I think she will come to understand that you meant her no harm."

She took a deep breath to steel herself to go on, collecting her faltering words. "I have done something far worse- a thing that shames me. I harmed both you and her in what I did."

His eyes stared into hers in a kind, nonjudgmental way. She stumbled through the story: the lust, betrayal, taking the money and the buying of things to help her mother. Finally, she told him of the day just gone, when she met this man again and how she took his money again in return for telling him what Ross had told her. She saw pain wash over his face as she told of that- a wince. He did not look away.

She finished by saying, "After I saw the video, I could not bear to touch the money. It is still in my drawer. I feel, having already sold out, I should take it to use it to buy the thing for which I paid the price. Then, a small piece of good can follow the bad. But I cannot bear one more betrayal. Before I saw her face and terror, I pretended I was harming no-one, although it was a lie.

"I cannot pretend anymore. In her face, I saw the harm I had done to her- now and before. So, if I cannot repair that, I must do no further harm." Beck's body was shaking as she spoke. Her mind felt a tearless horror.

Ross did not speak but simply put a big arm around her shoulder. He pulled her in against him and cradled her head like a child. They sat like that for some unknown time.

At last, he spoke, softly, "What you did was a bad and selfish thing and cannot be undone. For that, you will always carry shame. Now, you must learn to let it go. One day, should the chance arise, you must tell these words to those you have hurt- the girl and her man. They are good people, and I am sure they would forgive- as I do. Then, perhaps, you can begin to forgive yourself. In the meantime, we should do something good with that money. Not use it for your mother- I will make sure she gets the wheelchair she needs without you needing to lie and steal secrets. But you should use it to help others in great need. Ones you do not know. That way, the money will not taint them, too."

Beck put her arm around him and lay her head against his shoulder. "Did anyone tell you: you are a good man and a good friend?"

The weekend passed with them spending most of the time in each other's company. They were not lovers, but their friendship was a deep and intense thing. They had shared their deepest and worst secrets so, now, they felt as if they could each tell the other anything. On Saturday, they drove out to Litchfield National Park. They walked alone along a barren stony track for half an hour until it plunged down a hole in the hills. They swam together in a clear rock-encased pool- both a little self-conscious about their revealed, imperfect bodies. A late wet season water flow plunged over a sheer cliff into this shadowed place below. It sprayed them with a fine mist that flowed over their bodies and made surreal shapes as they drifted in and out of the fog into the gloomy light.

That night, Beck played host at her own house. While she worked away in the kitchen preparing food, Ross charmed her mother and the next-door neighbor. The neighbor was a regular visitor who covered for when Beck was away and was also a longstanding friend of the family.

On Sunday night, in fact early Monday morning, she went with Ross to the airport for his red-eye flight to Brisbane. She sat with him at a small table, sipping a coke. They kept odd snippets of conversation going but, mostly, just shared silence. Finally, when the flight was called, Ross took her hands, saying, "Thank you for a wonderful weekend. The best in my memory.

"I have been meaning to tell you but was not sure how to say it. I have been offered a job in Darwin. It would be working at the hospital in the Rehabilitation Unit, helping people with brain injuries, both from alcohol and traumatic causes. It sounds exciting but, in truth, half the attraction is because you live here. What do you think about me taking it?"

She gave a spontaneous grin, saying, "Well, I am glad that is settled. Otherwise, I would have had to find a way to move to Brisbane. That would have been tricky with my mother. In the meantime, I was thinking of flying down to Brisbane for another weekend. It would be just to see you again, and only if you are free, of course. This time, you can play the host."

Now, Ross gave Beck a huge smile in return, admitting happily, "I would really like that."

Chapter 26 – The Returning

Vic had heard the warning to move from Anne, via Alan, and took it seriously.

He had been shocked as he had looked at the record of Jane's interview, a few days later, with Ross and the barrister. Jane's upset manner on the day was bad, but she was over the worst when he saw her. Afterwards, she had a distant and reserved manner, so unlike her normal sunshine self, which had persisted for a few days. It was as if, for the first time in her remembered life, she had lost trust in someone or something- even though she had stayed affectionate to him. Fortunately, this had faded and she now seemed back to normal. Yet it still had reinforced his sense of her vulnerability.

Vic went back to Brisbane the following week for a two-hour meeting to decide on the contents of the video to be provided. They debated long and hard over what parts to leave in and what to cut. Vic insisted that all parts referring to him or her living in the north Queensland aboriginal community must be taken out, lest others who saw it trace her using the information. He also wanted the bit showing her acute distress removed. It was not that it gave anything else away, but it was far too raw and pain-filled to let others see- or so he had thought.

Ross argued, forcefully, that despite his question having been a mistake, her reaction was the thing which would work best in getting the government to understand just how fragile and damaged she was. The barrister supported Ross, saying this picture was far better than any words.

Even though Vic finally agreed to it remaining, the awful sight of Jane's terrified face frightened him to his core. He had already been thinking it was too dangerous for them to keep staying so close to Brisbane after the series of meetings he had been to there.

It would not require Einstein to start checking the smaller regional towns nearby, particularly checking out the temporary places where people stayed like caravan parks. He considered renting a house in one of the towns around here. However, that was fraught with its own problems, like the identity documents and references being needed for leases. Perhaps he could look for a farmhouse in return for farm work, but his contact network did not run deep in this place and the act of looking would bring him into public view.

Vic hated the idea of randomly moving Jane and their children around, as much for the children's sake as hers. They all needed stability and new roots, not an endless, half fugitive existence.

It was a devil's choice between two evils: the evil of a forever fractured existence, of links broken over and over when only half formed, and the evil lurking in a buried place in her mind, threatening to break out and overwhelm her. He did not know what to do, since each choice was not a good one.

With the message about the threat of exposure, Vic learned the fact of an agreement for a pardon. The other thing Vic had thought about and talked over with Anne, was the need for Jane to have new identity documents. They were needed for marriage, which she mentioned regularly, and they were needed for travel. They were also needed for the thousand other normal things a person did, things such as: health insurance, education, driver's license – the list went on. Of course, the primary identity of Susan MacDonald was an English one, so the identity change had to begin there.

Vic had a half-formed plan of her needing a new passport in the Jane Bennet name. That would mean a legal name change in England. This part would not be hard to achieve if Jane could remember her former self and give a signed instruction for her name to be changed. However, it needed to be done without public knowledge. Also, it needed to be done on her behalf by someone else- which meant her parents, in this case.

He had talked about it with Anne and bounced ideas around with Ross, too. They formed a plan for Ross to provide a report confirming Jane's loss of memory and how she had created a new identity. Ross would say she needed to be given identity documents in this new name- as it was likely to be very harmful for her to be forced to confront her previous identity.

At the same time Anne would use her legal connections in London to work out how this could be done both legally and in a non-disclosed way. Her idea was simple: Jane's parents could sign forms authorizing a name change and then new identity documents could be issued in the Jane Bennet name.

With the wheels in progress for a pardon, Vic thought he should seek agreement from the NT government for this course of action. Alan had already shown he was pretty good at getting things like this sorted out, so Vic planned to ask for his assistance.

Vic was hopeful that, within four to six weeks, Jane would have identity documents in her own name. This would also be shortly after the pardon was granted. Then, using these documents, they could get on with their lives together, in a faraway place.

This did not solve the conundrum of where to go now, though. He knew they needed a new home, one not easy to get to and one where the people could be trusted not to let the cat out of the bag. It had to be a place where there was control of others who came and went. Most importantly, a place where Vic could do something useful while he waited. He tried to think of all the remote parts of Australia where he had not been. Vic was at first thinking, if he was unknown there, no one would guess to look for him in these places. At the same time, if he did not know the people in a small place, he would stand out like a proverbial 'sore thumb,' as would Jane and their children. Their unknown status would make them the subject of idle gossip and curiosity. All the unwanted attention could bring new danger.

At last, it came to him. Vic had to go back to where he was known and trusted because, with that, came a trust in others. One of the stations at the outer edges of the Alice Springs district would be best. These were small family-owned units, despite their immense size. Many had extra houses for workers or outstations. As of now, most stations had yet to take on workers for the cattle season. He could think of several such places. It would take a bit of careful inquiry to work out which would serve best- for both the place and him. In such a place, the only person who would know he was there would be the station manager. Most of these managers were already personal friends of his. And importantly, people from outside could only get to these stations with the manager's agreement.

It seemed like a neat solution, at least for a couple months, until the pardon and identity stuff were sorted out. He remembered he had an uncle who worked out on a place north-east of Alice. He lived alone now since his wife had died and his kids had moved to town. He was head stockmen when there was a stock camp. The rest of the time, he maintained the windmills and made sure the stock had water. Vic had not seen him for several years, but he had visited him often as a boy. It was an obvious place to go.

Vic would call his sister to ask her to try and get it arranged. At the same time, he would tell Jane he wanted to make a trip to Alice Springs for her to meet his family. Jane had announced before that she wanted to get married there, so it was also a step towards this idea. If Vic was honest, he liked the thought of marrying her as much as she did him.

Jane and the children were delighted when he told them. They decided to leave the day after tomorrow. They all had really enjoyed the Christmas car trip to the farm. This now promised to be another family adventure.

Vic made Jane promise not to tell anyone where they were going. He said that, once the arrangements for the wedding were made, she could call and tell people. For now, however, he wanted to keep it a secret. He could see she was torn in wanting to tell Thea, but she agreed at last. He knew she always stuck to what she said.

A week later, they found themselves crossing into the Northern Territory from Queensland. They had come across from Boulia and crossed the multiple flood outs of the Georgina River. It had rained two months ago. The country was lush with fat cattle, myriad wildlife and water birds. They came onto the Plenty Highway as they entered the Territory and followed it as it skirted around the northern margin of the Simpson Desert. Part-way along, they turned into the station homestead road they were heading for. After another hour, they were there. Vic's uncle was there to meet them- along with his sister and mother, who had driven the several hundred kilometers for a family visit. They were entertained royally in the station homestead on the first night.

The next day, they all climbed aboard a Toyota Landcruiser Station Wagon driven by Vic's Uncle Jack. Jack brought them to the outstation where he lived and showed them to a two-bedroom cottage next to his house. He said this was their new home for as long as it was needed.

The house had a telephone so they could call the outside world. A mail plane came to the main station each week, delivering mail. The station cook went to town once a fortnight to buy food. On the following day a delivery was made to his uncle's outstation. In return for this place to stay, Vic would do work on the station, things like helping his uncle fix roads, fences, and machinery, along with checking waters and doing general stock work. He wanted no wages for this work- just a place to stay for him and his family.

Finally, Vic felt safe knowing no one could find or reach them here. The only people who knew where there were staying now were his own people, ones he would entrust his life to.

Chapter 27 – Another Family

Jane was surprised at the joy she felt in discovering a new family: Vic's mother, sister and uncle. They were all affectionate to her and kind and wonderful with the children. They were also full of stories of the land. She found she could sit and listen to them for hours.

She loved the fact they shared Vic's blood and some of his looks. Their dark skin and eyes were just the same as his. At the same time, each had their own special bits to their appearance which set them apart from one another: his sister had blond highlights to her hair, which Vic assured Jane were natural for some desert people. His mother had beautiful, glossy-back skin and hair, which shone when she brushed it. His uncle, Jack, had a tough, wiry body so much like her Vic. However, Jack's hair was now a grizzled grey.

Vic's mother and sister stayed for a week. They lived next door in the uncle's house, although in truth, they were as much in her house as his. Jane loved it that way. The third day, Uncle Jack appeared with a quiet horse. He led the children around the yard on it. The next day, he came with two quiet horses for Jane and Vic to ride, while his mother minded Anne and David.

Jane and Vic followed Jack as he rode around the home paddock. First, he took them to a little rocky hill where the heavy-bodied kangaroos, which he called 'big boy wallaroo,' grazed. From here, they had a panoramic view and he showed them the lie of the land. They rode on, checking the fences. Jack showed them his special places and the signs of the land: the sweet open grass flats where cows and calves played, the places of water along the creek, the places in hidden trees where the cattle camped and two more little rocky hills where more kangaroos grazed.

Jack finished by saying, "Now, I know you not get lost. More better, you stay inside fence unless you come with me. Don't want picaninny belong you lost in outside bush. Too hot, no water, big snakes and maybe the devil man."

Vic grinned and punched his uncle on the arm, saying, "Ah, go long with you, Jack. Devil man only a children story. Me, blackfella, too. Not get lost. But, still, we best be careful with the children in the bush."

Jane nodded to show she understood Jack's and Vic's warning that this could be a dangerous place.

After a week, Vic's Mum, Rosa, and his sister, Jill, went back to Alice. They said they had a wedding to organize while giving Jane and Vic a sly wink. Each week, Jane called her parents and Anne. David and little Annie had now learned to take turns to say hello, too, and tell simple stories like "today the chooks laid three eggs," or "yesterday we saw a big goanna."

At other times, Vic rang his wider friends to check on the wedding arrangements- at least, that is what he told Jane. She knew it was a bit more than just that. She was fine with this. She knew Vic would tell her anything she needed to know and she trusted him.

One day, when Vic was out fixing a grader which had broken down on the main station road, there was a knock on the door. It was Uncle Jack, who had been out checking windmills. He was finished for the day. He said, "Today, Vic's not home till late. Better you come and have dinner with me."

Jane followed Jack to his house with the children and went to help him prepare dinner. He shook his head. Instead of accepting her help with dinner, he showed her to a chair and gave her an album of photos to look through.

Jack said, "I good cook. I fix the dinner. You marry family, you become part of family. So, this is family photo book from great grandfather to now. You look. That way you know your other family, too."

After this, Jane sat and began to turn the pages. First, she was looking at old sepia photos: men with big hats, ladies with long heavy skirts, other men leading and driving camels and men with black skin and few clothes carrying big spears and throwing sticks. There was also another one with a proud black man carrying a big kangaroo on his shoulder. Last, there were photos of several men riding horses behind cattle, horse races and a collection of old cars and trucks with their proud owners driving along scrubby roads.

As Jane worked her way towards the back, she recognized the clothes were becoming more modern and the cars were newer looking. She recognized a lady who was a young Rosa. She had three children standing around her and a small baby in her arms. She looked carefully at each child around Rosa: two boys, like Vic but different, and the girl, perhaps five or six in this photo. She realized the little girl was Jillie. Vic must be the baby in his mother's arms. Rosa looked so very proud with her children-particularly, her little baby.

It made Jane smile inside with pleasure. She realized that, but for change of skin color, it could have been her when she held her babies, David and Annie. She knew and owned that look too. On the next page, there was a picture of a shiny, new helicopter and a proud, young man standing beside it. Then there was a second picture of a tribe of black kids climbing all over the helicopter as the same man watched over them- his smile huge with pride.

Uncle Jack walked over as she stared at her Vic in the flush of success. "Fine looking boy, heh. Not bad for a desert blackfella to own that thing. Good thing about our Vic is he never forgot his blackfella roots. He spent half that first day taking all the nieces, nephews and then, the rest of the town camp kids for rides in that machine.

"Only pity was that boy could have been a football star. He was so quick and balanced. If only you could have seen him running down the ground, cutting his way through a mob of players. He would step one way, then swerve another. He kept the ball at his fingertips and moved so fast, no-one could even touch him. He was pure magic, he was. Could have played for a top Melbourne AFL team, made lots of money and seen his name in lights. But, his big sister, Jillie, she would have none of it.

"She would tell him, 'Sure you could make the big-time boyo, but what then? What when you'se 30 and all smashed up?'

So, she made him stay at school, do his lessons, get an apprenticeship and learn to fly. The day he bought that machine, I had to tell her she was right. But a part of me always wanted to see him running down the field with the ball on a string. Kicking it straight through the center of the MCG goals- it would have been a pretty sight."

Jane folded the book closed. She walked over and hugged the Jack, saying, "I suppose being married to Vic makes you my family, too. I like being part of this family and having an uncle like you. You must tell me all the stories of Vic as a little boy- along with stories about your own children."

They shared a meal as he told her story after story. Most of the stories were funny, but some were sad. As he talked more and more, she felt she belonged here. This was her real family now and she was joined to them. When the meal was finished, Jack went to a drawer and pulled out a package wrapped in a tattered piece of oil cloth. He placed it in her hands.

She unwrapped it. It was an old book, bound in a leather cover with its edges frayed and marked. It was tied closed with a faded, red ribbon. She carefully untied the ribbon and opened it. There was something old and precious in the feel of this manuscript: its weight, the heavy paper and the marks of all the hands which had held it. She turned the pages slowly, seeing brightly colored ink drawings and delicately drawn lettering. She could not read the writing as the characters and words were unfamiliar to her.

Jane looked at Jack with inquiring eyes, "What is it?"

Jack answered, "I do not know. It belonged to my Grandfather Vikram and has been passed to each generation for someone to mind. It should now go to Vic. As you have more education, maybe you could find out the story it tells. Does it tell from where he came? Or is it a religious book, like a bible? Now that there is a new generation in our family, it is a thing for you and Vic to have. But, before it passes from me, I would like to know what it says. What is the story it tells? Could you find out for me, so I can know its story?

"I have held it in my hands many times. But its inside is a mystery to me. I do not have the learning to discover what it says. I would like if you can do that for me. Then, when I give it to Vic, I can give him proper instruction in its meaning. I think that is what I should do before I pass it on."

Jane nodded, agreeing, "I'm not sure quite where to begin. But I'm sure I can find out. So, yes, I will do it for you. It's best if you keep the book, keep it safe. But I will take photos of its pages. That way, I can find a person who can read these words and tell me what it says. Then, I can tell you in turn."

The next day, Jane borrowed Vic's mobile phone, which had a camera, and worked her way through this old book. She carefully turned each thick, yellowed page to take pictures. Some pages were smudged with dirt or had fingermarks. There were about 150 pages with writing and a few blank pages towards the end. The writing was like nothing she knew, but a few of the pictures seemed to have a familiar feel about them. One of these pictures was a brightly colored parrot. She was sure she had seen a similar bird flitting through this desert landscape. There were also a couple of images of men in long, flowing garbs leading and riding camels. Last, there were a couple landscape type pictures which had been carefully drawn using a range of ink colors which seemed to be Australian in origin. There were also drawings of landscapes with jagged, high snow-covered mountains and lush valleys. These pictures seemed to be of another land- perhaps around the high mountains of the Himalayan ranges.

However, the writing gave no clues to its origin. There was also nothing written in a language Jane could understand. The script seemed different from any language she had seen, for it contained many letters or symbols with complex curves and curls. She decided she needed to talk to a university professor with knowledge of languages from the Indian subcontinent or Middle East to begin to decipher this story.

Chapter –8 - Search for the Elusive Susan

Jacob felt bemused and a bit frustrated as he left Beck behind. The aborted sex had left him full of desire – not just for Beck, but for any raunchy, hot young thing between the sheets. By the end of the night, he had satisfied this itch with another girl he had picked up at the hotel bar. He only had to buy her a few drinks and sweet talk his way into her pants.

But, after he had her a couple times, Jacob found he had little to talk about with her. She was just a good-time girl and was happy to go on her way to look for more adventure before the night was done. When she was gone, he fell into a deep sleep.

He woke up early and found himself wishing Beck was lying beside him. He would have liked to start his morning off by having sex with her, but even more he enjoyed talking to her- almost more than the sex. Her mind was sharp like his own and she challenged him.

However, Beck was not there. He knew she was torn about what she had done, with a guilty conscience. He wondered what led to her change of heart. Had she found out something she was not telling him? In the end, he decided it had been a fair trade- the money for the information she had given him. Now, they could both get on with their own lives.

As Jacob showered and dressed, he felt re-energized. He could sense this story was now within his grasp. It had that feel to it. His gut instinct told him it was able to be cracked wide open. This girl had gone into hiding under another name. He now had that name, a first name at least, and an approximate location for where she now lived- a coastal town somewhere within a hundred or so kilometers of Brisbane.

He spent a few hours on the internet in his hotel room to familiarize himself with the geography of this area. After his searching, Jacob decided that either the Sunshine Coast, the Gold Coast, or, perhaps, the very north of NSW were the most likely places she would be. There were loads of apartments for rent in the Gold Coast. Also, there were lots of other short-term accommodation options for backpackers: caravan parks and the like.

A backpacker place was also unlikely with two small children. Her place was also unlikely to be at the top end of the market as these would want references and identification. Plus, two small children would be a negative for these places. That is unless she now had a sugar daddy- he could not discount this. She was known to pick up men easily with some sort of sex and charm offensive. However, her new boyfriend sounded like someone more her age- meaning not some old rich dude.

He focused on the bottom end of the real estate market: the scummy flats which took cash for rent and asked no questions. Perhaps there was a caravan park where she rented a van with cooking facilities- but that did not feel right. The Gold Coast had a lot of these places, but once you went down to the bottom feeders, the pickings thinned out. There were also a lot of these places between Tweed Heads and Byron Bay, in the far north of NSW. Then, there were a lot more places in Sunshine Coast- from Noosa to the south but, overall, these were of higher class with less chances for anonymity.

Jacob decided he would begin at the bottom end of the strip, fly to Brisbane, rent a car and work his way north. He figured two weeks south of Brisbane would let him work his way through northern NSW and the Gold Coast. Then, he would need another week to cover the Sunshine Coast. If he found nothing by then, he would rethink his options and try a different tack.

Having made his plan, Jacob booked the lunchtime flight to Brisbane and booked a luxury hire car for him to collect from the airport. He decided he wanted to play the part of a high-end private investigator, employed by Jane's parents. His invented back story was they were desperately seeking to trace their daughter, who had left London after a family falling out. She had gone off travelling on her own without keeping in touch with the family. Her mother was now critically ill with advanced cancer and the family urgently wanted to find her to give her the news. They hoped she would return to see her mother, again, before she died.

He would tell people her last known address was in Cairns. When she was there, she had a baby, twins actually, born about a year after she left home. These children would now be about two years old. She had sent her parents a card telling them this news from Cairns, but that was her last direct contact. It was also known she'd left there a few months ago and travelled south. He said he knew this because she'd called a friend in Brisbane, to say she lived in a coastal town not too far away from them but had not given them the address. Now his job was to try and locate her, to ask she urgently get in touch with her family. He implied a substantial reward was on offer from the family to anyone who could give the information which found her.

Jacob knew he could tell this story convincingly. He had cards printed up giving his contact details as a private investigator with a confirmed London firm. As he travelled, he would leave these cards and photos of her with people he met along the way.

On the bottom of each photo was written: *Have you seen Jane? Reward for information about her location,* along with his mobile number. The photo was of Susan from earlier in her life when her hair was cut shorter and her face was rounder. It was a sufficiently different appearance from the public view of the NT Crocodile Girl so as not to easily link her to this famous woman, but with enough similarity to uncover some possible sightings.

A week passed as Jacob worked his way north and then a second week. He had been to lots of places, talked to many people: building and caravan park managers, small neighborhood shops and cafés, children's playgrounds, childcare centers, toyshops and those who sat around just watching others.

Jacob had run to ground a few leads which had turned into nothing. Overall, people bought his story and the reward mentioned sharpened their interest, but there was nothing convincing about any likely sightings and no substantial leads. He had given away over a thousand cards and photos in his travels. He felt that, with all this, something should come back to him- if she was around here.

So far, nothing had. Even though he was not ready to give up, it felt like a lot of effort for so little progress.

Tomorrow, he would begin at Noosa and work his way back down the Sunshine Coast towards Brisbane. If that yielded nothing, then he would need to rethink how to do this.

Another week passed by. Jacob had gone through all the towns of the Sunshine Coast- both those on the coast and the near inland ones. The only one he hadn't gone to yet was Caloundra. After searching this town, all that remained was the bayside villages and towns along Moreton Bay until they were hard up against Brisbane suburbia. Once he got there, if her found nothing, he would have to admit he had failed to find Jane.

Today was Caloundra. He would start at the southern tip, going to a caravan park, and work his way north. At 8:30 am, he knocked at the caravan park office and was greeted by a middle-aged couple who announced they were the park managers. He asked if they had seen a girl named Jane with two small children, twins, aged around two years old. He knew, in an instant, he had a hit, for he saw recognition in both their eyes at the name, Jane.

"Yes. We had a Jane who stayed here until about two weeks ago. I'm afraid I don't have a forwarding address. She left suddenly with the man she was with. We'd thought they were married. They really seemed like a family, but Jane told Thea they were heading off to get married. She did not say where. Thea has gone to the shops, but she said she will be back in an hour or so. You had best talk to her- as they were good friends. She's the one most likely to know anything further."

With this information Jacob sat in his car and waited. He tried to calm his jangling nerves with some soothing music. At last, a girl of a similar age to Susan came driving in. She looked like she belonged here. A few seconds later, the manager came out, pointing to her car and her unit.

Taking this as an invitation, Jacob went over and knocked on the door. "Coming," came a voice through the door. In a few seconds, she was there looking out at him. She was not quite suspicious, but there was something guarded about her.

Jacob went through his story, but he could tell this woman did not believe him. As he spoke, she became even more guarded and cautious. The mention of a reward only served to make her even more suspicious.

Finally, she said, "I am sorry. I can't help you. I really did not know her that well. We just chatted a bit as we made up beds and things like that. Then, one day, she just upped and off- not saying where she was heading."

Jacob knew she was lying because of her whole defensive demeanor. He knew he was wasting his time. He decided he'd better try another option to find out more, and before the suspicion she showed was conveyed to others. He thought the wedding story was likely true,. He saw it in Thea's eyes when he mentioned hearing of this. He backed off, thanked her and left. He decided to try and get a bit more about the man Jane was with. He would go back to the park managers and ask them about him- and do it before Thea could warn them to be careful.

With to this plan, Jacob returned to the office, thanking them profusely for all their help, and saying it was a pity Thea had not known where they had gone. As if in passing, he added, "Oh. She told me the man's name Jane was with, but I forgot to write it down. Could you prompt my memory?"

"Vic," replied the man, at once.

"You don't know a surname?" asked Jacob.

The man thought for a minute and said, "Bennet.".

"Nothing else you can think of about him?" asked Jacob.

The man scratched his head, obviously giving the matter some thought. "Only that he was a dark one. Skin halfway to your color. I've a feeling that, one day, Jane said his Mum lived in Alice Springs. She was a sweet girl, she was. She thought the sun shone out of our Vic. It was something she said, one day, about how she really wanted to go to Alice Springs to meet his family- particularly his Mum, who lived there."

Jacob felt huge and rising elation. He would bet London to a brick he had them. He had thought Vic had gone overseas. Obviously, he did not.

Jacob had been informed about the boyfriend, Vic, being heartbroken over Susan's disappearance. He was told Vic had caught a flight to Canada right around the time the first rumors of Susan's reappearance surfaced.

However, it seemed the sneaky bugger had been smarter than Jacob had credited him. Vic had obviously set this rumor up as part of a disappearing act. Meanwhile, he'd hooked up with his girlfriend, again.

Jacob knew it was only inference at this stage, but how many blokes had skin that color and the name 'Vic' who lived in Alice Springs?

He could have asked these people for a better description of Vic. He could have even got a photo and shown it to them to confirm it was Vic. However, he did not need to do that. Instead, he went out to his car and put $2000 cash in an envelope. He passed it to the man and his wife, saying, "My employer is a well-to-do, generous man. He would like you to take this for your trouble. Perhaps, you could treat yourself to something nice with it."

With that, Jacob gave them a wave, climbed in his car and drove away.

He knew the end of the chase was very near.

Chapter 29 – The Wedding

Vic looked back at the month which had passed while they lived in seclusion in their desert hideaway. He had loved this uninterrupted time spent with Jane and the children. Even though he knew another man was their father, it felt like Jane's children were fully his now. He had worked hard on the station in return for room and board, but the work was a pleasure to him. He was mostly doing things with his hands and knowing, each night, he would return to his family. They always greeted him with ferocious joy.

Now, the weather was cooling at night. At the main station, a stock camp had been assembled to start the season's muster. Next week, they would draft off the steers for fattening in the river paddock and brand all this year's calves, from the close in paddocks, before they went mustering further out. Vic and Jane mostly stayed in their outstation cottage but, a few times, they had gone to the main homestead to join the others for dinner.

His Mum and Jillie had visited, again, the weekend before last, to tell them about all the arrangements made for their wedding. Jane had sent Vic across to talk and drink with his Uncle Jack for the afternoon The children were playing at his feet. She had closed the doors and put blinds across the windows so he could not look inside while she brought Rosa and Jillie in to help her select a wedding dress and make other style arrangements.

Vic understood from Jane that her two bridesmaids would be Jillie and Anne. Little Davie and Annie would carry flowers and follow Anne. He also knew that Jane's mother, father and a few other key friends would attend. He wanted to keep it low-key, but this was easier said than done. Jane had a penchant for issuing instant invitations as she did not see the need for secrecy. That meant it was hard to keep it quiet. Overall, however, it seemed to have worked.

Sorting out the legal complexities had been tricky, too. Vic knew he owed a great debt to Buck, Alan, Anne and many others. In the end it had all come off as well as he could have hoped and much better than expected.

It had been worked out in two places at the same time.

After viewing the video, the Northern Territory Government agreed to grant a pardon to 'Susan Emily MacDonald.' It would be signed in two days- on the Friday evening, at the end of normal business hours, before their Saturday wedding. It would not be announced until the following Monday, to limit the chance of journalists searching for her.

At the same time, the English Government had privately organized to grant new identity papers. These were also to be released on the same Friday- but on English time. This would only happen once the NT government confirmed the pardon was signed. These documents, which changed the name of 'Susan MacDonald' to 'Jane Bennet,' had been lodged on Jane's behalf by her parents and with the support of the psychiatrist, Ross Sangster. Ross confirmed her memory loss and the risk of severe mental or physical harm if Jane was forced to become aware of her past identity.

His statement was supported by an eminent English colleague who had been given the transcript of his previous interview with Jane, along with the video and a summary of the trial information. He had fully concurred with Ross Sangster's opinion. The English lawyers from Anne's former firm had obtained a court order to suppress this identity change from public disclosure for a five-year period.

Therefore, barring any unforeseen hold ups, it would all happen like clockwork. Scanned copies of the NT documents would be sent to the UK once they were signed. Then, scanned copies of the new UK passport and other identity forms would arrive in time for the Saturday wedding ceremony. The originals would be couriered in both directions on flights, leaving Friday night, from both London and Darwin. They would be available in both London and Alice Springs at the end of the following day. This was so the original documents for the wedding could be lodged the following Monday in time for official registration procedures. The English passport would also be in their hands before they boarded the plane on Monday morning.

The end result was that Vikram Campbell was marrying Jane Bennet. It would be decreed in the official marriage ceremony. It would all be legal. Vic lived in hope that no one, outside their immediate circle, would be any the wiser as to how Susan had become Jane, his bride.

Early on Monday morning, they would fly from Alice Springs via Cairns for a month's holiday in remote northern Scotland. There they would be staying on the family farm where Jane's last childhood memories remained. She would travel under this new passport issued to Jane Bennet.

After the holiday, they would see what happened with the pardon. They could then decide on whether they could become public people again, in either Australia or the UK, or whether they needed to establish a new life in some other unknown location- perhaps New Zealand. Vic liked the last idea as he had contacts who could arrange work there as a pilot. It would let him fly helicopters in the mountains, again, a thing he loved and had missed.

For now, Vic was happy to know almost nothing of the detailed wedding plans. All he knew was they would drive back to Alice Springs, tomorrow, Friday. Jane would stay in a private resort with her parents and Anne that night. He would have a night with his mates. He'd insisted on a low-key bucks' ceremony. He was determined not to have a hangover. He would stay that night at his sister's place with his Uncle Jack, in two of Jillie's kids' bunk beds.

Jillie and his Mum would bring him and his Uncle Jack to church the next day. They were going to the church his sister belonged to. Jillie had squared away with the pastor that there be no publicity and no uninvited guests. For extra security, Buck and Alan would take positions by the back door to ensure only invited guests came inside for the church wedding ceremony.

After the ceremony, they would head out to Desert Springs Park for a private evening reception. This included paid security, also to ensure no uninvited guests, like photographers, turned up there either. Their wedding night, they would go to a private resort in a gorge in the West McDonnells. Here, they would have brunch with the wedding guests, the next day, before saying their goodbyes in preparation for Monday's early departure.

The whole plan was not totally foolproof but, since the early leaks when he had faked going to Canada and had actually brought Jane away, there had been no further leaks. Based on this, Vic was quietly confident it would work out and they could fade into the sunset- just like any other newlyweds.

Saturday morning had a slow, dreamlike quality. Vic sat at his sister's kitchen table, with a minor hangover, drinking endless cups of coffee. Jack had gone uptown shopping, after having been harassed by Rosa to buy a new suit, to ensure he looked the part of the head man of the family. Vic's own suit hung in the cupboard. It had never been worn, but he was confident it would fit. He would do it all in the proper way, even though, this part of ceremony seemed unimportant to him. He wanted it to be perfect for Jane. He could not quite believe his luck in marrying this delightful girl. After all, it was an unimagined dream of barely six months ago. He promised himself to make their life together extra good from here on. He could not wait to see her or their children again. Vic even wondered if a third one may have started its spirit journey during one of their nights of loving out in the desert. It was a wonderful thought.

The time drifted away until his sister harassed him into showering and dressing. He polished his shoes an extra time, adjusted his bow tie in the mirror and decided he looked pretty slick.

Then, it was time to go to church. After a brief hello to a few friends, he moved to the front of the church to await his bride. The waiting was agony! All Vic could think of was all the things which could go wrong. Every second seemed like a minute and every minute seemed like an hour.

At last, he heard the distant noise of a car's arrival along with muffled voices. This was the moment the waiting ended. He looked down to the far end of the church. A shimmer of light started to drift through the door-part sunlight and part gossamer.

Vic realized it was the flounces of a wedding dress as Jane paused for a second before coming through. White, tiny patterns of a faint blue to turquoise that he could only just make out. They drifted in and out of view in the breeze. Then, this gorgeous apparition wafted through while lightly holding her father's arm. She was so very beautiful that she took his breath completely away. A huge lump formed in his throat and his hand brushed tears from the edges of his eyes.

Jane drifted towards Vic like the strand of gossamer which floats above air eddies. She was weightless with her own exhilaration. Their eyes met in an iridescent smile. Just a trace of amusement was in her smile at his discomfort.

The service had a mesmeric quality to it. The words were spoken: "I do, I promise." Finally, it was done with a ring being placed on his and her finger along with the signing of the register. Her kiss was the barest brush on his lips. They joined their arms together to walk back down the aisle.

They emerged through the crowd of well-wishers. All of them were laughing, hugging and shaking hands. Vic was still unable to believe his luck.

Suddenly, a man stepped forward. Dark-skinned but different from his local black brothers. Vic thought he was coming towards him, but then, he realized it was Jane the man sought. As the man reached them, a microphone was pushed forward. Vic saw a camera on a tripod a few feet behind him with its red 'record' light running.

Words spilled from the man's mouth, "Hello, Susan Emily MacDonald. How does it feel to have married the best friend of the man you killed?

"This is Jake SS reporting for 'The Truth' in downtown Alice Springs."

Vic felt overwhelming rage. He knew that name well. He had read his by- line in the newspaper on the day in which Susan had vanished. He was the author of all those hateful words and still it was not enough.

Vic stepped forward, tearing the microphone free with one hand and casting it aside. He felt his fists move and heard dull thuds as they connected with the hateful face- once, twice, thrice with each hand. The man slumped forward. Vic hit him in his chest and body- as his rage powered him on.

Vic felt himself being grabbed from behind and pulled back. The man was slumped on the footpath near the edge of the road. Buck moved across his view, picking up the camera and smashing it into the road. Then, Buck grabbed this man and hauled him to his feel. Alan was by Buck's side- a posse of two. Each held an arm and kept the man upright.

Buck's voice spoke, vehemently, "Listen, you scumbag. You are lucky we pulled Vic off before he killed you- because he surely would have. I don't want him to end up in jail for fixing filth, like you, on what should be his perfect wedding day.

"But I will give you a tip. If so much as one word of what happened today ends up in your scummy paper, I will come and find you. I will string you upside down, hanging by your balls and dick, until your precious bits come away. Then, I will take what is left of you and give it to the crocodiles- the ones that interest you so much. If you don't believe me, just try it on."

Alan nodded, "To be double sure you shut your filthy mouth, I will be there to help him, too. This man and woman who got married today are both worth a hundred of you. They have earned the right to be left in peace."

With that, each took an arm and flung him backwards towards the road. Jacob lay there, on his side in the gutter, with a stunned look on his face. There was blood oozing from cuts on his face and lips.

Vic felt his anger slowly cool, watching from the edge of his vision as this man sat there unmoving, making no attempt to interrupt further. It almost looked like an expression of shame had come onto this man's bleeding face. Vic decided he would not to let it spoil his day.

Anne and David, along with other family and friends, had formed a tight knot around Jane to shield her from view and further intrusion. This simple act pleased Vic while he got his anger under control. Alan and Buck stayed nearby, not crowding him, but giving unspoken support and plenty of time to let Vic get himself back together.

Vic felt a tug at his elbow. It was Jane's father with a big grin on his face.

"I always told her she needed to find a man with balls, one who would stand up and fight for her. I think you just proved you're that one. It was the prettiest boxing exhibition I have seen. It was barely five seconds and had eight lovely punches. Someone should put you in a ring against a pro. You could show them a thing or two."

Vic found himself grinning and laughing. His anger evaporated. It seemed the words had passed Jane by, not understood, so no damage was done. He sensed, from this guy's demeanor, he would tell no further stories.

Time now to enjoy the night with his ravishingly beautiful wife!

Vic eased his way back through the crowd to her. Jane rewarded him with a smile which melted everything inside him.

"I belong to you. I love you and we are married," she whispered with unadorned delight.

Now, Vic kissed her and savored every inch of her wonderful body as it pressed to his. Then, it was David and Anne, both the big and little, who joined the hug circle. Next, it was Jane's mother, father and brother, too. Soon enough, his own mother, sister and uncle. Last, the hug was joined by every person who was there- all except one.

After a minute, a second person detached from the group and went to the man on the ground. She took his hand and spoke to him briefly.

Then, she pulled him to his feet, put her arm around his waist and led him away.

Vic did not recognize this person- not someone from his family or friends and not anyone he had met from Susan's side. She had grey-streaked hair and looked old- perhaps fifty or sixty. However, she walked with the firm decisive manner and had the spring in her step of someone half her estimated age. *Curious*, Vic thought.

Gradually, the people hug-knot unwound and they made their way to their cars. For Susan and Vic, it was only a short trip to an open place where a helicopter stood resting. It was waiting to whisk them off to afternoon photos and then on to the reception. The children would travel with Jane's and his parents, along with the rest of the bridal party, to join in the photos. Other guests would follow along in an hour or two.

Chapter 30 – In the Gutter

Jacob pulled himself to a seated position on the edge of the gutter and waited for the pain to ease. Long minutes passed as the pain continued. His whole face and body were hurting, but it was a small hurt compared to the one to his pride. Five minutes before, Jacob had been feeling so pleased with himself for, finally, having run the witch-bitch, Susan, to ground. He had thought of hiring a camera man to capture the day but, in the end, decided not to. He did not want to share his glory with any other.

It was a simple shoot. Jacob knew exactly where they would be when they came out of church, making their way through the gathered people and walking down the steps to the outside. He put his camera on a tripod and filmed them as they came out the back door, following their slow progress, unnoticed, as they made their way through the wedding guests, handshaking and kissing friends. He focused the camera on the bottom of the steps with a wide enough view to capture them coming down. As the camera continued to record, he stepped forward, holding a microphone connected to a recorder in his pocket.

Susan looked different to when he had last seen her: she had a much fuller body and face and appeared much more like a woman, overall. Her hair was also done differently. She looked stunning in her floating white dress with little blue-green flowers within the fabric. Despite the changed appearance, it was unmistakably her. Her blue eyes and an aura around her were recognisable as Susan. Jacob knew for certain he had finally found her.

Seeing her bedecked as a beautiful bride seemed a fitting way to end the story, the ultimate betrayer image, the perfect deception story undone.

As Jacob had said her name, he expected to see a look of fear and horror come into her eyes at being caught. Instead, all that came into her eyes was a blank, bemused look. He knew in that instant that she really had no idea what it was all about. There was no guilt or anxiety on her face. As good of an actress as Susan had been, Jacob knew she was not good enough to hide this. Instead, here was a person filled to the brim and overflowing from happiness who merely showed a warm, kindly face towards an unknown stranger. Someone who had said something she did not understand. Jacob could see in her face that she would try to help him out of innate generosity.

This image was not right to him. In fact, it was totally wrong.

As Jacob saw it, his certainly about her guilt crumbled to dust in that instant. Instead, he felt ashamed at what he had done.

In the second of watching her face, Jacob had forgotten about the man standing beside her, Vic, through whom Jacob had finally found Susan.

He felt surprised as this man loomed into his central vision, tearing the microphone free from his hand and throwing it away. Then came more surprise as the flying fists connected with his face and body. Jacob felt his head jerk back and forward with each impact and his face mashing under hard knuckles. Normally, he was quick on his feet. Jacob had grown up in a tough place where self-defense was a survival skill. He knew he should protect himself or get out of the way. But surprise rendered him immobile in those seconds. He just stood there and let the blows fall.

Jacob felt burning pain in his chest and belly as more blows fell there. This guy had fists like sledgehammers despite his modest size. Then, before he could react, two human gorillas stepped in. They were not so much big as they were strong. With hard faces pushed into his face and hard hands on his arms, they both told Jacob they would finish what Vic started, if he spoke another word of what he had found out here, today.

Jacob knew he would never tell the rest of this story- but it was due to their threats. It was a thing inside his brain called his 'conscience'. It told him he had got this story awfully wrong. To mislead further would be the greater wrong. It had never occurred to Jacob before that he had a thing inside him called "knowledge of right and wrong." He realized it must have been first instilled in him as a child while in the church with his mother. This part of his mind now said, *Enough!!*

He felt mortified with himself as he lay there. It was a blow to his manhood and pride. He could have stood up for himself and fought back. However, they were right. She deserved to be left alone. Even if they had not smashed his camera, he could not use it now, not if he had any shred of remaining decency.

This girl was a victim- not a monster. Jacob could harm her no further. He had first glimpsed it in Beck's face on the last day they had spoken. Then, he had ignored this intuition, in his desire to pursue Susan, anyway.

After visiting all the coastal towns around Brisbane, Gold Coast, and Sunshine Coast to search for a 'Jane with two small children,' Jacob had found her trail in the caravan park in Caloundra. There the manager had confirmed her identity and told Jacob the name of the man with her was Vic.

At that point, Jacob knew how to find him- Vic, helicopter pilot. He guessed they had gone to Alice Springs and came to this town to look.

At first, nobody amongst his wide group of former mates in Alice had known anything about Vic's wedding plans. Jacob kept clear of the immediate family and close friends, for fear they would warn Vic. Instead, he focused on 'friends of friends' knowing some secrets were bound to pop out.

Only last week, he finally cracked it. He'd found out, from a friend of a friend, that Vic was indeed getting married this Saturday, at his sister's regular church, in the main street of Alice Springs.

Jacob paid a visit to the church prior to the wedding. The office lady asked pleasantly how she could help. Jacob said he was assisting with accommodation for guests coming to Saturday's wedding of 'Vic Campbell.' He'd mislaid the wedding invitation and needed to know the time of the wedding. As he was walking by the church, he decided to pop inside to ask.

She answered, without hesitation, "It is at three in the afternoon."

Jacob made his plan to be there for the wedding. First, he had thought of setting up to catch Susan on the way into the church. However, he thought there would be lots of people standing around beforehand and it might be hard to get close to her. In the end, Jacob decided it was best to let the ceremony proceed and catch her on the way out. That way, the element of surprise would be the greatest. And, with everyone inside, he could set everything up in the perfect position to record the newly married couple exiting the church.

Tomorrow, Jacob planned to have his story and pictures syndicated to the front pages of the London and Australian tabloids. It would be a huge story! He would make sure to have the picture of the wedding girl in the white dress alongside the ones of the evil monster whom was presented to court for murdering her lover and feeding him to the crocodiles. Jacob would tie the two pictures together along with the picture of her shocked face when he asked his first question after finding her.

It had not worked out the way he had imagined. Jacob knew the actuality of this situation was a better and more decent conclusion to the 'Crocodile Girl' story. Even though his journalist career would go up in smoke if he did not submit the story, as promised, to all those who eagerly awaited it, Jacob knew he wouldn't write it.

Part of him felt strange relief for having not succeeded in his final assault on this girl. Jacob sensed there was a justice in him being thwarted. Another part of him felt mortified at his inglorious treatment and thrashing. Now, he looked like any other black drunk sitting in the gutter. He felt he should get up and crawl away to some obscure location to sleep off the pain and shame, in the same way another black drunk would do.

Yet Jacob stayed, transfixed, carefully watching the unfolding scene. The family and friends immediately closed around the married couple. They were enfolding them in friendly protection. The mood of the guests lifted, again, even if they were a bit more subdued.

Jacob decided they were right. It was their time in the sun to enjoy. It was a special occasion which no one else should take away from them.

Yet, Jacob was still a journalist who needed a story. He wondered if he could do an: "I was wrong. They are really decent people," story. He could tell of his 'road to Damascus' conversion.

No, it would not work. The story would reveal their location to others of his kind. Those people would keep his previous version of the story running. His stepping aside would hand this story to them on a silver platter. Jacob knew the new identity of this girl, Jane Bennet. Once this fact got out, hiding would no longer be a realistic option for her. She could not keep running, nor could Vic vanish easily, again, either.

Jacob noticed that something had changed in the wedding group. They had all formed into a tight circle with their arms around each other and the bridal couple in the center. It was an enormous 'group hug.'

There was such a sense of solidarity in these people that Jacob found himself profoundly moved. He knew he was not welcome- but a part of him felt an urge to join them in this hug. It reminded him of the family gatherings of his childhood and of the community of his home. He felt a wistful nostalgia for that time and place along with its simple, innocent goodness.

As Jacob watched, a grey-haired lady detached from the edge of the group. It didn't seem she quite belonged, yet she'd been moved to express shared pleasure with them, regardless, by joining her arms to their bodies.

Now, she moved purposefully towards him. He feared she would ask him to join in and he could not do that. Instead, she spoke to him, gently, "I do not really know them. However, I wanted to wish them well- particularly the girl, Jane. She and I are fellow travelers.

"When I saw you sitting here, alone and lonely, with your cut face, I thought I would come and talk to you. You do not know me, but I know of you. I have read some of your stories: true in parts, untrue and unkind in others. But, at least, you are a searcher for the truth. It seems this story you planned to tell has got away from you and will stay untold.

"Perhaps, I can give you another. It's time to stop running from my past.

"I am Cathy- one of the four Lost Girls."

Chapter 31 – Cathy's Tale

Jacob allowed himself to be led away by this strange looking girl. His mind had barely comprehended what she had said. However, she had a power in her eyes and her face that compelled him to action.

It was funny how he had first thought of her as old. It was her grey hair which had made him think this. It was streaked with grey and appeared thin, giving her a worn demeanor. Her clothes were ragged and in the style of what an old woman would wear. But, upon closer inspection, Jacob could see they all gave the lie to her true appearance.

She was actually quite youthful. She appeared something around his own age. Despite her raggedy demeanor, she was distinctly pretty. She had a pert, button nose and sweet, soft mouth. Most of all, she had a 'look' to her.

Jacob struggled to place where he seen such a 'look' before. It was hauntingly familiar. At last, it came to him. It was the look of Susan on that first day in court. It had been a day when she should have been pleading for her deliverance and freedom. Rather, she made a guilty plea with something like gloating mischief on her face. It was a look of sparkling vitality which she could not hide. That moment, Jacob hated Susan's cocky joy. It made him angry. In response, he was determined to wipe that look from her face. He was going to make her pay for what she had done. At that time, he made himself the sole judge of her actions. His words would be his tool of justice.

Now, Jacob understood Susan had been the actress- playing a deliberate role to turn the crowd against her own self. She had been mocking the gravity of the court, refusing to bow to fear. Despite her central role on a day of horrors, an ineffable part of her soul's defiance bubbled out into a 'look.' This lady had it, too. It was her willingness to look true horror in the face and smile, unbowed by it.

In that second, as Jacob saw this similarity, he knew what was missing from today. It was what had crumbled his desire to pursue Susan. The thing he hated most in her was gone. Gone was her defiance of the world. But, in losing it, she had lost most of herself. He could see her soul was missing. What remained in her body shell, was a simple, kind person. A person who had lost their devil spirit and, with it, their life's fire. He knew of his hand in this loss. From this realisation came shame. Jacob had done his part in a thing which had destroyed her essence. A thing which had broken an essential part of her humanity and being.

However, this other woman who stood beside him, holding his hand in hers, still had that life force. She had the yin and yang of a full soul. With this soul came the courage to look at the worst of the world and spit in its face.

Jacob would go with this woman and hear her story. This story mattered, no matter what. Yet, it was the power of the life force in her soul which really drew him in, and he fed on its power now.

Jacob looked carefully at this woman as she turned her face to him. If you put aside the raggedy hair and outdated clothes, she really was very beautiful. Their eyes connected and he felt a sudden jolt. It was not lust. It was the jolt of two souls sharing knowledge and pain- their own and others.

Jacob said, "What did you say your name was, again? My mind was inside my head, until now, and I did not properly hear what you were saying."

She said, "Today, most people call me 'Kate James.' My few friends call me 'Cathy.' However, my true name is 'Fiona Rodgers.' As I said before, I am one of the 'Lost Girls' in this story you and others have been writing. Today, I came here to show solidarity with another Lost Girl, Susan- now called Jane.

"I came in when most guests were inside and sat, quietly, in the back of the church. I was unknown and unseen. I wished her a new joy in life after so much horror. I intended to leave, quietly, too. I planned to slip away and return to my quiet, unknown life, with my own story still unknown.

"In that moment, when you tried to tear her story from her, I knew that there was another story that must be told. I decided, in those seconds of your confrontation and beating, to seek out her friend, Anne. To ask her to tell my story. She knows I am alive, but not where. I wanted to give her my story.

"But, when I saw you sitting in the gutter, beaten and shamed- I knew that it was you to whom I should tell my story. You have been a seeker after the truth, even if blinded by your own cleverness. Now, you have understood the pain done by your former words. Their ability to harm as well as heal. I think you are ready to hear, take and tell my story, if you will.

"So, I will tell it to you. You must find words to tell it to the world with kindness. It, like Susan's story, is a story with power to harm. But my hiding it for so long has caused even more harm. Now, I know it must be told."

Jacob and Cathy found a café where they sat for two hours while he listened as she talked. It was the story of the life of an innocent young girl who trusted her uncle. It told of her sister's rape and suicide. It told of her own rape, and then, of her seeking escape in the selling of her body. She told of her flight from that life to Australia. Then of her meeting the man, Mark, and travelling with him for a week, how they first traveled as friends, then as lovers. She said they only shared love for two nights. She told of a first, wonderful night in which she had told Mark of her own awful childhood. He had held her and comforted her. In that night, she had loved him and known he cared for her.

Then, Cathy told of a second wonderful night when she had joined her body to Mark's. It seemed he had loved her in return, for he had told her of his awful secrets: the killing of Isabelle to save her from the crocodiles along with the killings of Josie and Amanda. Despite knowing all of this, she had loved Mark still.

Then, Cathy told of the awful realization which came to her in the early light of next morning: that Mark was too dangerous to stay with- not a danger for her, but for her family. He slept still as she arose and quietly dressed. She knew she must leave him, to protect him from himself.

The knowledge had come to her in the darkest part of the night. At first, she had not understood it. Now, in the morning light, she saw it clearly. It convinced her she must leave. Cathy saw in Mark an uncompromising hatred of those who harmed small children in any way. Hatred of any who abused them or destroyed their innocence. In that moment, she knew he would surely kill her uncle, her abuser, when the chance arose. He had said it to her in the night. At the time he spoke the words, full of the rapture of love, she had not really listened.

His words were, "The only way to fix those bastards, ones who do bad things to little children is kill them. I will fix him. He will never harm another."

In the morning's first light she had known, if she stayed with Mark, he would act on these words. She could not bear for him to further kill a part of the goodness in his own soul through the killing of another. Despite her hatred of her uncle, she did not wish for his death. It would only bring yet more pain to her family. Knowing this, she had fled, taking rides along the highway to Alice Springs. She left all her things in his car- except for her purse, which contained a few hundred dollars. She had picked it up as she got out of bed.

Once in Alice Springs, she had stayed there. She changed her appearance so no one would know her, found a cleaning job for which she was paid cash and did not require identification. Now, more than three years had passed.

Cathy lived alone in a tiny room with a gas burner to cook on. She mostly read books, when she not working. In the early mornings and evenings, she walked along the sandy riverbed and beside the red hillsides. As people thought she was old and slightly mad, no one troubled her.

Her only real friends were a few aboriginal people who lived near the river and some other people who walked amongst the hills to collect bush foods. In this way, she had met Vic's mother, Rosa. Over more than two years, she had run into her at odd times.

Over time and with story sharing, Cathy had realized that Rosa's son, Vic, and Mark were friends. She had then connected Susan to them through the story of Mark's murder and the trial. Then, when Susan vanished, Rosa had told her how cut up her son had been: searching for, but never finding this girl. Then, one day, Rosa was smiling again. Cathy knew Rosa had a happy secret, but she did not probe. Another day, Rosa had told her of this- unable to keep the secret any longer. Cathy was sworn to secrecy before being told that Vic had found Susan, again. Also, a few months later, Cathy was told of the marriage plans.

Cathy had quietly come to the wedding and sat alone at the back of the church. She was unknown to all- but Rosa, who had given her a friendly smile and waved her in past Buck while whispering, "Later, you meet Vic and Jane."

Instead of this meeting, she now was sitting here with Jacob, telling this story. She was saying that, once she had talked to Anne, he could write it.

Jacob sat and listened, spellbound. This story would bring him back to the top if he chose to tell it: rediscovery of another Lost Girl. The tale of her being returned to her family- along with the telling of the childhood abuse which had brought her to this place. However, he was no longer sure he wanted to tell it.

Kate's family, like Susan's, had suffered enough pain. They needed to know their daughter was safe; and she needed to have a family again- this was true. Yet what good could come from the world knowing of her childhood and of the harm done to her and her sister? It would not bring her sister back. It would not take away her pain. In fact, it would only give new pain to her parents. Perhaps Jacob could help her to give her evidence to the police. Doing this would prevent her uncle from harming others. Perhaps that would be enough. Maybe, in a small way, this good may help to balance against past harm he had done.

He told her of these thoughts and she nodded, saying, "Yes. I must tell my parents- but I am terrified. Would you help me do this please?"

Chapter 32 - Across the Ocean

It was almost dark when Vic and Jane arrived in Abu Dhabi- a stopover point on their flight to London. They approached over the clear waters of the Arabian Gulf and glimpsed high buildings at the edge of the water before settling onto a runway which shimmered with heat eddies in the late afternoon light. They had three nights to spend here. Then, their flight went on from London to Glasgow, where Jane's parents would be waiting for them.

Vic had read the Sunday and Monday papers with trepidation as they waited to depart from Australia, but there had been nothing about where Susan was or linking her to his Jane. He was not convinced the hunting of her was finished, but it was out of his hands now.

Vic decided that for now he and his new bride, along with little David and Annie, should enjoy this visit to an exotic location. Tomorrow, they would do a boat trip to sightsee in the Gulf. The next day was a rest and relaxation day in which they would visit the shopping centers and big buildings. They would have an early departure on the third morning for the London leg of the trip.

As the family left the airport terminal for a taxi to the city, the baking heat hit them. Vic felt at home in this desert place. It was a different landscape than he was used to but with a similar 'air-feel' to his home. He wondered how he would handle the cold rain and mist of Scotland after this place's blasting heat, which barely eased with the setting sun.

Their days passed like a magic interlude. They went out in the sparkling Gulf waters on the next day where they looked back and saw the heat shimmering off the shore horizon. On their last full day, they mostly lounged around the pool, teaching their children to swim, with a brief lunchtime foray to a huge shopping center.

As Jane lay in the circle of Vic's arms on the last night in the Gulf, he asked her if she was still as happy to be married as she thought she would be. They had not talked about what happened on the day with the journalist. With all the other activity of the wedding, it had largely passed her by. He hoped he could now consign it to the dustbin of history.

However, rather than giving an immediate answer in her normal way, he felt Jane pause- as if she were thinking. Vic looked at her closely. He found himself sinking into her blue eyes. Just when he felt himself losing all other threads of memory in this pool of light, she spoke, "I was fully happy before and now I am glad to be married. It has a feeling of rightness for me along with making you the father of my children, officially

"One thing I do not understand though is: who that man was, why he asked that question, and what it meant? I most don't understand what it was that made you so angry. I have never seen you angry before. With that man, you frightened me. Not because I thought you would hurt me, but because you were so quick to act against him. There was danger in you, in that minute, that I did not know existed.

"If I have done something that caused your anger towards him, I feel I need to know and yet, that knowledge scares me so. The only thing he said that made sense to me was my name.

"One day, last Christmas, at the farm in the country, I saw a piece paper with the travel bookings for Tom and Elinor MacDonald. I knew it must be my parents because people had called them Tom and Elinor. That information told me, as their daughter, my surname must have been MacDonald, too.

"I could not remember having that name but knew it must have been so. So, I thought, *I have been married before and that is where my babies came from. That man's surname must have been Bennet.*

"When Ross Sangster was asking me questions, he asked me to try and remember being a little girl. I told him I remembered going to my grandparents' farm in Scotland. Since that day, I have remembered how people called me Susan, or Susie. Sometimes they called me "little M"- after my aunt, Emily. So, I knew that my other names were once: Susan and Emily.

"When that man came up to me and said, 'Susan Emily MacDonald,' I knew he was talking to me and I wanted to help him.

But when he asked me about marrying the best friend of the man I killed- I did not understand. "Did I crash a car and kill that man? In doing so, did I lose my memory? Or did I cause some other accident that killed him? If so, what was it?

"And why did him saying that make you so angry that you punched him, over and over again, until he fell to the ground?

"So, it has not spoiled my opinion of being married. But, each day, my mind asks these questions. Even though it frightens me, I think I need to know the answers."

Now, it was Vic's turn to think. He needed to try and wrestle a safe answer out of his mind which was true but also not dangerous. To mask his uncertainty, he put his fingers in her hair and kissed her. She kissed him in return. Soon, the question was lost in other pleasures.

After, as she lay with hair spilling into his face, she reminded him, "My question still remains from our wedding day."

He said, "I will start to tell you, one little bit at a time. But if I frighten you, please tell me to stop."

"Before I met you in the town with your children, you were with my best friend. His name was Mark, Mark Bennet. He is the father of your children. One day, he died. I don't think it was your fault- but some people said you killed him. The man I hit wrote about it in a newspaper, along with saying other bad and untrue things about you, too. So, on our wedding day, when he asked that question- I got very angry."

Jane nodded, "I am glad that is all it was. That is all I need to know."

Vic felt relief that Jane had asked for nothing further. At the same time, though, her lack of curiosity also troubled him.

Instead, she placed his hand on the bottom of her belly and put her own hand over it. "Now, I have something to tell you. Under our hands, a new person is growing. I can feel his spirit touching mine like butterfly wings. His name will be Vic. He will be our child- the product of love and bodies joined."

Vic lay there, keeping his hand pressed to that place, lost in the amazement that a part of him had created a new life within the body of this gorgeous woman. He felt overcome by a joyous wonder that it could be so.

The next day, they came into London. Then, they flew on to Glasgow after having decided it was safest plan to go straight there. From there, they caught the train up into the highlands to be with her parents. They marveled at the glorious scenery of lochs and snow-covered mountains.

Jane found more and more childhood memories returning to her as she saw this place. She instantly knew the mountain and lake names and remembered the little villages. Finally, as they drew near to their own stop, she was bubbling over with excitement. As they came to the small village railway stop, she could feel herself bursting with impatience.

Jane saw her aunt in the distance and knew her name without any prompting. "Aunt Ada," she called out as she ran into her arms. "It's so good to see you and remember you! I feared you'd all be strangers! I'm so happy to know you, even though it is only a memory from when I was a little girl."

They brought their new family to their country house. It was not so large and grand as the memory held in her childhood mind, but it was warm and comfortable. It was tucked into a hill with a lake below and with her grandparents' house just behind it. As they looked out over the view, a late afternoon mist was rising in the valley. Far across the heather hillside, she saw deer heads raising proud and tall against the skyline. It felt so good to have returned to this familiar place, which was alive with so many memories.

Chapter 33 – Anne's Meeting

It was now the Monday after the wedding of Vic and Jane. Anne and David had decided to treat themselves to a couple days in Alice Springs, before flying to Darwin for the rest of the week, to ensure all the legal issues about Susan and Vic were properly tidied away. Despite the minor hiccup of the arrival of the uninvited journalist on the wedding day, which they had only glimpsed and not spoken of since, it had been a wonderful few days.

The bride, still Susan in Anne's mind, looked radiant and spectacularly beautiful in her dress of fine, pale turquoise flowers set into delicate lace. Anne, as a bridesmaid, also had a soft turquoise-toned dress. It matched perfectly with both her auburn hair and the rich brown skin of Jillie, who was similarly attired.

She had found Jillie and all Vic's family to be delightful people. They were so warm and welcoming to her and Susan- who, of course, they called Janie now. It was funny how names rolled off the tongue in this place: Annie, Jillie and Janie as the bride's group. Little Annie and Davie were the flower and ring carriers. Little Annie was dark-haired and cheeky while Davie was blonde and serious.

Anne felt incredibly connected to these children. Perhaps this was because their names had come from her and David. Also, Anne and David had been named their godparents, even though they missed the baptism. But they had taken the promises given to ensure these kids were okay very seriously- should something happen to the mother and newly named father.

Anne felt so blessed that her prayers were answered of having her friend returned to her. Even though the damage to Susan was still evident, largely in the vacant parts of her mind and in her simplicity, she was with them again. That fact alone was infinitely precious.

Today, they had all waved their farewells at the airport as the Cairns jet departed. Then, they had all come back to town together with a loose plan of each couple or group enjoying a mixture of their own private time along with some group activities before they went their separate ways in a day or two.

Tonight, they were having a private group dinner of all the remaining family and friends, as a way to both say goodbye and give thanks for this wondrous time they had shared. Now, she and David had decided to have their lunch in the mall along with seeing the local sights and doing some shopping before having a quiet afternoon by the pool. Tomorrow, they would do a tourist trip out along the McDonnel Ranges to the gorges.

Anne and David settled into a simple salad lunch after a surfeit of rich food. She was reading a magazine and David the newspaper.

A woman came to their table. She was not a waitress and was clearly seeking Anne out. She must be older as her hair was grey. Something about her felt familiar, although Anne could not recollect from where.

As she stood in front of them, she said, 'Excuse me, could I talk to you for a minute." Her voice sounded unexpectedly young. It was soft spoken and her manner was very polite.

Anne looked up at her intently, trying to place the familiarity. She remembered she had glimpsed her briefly at the wedding. At that time she had been walking away, leading the journalist in a kindly manner. But that was not the source of the familiarity that Anne felt. It was found in her face. On the wedding day, she had only seen a back view of this woman.

The woman said, "You are probably wondering who I am and why I have come to you. My name is Cathy, once Cathy Rodgers, though I use a different surname now."

With those words, it all came clear in Anne's mind. "Oh my God," was all she could say. No other words could come to her.

David looked up. He had been impervious until now, but she could see his brain was working fast, replaying the words and joining the dots, "That Cathy. The one we have sought for over two years now."

Standing a few steps behind, as if awaiting the outcome, was the black man Vic had punched. David felt his gut tighten with anger at what this man had written, the source of so many problems. But this girl was so polite that his anger stayed contained. He invited her to join them. Then he asked her, forcing politeness into his voice, "Is the man behind you with you, too?"

She looked at Jacob and nodded, answering, "He has come to make an apology for the harm he has done. I thought he should begin with you, her best friends. But that is not why I came. I came to seek your help for myself. I realize I cannot hide away any longer- but I do not know how to rejoin the world. I have disguised myself and led a simple life for over three years now.

"I suppose I should just ring my parents and ask them to come to me- but I find myself unable to do so. Too much time has passed, with too much pain involved, to just go home again. But I am tired of running. I am tired of hiding and I don't want my parents suffering to continue. I have asked Jacob to help me to tell my story, perhaps in public. He has said he will. He will write no more of Susan, for she has earned her right to a new life.

"So, now, I ask that you hear what he has to say first. Then, allow me to tell you of me and what has brought me here."

David and Anne both nodded consent. Cathy invited the man to join them. His words were simple as he sat down, "I have done your friend a great wrong, in what I wrote and spoke. One day, I will apologize to her, myself. But today, my apology is for you- her friend who has walked in her shoes and suffered along with her."

Anne took his hand, "I thank you. I cannot speak for her, but what you have said now is enough for me. The past is the past and it cannot be undone. The future is what we can change."

He nodded and said, "Thank you."

David held out his hand, shaking Jacob's hand, "She speaks for me, too."

With that said, they sat and shared their stories.

Cathy told the story of her three years of living a simple hidden life as an old woman who cleaned around the town. She told of how she had befriended Vic's mother, thus hearing of the wedding.

Anne told them the story of the diary, specifically the parts in it where Mark had written about Cathy. She shared how Mark had told of Cathy's early life and its pain, parts which the inquest had deliberately withheld. She explained how the parts had even been withheld from Cathy's parents- lest this information cause further harm.

Anne said, "I know what your uncle did to you as a child and I know why you fled. I also know your uncle has been missing for nearly three years now. It is not known if he has gone into hiding or if it is something else. But it is clear he has disappeared. Because of what he had done, we chose not to tell that part of the story."

Anne asked if she could ring Cathy's parents to tell them of meeting her.

Cathy shook her head, explaining, "Soon, I hope, but not now. I need to know fully about my uncle first. I cannot see my parents and tell them all this until I know the truth about him- whether he is hiding or he is dead.

"Before I knew what you have told me about him being missing, I had decided to confront him with Jacob present. I would have asked him to admit to what he had done, to give him the choice to go and tell it to my parents and the police- or I would do if for him.

"Now, it seems we cannot do that. So, now, we must try to find him for ourselves. If he is out there, I may be able to reach him when others cannot. Jacob has the skills and contacts of an investigative journalist to help in this.

"If we locate him, it will be as I have said. We will give him a choice to turn himself in and admit publicly to what he has done. If he does not, then Jacob will write and publish his story for the whole world to read. That is the only way I can see for real justice to be done."

David and Anne agreed to help in this quest. They offered money, but Cathy said she had more than enough. Instead of financing the search, they offered to arrange an introduction to Alan. He was dealing with the English Police in their search for this man.

Cathy said, armed with this information, they would conduct their own search for him. If her uncle was hiding somewhere, there must be others who knew where. She would try and find a way to reach him through people who knew him. It may take several months, but that is what she and Jacob would do. She said she'd give it six months and then, if no trace was found, she would contact her parents to tell them the truth.

Two days later, Anne and David again met with Cathy and Jacob in Darwin, this time at the police station. Information was exchanged along with the promise that, should anything further be discovered, Jacob and Cathy would let both the English and Australian police know.

Two days later, Jacob and Cathy were on a plane bound for Iraq.

Chapter 34- Crocodile Sisters

Beck and Ross were together again in Darwin. This was shortly after a wonderful weekend spent in Brisbane, when they had crossed the bridge from friends to lovers. Beck was very busy sorting out final arrangements for the pardon, preparing briefs to all and sundry. The need to keep strictest confidence was a challenge.

Ross was now very cautious about what he said about this whole thing following the cautionary tale about the leaking and consequences. They knew there were others who could also be the source of something getting out. He and Beck both waited in trepidation for the journalist from London to spring a discovery of Susan's location, but all remained silent.

At last it was all done. The pardon had been signed and delivered, the wedding had occurred and Susan and Vic had flown away. Of Jacob, nothing further was heard. He seemed to have faded away without sign. Both Beck and Ross breathed a sigh of relief as their day-to -day lives continued.

A few days later, Alan came on the phone to Beck, saying, "The word is around town that you have a new man. Sandy and I would like to invite you both out to dinner with a dear friend of ours, Charlie, otherwise known to friends as the real Crocodile Man. His wife is making her legendary catfish curry this Friday night and she told us to bring any extras we can find. So, I thought of you- particularly as I hear that you and that Queensland doctor who saw Susan, are now an item. I thought you might like to meet a few of the locals and hear a bit of the back story about how this all unfolded."

Beck had no hesitation in accepting. Alan and Sandy were great company. Also, it was great to be out in the open with Ross. This relationship somehow felt different from her previous one-night stands and she wanted the whole world to know about them.

Beck and Ross drove to the address given, carrying beer and wine in their arms. Charlie greeted them at the door. She had seen him from a distance at the previous legal proceedings, but had never spoken to him directly.

Charlie's eyes twinkled as he met them, saying "Aha! More friends of the girl with the crocodile stone."

Beck looked puzzled, saying, "You've lost me there."

Alan came over to welcome them and bring them inside. Seeing Beck's inquiring look, he explained, "Charlie means 'Susan.' I suppose you could call us all the 'Save Susan Committee', not that she knows about us that way. But now, you have played your part of helping her and, as a result, she is on her way to the other side of the world. So, we wanted to welcome you to our group celebration."

Alan brought them over and introduced them to two others who Beck also knew by sight: the flaming English redhead, Anne, now a significant TV celebrity, and her drop-dead gorgeous boyfriend, David. Beck knew he had been engaged to Susan before- and was now with her best friend. He was also something of a TV celebrity with all the publicity of the case.

At first, Beck felt a bit over-awed with all these people. However, in the course of a few drinks and lots of plates of curry, the ice was soon broken. Within an hour, they both felt like they had all been friends forever.

As they talked, Alan filled in more about the details of the wedding which had been held over a week ago now. He said how the journalist, Jake, waited outside the church with a camera and microphone in hand for them to come out, once married. He recounted how Vic had dropped him with some well-directed punches and how some other nameless people had warned him off. They left him nursing a cut face sitting on the gutter at the edge of the street.

Alan then told how the girl, Cathy, who had been long lost, had gone over to Jake, taken him in hand and led him away. Beck and Ross listened in trepidation, and then relief, as the story emerged from Anne and David about how they knew for a fact that this man, they now regarded as a friend and called Jacob, would trouble Susan no more.

It felt to Beck like a stone of fear was lifted off her heart, hearing how this huge threat had been taken away from Susan, and she could get on with her life. She said a silent prayer of thanks for this deliverance.

As they sat there in a loose circle, talking, Charlie came over, and asked Beck to first close her eyes then put out her open hand. Into it he placed a flat, round item which rested neatly in the palm of her hand. It was cool and heavy. It felt like a stone.

She asked, "What is it?"

"What you think?" replied Charlie.

She closed her hand over it, kept her eyes shut, and focused her mind on it. It was clearly a stone and yet was more than that. It seemed imbued with something- a presence. Beck tried to focus only on this presence. Slowly it sharpened into something more distinct. She could sense an ancient being, which lived in places such are rivers and deep water. She could not see its shape, just a sense of being inside and looking out into a watery world.

Sandy came over, by herself, and took Beck's hand. Now, it was like there was a link formed between their minds. Sandy could see and feel what Beck felt. Beck could see and feel what Sandy felt.

She asked Sandy, curiously, "Why is this? What it this thing that makes us connected? I can sense its presence, but I cannot see its shape. I only know it is a creature of the water: a giant fish or turtle, perhaps."

Then, it came to her- as if an insight from inside Sandy's mind, "I know. It is a stone which belongs to a crocodile, infused with a crocodile's spirit. It sits inside a crocodile. It allows one to look out, as if with the eyes of a crocodile."

Sandy nodded, "I suppose you could call it a crocodile spirit stone. It is a stone taken from the stomach of a crocodile where it had sat for many years, becoming infused with its presence. A part of it lingers still. Only some can see and feel it, most cannot. Susan could, I can, and it seems you can too. I guess that makes us all 'crocodile sisters.'

"When Susan sat in jail, in her moments of terror when she thought the bad crocodile spirit of Mark would overwhelm her, she would hold this stone and keep it touching her skin. And, when she did, the crocodile spirit within this stone would free her from other outside spirits trying to invade her mind. She must have let some parts of them in on that fateful first day when she killed Mark, and they grew ever stronger when was in jail.

"But, as the madness seized her, she did not want to hold this anymore. Back then, I feared the other spirits, bad spirits of crocodiles at that cursed waterhole, would overwhelm her. I feared they would draw her back to them and consume her.

"Now, I hope and pray she has escaped their hold. But the thing you saw on the video- Alan told me of that. It means that part of a bad crocodile spirit lurks somewhere, deep inside her, and it still has the power to tear at her soul. So, we must all help her be safe in whatever way we can.

"There may be something you can do to help her in return for what you have done against her. I have seen your secret in your mind and know it, too. I am not one to judge- none of us are. But should she have need of us, then we are her kin. We will help her in the way sisters do. Anne is her best friend and that, itself, is a powerful bond. But it is only you and I who share her spirit sisterhood."

Chapter 35 - Northern Seas

Vic was pleased with the positive change in Jane as the family settled into the routines of the Scottish hill farm life. She seemed to pick up from her past life as a 12-year-old girl, which was when last she remembered being here.

She had even taken to using her original names of 'Emily' and 'Susan,' some of the time. These were what her grandparents, aunt, uncle, and cousins called her, without thinking. They mostly called her Em, or Emily, the name of her later childhood. Sometimes they'd call her Susan- her small girl's name and the name which best connected her to the memories of this past.

One day, Jane told Vic that, now she had his surname of Campbell as her married name and she was getting used to the names of 'Susan' and 'Emily' again, she did not mind him using these names for her, too, if he wanted.

He found all three names were now connected in his brain. Due to this he could use them all and move between them without effort. However, more and more, she became Susan, again, to him in his mind.

One day, Jane asked Vic if he thought she should change her name back. He said he did not mind if she added back the old names, but he did not want her to lose the name he had rediscovered her under. There was a sweet and innocent part of her which was still Jane to him.

While her aunt and parents mostly called her 'Emily' and her grandparents mostly called her 'Susan,' he called her all three as the mood took him. Sometimes, Vic even used them all together: 'Susan-Emily-Jane.' They were all parts of one fused person and he loved them equally. Their children, of course, just called her Mummy, so it did not matter to them either way.

Vic could sense this place, with its quiet and peaceful routines, was good for the healing of her spirit and mind. He was pleased it was so.

There was also an endless flow of people wanting to meet the children: cousins, friends of cousins and village neighbors.

Tom and Elinor stayed for the first two weeks. The children were rarely out of their grandparents' sight. Sometimes, they would make their own visits to Great Gran and Great Pa to tell them their stories of the day.

Vic worked alongside the farm manager most days to have an outlet for all his bursting energy. He found he needed to spend most of his time outdoors or he would feel a restlessness grow inside him, like a caged animal.

Jane seemed content to spend hours inside with her grandparents, parents, aunts and cousins, chatting while drinking cups of tea. He loved her dearly and he found satisfaction in the stability she seemed to have gained. Sometimes, he wished Jane had a bit of the fire which had burned inside the old Susan: the ferocity and anger as well as the gentle softness. However, he knew that trying to bring this person back was fraught with danger. He did not want to risk opening up any cracks to her missing years.

Still, it was as if what she was now was a sweet, twelve-year-old in an adult's body. She was without the edginess of maturity. Her boundaries were very contained things and she seemed to live contentedly within them. Part of him, deep down, ached to have a bit more of the old Susan back.

So, to keep his worry at bay, Vic put in hard, physical days outside. He loved the bare open Scottish hillsides- even though, a spring day here rarely reached the temperature of an Alice Springs winter day.

The day before Tom and Elinor were due to leave, Tom brought out two rifles and suggested Vic walk out with him to try to bag a deer. He said that, once, he would have loved to do this with Susan. However now, she seemed to have lost her desire for the outdoor life. There was a wistfulness in Tom's voice as he said these words.

Vic looked at him, sharply.

Tom returned his look, "Yes, I know," he said. "We should just be happy to have our daughter back. Truly, I am so grateful, and to you for your part. But I miss the fire she used to have. She does not argue with me anymore or challenge anything I say. She does not burst with the uncontained energy of before. I would not lose what we have for all the tea in China, but a part of me aches to have my little, fiery Susan back."

Vic nodded, "Me, too. Sometimes, I cannot bear to sit around the house anymore. I am a person who is used to doing physical things. I suppose we could go off and travel- but I do not want to break up her pleasure in rebuilding her family and her memories. But, I too, find I want more. I want to work hard in something that pushes me to the limits. The farm work is good, but it's a bit too easy on my mind."

Tom said, "Yes, I know. I have been thinking about it. You are not the sort of bloke to sit around twiddling your thumbs. I hear tell you're a helicopter pilot- a damn good one at that- so your friends say. Are you still up for that?"

Vic nodded profusely, although not seeing where a job like that would come from, over here.

Tom continued, "Well, I know a good few people in the North Sea oil industry business. They have oil rigs, lots of them, off the coast not too far east of here, out in the North Sea. They use helicopters to ferry people and goods out and back. They use ships, too, but often a helicopter is best. It gets in and out quickly, which is safer with the bad weather out there.

"So, I could ask around with some of the oil company bosses I know, see if there are any jobs supplying the rigs, even maintenance might be the go. I am not sure what you would need to do to get a ticket to fly one, but I heard tell you are also a qualified aircraft mechanic. So, it got me to thinking that even that would be something to get you out of here. Once you get a foot in the door there, you never know.

"Anyway, I will inquire if you like. After that, it will be up to you to impress them. Not that I expect you to have too much trouble, if you can fly like you can box. Working a machine amongst the trees while chasing cattle is probably a bigger test than doing a ferry run to an oil rig."

Vic said, "Thanks, Tom. I would love if you'd ask. I think I will need to do something soon or I will go mad. But I don't want to tear Susan away from here, she seems so happy to be back with her family, again."

Tom nodded and the talking was done. They walked many miles over the heather. Late in the day, they got their deer, two stags with fine heads, before they headed back home, struggling under the weight of the meat.

The next day, true to his word, Tom made some calls. A visit to the helicopter base was arranged. The day after, Vic was on his way, driving to Aberdeen two hours east of there, where he was to meet the head pilot.

His name was Jim. He was a big brawny guy with a shock of red hair and he spoke with a thick Scottish accent. He was standing in the hangar as they stripped down a big jet turbine machine. He began by asking Vic odd questions as they both watched the work, standing side by side.

He quizzed Vic on his maintenance skills and the need to see his ticket for this. Then, he asked about the machines he had flown. He had been expecting, from the story which had come down from the big boss, that Vic had only flown the little stuff which was light and maneuverable. This would not really make him the type of pilot required for this work.

Vic told Jim he had endorsements for most of the main types. He said he had done a lot of work for the mining companies with the big, heavy lift machines used to bring machinery and spare parts in and out of remote Northern Territory and Kimberly mines.

The work on the machine was finishing now, so Jim said to the head mechanic, "Well, roll her out. I want to give it a test flight, just to be sure she's right, before you sign her off."

"Aye, aye sir," the mechanic replied.

Vic stepped back, expecting his meeting was done for now and he would hear more later. Instead, Jim turned to him and said, "Well, what are you waiting for? Do I need to invite you to come, too? I imagine you want to get the feel of your bum in the seat of a metal bird again, back in the air."

Vic grinned and nodded. Soon, he was strapped into the copilot seat while Jim took command. The sound of the turbines spinning up was sweet music in his ears. Then they were up and away. The ground fell away as they climbed steadily, heading into a grey eastern sky over an even greyer and lumpy ocean. They leveled at 1000 feet heading due east at about 150 knots.

Jim turned to Vic and said, "Over to you, sonny boy. Put this old girl through her paces and show us what she can do."

Vic realized Jim had taken his hands off the controls and it was now up to him. He had never flown this exact type before, but it was pretty similar to some other big birds he had worked. He took the stick in hand and steadily pushed her into a slow bank. Then, he pulled back to feel how she responded to a climb. She was slow and heavy. The engine revs began to dip. He piled on the power. Now, she was responding as the turbines roared up the range.

Vic felt fully alive for the first time in ages. He looked across at Jim with elation. He asked, "Do you mind if I work her through the paces a bit more?"

Jim nodded, "Be disappointed if you don't."

With this, Vic focused all his attention on getting to be as one with this huge bird. He began dialing up the power to feel the limit of her climb. Then, he did a gentle bank, which he tightened sharply into dive and, at the last minute, a flare to pull her up above the waves. Vic kept her straight and steady, just above wave skipping height as he pushed her forward. He began steadily increasing the speed until she was roaring through the spume, skimming above wave tops at over 100 knots. Then, gradually, he brought her back to the original height, straight and level, almost exactly as she had been ten minutes earlier when he first began flying her.

Vic turned to Jim and said, "Well, I am a bit rusty yet. She is a wee bit different from others I have used, but I feel I am starting to get her to sing like a friendly bird for me."

Jim looked at him and nodded, "For someone who has not flown in over six months, and with a new machine type in a different place, I think you have pretty much nailed it. I would have been hard-pressed to do it any better and I have over 1000 hours on this type. Next, we had better go and see my form filling secretary to work out all the dozens of forms and papers we need to get you on the books."

It took a month until Vic was fully legal and able to fly on his own. In the meantime, he shared copilot and mechanic duties. He would go home twice a week to spend a day and night with his beloved, Susie-J, as he'd taken to calling her. The rest of the time, he was a North Sea pilot. Jim seemed to have taken a special liking to Vic and was always looking for when he could give him good jobs and opportunities.

Summer passed with mostly good weather. Now, each week, Vic typically flew three days doing ferry trips out to the rigs. He spent two days at base to check his machine, arrange trips, or do various training and certification courses. Most weeks, he had two days off at home. They were sometimes days together and sometimes single days apart.

Susan was always glad to see Vic. Their days and nights together were a delight. But, with all her family around, her need and dependence on Vic had become much reduced.

Susan's pregnancy was now beginning to show. In his nights with her, Vic took great delight in placing his hand on her belly to feel the tiny movements within. It still blew his mind to think how he had helped to create this new life inside her body.

It was a two-to-three-hour drive from the highland farm to Aberdeen so, when at work, Vic stopped over in a small pub in the center of town near the oil rig helicopter base. He gradually got to know both the other pilots and the other crew members who flew and maintained the machines, along with locals from the town- particularly the fishermen who crewed the many trawlers based here.

They would tell tall tales of scary winter trips, huge seas and wild weather. Several had lost good mates in storms in that unforgiving place out over the horizon called the North Sea.

One of the things Vic had undertaken as part of this work was emergency rescue training. That way, when ships got into trouble in the bad weather, a not infrequent event for the many sailing boats and fishing trawlers which plied the North Sea, he could respond if he was closest to hand.

He had been assigned a skilled crew for major search and rescue events of two others: a trained observer Andy, who also served as winch operator and a rescue man, Reg, who would strap himself to a line on the winch, to go down when required.

The three of them did a weekly training run which involved him holding a hover while the winch team practiced a retrieval. They were getting pretty slick in this operation. They could scramble and be in the air in less than five minutes. However, as Jim- an old and experienced rescue pilot- told them, it was one thing to do practice drills in good weather. It was entirely different to do it for real in a howling gale.

In the autumn, the first of the winter storms came. This first storm was only a moderate event with force five to six gale winds. So, Vic continued his ferry operations, but got his first taste of bad weather flying in this part of the world. He marveled as the sea transformed from a one to two meter rolling swell to a five-meter broken, lumpy ocean which whipped into whitecaps. His skill was tested by holding a flat hover over the rig with a 40 knot nor-wester. However, the big, heavy machine rode the buffeting well and his hands were now attuned to the slightest wind changes.

Vic found he could hold it steady better than most. He enjoyed the challenge of the wild weather. It was a test for his skill and he rose to the test, improving steadily with this real-life practice. Soon, the weather settled again to a glorious late autumn. He enjoyed his drives to and from the highlands where he watched the low-slanting sun carve through a glowing sky to add to the brilliant colors of the falling leaves along the roadsides.

One day, in early November, as he was driving back to Aberdeen and the weather was at its brilliant best, he heard a news flash. There was a sudden intensification of a low-pressure system in the mid-north Atlantic. It was located south-west of Iceland with a bearing for the north of Scotland and Ireland. The bad weather was set to intensify over the next twenty-four hours. A Force 8 wind event was predicted. They would not fly past Force 7, except for major emergencies, so he thought he might end up sitting in base. However, they still needed to be ready to mobilize for emergencies. At the base, there was frantic activity. They were seeking to jam several ferry trips in today, to get excess machinery and people on and off the rigs, before the weather turned bad. Vic flew four trips out and back. He was mostly carrying people to get the non-essentials workers off the rigs and doing crew changes, wherever possible, before the several days when they may not be able to fly.

The next day, the weather was bad, even in the shelter of the port. There were gusting winds, driving rain and endless grey skies. There were no flights as, even though the weather was just within allowed flight limits, it was deemed unnecessary as the essential work was done the day before.

Mostly, they sat around the base and listened to the radio. They did minor maintenance but stayed on high-alert, lest a call out came. In the fading light of the four o'clock news, a new alert came out, predicting a major intensification of the system later tonight to a Force Eight or even Nine event. Shortly after this, a Mayday call came from a small fishing trawler in trouble in the North Sea, 100 miles north-east of Aberdeen. Vic was listed as the first responder, so he called his crew. They rolled the machine out of the hangar. He warmed up the engines while they waited to see who would be given the task, whether a boat nearby could respond or whether a helicopter would be called in. This was a call which the full-time helicopter rescue base would normally respond to, and he was waiting merely as a backup.

There was a static of chatter across the airwaves, saying the nearest ship able to respond was 1-2 hours sailing time away. With heavy seas, it may take longer. The regular helicopter rescue machine was already out, having just done another job. It needed to return to base to take on fuel before it could get out to this Mayday call. It was an estimated 45 minutes flying time for Vic on a normal day. However, the weather was still deteriorating, meaning it was a marginal call whether it was still safe to fly. In the meantime, one of the crew was on the phone back in town to see if he could get better information about the fishing trawler, as it was Aberdeen based. It turned out several of the trawler's crew were locals who were well-known in the town.

That information did it for him. Vic called in, saying, "We are best placed to respond. Flying conditions are still suitable, just – he muttered under his breath, so clearance is requested to respond."

Clearance was granted, but with the added statement, "Pilot to return to base if conditions deteriorate further." Vic blocked out hearing the second part, for he had a job to do. He did a final check of the machine while the crew checked their gear. Then, they were away.

The wind was at 90 degrees to their course and gusting to over 50 knots as they cleared the port. They proceeded with a crab-wise angle, but still maintained a hundred knots plus ground speed. This gave them an estimated time to arrival of 45 to 50 minutes. The trawler had lost its engine and was rolling in ten-meter swells. The crew was considering abandoning ship to a life raft as the big waves threatened to overwhelm it without steerage being available. The mechanic was working furiously on getting the engine going again. Vic had connected to the boat on the radio so he could talk himself into their precise location.

As they were holding a steady course, a massive buffeting gust pushed them offline. His wind speed measurement kicked up to over 70 knots. He knew, at this point, it was beyond safe limits for the machine. He should return to base.

But, hell! Vic thought. These people are locals of the town, his mates regularly drunk with them and they were in deep trouble. He could not leave them out there, without an engine. He pushed on. Now, the wind was so strong he was down to 90 knots going forward, pushing his arrival time out by five more minutes.

Fortunately, the machine still felt solid and stable despite the buffeting as the wind bounced around. Some of the gusts were now getting close to 100 knots, Vic realized as he closed in on the trawler. Finally, they spotted it, just a tiny dot between some massive waves.

As Vic drew level with the vessel, he turned the machine to face into the wind. Slowing to a hover above the stranded vessel, he saw his airspeed still read 85 knots. He knew attempting a winch rescue in this wind was foolhardy and dangerous to both the helicopter and crew- particularly the man on the rope. He asked Reg, who would be going down, whether he wanted to go ahead. It was really past the limits of what they could do.

Reg answered, without hesitation, "These guys are my mates. I drink at the pub, most days, with them when they are in port. So, you hold her steady. I will go get them."

Vic nodded and looked out towards the horizon. Barely a kilometer away, he saw a massive bracket of at least three waves. If those hit the boat, it would roll over and that would be the end of it. He called out to Reg and winch man, Andy. "Only got a couple minutes with that bracket coming. I will get as low as I can, that way the down draft will keep you more flat."

Vic brought the machine to a bare fifty feet above the trawler mast. He held it as still as possible. The twin-turbines were roaring with the strain.

He nodded to Reg. Reg was down and, in a minute, he was up again with the first two of the crew. Then, Reg was heading down again for the final two.

Vic spared a glimpse towards the horizon. The waves were getting really close now. There were the three big ones in a bracket, and behind them, a total monster. He knew, in that instant, the boat would be unlikely to ride out the first three. If, by some miracle, it did, the last one would definitely turn it over. That would be the end of anything below him.

Vic called out over the radio, "Need to be away in less than thirty seconds. Once those waves hit, I need to get up into the sky. I won't be able to hold steady above them at this height." He could see Reg on the lurching deck now, clipping on the harnesses to the other two. The first wave was almost upon them and was towering up to the helicopter's height. In ten seconds, Vic would have to dial on the power and pull up to keep clear.

He called out, "Ten seconds max."

Now, the boat was rolling into a forty-five degrees angle and the man was still fumbling with his harness. Vic called to the winch man, "Andy, I am going up. Let out more line against me- they need a bit longer."

As the machine responded to the power and came up just above the wave crest, Vic looked below. The boat had come over the wave and just righted. It was now much deeper in the water, as if it had half-filled with water in the roll.

Vic knew the next wave would finish it. It was even bigger than the first set, so he needed more height to get above it. He watched it thunder towards them and held as steady as he could while the precious seconds ticked by.

Just when he could wait no longer, the call he had been waiting for, came in, "Up and away."

Vic powered into the sky, pulling the three men on the line clear of the wave by, what looked like, inches. Then, they were up to a safe height and the three came fully into the copter. The trawler was now lying on its side in the water. It was still there after the third wave passed by.

The fourth wave sounded like a freight train as it thundered towards them. They could hear it even above the engine roaring and wind howling. It seemed to pass bare meters below the machine as it sat there, waiting while the winch man got all the men from below on board. Then, he directed them to go home.

Vic held steady for a few more seconds until the wave had gone fully past them. Of the trawler, no sign remained in the sea below.

He turned the helicopter for home. He felt it shoot forward, like a stone from catapult, with the wind pushing behind it.

Chapter 36 – Reluctant Hero

As Vic came in to land, a crowd was gathered at the helicopter base to welcome them home with cheers and claps. As he shut the helicopter down, he saw Jim heading his way with a concerned look on his face. It seemed out of character with all the well-wishers. He wondered what he had done.

Vic walked over to him and Jim pulled him away to the side of all the people, saying quickly, "Well done, young fella. I gather that was a neat piece of flying to get them out. But- other news is more important right now.

"Your wife's aunt rang about half an hour ago to say your wife has gone into labor. So, I thought you might want to escape the celebrations and head home. It is not the best driving weather, but it is better than flying. I gather all is fine, but the aunt thought you would want to be there.

Vic thanked him and slipped out the back, unnoticed, to his car. The drive was wild, wet and windy. Despite his anxiety to go fast, he kept his speed under control. He did not want to slide into a ditch.

It took two hours of intense concentration to reach the local small-town hospital where Susan was waiting. She was pale and drawn. A contraction came as he entered the ward. As it passed, she greeted him with her usual smile. It was again interrupted by another spasm.

He held her hand. They talked, quietly, in between contractions.

The midwife advised them that all was proceeding normally. The baby seemed strong- even if it was three weeks early. It was just a matter of letting it happen in its own, good time.

Vic had spent a very little time in hospitals. His only real past experience was when they had operated on his broken leg. Then, he had left early to search for a missing Susan. That seemed a lifetime ago. He told himself he should feel blessed that she was here, again, with him and today was the product of their new life together.

Vic said a silent prayer for the day to go well. He felt a deep buried fear of yet another problem arising. He thought about how the unforeseen had a habit of rising up each time their life seemed to be comfortable.

He calmed his mind. This hospital seemed like a good place. The nurses were reassuring and the doctor was quietly competent. It was just Susan's aunt and him with her, now. Her parents were to return in a fortnight to mind the children for her original, predicted delivery. They were now on their way after hearing the news of her labor beginning. He welcomed the thought of their quiet and calm steadiness.

Vic felt he should be in control and reassuring, but he was scared. Despite having seen it often in livestock, this birth business was no joke. He found himself more anxious for Susan and the baby than he had been in the middle of the Force 9 gale while trying to hold a lurching helicopter steady.

Each time she had a contraction, his body contracted, too, in a fear spasm. It proceeded along slowly. A contraction following another contraction, with them becoming ever more frequent until they were almost continuous. The midwife checked and announced Susan was fully-dilated. It would happen very soon.

They gave Susan gas to breathe in and told her to get ready for a final push. Vic held both her hands as her face contorted and she cried out. His heart was in his mouth. Then, suddenly it was there. the black head pushing out between her legs. An almost-pop was heard as the body slithered through the opening and into the waiting hands.

After a quick wipe and shake to clear the mucus, this little creature was drawing breaths. Its color went from bluish to pink. The nurse wrapped it in a small blanket and passed it to Vic to hold. He looked at the unknown object and saw a little face with perfectly formed eyes, nose and his black hair.

In that moment, it was no longer an object to him but a living, breathing person they had made. The emotion of what they had created almost overwhelmed him. It was the most perfect day in his life: to have lost this woman and found her again, now to share the birth of this person with her, to hold it- a joined part of them both. He could feel tears streaming down his cheeks as he gazed at their baby.

Vic carried the small bundle over to his most beautiful darling and placed it in her arms. Susan looked at them both with a radiant smile. Then, she tucked the bundle and him inside her arms. It felt unbelievably good.

She stayed in the hospital for five days. It was not really that she needed to, but the baby was a bit on the small side so the doctor wanted to make sure it was well-settled and feeding well before it went home. In addition, the hospital was hardly busy. There was just Susan and one other mother in the maternity ward so there was no rush to get them out.

Vic barely left her side while her other relatives ferried brother, David, and sister, Anne, in to see their new baby brother. Susan announced the next morning that this baby was named Victor Thomas or Vic junior, for short. She did not ask Vic about it. She just said it was what she wanted. Who was he to disagree with her?

On the third day, the weather cleared. The storm had blown itself out somewhere across the middle of Europe. As they ate a leisurely breakfast in the hospital bed, the nurse came in with a newspaper held out before her.

"Didn't know you were a hero, did you?" she asked Vic, with a smirk.

There was a photo of Vic making his exit from the helicopter. It was from his return to base after the rescue.

The story began below the picture:

HELICOPTER PILOT HERO.

But for a remarkable piece of flying by helicopter pilot Vic Campbell, four men would have lost their lives when a fishing trawler foundered in the North Sea in this week's huge storm.

Yesterday we told of the remarkable bravery of the man who went down to winch the four crew of the trawler to safety. But all those involved say the true hero of the story is the pilot. He brought his helicopter down to wave height and held it there as four huge waves came crashing in, holding position as wave after wave rolled past, first capsizing then sinking the boat as the sea thundered over it. All the while the pilot held the helicopter steady allowing the men cling to life and be lifted out on a flimsy line.

With waves of 50 feet bearing down and a Force 9 -10 gale only pilot skill allowed the crew to be winched up to safety. The pilot somehow kept the helicopter bare feet above the wave tops, so the down draft allowed the winch to operate despite the hundred mile an hour gale. Those who saw it describe it as the most skillful and courageous flying feat they have witnessed.

But where is Vic, reluctant hero. Rumor has it that on this same night his wife gave birth to a child. So, Vic drove through this same storm across

Vic winced as he read it. He knew he should have felt flattered. But now, as a local hero, all the reporters would descend on the hospital. It was no secret here who the new mother, Susan, really was. In days, the story would be out.

Vic was tired of running away. Susan had done nothing to be ashamed of, nor had he. He knew it was now far out of his control, but he was not going to hide from it, ever again. He would hold his head high and, if any reporter came to him saying nasty things about his wife, he would punch him in the mouth, like he had with the last one. This time, he would let the story run its course. He hoped it would all end up 'OK,' but he would not hide away. At least, this time, it was Susan who was in hospital, not him. She was almost totally blind to the outside world and utterly captivated by new little Vic.

Surprisingly, for the next week, it was only a local story. Vic actually thought it might all die down. Susan was named in some of the stories- but only of minor interest. Vic was the one most talked about: the boy from the Australian Outback, a true bush hero.

After a week, someone connected the dots. This story was featured on the front page on a London tabloid. Vic knew that, tomorrow, it would be on the front cover of all the papers. Next the story would be on the TV news.

Vic waited, anxiously, for the next day to come while expecting the worst. Instead, now that he was a national hero, there was no space for any bad story about Susan. Even though the first tabloid had made the connection and tried to give some hints about Susan's past life, it was pushed down by all the other papers and programs the next day with stories like:

HELICOPTER PILOT HERO AND HIS REMARKABLE WIFE.
Despite rumors in our disreputable competitor, we can report that both Vic Campbell and his delightful wife Susan are true heroes, she for surviving

the ordeal of months in jail for a murder she has now been pardoned for, he for first having made an extraordinary journey to escape from his own helicopter crash in one of the remotest parts of Australia and then having performed a second extraordinary feat to rescue others in a similarly terrifying situation. As modest people they now just want to be left alone to enjoy their beautiful little baby and so we should respect their wishes.

The only comment made was a single interview with her father. He simply said he and his wife were incredibly proud grandparents. He asked all to respect the privacy of his daughter and son-in-law.

Within a week, it was just another story which was barely mentioned. In another week, it was gone completely. There was no appetite remaining for the sensation of the 'Crocodile Girl' story. It seemed to pass Susan by. They did not deliberately hide newspapers from her. For the first day or two, she had proudly read about Vic. By the time she became a character in the story, she had lost interest and these papers stayed unread.

Chapter 37 – Mind Picture Flashes

Susan found little Vic to be a delight. He was an easy baby, full of life when awake, but also happy to feed and settle for good long sleeps. His eyes were now fully open and she loved to meet his eyes. She thought he was beginning to recognize both her and Vic, and give her tiny smiles as his dark eyes gazed at hers, intensely.

Susan was also full of pleasure as she watched Vic hold his child. He was trying to talk in an overly grown-up way, telling the tiny boy of the first ride he would have in a helicopter, how they would play football and of all the other things they would do together in the future. All the while, the baby would look up at him with dark, serious eyes.

On the day Susan brought Little Vic home, she had felt no anxiety for she had done this before. That time she had been alone. Now, she had helpers by the score. All things considered, it was not hard.

As she settled back into life at the farm, she found it almost too easy. For the first time, since she could remember, she felt strangely restless. It was an unfamiliar feeling. She wondered, *why now,* when everything was so perfect.

Susan felt a sense she needed to bring order to her life. She needed to do something more constructive than just mind her baby and her twins, particularly when she had so many other helpers.

She decided to organize their room. She did this by re-arranging the furniture, bringing in bright pictures from the hall and buying exotic imported flowers in the town.

As she was sorting through all her things one day, she came across a book, wrapped in cloth, which she had forgotten about. As she unwrapped it, the memory came flooding back. It was the gift of Vic's uncle from a couple weeks before they got married. She had promised to try and find someone to decipher the strange writing within it and comprehend its contents.

At that time, she had photographed it on Vic's phone and meant to seek out someone who could make sense of it. However, in the activity of the wedding preparations, it had been forgotten. the pictures were left on the memory card of Vic's phone- which now sat at his sister's house in Alice Springs. The book had been put into the bottom of her suitcase. It had stayed there while it accompanied her across the world.

Susan decided this would be her new project. It would be something to keep her busy in her free time, of which she had plenty, right now. She needed to find someone who could read what it said. It was unlikely anyone in this small community would be able to do this. She needed to go to a city to find someone who could do this translation. Perhaps she would go to Edinburgh or Glasgow, where University scholars abounded. Or, perhaps, down to London. She remembered her mother worked at Reading University, in a medical field. Her brother had also attended there. Between the two of them, they may know someone who could help.

Susan had promised her Mum and Dad she would come to stay with them with the baby very soon. She had a half-formed plan to go next week. She could catch the train down there and stay for three or four days. She would do it while Vic was away in Aberdeen on one of his flying trips. She could fit it in then.

She wanted to keep the old book safe during the travel. It was, after all, a family heirloom of Vic's family and had been entrusted to her for a purpose. While, in due course, she wanted to show it to various people to get their opinion, she did not want to hand it over to others just yet- lest it got lost or damaged. She decided she must photograph it again, before she showed it to others. That way, she could pass over a digital copy while still retaining the original. Her Mum and Dad were always taking photos of their grandchildren on a fancy camera. She could borrow this from them while she was visiting.

The following week, she was on the train with David, Anne and little Vic.

Vic dropped her at the station as he was en route to Aberdeen for four days. He would collect her on his return trip- which he had timed to fit in with her travel plans. David and Anne were thrilled with the train ride. They were looking out of carriage windows at mountains, lakes and, as the highlands fell away, at rolling green fields with sheep and cattle scattered across them. However, as the novelty went away, they were just two, bratty toddlers. They were hungry, restless and endlessly complaining as boredom overtook them.

Susan was glad to arrive at Reading, after several long train hours, and pass her children to her mother. They soon came to her old house.

As Susan walked inside, she felt the weight of memories flood in on her. It had been her home for most of her life. Even though she had no memory of it since she was little, there was so much of her life from before which then came pouring into her mind once again.

Her Mum called out to inform Susan she was taking David and Anne to visit a neighbor who had promised them a cake. She should follow them over there in half an hour, as they were invited for afternoon tea. Baby Vic had fed shortly before arrival and was now sleeping soundly, so she placed him on a rug on the floor. Then, she asked her father if he would keep an eye on him while she set out to explore the rest of the house.

Susan found her old bedroom, not so large and grand as she remembered, but with her familiar favorite teddy on the pillow. She picked it up and hugged it to herself. As she did, more memories came back- some were even fully remembered. Others were little more than shadows which teased at the edge of her mind. Today, she felt her mind was a place of sunshine and shadows with the remembered, happy memories like bright, sunlit spaces. Alongside these bright spaces were other places where she knew she should remember, but she saw only shadows with vague glimpses of things which had been before. For the first time, she felt her curiosity piqued. She suddenly wanted to know about all that had gone on in her life from before, particularly in those missing years.

Susan started investigating her drawers to look at the clothes. None were what she remembered: tight denim jeans with a bright sparkly top, floral summer dresses, lots of make-up and accessories. None of these had belonged to a twelve-year-old.

She opened the bottom drawer, still searching for something which may be familiar to her. Instead, under jumpers, she found an expensive looking camera. It tore at her memory strings, but no clear knowledge appeared to tell her it had been hers. Still, as she picked it up, she instinctively knew how to use it and the controls were familiar in her hands. She flipped the power button on. Surprisingly, it still worked. She thought the batteries would be dead from years of non-use. The battery warning light was on, but it still lit the back screen.

Susan pushed the buttons to display the photos on the camera. One by one, they flashed by. There were photos of her with friends and family, both at home and on holidays. Apart from her family, the only other person she knew was Anne. She saw photos of herself in a pale-shaded bikini holding the hand of a handsome, blond tousle-haired man. He must have been a past boyfriend- though she could feel no trace of him left in her mind.

It came to her, suddenly, this camera could provide a solution to taking photos of the old book she needed to get translated. It had lots of space on the memory card and just a new set of batteries were required to get it ready. Then, she could get to work. It would take a few hours, tomorrow, to photograph all the pages. After, she could print off some sample pages and go looking for someone to translate what was written.

That evening, she talked to her parents about her plan. After dinner, her mother suggested she show them the book so they could think who might best be able to help her with deciphering it.

Her father looked at the complex curls of characters on each page and said, "I think it looks a bit like Arabic, so we should start there. If it is something else from the Middle East or India, there is a good chance that they can direct us."

Her mother somewhat knew a Professor of Arabic Languages at the Reading School of Literature and Languages. He had helped her with a project, some years ago, about Arabic medicine from the time of the Moorish Empire. She took a few photos on her phone while saying she would show him these tomorrow to seek his advice.

Her father found new batteries for the camera. It now showed it was fully charged. Susan's other grandmother, who lived nearby, agreed to come over tomorrow to mind the children, so Susan would have a few, undisturbed hours to take photographs. Susan found she was looking forward to the challenge of doing something which felt important and complex.

After breakfast the next day, she got to work. Her Gran was there early, and the older children were keen to go with her to a nearby park. Then, they would head on to visit neighbors while Susan worked away. She had just fed them and she would have several hours of solitude to work.

Susan opened the book and began at the front. She started by doing it page- by- page, checking to make sure the quality of the first few photos were acceptable on a laptop her father had lent her, before she continued taking more photos. They were fine.

As she returned the memory card to the camera, she was seized by a powerful sense of déjà vu. It felt so familiar- her using this camera to photograph this – the word 'diary' came unbidden into her head-and she wondered where this thought had come from. It may, in fact, be a diary. On the other hand, it could equally be something else: like a religious book of devotions or transcribed stories.

Susan told herself, *no it is not a diary, it is a book*. Yet, every time she turned the page and took another photo, her mind said, *now you have captured another page of the diary.* She had a sense that it was now not one book, but two: this book in a strange language in her hand and, another book. The other book was a diary in neat, but cramped, English and with a bit of French thrown in. She could even picture a page of lovely flowing, French cursive script though her mind but did not have knowledge of its meaning.

Susan shook her head to clear this complexity of layered pictures. It was like two sequences of images overlaid in her brain: one from now, one from some other time. She made a conscious effort to block out the extraneous thoughts and just concentrate on the task at hand – turn the page, focus, click, check image on back screen of camera and begin over again.

An hour passed. Then, two hours were gone. Now, she had all the pages captured. She just needed to check their quality, in detail, and label them on her computer. She would cross check the accuracy of the sequence with the original book as she went. She began at the outside – Label - Outside Front Cover – correct. Inside Front Cover – correct. She clicked to the next image on her screen and reached for the book to open its cover again and compare. Now, however, this dark brown cover with a few curly symbols transposed in her mind to a red brown cover with the words 'Mark B' in clear handwriting.

She shook her head. This was seriously weird.

She pushed on but it was hard to concentrate. Each time she turned the page, another image, different from the book in front of her, jumped into her mind for a few seconds before it faded.

She forced herself to ignore these unwanted images and go on. As she was getting towards the end, she saw a transposed page with the word 'Kate' written on it. She tried to think of any 'Kate' she knew, but she could not. A few pages later, the word 'Susan' jumped out at her. Somehow, she knew this half-seen page in her mind was a page about her.

Susan could not begin to imagine why she was seeing a book, actually a diary, which had parts written about her. It was not written by her for she knew this writing belonged to someone else- *an unknown man*, she thought. She also knew the lovely French script was written by another woman.

The strange thing was: if she tried to see this other book more clearly, it would fade and drift out of her mind. But, if she looked at the book in front of her, its images were overlaid with sharp images of the other diary.

At last, she was finished and went to make herself a cup of tea. Her head was feeling overloaded with so many images. As she sipped her tea, the jumble of pictures left her mind and only the ones of the book she had photographed today remained. It felt like a relief to get her mind back under her control again.

Susan looked at the clock. It was lunchtime and she was hungry. Her Gran and the children should be home soon. Little Vic would wake up hungry, too. She set to work to make sandwiches for the others when they arrived. As she worked, the phone rang and it startled her out of her reverie.

It was her mother, saying, "I have just met the Arabic Professor over our lunch break. He tells me the language of your book is not Arabic, but it has some similarities. He thinks it may be in a language from the Indian subcontinent, something like a Kashmiri script. He is unable to work it out, although he can guess the odd word. However, he has a long-standing Kashmiri friend in Wokingham who has offered to have a look. He rang this friend while I was there. The friend has kindly offered to meet you and myself mid-morning, tomorrow.

"So, I have blocked out the morning for this- if it suits you to come. If Gran is there, I will ask her to mind the children, again. This man would like to see the original, as well as the copied images. He said that if he can look carefully at the cover and binding, it will help him to know exactly where it is from and the period when it was written."

The next morning, about half past nine, when the morning traffic rush had died down, they set out. It was seven miles to Wokingham. In less than half an hour, they were coming into this lovely, old town. It felt achingly familiar to Susan- but this was no surprise to her for she had probably been here many times in her lost memory period.

They met an elderly, Indian-looking man who introduced himself. As they waited for coffees, he reverently unwrapped the book from its covering.

"Ah. It is beautiful, as I thought it is written in Kashmiri. It is a variant that is a different from the regular script. But I can read most words. With a bit of practice and research, I will be able to transcribe and translate it for you.

"It is a book which has been written over several generations. It covers at least two hundred years. It contains some religious tracts, but also family stories. The last part describes the journey of a young man who left his home and family to travel to a faraway land while bringing camels with him.

"It will take me a couple months to work my way through it, but I would be honored to do this task- if you will allow me. Could you tell me as to how you came by this book?"

Susan described its history, saying it had been handed down over many generations through a part-aboriginal family in Alice Springs, a town in inland Australia. She had an understanding it had originally been owned by an Afghan Cameleer who brought it to Australia.

"That is all I know- except that this Afghan man was my husband's great grandfather. His uncle told me the book is to go to my husband and, one day, it is to be passed on to our children to keep the old man's memory alive. So, this uncle would like to know what it says. He would like to know the story of his ancestor so he can pass this on, too, along with the book.

"So, I am happy for you to do this, but I would ask you to take great care of it. It is the only surviving piece of family history of that man."

As Susan spoke these words, she knew it was a silly request. The reverent way in which this man handled this book meant he gave it a value far higher than she had perceived.

He nodded, agreeing, "But, of course. It is a very precious object. I will take very great care. I understand you have photographed the pages. I will work off those images, but I would still value having the original as I work. Sometimes, it may help my understanding to hold it, look at it more closely."

It was agreed. He would copy the memory card images onto his computer and she would retain a copy as well. Each week, he would send her a letter with a copy of the pages he had translated so far. She and her husband could read this story as it unfolded and from time to time she would send a copy back to Vic's Uncle.

It was now almost lunchtime. Susan's mother needed to go as she had an afternoon appointment at the University. After shaking hands and thanking the man profusely for his help, they started to drive out of town. They followed a different road to the one they had come in on.

As they left the town, some shops located behind an industrial building came alongside them. Something buried deep in Susan's mind screamed out. "Stop," she said.

Puzzled, her mother pulled to the side of the road. "What is it?"

Chapter 38– Contents of the Locked Box

Susan said to her mother, "There is something inside there I need to get. I left it here before. It is inside a locked box."

She could feel herself tugged towards the building. It was here- she knew it was, the diary she had seen was locked up here. She walked off without reply, leaving her mother in the car. He mother parked and followed her.

Susan found the front entrance and let herself in. A middle-aged man came to the counter to help, "Yes. How may I assist?"

The words came out unbidden, "It is Locked Box 972532. I need to open it and retrieve the contents. The security code is 679013."

The man looked up his list on the computer and wrote down the numbers she had given. Then, he nodded. As he was about to speak, Susan's mother joined them, so he paused until she was alongside as well.

The man said, "That box was in use with that security code for two years, until a bit over a year ago. However, at the end of the rental period, the owner had not returned to collect it. Therefore, its contents were removed. It is now in use, again, with a different security code."

Susan felt panic flood into her mind, *it could not be possible that the contents were gone! She wanted, no, she really needed to see the diary that she knew was inside!*

She calmed herself and said slowly, "Do you know what has happened to the contents since they were removed?"

The man shook his head and replied, "No, but I can find out. Generally, we hold the contents for a further 12 months before we dispose of them. However, in some cases where the contents are clearly valuable and we know we can recover the cost of storage, if needed, we will hold them for longer."

He picked up the phone and spoke a few words. In another minute, they were joined by a lady of similar age who was introduced as the person who managed recovered objects. This lady brought them into an office and keyed the details into a computer.

"Yes," she said, "I can see what happened. The security box had two things inside: a book which looked like an old diary and a pouch with some jewelry inside. Our preliminary estimate was the diary is of no particular value, but the jewelry is highly valuable. Therefore, we stored them in a new secure storage compartment in the off-limits area. It is our policy to hold items of this value for five years before we consider disposing of them."

Susan could feel relief flooding into her. She did not know why these things were important, but she knew they were. They were a vital part of her life from before and, even if she could not remember them, she needed to have them back, to see what they told her.

She asked, "Are we able to collect them now?"

The lady looked carefully at her, as if assessing what to do. She hesitantly said, "Well, there are two things to cover, first. One is to confirm your entitlement to the objects. The second is to pay the outstanding fees for their storage. You have confirmed you know the security code, so that is a start. In addition, at the time you stored the objects, we recorded your driver's license number to give us an independent way of confirming your identity- should the need ever arise."

Now, Susan felt flummoxed again. She had no memory of where her past license would be.

She said, "I don't have my license with me. Do you really need to see it?"

The lady shook her head and said, "No. Just the number will suffice."

Unbidden again, the number came into Susan's head. She recited it and the lady wrote it down. It was matched to a field on the computer screen.

"Well, that is all correct. Now, there is just a matter of $300 pounds: that is for two further years of storage fees along with an additional charge for the removal and storage of the items in a new location."

Her mother pulled out her credit card and made the payment.

In five minutes, Susan was holding these two objects in her hands.

Her mother looked at her, curious, "Do you want to check the contents?"

Susan shook her head, "No. I just want to bring them home. I will find time to look at them properly, later."

Her mother shrugged and they drove home.

*

Susan sat alone in her room in the late night. She had suppressed her desire to look at the diary and the bag of stones immediately after she got home. She knew it had been a subject of conversation with her mother, father and her Gran, who had stayed for dinner. She had walked into the room as they were talking and felt the conversation fall into a lull on her entrance.

Finally, her father had blurted out, "Your Mum was just telling us about your visit to Wokingham, today. The meeting of the Kashmiri man and his kind offer to translate the book. Also, he said about your stop off at the storage place on the way home. How you remembered that you had left things there from before you went away."

He stopped there and waited for her to say something. A silence ensued. Finally, realizing she was being rude, Susan said, "I don't really remember what it is. But I feel like I need to have a look with Vic- before I show whatever it is to others. He may help me understand what it means.

"So, I plan to bring it home, tomorrow, on the train. Then, we can have a look together. Once we do that, I promise I will tell you all about it."

They all nodded, but she could see a disbelieving look on all faces. She felt bad. She could not remember lying deliberately before. Doing it to these people, who had been so wonderful to her, felt unworthy.

However, she could not bear to open something so significant and private with anyone else looking on- not even her Vic. This book was a story of the life she had lost. She must know what it said. It was just for her and her alone, to begin with.

After that conversation, no one raised the topic of the contents of the locked box anymore. The night proceeded with lots of laughter and fun, entertaining the children as her parents and Gran told stories about her when she was a little girl, along with stories about her brother. Now, they were all gone to bed. The older children were in their own room and little Vic was in the crib alongside her bed, sleeping soundly.

Susan sat on her bed with the book in her hands, looking at a reddish-brown cover with only "Mark B", handwritten, to distinguish it. It was just as she had remembered it from when she had photographed the other book. She knew that inside would be the 'words of writing' her mind had glimpsed.

She felt no real interest in the stones in the cloth pouch. The lady had said they were jewels, but they felt like small stones to her.

One day, soon, when she had read the book, she was happy to open the pouch and show these stones to others. She did not care about them. If they were valuable, all the better. However, it was of minor importance.

The story must come first. She knew, with a deep clarity, this was her story. It was the key to unlocking a part of her mind. She held the book in her hands and immersed herself in its presence. It had its own presence-the essence of a vanished spirit, perhaps this was Mark B.

Chapter 39 – The Ghost of Mark

Susan kept holding the book and let it fill her consciousness. It had its own clear presence. As she thought of it, she felt it enter her mind. It had a face: half human and half crocodile. She should have been frightened like she was on the day when she glimpsed the crocodile tearing at her children. However, there was none of that. She could only feel the faint, regretful curiosity that came with wondering where this man had gone.

Now, his crocodile part dissolved and only the man remained. It was a regular man's face: weather beaten edges, an eye-crinkling smile. It was not quite handsome, but utterly arresting. It looked into and captivated her soul.

With a pang of pain, Susan knew she had utterly and totally loved this man. His departure had been the most devastating thing she had ever known. She loved Vic no less, but the sense of the loss of this earlier love was so powerful and poignant at this moment- it dwarfed all else in her mind. She could feel tears trickling down her cheeks.

Susan turned the pages forward a little way and started reading. She was reading the story of 'E' or 'Elfin,' later to become the 'Elfin Queen.' This man had loved her, too- fully and completely. It did not take from what Susan knew was his love for her and hers for him. As she read of how 'E' had died and he buried her in the boat he had made, somewhere out in the desert by a river, she felt tears streaming down her face. He was totally desolate and heartbroken. She shared in his heartbreak.

Susan read on. There were various odd stories interspersed throughout the diary. There was even one about a metal bird and a man named Vic. She realized, with a shock, this was her Vic! He had been this man's friend. They had shared a lot together.

There were more stories about Vic and other characters over the pages which followed. There were also many other stories that were set in the Australian Outback. They told of musters, cattle, horses, more helicopters, shooting, fishing, and crocodiles. In the diary were lots of places with crocodile stories and images. There were some references to other girls, too. These girls seemed to pass like ships in the night. They would light pages, but only for brief spaces and then their lights were gone.

Then, a second significant person came along: 'B' or 'Belle.' As time went by, she was referred to as "my beautiful B." It began as a lovely story of friendship involving meetings and re-meetings. Then, it told of a road journey together to a faraway place in part of Australia called the Kimberly. They had started from Broome and headed north.

It was a trip of joy, wonders and a friendship morphing into a deep love. It was clearly a two-way thing: she read it in Mark's words and read it, also, in the elegant cursive script of Belle. Her parts were written some in French and some in English. Belle told of her delight in her newfound lover, her plans to bring him home to meet her family and her plans to make babies with him. It was utterly gorgeous.

Then, Susan turned another page. She was devastated. Belle had fallen into a pool full of huge crocodiles, beasts which would tear her body apart. Mark, using the only weapon at hand, had finished her off, before she could suffer, with a single shot into the head he loved so much. Belle had felt nothing. The crocodiles got only a body for the spirit had already departed.

However, Mark had killed the one he loved. Rage and grief tore apart his soul. It left something else in its place: a dark, malevolent crocodile spirit, now become a hunter and destroyer.

She could bear to read no further. She had no tears left to shed, just a heart full of devastation as she shared his pain. She did not want to read on. She knew nothing good could come past this point in his story.

She lay in her bed, with the light off, and dreamt awful crocodile dreams. This time, however, they were not of her children but of a girl. She was dark haired and looked, somehow, like Susan. Susan watched, through eyes which she knew weren't her own, from high above, as this girl's body was torn apart, and then as the monsters feasted on her. Limb was torn from limb as blood darkened the water- all while the man watched in anguish. Then, it was his body they tore at. She first thought he had thrown himself in the pool with Belle, being consumed by grief at her death. But, as she watched, she saw these were other crocodiles located in a different place and time. The eyes which watched this time were hers.

In the morning, Susan woke up with the book on her lap. She had only vague memories of her dreams and the man featured in them. They felt like they belonged in another place and time. However, a portent of unresolved doom which had tearing crocodiles at its center, remained in her mind.

Susan pushed it from her mind. She was determined not to let these dark thoughts spoil this, her homecoming day. She felt mounting excitement to be on her way back to her husband. She loved the sound of that word, and she particularly loved the thought of his intense, smiling face.

She was upbeat now. She wanted to share this discovery with him. Then, she thought of how good her parents had been to her. They deserved for her to be more forthcoming with them, too.

Susan knew what she should do. Even though she was not ready to let them read the contents of the diary, she could share something else with them. After all, Vic did have the first right to see diary. Instead, she would open the contents of the pouch with them. It was only bits of old jewelry. Going on what the lady at the bank said, they may be some semi-precious stones. Perhaps, they were worth a few thousand pounds. This would be at least enough to ensure their storage bill was paid.

She put the dairy in her suitcase, underneath her clothes, in the place which had held her Kashmiri book before. Then, she took the pouch in her hand and went out to see the others in the kitchen.

Her Gran had stopped over last night. The children were already up and eating breakfast. The kitchen was a babble of noise. She walked into it, unnoticed. As they sensed her presence, they all looked up.

She said, "I thought, before I go home today, we should open this pouch of 'supposedly' old jewels, to see exactly what it contains."

She handed it to her mother, saying, "Perhaps, as you were there with me when I collected it, you should do the honour of opening it."

Her mother nodded, looking thoughtful and a bit tense. She untied the strings and tipped the contents gently onto the table. As the stones rolled out, she let out a small gasp. It was mirrored by her Gran and her father.

There were about fifty stones inside the bag. There were only two which had been made into settings. These two were a set of gorgeous milky, pale blue stones made into a ring and a pendant. She saw these two stones were almost identical and she could see their blue clearly for what it represented.

Susan felt her eyes riveted to just these two objects. Without knowing where they came from, her words came tumbling out, "He said he chose them to match the color of my eyes."

She shook her head, "I don't know why I said that. I don't even know who 'he' is, but I know he gave them to me."

The others seemed to have barely noticed her words. They were gazing, as if awestruck, at the rest of the pouch's contents. There were big stones in many different sizes, shapes and hues. Susan saw there were many colors, although she could not fully make these out. Only the two blue pieces had real color to her eyes.

Her father was shaking his head, saying, "Unless I am seriously mistaken, this is a lot more than some bits of old jewelry and semi-precious stones. See all the colors: red, blue, orange, green, milky, clear and sparkling. I think this is the real stuff: opals, rubies, emeralds, sapphires, diamonds and nothing else but the very best.

"I would not begin to guess what these are worth. It must be a huge amount. At an estimate, each stone is worth at least ten thousand pounds, and many of them are worth much more than that. So, I think we are looking at upwards of half a million pounds on the table."

Susan looked at her dad as if he was crazy and said, "Dad, you are joking. Why would someone put such things in a locked box and forget about them?"

He replied, "Sweetie, I don't know. I did not put them there. But look for yourself. Then, tell me if I am wrong."

Susan took a real look at the stones for the first time. While she could not see the many colors, except for the blue of her amazing opals, she realized it must be true.

Her dad said, "This stuff needs to go into a bank vault, at least until we can make arrangements to have them properly assessed and valued. Whoever's this is, they are far too valuable to just leave lying around."

Susan felt disappointed. She had been looking forward to taking these home to Vic and admiring them, together, "Oh, Dad, I don't know. Can't I just take them with me, home on the train, to show them to Vic? I can't wait to see his eyes open wide when he sees them. I want to surprise him."

Her father shook his head in disbelief, "Susan, what a crazy idea! What if something happens to them? What if they get lost or stolen? They are far too valuable to be careless with them."

Now, she felt annoyed. "Dad, they have been sitting, forgotten, in a box for three or four years. Before that, God only knows where they were and for how long. Yesterday, I carried them home in this little bag in the car without anybody thinking anything of it. Then, last night, they sat in my bedroom without any lock and key. We are the only people who know about them. Why would something suddenly happen now? Not to mention that, if I had not remembered that code yesterday, they could have sat in that storage place forever."

She could see her mother and Gran nodding with her in agreement. Reluctantly, her father gave in, saying, "Well, I suppose that is true. It is like you were meant to discover them. But you must let one of us come with you on the train. I am sure your Gran would be glad to come with you."

Her Gran nodded, "Of course, pet. I am free and would love to come. I have barely been introduced to your children. A day with them on the train would be wonderful. And who is safer than an old lady with a walking stick?"

Now, they all laughed and agreed. Today, she and her Gran would go on the train to Scotland. Tonight, they would show the gems to Vic. Tomorrow, the gems would be taken and stored in a bank vault in Edinburgh or Glasgow until they were appraised.

The trip home was uneventful. Vic was there to meet them all. He encased everyone, Gran included, in a group hug. Susan felt her news bursting on the tip of her tongue, but she held it in. She would save it for after supper- when it was just the two of them. Then, she would show him both the diary and the stones together. In doing this, Susan knew she must ask him to tell her about this Mark person who was his friend. She could run away from this knowledge no longer.

As they were sitting over supper, chatting around the table with the whole family, telling of the trip and the book from Kashmir, the phone rang. Her aunt got up to answer it. In a minute, she had a puzzled look on her face.

Finally, she said, "Just a minute," and turned to address Susan, "There is a girl, Cathy, on the phone. She says she has a letter of introduction from your friend, Anne. She has just arrived from Australia. She asks if she could come over here, now, and give this letter to you. She is staying nearby and could come straight away, if that's alright."

Susan was looking forward to the rest of her night alone with Vic but could think of no polite way to say 'no' to someone who wanted to meet her and had Anne's blessing. With nothing else to say, she shrugged her assent.

Chapter 40 – Meeting a Lost Girl

Soon there was the sound of car tires crunching on the gravel drive. Then, there came a knock on the door. Susan went to the door and opened it.

Standing before her was a girl of somewhere around her own age, with darkish hair cut short. She could also see a dark-skinned man still sitting in the car which was parked some distance away. The girl held out her hand and said, "Hello, I am Cathy. I was just talking to your aunt on the phone."

Susan invited her in, but the girl replied, "Thanks, but no thanks. At least, not tonight. I just wanted you to have this letter, sooner rather than later.

"I'm hoping to have a chance to meet with you and talk about what it says in the next couple days. Tonight, we are jet-lagged and need to sleep," she said, pointing to the man in the car. "I want you to have chance to think about what we are asking and say no, if you want, before we go further."

Susan took the letter she proffered, thanked Cathy and watched her walk back to the car. Cathy drove away before Susan came back inside.

The others all looked at her with interest. Susan briefly explained what had happened, saying, "If Anne wanted to give me a message, it is funny that she did not call me and tell me directly. It must be something complicated, that I need to think about, for her to have written to me, instead."

Vic yawned. It made no sense to him, too. And he was tired, after a long day of flying and driving.

Her aunt took the initiative, "Actually, I think we all need to head off to bed now. It's getting late and you both look tired after your trips. Maybe, you should leave reading the letter until you wake in the morning with a fresh mind. I will pop your kids in the bath and put them into bed. Susan, you go a have a rest with Vic and your baby, now."

Susan felt happy to oblige. Since coming to live here, David and Anne always seemed happy to go off with others. In truth, after her bad night of sleep last night, she was suddenly, very tired.

She took Vic's hand. They went to their bedroom. They were happy to be together with their baby and knew talking could wait. As she lay beside him, she said, "I have much news, but I need to rest before I tell you."

Vic tucked their baby in between them. He put his arms around Susan and they soon fell asleep.

She dreamt of meeting Vic, for the first time. He was standing next to a helicopter. She was travelling with another man whose face was hidden. But she was happy. Everything around her in this dream was bright and full of colors: green trees, blue sky, golden sun, red dirt, and Vic's berry-brown skin. The colors were unbelievably beautiful. She did not want to wake from her dream. It was a warm, happy place which she did not want to leave.

Susan woke to find Vic staring, intently, at her. She told him of the dream. He stroked her and held her close, telling her she had remembered the first day they met. Still in this happy place, she returned to sleep.

The sky was just glowing into a clear, cold daylight when she woke again. Her baby was restless, seeking food, so she gave him a breast. She watched as he sucked, greedily. She snuggled into Vic. She was wanting to postpone the telling which needed to be done. It all seemed too complicated and hard to explain now. Plus, she could feel his early morning desire for her. She wanted that, too. They postponed the talk a little longer with joined pleasure. She dozed again. Her mind snapped suddenly awake. It was time to speak.

Susan began by telling him of it as it happened: the taking of the pictures, those images of another time which kept coming into her mind, ones of the diary and the man with the crocodile face. Then, she told how she had driven past and seen the place where the things were stored and had known they were there. She had even known what the code was, although she had no remembrance of leaving things there three of four years ago. Having told Vic up to this part, she went to get the items from the box. She took the book and the stones from her bag to pass them to him.

"It is time for you to begin to tell me who I was before," she said. "I need to know. I cannot block it out anymore."

He nodded and looked at the book with wonder., "It is hard to believe I am holding it. I have read parts. Anne read it all- not this exact book, but a copy. You must have copied it, as you did with my book, and then stored the original for safe keeping, along with the stones. They belonged to Mark too. They are all yours, now.

"The book, this diary, is the story of Mark. He was your lover before me. He is the father of Anne and David. He was my best friend and I miss him, still. It is a hard story. It tells of bad things that Mark has done. I can tell you parts, Anne can tell you more.

"If you wish, I can read this with you. Or I can sit with you while you read it for yourself. Only a small part of it is a story about you. You came last- his final, great love. When I knew you then, I was only a friend. A friend of Mark who took you both flying for a magic day of scenery and fishing. By the end of that day, you were my friend, too. After that, you travelled on with him, but I never saw you together, again.

"When you left him, he was dead. In that you played a part, but it is not something to take blame for. Mark saw there was no other way for him. He could not escape his past. Knowing this, he chose to give his body to the crocodiles. That is why you see a crocodile face. When he left, what remained of him was a crocodile spirit. Sometimes, this spirit has haunted you, too.

"As to the stones, I knew he owned some such. He was a rich man. He once told me, an old timer had shown him a fabulous opal mine, far out in the desert. It gave him more money than he ever needed. Instead, he chose to live and work in the outback, the only place where he felt at home.

"As part of this life, he bought and traded gemstones with other miners- always at a fair price. He would keep the best stones for himself, saying he loved to have these things of beauty. I think only Buck and I knew of this. Sometimes, he would give them as gifts to friends.

"Even though he was rich, he lived simply and spent little on himself. His needs were always few. So, those stones were his own collection. When he went, he gave them to you to do with as you wish."

Vic picked up the book and turned the pages until he came to where Susan first appeared. He said, "Here, he tells of when he first saw you."

He read the words out loud:

"Beach Girl, beautiful. She stands there with her toes in the little waves, hair flung back like a Greek goddess, arms stretched out to the morning sun. She is enchanting and I want to know who she is. I stand on the shore path, watching her in the bright light. When she looks my way I move

behind trees, now I can only glimpse her. Then she comes my way, I keep out of sight, it might look like I am spying.

"She has stopped at an ice cream stand. Now she walks on, licking a cone with such pleasure, the ice cream trickles down her fingers and she licks it off. I wish I was an ice cream drop."

Vic finished by saying, "I wish I could write as well as he did. In the moment I first saw you, I felt something the same, too. Part of me was jealous of Mark, but part of me was delighted my friend had found such a wonderful person.

"I could not believe it when I heard he was gone. Even though I wanted you for myself, I also felt entrusted by him to look after you."

Mark's words and Vic's words both moved her greatly, although it was only Vic she knew. She still didn't remember Mark at all. That 'Mark' was only flashes of a face at the edge of the light, like a shadow in the last sunlight.

Susan moved in against Vic and held him, telling him she was very happy to be entrusted to him. Then, she joined her body to him again. They drifted back to sleep once again.

It was mid-morning when she woke again, saying, "Now, I must read that letter from Anne, the one which Cathy, gave me last night."

She found the letter and opened it. She took the folded sheet in her hand and spoke the words out loud:

Dearest Susan-Jane,
I hope this letter finds you well, and congratulations on the great news about your little boy, Vic. I know I have said it to you on the phone, but I still find I want to write it too. I am so, so, SOOO excited for you.

I have also read about your heroic husband, and the stories which are now beginning to be told about his heroic wife, although last time I talked to Vic he said you had little interest in reading these stories, they had largely passed you by.

So, if you do not now know about your past life or choose not to want to know, please put this letter aside without reading more. I would not have brought this memory back, but this story is not only about you.

I started trying to find out about you, my missing friend, but along the way I found the stories of others, those I called the "Lost Girls". I have told these stories as best I can, and that would be the end, except that one girl is lost no longer, that is Cathy, who you have now met.

She has decided her story will cause much pain and yet it must be spoken. The man who is with her is the man who wrote awful things about you. He is the man who Vic punched and left in the gutter at your wedding. Now he is ashamed of what he did to you, knowing much he wrote was untrue. He has played no part in the recent stories about you and Vic, except to write a piece asking others to respect your privacy.

However, now, he is helping Cathy tell her story. Like you she has suffered much, but she wants the truth to be known. It is a hard story for her family to hear, it will be a hard story for her to speak of, yet she feels she must.

But, before she opens her own Pandora's Box of secrets, she has set one condition, not to protect her family but to protect you. If you decide, after having met with her, that you want this box of secrets kept closed, nothing further will be told. Then she and Jacob will say no more, lest it harm you.

They say that, after the harm done to you in what Jacob wrote, their first consideration is to harm you no more. So, Cathy has asked to meet with you, if you are willing, to tell you the story of her life and what she knows of Mark.

Then, she can decide if she is brave enough to tell the story of her own life for others to hear, her parents first and then the world.

If you are willing to know what happened from part of that time lost to your memory, then meet her, listen to her and hear what she has to say. If this is too hard, no one will blame you. She will speak of it no more and trouble you no further.

So, I leave it with you to decide whether you want to hear her story. I know it and it is a brave story, but it is not mine to tell.

Please give your baby and your other delightful children lots of hugs and kisses from me and David and from all your other Australian friends.

We all miss you and Vic greatly and hope to see you again soon.

Your closest and ever-loving friend

Anne

Vic and Susan began to talk in earnest as she put the letter aside. It was the narrative of a lost year of her life which he told her. He did not know of the years before she came to Australia, but their importance was minor and others could fill them in if needed.

However, Vic knew the story of his wife from many sources: from the documentaries on the lives of the 'Lost Girls' which Anne made and which he had forced himself to watch, despite the pain, and from reading some bits of Mark's diary. He had only really read the parts about himself and Susan.

Due to the sensitivity of some of the parts, the full transcript had not been released. However, Anne and the police had gradually worked through the different parts with the named parties, checking facts and verifying contents. Anne and Alan had spent many hours with Vic going through the parts where he was mentioned, where they concerned Susan or where the locations and other things may be within his knowledge.

At that time, all had agreed, the diary was Mark's bequest to Vic since Susan was gone. It was also Susan's gift to him in another time. Although he had never fully looked at it before, it was agreed he had a right to it.

While Vic did not know all its contents and had largely avoided the parts which told bad things about his friend, he knew the main facts. He had learned these through him and Anne sharing knowledge, which was done as they searched for Susan.

Slowly, over the whole morning, he filled in the story. Their bodies lay, almost together, in bed. There were times when it was hard to continue and tears flowed, a sadness for both of them at the unfolding tragedy of this man. But Vic knew that, now the telling had begun, it could not be stopped until an end was reached. So, the telling continued. Mostly, it was Vic's words being spoken. She had no memory, other than of those tiny fragments, which had only come to her two days before, when she had been taking of the pictures of Vic's family's book.

Susan watched as Vic spoke. She was looking with a rapt face and intent eyes. Occasionally she asked him to stop and sometimes she would seek for him to hold and comfort her. It was late morning when he finally finished. They knew others of the family had attended to their children, David and Anne. Susan had stopped once during the telling to feed baby Vic again. After the telling was done, they lay together and barely moved for a long time.

Finally, she roused herself, saying., "Thank you for telling me. Perhaps it is good that I don't remember, although right now I feel a huge void in my life. Before it was just an empty place, like a blank sheet of paper, with nothing written on it.

"I don't know why I can't remember. Perhaps it was protection for my mind so the awfulness could not reach me. Now, part of me wants to stay in that place of forgetfulness. Another part wants to know it within my own mind. I fear the memory will tear its way through- whether I want it or not.

"But I cannot go back to the place of unknowing- I must go forward. So, I must go and meet with Cathy to hear her story. Before I do, I will read what Mark's diary says about her so I know, at least, a part of her story and can spare her telling me that again. I will do it this afternoon.

"Then, perhaps I will read more of what it tells of me. For now, I cannot bear to read the middle part, the part which tells the worst of the man known as 'Mark.' I find that this part is something I do not want to know.

"Will you come with me when I meet Cathy? Along with her will be the man, Jacob. If Jacob is helping her, then I must help him. I know you fought with him to protect me, but that is past. I cannot hold anger against him."

Vic nodded, "Yes, I will come. Also, I will not fight with him."

*

Next morning, they all met in a café in the local town. They jointly decided on this location since it was neutral ground.

Vic opened the meeting by shaking hands with Jacob, saying, "My knuckles hurt for a week after I hit you. I do hope your face did not hurt for too long."

Jacob answered, "I like people who fight for what they believe in, although it was a month until I could eat without pain in my mouth. However, it is in the past. I feel no pleasure in what I did and wrote."

With that said, they shook hands and walked off to look at the countryside for five minutes while the girls talked alone. It was an intensely, private thing for Susan to tell Cathy that she had read Mark's words telling of her most intimate and private memories, things which

Cathy had told him when he was her lover. Susan said how Mark's words had told of her rape as a child and the death of her sister. It was all said in only a minute. Then, they just hugged in the same way which sisters do. After that was done, they talked for half an hour until the men returned.

Cathy and Jacob then told how they had met with Alan. He had told them he had passed this same information to Scotland Yard, about a year and a half ago, for its investigation. What was strange was: they had passed over the information in a case where the accused was now a missing person. Cathy's uncle, George, disappeared almost four years ago now. He went missing bare months after Cathy met Mark and before Susan had first come to Australia.

George was on a tour of duty in the Middle East. He had been providing support and intelligence in Iraq at a time when information emerged about a child pornography ring he was linked to. There was nothing definite, but he was sought by the police to interview. The contact was only with a senior officer. He should not have known of the police arranging to send an investigator to Iraq to meet with him. But it seemed he was tipped off.

One day, he had not come to work. All inquiries since found no trace of him. He was skilled at working and operating undercover. Perhaps, he heard something and went underground. All that was officially known was he could not be located, but there were not any specific fears voiced for his safety.

Four years was a long time, so it was hard to know what to make of it. It was particularly hard for Cathy's mother. He was the younger brother and she did not know of what he had done to her daughters. And now, he was missing, too. It was as if she had lost one daughter, and then another and now, lost her brother. But Cathy was the daughter who had returned. With Susan's permission, she would no longer live a lie.

Before the meeting was done, Susan found herself offering to come with Cathy while she told her parents what had passed. Cathy was determined it must come out. She had now moved past secrets and the harm they caused.

That very afternoon, it was just Susan and Cathy who sat in another Scottish living room. They told a story, one which no-one wanted to hear.

Mark and Jacob collected the children and drove in the countryside. David had taken a real shine to Jacob and sat on his shoulders as they walked in the woods and hills around the villages they visited. Annie was happy to have Vic's undivided attention. As they walked, the men talked. They shared childhood tales, ones about: the boy who was mostly black and grew up in a rough London neighborhood but fed his imagination on his mother's Caribbean tales. And the other boy who was similarly black and grew up in a rough town camp in the middle of Australia but was dragged into being something better by a sister with high expectations. By the end of the day, they were good friends. Each loved a woman who was alike: a survivor of something awful. the women could comfort each other in the way of sisters. Considering this, they decided they must be like the brothers and they felt like brothers, too. It seemed right.

They returned as the winter sun was setting to a somber living room. Tears had been cried, now there was forgiveness and the relief of knowing.

Cathy, having got her story out, decided it did not need to be spoken of further. She had been reconciled and only a vanished man remained. Grief must be endured as the family faced the truth. All agreed the story would end here, unless this man was found.

Vic agreed it was better this way. Cathy's family had more than enough to deal with, without having the story of such a man told and retold outside their family circle. At the same time, his unexplained absence made full closure impossible.

Chapter 41 – Fading, Fading Colors

Vic and Susan spent most of the next two days with Jacob and Cathy. By the end of this time, a fast friendship between all had formed.

Jacob took Susan aside, before leaving, saying, "I cannot believe what I wrote about you. It is so untrue. I had blinders on my eyes. I was so angry that you dared to challenge the world, not bowing to its power. I confused that courage with mockery. Now, I see that what you were doing was refusing to give in to awfulness. It is good you do not remember that time. I would rather you never read what I wrote about you, then."

Susan said, "We did not know each other then. Now, we are friends. As I do not remember, it does not hurt me. So, I will never read it."

Then, Jacob and Cathy were gone. They were returning to London to talk again to the English Police. Then, they would head onto Australia, via the Middle East, for one last attempt to find the uncle who remained elusive.

It was strange how, despite both Jacob and Cathy being UK citizens, they'd decided to spend their lives in Australia for now. Both said it felt like home. It was where they had found each other and a wholesome, new life. Even if Cathy never found her uncle and Jacob never published any parts of this story, they had reached joint acceptance. Now, their lives had moved on.

Vic felt a pang of regret that it was not Susan and him on the plane, returning to his home. As winter ground slowly forward in Scotland, he really missed his Australian life- particularly the endless, bright sunlight.

As Susan said goodbye, she felt amazed at how far their lives had moved on in the last six months. For her, their past life in Australia now seemed like a barely remembered shadow. She did not miss it. She was less sure if Vic felt the same way. She wondered if she was a selfish burden on him: trapping him in this place with her family and offering little in return for what he had left behind. Still, at least he was flying helicopters again.

Over the month which followed, Susan made herself know the full story of her missing year. She listened to the tapes of her own voice telling it, which Anne had sent her. Also, she watched the documentaries of the 'Lost Girls Series.' In addition, she heard the same stories from Vic, making him recount all he had seen and done. But it was only knowledge, not memory. It seemed like it had happened to another person, someone unrelated to who she was now. No new memories of then broke through whatever the block was that had sealed off this part of her mind.

A week before Christmas, Susan got another letter from Anne. It was a wedding invitation. This time it was for her to take the bridesmaid role. It was to be after Easter in Reading, four months from now. It would be when the spring days were growing long and all the flowers were out.

David and his family would cross the world for the wedding. Susan found herself thrilled with the idea of this occasion. She would chatter to Vic about it, asking for his advice about the various arrangements which she had offered to help Anne with. Vic was of little help, telling her to ask her mother. He told her how his part in his own wedding was simply to turn up fully dressed. Vic said this was the limit of what he could manage. Susan did not push it, for she liked this new challenge.

Three more wedding invitations turned up at the end of that same week. This was to be three weddings in one, all for the end of May. All were to be held in Darwin on the same day. They were for Alan and Sandy, Cathy and Jacob, and for Ross to a person named Beck. Vic knew and told Susan of Beck's role in arranging her pardon.

Neither Vic nor Susan had met Beck, but both liked Ross Sangster. His opinion, after all, allowed Susan to go free. So, while he was little more than a face to them, they thought well of him. Now, he was a good friend of others they knew. They figured that soon they and Beck would be their good friends, too. It seemed strange to have decided to have three weddings all on one day in Darwin, but it would make it easier for them to attend them all.

They booked their flights to return to Australia in the middle of June. They planned to fly from London to Darwin for the weddings, spend a week in Alice Springs with Vic's family, spend a week in Sydney with David, Anne and Susan's cousins, and then, a final week of holiday time in Cairns before they returned to Scotland.

They had never discussed a future beyond this place. It seemed Scotland had become their new home. Vic's flying career had risen with the publicity and the money was good. Susan's life was full, with her children, the book translation pages arriving from the Kashmiri book and helping around the farm. So, for now, they both accepted they would return here.

Susan and Vic were even making plans to have another baby around the end of the year- God willing. A gap of a year seemed right. Of course, it was up to Susan to fall pregnant. Considering that it had happened with such ease before, there was no reason to believe it would be any different this time. Susan would stop breastfeeding in March in the hope of a New Year baby. With luck, it would be a little sister for Annie. She knew Vic would absolutely love that.

It was a white Christmas that year. All the hills around them were covered with snow. Susan's parents, along with other cousins, came up to celebrate. It was a day of great excitement- particularly for David and Anne for whom it was their first remembered Christmas. They were spoiled rotten with so many presents from so many relatives. In the afternoon, the men found toboggans in the shed and took turns racing each other down the snowy hillsides, with children on board.

In the New Year, life settled back into a quiet routine. There were periods of three or four days when Vic was gone. In return, there were two-day home periods when they spent most of their time together.

They read part of the diary each night and discussed what it meant. They were half-way through but had already jumped forward and read the later bits about Susan, early on, as a way of her knowing her past. It felt like embarking on a joint voyage of discovery. They would read a two-page section each night and discuss what it meant, before sleep.

They were reading about 'J', or 'Josie' as Vic thought her to be. She had just arrived in Katherine and Mark had taken her in. He was describing his feelings for her being like those for a little kid sister, but it was clear she was looking for more than that from him. By the end of this night of reading, Josie had found her way into his bed. They both felt secretly pleased for this comfort Josie had given Mark. His life had been very dark and empty since Belle was gone.

They drifted into a dreamy sleep as they put the book aside. Their bodies were not quite touching but with touch connections between hands and feet.

Vic awoke to hear Susan call out. At first, he thought something had happened, perhaps to one of the children. He thought she was summoning him to wake up. However, he saw she was still asleep. He watched her for a moment. Her face was reflected in the soft light placed behind little Vic's crib which allowed them to find their baby in the dark.

Suddenly, Susan sat bolt upright in the bed, waving her arms and saying "Please. Please. Don't let it end like this. I will stay with you on any terms. We can make a new life together in a place where we know nobody. I love you. I will never tell what you have done."

Susan held out her arms, imploringly. Vic could see desperation in her face and pleading. Then, it seemed as if she had been struck an invisible blow. She recoiled and, as if rejected, turned her face away while softly crying and lying down on her side.

Vic wanted to put his arms around her to comfort her. However, he knew in this dream, she was sharing life with another man. She was living out a private agony of the ending of that life. He did not feel entitled to share that with her. He had heard the story before, told with her voice on the tape, the story of her final night with Mark. How she had implored Mark to stay, yet he had turned his face away from her.

In the morning, when she awoke, he asked her if she remembered any dreams from the night before. She shook her head, puzzled, and said, "No. Maybe I dreamt of colors and sunshine."

The next night, he awoke to her dreams again. This time, he found her pacing the room, as if in a trance, talking to a person he could not see.

Vic said her name, "Susan."

She did not seem to hear him. She continued on with her conversation. Then, she put up her arms and started to move and sway in a rhythmic pattern. He realized she was dancing, moving in time with an invisible body. It felt both private and weird. As it went on, Vic was consumed by jealousy. Eventually, she came and sat on the bed- the dance and conversation now over. He eased her under the covers, tucked them around her and she settled back to a deep sleep.

Again, the next day, Susan said she remembered nothing of her dreams when he asked her.

The next night, he was gone to work. Before he left, he asked her aunt to check on Susan in the middle of the night. He told her he was worried she would sleepwalk as he had found her sleepwalking the night before, but she remembered nothing of it.

When he rang and asked about Susan the next day, her aunt said she had been sleeping soundly when she checked. However, that morning, Susan had told her of having a dream full of colors. Susan had said she could not remember what happened in the dream- the colors were the only thing she could remember.

When Vic returned after his three days of flying, Susan had a tired and drawn look to her face. Her aunt said she had been irritable for the last two days. This was very unlike her for she was normally so calm and sweet.

Next day, Vic brought Susan walking into the hills with him. It was late afternoon. The sky was alive with streamers of cloud in the flat, slanting winter light. He was entranced by the beauty of these streamers of gold and other fiery colors. He held Susan in front of him, arms wrapped around her and body pressed to his. He asked whether she saw it, too- the glowing light and colors.

She showed no interest at all. She said it looked like nothing much to her- just a dull, grey color as the light was fading.

That night, Vic kept his arms around Susan all through the night. He was determined to hold her and, thus, keep her for himself. He was not going to let any other invade her dreams. It felt as if this person of her dreams was stealing her soul from him.

She woke up in the morning with a sad, wistful look and said, "Vic, your skin used to be brown to me. Now, it has gone a dull and dirty grey. I can't see your color anymore."

Susan went to pick her baby up from the cot. She came back with empty hands and tears streaming down her face. She cried, "Something has happened to my eyes. Now, I can't see the color of my baby's skin anymore. He is a dull and dreary grey, too. He is the same color as you."

"Everything looks the same color now. That is: no color, all the light has gone. It is only when I dream that the light and color returns to my world."

Vic thought of taking her to the doctor, but it did not seem a problem which a doctor could fix. Vic knew it was in her mind, not her eyes.

He took Susan in his arms and brought her back to bed. He was seeking to comfort her. He made love to her with all the tenderness he could find.

Vic remembered how, once, he had wanted a woman with a fire which raged at the world. Someone who could see the shadows as well as the sunlight. Then, he had found a woman who only saw sunlight and he had loved her for her simple goodness.

Now it seemed, she only saw shadows in her waking hours and the sunlight was only for her dreams. More than anything, he wanted the sunlight to return to her waking eyes. He wanted to see the bright light in them again.

After that revelation, he let her to her dreams each night. It seemed to refresh her spirit but, at the same time, it left her tired and irritable in the day. It was as if some of the color of the night carried forward into the next day. By the evening, the light in her eyes had faded. Susan would take to their bed early so she could return to her dreams.

Vic found himself hating the spirit which shared this time with her. At the same time, he could not withhold this from her, lest all the color fade completely from her daytime eyes.

The thought that she could not see the color of him anymore was hard to bear. The thought that she could not see the color of her baby was impossible to bear and made him feel like his heart was being torn apart all over again. He hoped and prayed that, as the sun returned in strength to move the winter sky back towards spring, so, too, would the light come back into her days. Then, her need for nighttime dreams of color would fade.

January merged into February. The sun grew brighter and the days grew longer but, yet, the dreams continued. Her daylight colors seemed to fade ever faster. Now, they were barely lasting the morning. Sometimes, he would find her gone to her bed and sleeping after lunch. It was as if she must return to the one place which was real for her. It made his heart ache to see her like this. She was his girl of fading, fading colors- except in her world of dreams.

Now, Vic often spent sleepless nights trying to understand who or what it was which invaded her dreams. But while she often walked and talked in her sleep, it seemed it was never again to a known person.

Susan never spoke any name. It seemed her partner was a faceless, soulless being. But, always, she returned to commune in this place of colored dreams. After each set of two nights watching her, Vic needed to return to the helicopter base to sleep.

Susan continued to be sweet to him, though now, she was often irritable with her children and others. But, more and more, it seemed her eyes no longer looked towards the daylight but only to the night. It was as if he and others of the world were fast fading from her view and, as they did, the colors faded, too.

Vic could feel quiet desperation seep into him. He had found this girl, his wife. He had loved her and she had come back to him in body and soul. Why had he not just taken her to a far-off place, one where she knew nobody and the past could never reach her? She had a new identity. They could have gone and lived anywhere in the world, unknown to all.

Instead, Vic had chosen to bring Susan back to the simple and comforting reality of an older familiarity. He had been trying to give her connections back to her distant past from which to build a new and different reality. But, while the past brought back connections, some were good and some were bad. It seemed she could not keep a separation between them.

Now, as the bad came surging back, Vic felt it was slowly tearing her apart. He could feel it making fractures in her soul and breaking apart the inner core of the new person he had found. It was as if her dreams opened cracks between two different people who were residing in one body. These cracks let in the colors, but they also let other shadowed things slip through as well.

Vic did not know for sure that the people or things of her dreams were bad. However, he could see them sucking her vitality away. Now, her life force was fully consumed at night and not enough of it remained for her daytime life with him and her family. He wished he knew what to do. His aunt had glimpses of this shadowed self. She had become a quiet supporter in his corner. Others saw less. His wife, the consummate actor, could hide it easily from them. Even the fact that she now was able to live a double life, spoke of the return of a duplicitous part to her soul. It had not been there when he found her, again.

Vic remembered how Susan had warned him on their first meeting, "I do not know if you can find her, or if you will ever be able to bring her back again." These words now resonated with a ring of truth. It was as if the more she discovered about the woman she was in her past, the less remained of herself in the present and for the future. He felt his despair grow at reliving all the loss anew.

He did not think it was a sickness of the body. It seemed to be an illness of spirit. It seemed as if another spirit, perhaps a malevolent crocodile spirit, was stealing away the soul of the person he loved.

One night at the helicopter base, when it was daytime in Australia, he rang Alan and told him of his fears. Vic asked Alan if he would talk to Ross and Charlie, to see if either of them could offer any ideas of what he might do. If it was a disease of the mind, perhaps their medicine could help. Or perhaps, if it was a spirit, whether human or crocodile, which was drawing her back, the way it had before- then, maybe some aboriginal spirit man could help.

The next day, Alan called him back. He said he had talked to Charlie and there was a package coming in the mail which Charlie hoped might help. It was heavy and had cost a good bit of money to express post it. However, he should have it in a day or two. Charlie said it was a powerful medicine against the dreaming spirits- a crocodile spirit to fight a crocodile spirit.

Ross called later that day. He had no solutions. He talked to Vic about psychoanalysis but admitted that, in her case, it was probably a waste of time. On the other hand, he thought Charlie's idea was worth a try.

Chapter 42 – Crocodile Stone

Vic returned from the base to the farm on the third day, nervous with anticipation. An express box sat on the kitchen table waiting for him. It bore his name, written large, in black Texta. He picked it up and felt it was heavy.

Susan was out visiting with her aunt, so he had the place to himself. Vic took the box to the bedroom and opened it. Inside it, nestled in bubble plastic, was a black stone. It was flat and round, as if river smoothed, but it was imbued with a dark, polished texture. It looked as if the stone was coated in an impregnable matter which had rubbed it smooth and into a dull luster.

Vic carefully lifted it out. It sat, neat and full, in the palm of his hand. He could feel it was infused with a presence and was emanating a silent force. It soothed his mind and spirit, like a healing balm.

He understood, without it being said, that it was intended for Susan to hold. It was meant to sit in the palm of her hand or rest against her body. Alan and Charlie had talked of the crocodile stone which had given her mind solace before. Perhaps, this was it and it could help again.

When Susan came into the kitchen, she was full of subdued brightness. It was as the light of the night was fading from her eyes already. Vic brought her to sit on the bed and asked her to close her eyes while putting her open hand out, palm up.

Susan complied without hesitation and Vic rested the stone in this place while closing her fingers around it. She seemed to want to open her eyes. So, he rested a finger on each eyelid and asked her to stay still and tell him what she felt. He could feel a calmness wash over both him and her. It was coming from her to him in the place where their skin was touching.

She said, "It is like a dream yet, I know I am awake. My mind is full of light- light and colors. I can see your color. I can see David and Anne's color. I can see my baby's color. I can even see the color of the sky. It is glorious and beautiful.

"It is as if, when I hold this stone, my mind sees through other eyes- eyes that are not my own. These eyes can see what mine cannot. But, because I am linked to it, I can see the things these eyes see, too."

Vic lifted his fingers from her eyelids. As he did, the shared vision faded. He watched her face intently as she looked at him. She said, "It is not so bright as it was before when you were touching me. But still- color remains. It is softer than before, but still a thing of beauty."

Susan kept looking at Vic with a beatific smile, saying, "The thing of most beauty I see is you. I had forgotten how wonderful you look."

Now, wherever they went, as she walked and talked, she carried the stone with her. It was mostly in an inside pocket where a part of it could rest against her skin. Sometimes, however, it was in her hand. It brought light back into her eyes and joy to her smile. It almost made her seem whole again. But, whenever she put it aside, the brightness faded and only the shadows remained.

Vic felt his anxiety fade as brightness returned to her eyes. It was not quite fully his Susan of old but, at least, when she held the stone, the fading colors became bright again. With them a light lit her face, like a shaft of sunlight.

Their life returned to a place of quiet joy.

He did not have her fully back but, having known the fear of losing her again, he better understood the preciousness of what he had regained. She had developed a renewed zest for life. He could see it flow out of her when she was playing with her children, talking to Anne, her parents and the old Kashmiri man or making plans for the upcoming weddings. However, it hid a brittleness. He felt it was just a shell encasing a shell- it was hollow inside.

Others seemed delighted to have the Susan of old back. *Perhaps,* Vic thought, *they had noticed more than he realized*. But he knew that, while it was better to have her in this place, he only held her by a thread. Only a thin line of contact ran between them, through a crocodile stone. The sickness was still in her soul. Sometimes, even now, he would glimpse it.

Vic wondered if, on the day she gave Mark to the crocodiles, whether a part of this crocodile's spirit had occupied her soul. Now, it seemed this part of the crocodile's spirit consumed her own spirit from a place deep inside her.

Vic knew he must find a tribal medicine man from the place of crocodile spirits, and see if he could heal her fully. The crocodile stone was working like a medicine pill would, keeping the disease at bay. However, it was no cure. The soul cancer was still there. Whenever the link with the crocodile stone was broken, the disease would return.

Still, it was something. It was a lifeline to buy time. This time was needed to find a full healing.

And somehow Vic now knew he must bring Susan back to the land of the crocodiles for this cure to happen.

Chapter 43– Last Will and Testament

It was now mid-March. It was only a little over a month to go until Anne's wedding and plans for it were well advanced. The days were much longer now. The grip of winter was easing and most of the snow was gone from the hillsides. The trees were all in bud, with early leaves. Flushes of early flowers were starting to poke up their heads in the meadows.

Anne was flying into England in two weeks. Once she arrived, Susan would take the children and stay with her parents in Reading for a fortnight. By doing this, she could share in the final preparations with her friend: going to the church rehearsals and the hens' night, amongst many other things.

David was flying into the country on Wednesday, three nights before the wedding. Most of the Australian part of the wedding party also arrived on Wednesday or the day after. Vic too would go there on Wednesday. He was taking the following week off from flying.

There was a bucks' night on Thursday. Vic would join other men from the Australian wedding party, along with Susan's brother and a couple of other 'down under' locals, to give David a proper Aussie send off. Friday was a quiet night before the wedding on Saturday. It was to be held in Greyfriars Church, a treasure of an old Franciscan building in the heart of Reading.

Susan and Anne had both been baptized and confirmed there, so it was familiar from both of their early lives. It was a place where Susan had taken Vic, a month ago, to sit quietly and meditate, when they visited her parents. That day, the old building, with seven hundred years of history, gave him a sense of calm and contentment as they sat amidst its lofty, soaring arches.

One night, when he was home from flying, Vic and Susan were curled up together in bed while doing their ritual of reading two pages of the diary together. It was an institution they had consistently maintained, resisting any temptation to skip ahead, determined to both know this man as fully as possible through the words he had written. They always took turns reading sections. Vic's concentration was a bit amiss tonight as he was thinking of the trips he was booked to make in the helicopter on the next day.

As Vic was reading his part, feeling dreamy, his eyes closed. The book slid from his hands. He made a grab for it and was able to just grasp the edge of the back cover. It fell open in his hand to a place without writing. A single sheet of paper fluttered out, floating in an unseen air eddy before it fell. Susan reached out and grabbed it. She turned it face-up so they could both read what it said.

Vic's eyes began reading the tight, small writing. He knew the hand which wrote it. Susan was looking at Vic, not the paper, saying, "I didn't know that was there. Perhaps I left a sheet of paper in it one day."

Vic shook his head. He had already read enough to know what it was. Part of him wished he could make it vanish, unread, for it was a love letter to Susan from another.

He knew the words belonged to Susan- but they both read:

Dear Susan,

If you are reading this it means I am dead. I know now that is the only way forward from here. One of us must vanish and I could not bear for it to be you.

I write this because I want to say goodbye. It seems important to me now to tell you that I love you and not vanish with those words never said.

They are words I have wanted to say to you since that first day on the boat when I met you face to face. I was already entranced by your image, glimpsed distantly on the Cairns shoreline, feet in little waves, hair flung back embracing the sun. What I must tell you is that I have loved you utterly since even before I first met you. It is only when brought to a place of no other choices that I can say it honestly.

"You probably wonder why I say this now and did not say it to your pleading eyes a short while ago. I cannot answer as I don't know. All I know is I couldn't give you false hope of a future together. That would have been an even worse lie.

There was a time yesterday when I was angry with you. Then I thought maybe I could kill you as I killed others. But I knew, in that instant when you tried to jump in front of the truck, that it was impossible. In a choice between me and you, you must live; my life is of less importance.

I'm sorry my actions have frightened you; I've seen fear of me in your eyes and I hate that. I understand why. Now I must hurt you no more. That leaves only one way. Soon, with the first light of dawn, that time will come, and my choice must be acted on.

I've just looked at your beautiful face as you lie sleeping. It's peaceful. I hope your dreams are good and you dream of happy times with me. There are so many memories of you in my mind now and the joy will never go away, it will be my last memory. I remember riding on the beach, sharing a helicopter dance, your eyes as I gave you the pendant and ring. Most of all I remember loving you, holding your body in my arms, your hair in my face, loving you over and over and over again. While I've had you like this so many times, as I watch you sleep, I ache to feel you again this way, just one more time.

Before I write a final goodbye, I must tell you a few practical things. In my briefcase, combination 2153, you'll find two things which I'd like you to have. Don't give them to others, at least not until you've decided for yourself what you want to do with them. The first is a pouch of precious stones. They're mine, bought and paid for in full by me. They're all of high quality. I think their value is at least two million dollars. They now belong to you. The second is my diary. It tells of what I've done over the last five years. I ask that you read it, so you know the good and bad of me. After this you may give it to the police or pass information in it to the families of others whose death I am responsible for. I wish I could feel guilt over them, but I don't, I didn't set out with the purpose of harming any of them. However, you must judge this and me with your own eyes and conscience.

I have made a will. It is set between the back leaf and cover of my diary, inserted into this space which is glued closed. It was witnessed by two friends I trust. It leaves all I possess to you and gives details of what I own.

Now all is said and I must say goodbye. I leave this where I hope you will find it, alongside your English passport which contains a picture of your smiling face. I have just touched and kissed this one last time. I would kiss the real face, but that may awake you too soon.

Now I go to the water's edge. My own crocodile totem will talk to the dreamtime crocodile spirit of this place until our spirits are as one. Then I'll swim out to join the crocodiles and offer my body to them as a gift. I'll wait until your eyes are open, before I go. I'd rather not give you this pain, but you must see me go to know I have gone, so as to have freedom from me again.

Vic and Susan sat in silence, for a long time after each had read the letter. Susan seemed less moved than Vic was- even though the letter to her.

Vic sat there with tears oozing from his eyes and breaths feeling like sobs. He thought of the bravery of his friend and of what might have been. Mark had given Vic his blessing to take and love this woman.

This paper was a message to Vic as much as to Susan. It was a message from a brother. Part of him wished this brother had lived to share this joy, instead of Vic. To be able to watch his children grow and throw them in the air while smiling his roguish grin.

For Susan, Mark was but a name and a few disjunct images. He was not the life force Vic remembered. It was left to Vic to grieve for what Susan had lost. Vic grieved for the loss of his friend, a full life unlived. Now, he felt he was back in the river, with his friend pushing him ever on. God how Vic missed Mark!

Susan, in contrast, was practical, saying, "He talks about a will. Did you know of a will? Were you one of the witnesses?"

Vic was too distracted to talk of this or look into it any further at this time. He told Susan to let it wait for another day. She nodded, cuddled into him and fell asleep. For a long time, he sat and stared at the sheet of paper.

It was written for her, but the words were balm to his soul. Sometimes, in the dark days of the winter past, he had felt rage and anger towards this man. Vic had blamed Mark for stealing away the soul of the woman he loved each night while also dimming the light in her eyes. Even if it was true, and he felt it was not, Vic could not begrudge this man a part of her. He, Vic, was the inheritor of the sunlight while this man lived only in shadows.

Vic felt a great sense of responsibility to carry out his friend's wishes. He had witnessed the will and intended to carefully ensure it was done. He would do all he could to fulfill the trust he had been given to care for the woman they both loved. It was enough.

Vic was roused early, with the daylight but a gleam. It was by Susan, saying, "You asked me to call you early to drive to work. Now, you must go. I will leave the will for your return."

It was four days before he returned. Then, their lives were busy for the next two days. The diary got left aside. It was sitting on the dresser in the corner for the whole visit, and for the next and the next. They both thought of it, but neither wanted to open it and take from it the hidden will. It had already waited there for more than three years now, what was a little longer?

The next thing they knew, it was time for Anne to arrive the following day. Their free time went into packing and preparations for Susan, and the children, to go to Reading. Vic took them to the train, waved goodbye to them and drove back to the farm. Early the next day, he would return to Aberdeen for five days more of flying before he joined the wedding party.

It was quiet in the house, on this night, for it was just him and his aunt. Absent was the usual sound of children's play and laughter. He went to the bedroom and put a pillow to his face, in order to feast on the smell of her which still remained. He saw the diary in the corner. It was time.

Vic could see how the back cover bulged slightly. He found a penknife and lifted the glued sheet which bound the cover. There were several sheets of paper in the space, divided into two sets. He extracted the first set. It was familiar to him and was titled:

LAST WILL AND TESTAMENT OF VINCENT MARCO BASSINGHAM

It was relatively straight-forward. Other than pages which referred to as Attachments 1 and 2, which sat behind the signed document, it said:

I leave all those things I own and possess to Susan MacDonald, except for the bequests I make as detailed in Attachment 1.

Attachment 2 provides a list of assets which comprise my estate and which I authorize the trustees of my estate to dispose of as they see fit.
I name as executors of my estate, Vikram Campbell and Buck Mathews.
I further ask that the executors contact and make arrangement for the ongoing support and protection of my African child, Nathaniel Mark Nockezume. I give them full discretion as to the manner in which they do so. He lives with his grandmother in Mozambique at the address in Attachment 1

Below this writing were two signatures. Vic recognized these as Buck's and his own. A third signature of Vincent Marco Bassingham, the man he only really knew as Mark B, sat below their signatures. Mark was still the best friend he'd ever had and he would follow Mark's instructions to a T.

Chapter 44 – African Boy

David's 'Buck's Night' was a night straight from his Australian home. To Vic, it seemed that most of the voices in the crowd had broad Aussie accents. Buck and Julie had come over as part of the gang. Their trip for the wedding was to be followed by some European sightseeing. Alan and Sandy were here, too. They were talking of the plans for their own outback wedding in Darwin. The night started at the hotel where they were staying. It began with pre-drinks for the whole Aussie wedding party and was gradually added to by locals, such as: Anne and Susan's joint friends from their English lives and a few well-heeled, legal eagles from the city firm which Anne had worked for previously. Once all the boys were assembled, they took a bus and moved on following the best 'Aussie style' towards central London. They preceded to do the whole nine yards with a succession of pubs and increasingly raunchy venues. They finished the evening by going to a late-night stripper. By then, though, David was in no state for any serious action.

Sandy professed disappointment at being unable to come with the boys. Instead, Sandy, Julie, Susan and Anne and Susan's Australian cousins decided on their own impromptu girls' night out together. They decided to have this night in a different part of the town to ensure their paths did not cross.

The next day was not wonderful for the boys. Hangover cures aplenty were passed out: greasy bacon and eggs or hair of the dog. None of these cures really worked. But slowly, as the day wore on, the passage of time ensured they all began to feel better.

The Australians, and others from out of town, had taken over a large part of the hotel in downtown Reading. The smoking room was now the place of the boys. They wore dark glasses to avoid the glare and nursed watered down drinks. They were accompanied by female partners who showed a complete lack of sympathy for the men. This was evidenced by how they sipped Gin and Tonics, consumed plates of fries and mocked their men folk for being soft and not able to handle their drink.

Vic was one of the better off amongst them, although he had still enjoyed the best night out he'd had since he left home. The 'Aussie' humor worked best for him, as it was full of mocking asides and little put-downs. David was mocked by brothers and others both.

However, that was last night. Now, he needed to talk to Buck, his fellow will executor, about Mark's bequests and directions. Vic and Susan had only spent brief moments together since his arrival at her family's house, getting there after dark the night before last. She had been busy with a church rehearsal once he arrived and, by the end of a night filled with many meetings and greetings, they had both slumped into bed, exhausted.

Yesterday morning, Vic had only mentioned the will to her and told her, briefly, of the contents. He wanted to talk to Buck first. It was up to the two of them to work out the details. Susan was the main beneficiary, once all the dust had settled. However, their job would have to come first: to interpret and follow Mark's written instructions.

The stones Susan had discovered were now stored in an Edinburgh bank vault. There was a conservative estimate placing their value at two to three million pounds plus. It was likely a big plus, due to their quality. However, they were Susan's private inheritance, as the letter from Mark made clear. Even though Susan said they should be considered as part of the estate, Vic did not agree with her on this. For now, he planned to forget about them.

Vic had to give it to Mark- he knew his rocks and had collected the best ones. The two gem assessors had drooled over them and said they might be worth up to five million pounds, maybe even more. Perhaps the real value of what was sitting in that one little pouch was equal to the rest of all his assets combined. However, that was the business of another day.

There was the pile of things in the will which he needed to discuss with Buck now. There was a long list of properties, shares and many other assets. Vic's own rough estimate was the list easily translated into upwards of ten million Aussie dollars' worth. In the currency of this place, it would be above five million English pounds. The bequests to come out were pretty simple: an amount of $500,000 for him, the same amount for Buck and few, smaller amounts for others such as Mark's Uncle and some other bush mates. Vic estimated these would add up to about another couple hundred thousand Australian dollars.

Whatever was left after these bequests was to be the property of Susan. This seemed doubly fitting as it would become Mark's own children's inheritance one day. However, Mark had not known this when he gave everything else to her. In due course, Vic and Buck would talk to

Susan together, in their joint role, about how to best realize this value. They would help her decide what to sell, what to hold and all those mundane details.

What Vic really wanted to discuss with Buck, most of all, was what to do about the African boy, Nathaniel. Mark clearly named him as his own child. He had asked them to ensure his care and support, as they saw fit. But, apart from a name and address, they knew nothing about him. They didn't know the exact place where he lived, what his circumstances were, or even an age.

They now sat and talked. Vic had two copies of the will in an envelope- one for him, the other for Buck. The original had been left with the family lawyer, where it was locked in his office safe for safe keeping. Vic passed a copy to Buck saying, "I see your signature here, alongside mine. I think you have seen this before." He sat silently as Buck read and digested it. When Buck was done reading, he let out a whistle.

"I knew the old bastard was loaded! It was obvious, despite his simple life. But all this! It somehow seems wrong to take it from him after what he has done. Perhaps the money should go to the families of those he harmed. What about you? I see you are named, like me, as a beneficiary."

Vic said, "I have thought about it, the same as you. At first, I thought I should not take it. Susan has plenty of money to meet her needs and I can make my own money. Then, I thought: *He was my friend. He wanted me to have it.* So, I will accept his wishes and take it with gratitude- as should you.

"You have always talked about buying your own place to run cattle, back home in Queensland. One separate from your family's farm. Mark would have wanted you to have that. He would far rather your farm be a continuance of what he once owned: good horses in paddock and cattle growing fat, rather than a pile of money or shares in a bank vault.

"For me, I have a yen to return to the land of my birth. I think Susan would like it, too. We have not properly talked about it, but since seeing her Aussie friends she has said it. She said she would like to live in bright sunlight and see her best friend, Anne, often. Perhaps, I shall buy a new helicopter to return to the life I once knew. I must talk it fully through with her first, but if she agrees, I think that is what I will do.

"However, the main reason I wanted to talk to you today is to decide what to do about the one other person Mark names in his will. The one he names not as a beneficiary, but as a child of his. I know nothing of Africa other than what Mark told me about how he once fought there, as a mercenary. The bullet fragments in his arm tell of that, too. But it appears he did much more than that: he sired a brat, a child with an African name. All I know is this boy lives in Mozambique somewhere. It must be a small village. I cannot find it on a map. Did Mark ever tell you anything of this?"

Buck shook his head.

Vic went on, saying "So, we must discover this child. We could pay someone to go and find him, using money from the estate. But I do not think this is what Mark intended- something done at arm's length. As he is Mark's own, I feel I must meet him and know him, to know best what to do. I don't just want to send money. Mark would have wanted more than that. I think we must make sure this boy has the chances his father never had. Education perhaps, maybe something more, not only things- but the care and support of Mark's friends. So, what do you think? Should I go and find him? Should I take Susan and the children or go alone?"

Buck said, "You are coming home in a month for the weddings. Why don't you leave a week early and fly by Africa? A flight to South Africa would get you close. Then, once you find him, you will see the way it is, what he is like, how old he is and what he needs. Only then will you properly know. Once it is done, you can fly on to Perth and up to Darwin in time for the weddings. I could come, too, but this is our first trip away to this side of the world. Julie has my life of visiting castles all mapped out. So, if needed, I could leave her for a part and come, too. But, in truth, I would rather it was just you. We'll talk on the phone, if needed. But I think it is something you should decide when you get there. And, yes, Susan must come, too. Any decision you make must be a decision of two."

With that said, that was how it was. The wedding passed by and was great. They returned to Scotland to pack up their lives there. They flew out a week earlier than planned to Johannesburg. From there, they flew on to Maputo. It was only two hours' drive from here to the village where the boy lived. They rented an apartment on the beach for the week. It was a place of white sand and a view out across the Indian Ocean. Somewhere over the horizon, to the north-east, sat the fabled land of Madagascar. The exotic sound of the name had always resonated in Vic's mind, along with images of its strange monkeys called lemurs. Further away, east, was his own home. It was a mere ten thousand kilometers away- if he could but glimpse it. It felt closer than it had for a long time knowing it was the next real land past the sea and sat over the distant horizon. It felt like a cord pulling him back.

On the first day in Mozambique, they rested and relaxed by simply enjoying their children's play on the beach. Little Vic was now six months. He sat like a Buddha, grasping handfuls of sand and trying to eat it, while goggling at his older brother and sister. Susan had bought a new bikini which showed off her 'back to flat' figure. Vic feasted his eyes on her. He never got tired of looking at her.

The second day they hired a four-wheel drive vehicle with a local guide to drive the vehicle, who spoke the language. He took them to the village by a mix of roads and tracks. It had an unpronounceable name. It was not much more than a collection of mud houses and a few houses made of tin.

Their guide made inquiries as to where the boy, Nathaniel, lived. Once he had directions, he paid the local boys some centavos to keep the car safe while they walked there along a dusty footpath. It was a simple hut, but better looking than most, as it was neatly swept and clean. As they came close, the word went around of who they were seeking. An old woman came out and conversed with their guide, who translated.

"She is Nathaniel's grandmother. The boy lives with her as his mother is long dead. She died of the wasting disease when the boy was only a few months old. You call it 'Aids.' The father lives in a faraway country, somewhere across the ocean, a land she thinks is Austria. He visits occasionally and gives her some money. It usually gives her enough to pay for him to go the village school, where the boy is now, and to buy books and food. The father has not been to visit now for over three years. The money remaining for school fees and other expenses is now running low."

Vic found an old passport photo of Mark and passed it to the interpreter to show to the old lady, saying, "Please ask her if this is the father?"

The woman looked at the photo and nodded intently. She let forth a stream of words where the name 'Marco' was heard.

The translator interposed, breaking her story into bite-sized bits, making her pause as he translated each part, "This man, Marco, is a good man. He loved my daughter. She was a prostitute until she met Mark. Soon after they met the sickness made her unable to work. Because we are poor here, she worked around the mines of the Witwatersrand. It was how she supported herself and me. She always sent me money, but I saw her rarely.

"One day, this man Mark, brought her home. She was expecting a baby and getting sick. He gave me money and asked me to care for her. He came when he could to see her, telling me he had met her when working in a mine. He was convinced the child was his. She had promised him that, since she had been with him, she had not been with other men.

"For six months, from when the child was nearly due and she was very sick, Mark stayed with us. He helped me care for her and the child until she died when the baby was only a few months old. He was very sad, but he said he had to work to make money and he could not care for a small baby.

"After that, he would come when he could- maybe every second year. Other times, he would send me money- at least twice a year. It was enough for me and the boy to live on and to buy books and pay for school when he grew older. But no money has come now for three years. I am too old to work so it is hard to survive.

"Nathaniel is a good boy, but there is nothing for him here in the village. He is too clever for his own good. He has learned to speak and read English. Before, he used to study and read many books. But now, the older boys and men of the village are trying to lead him astray. Because he is clever and can speak to strangers, they think it will make them rich. So, they get him to buy and sell things for them- even things they do not own.

"He listens to me, still, but it is getting much harder. He knows we need money. He thinks that their promises of riches will help. But I know trouble is coming. One day, he will end up in jail or beaten by bigger men.

"Can you take him away and give him the chance I cannot? You are his father's friends and I know it is what he would have wanted. Soon the boy will not listen to me. Then, I will be unable to control him and keep him safe.

"I am an old woman and will die soon. But I want a better life for the son of my daughter. I know that this man, Mark, would have wanted it, too."

They sat with her and she served them food from the little she had. They would have protested, but their guide said she would be offended if they refused her hospitality. They ate, dipping their fingers in a common pot of corn gruel and eating it with the accompanied pieces of coarse bred. There was also a tea-like liquid served in earthenware cups.

As they waited, they exchanged further stories. The grandmother told them stories of this boy becoming a man, of his own mother as a child and of the village. They, in turn, shared stories of their own families.

Vic, with his dark skin, was a source of general curiosity. This was particularly true when he explained how most of the others in his family had a darker skin than him. He explained it was nearer to the color of the guide and old lady. It was something they had in common and created a sense of kinship between them. Overall, it was a friendly exchange. However, since all the communication had to come through the guide, it was hard to fully understand. At last, a shout went up in the town. Morning classes were over and Nathaniel was returning.

Nathaniel was a sturdy boy with a serious face and the gawky, maturing body of someone in between childhood and adolescence. They were told he was twelve, soon to be thirteen. He was expecting visitors, hearing village gossip on his way home. He now looked awkward and self-conscious in the face of these strangers, ones who had come here solely to meet him.

However, once they explained their connection to his father, he was full of chatter. He particularly loved Vic, whose skin was almost the same color as his own, along with the chubby baby of the same name who had small brown hands and face. Soon, he had the baby on his own lap. Little Vic was chortling with delight at this new face to poke and hair to pull.

Nathaniel's English was surprisingly good. He proudly told them how, each time his father had visited, his father had taught him new English words and made him read from the English books which he kept stored in his part of the hut. After an hour of talking, they knew that they had reached a point of decision. They could either leave money and go, with arrangements for more money as needed, or they could try to do something further.

They asked the guide to make their excuses, for a minute, while they walked outside, following along the dusty track. Small village children rushed immediately to their feet, calling out at them with curiosity. Vic asked Susan what she thought.

She spoke without hesitation, "We must bring him with us, offer him the chance of a new life." Vic felt as she did, but knew it was not so simple.

He said, "We have five days yet in Mozambique. We had talked of making a trip to a national park and staying there for two nights to see the wildlife. Why don't we do that? We can invite Nathaniel to come with us. We can at least ask our guide about how that part of our trip can be arranged. Then, if Nathaniel spends those days with us and it still seems right, we can see how we can legally bring him out to live with us.

"If it is not possible, at least we can continue to be his friends. We can continue to support him and his grandmother. We can even visit them again."

With this being agreed, they returned to ask the guide how these things could be done. The guide said that, if his grandmother approved, Nathaniel could come and stay with them in Maputo until they left.

As for going to a national park, that part was easy. He suggested they go to Limpopo National Park. It ran along the mighty Limpopo River and adjoined Kruger National Park in South Africa. It was world famous for its wildlife.

It was a four-hour drive in the four-wheel drive vehicle they had hired. The guide said he would continue driving for them. Bringing one more person along with them really made no difference. All of them would fit in the car. The guide stated could continue to drive them, if they wished. He knew the road well and was happy to be their guide for this part, too. All it would cost them was another three days of guide fees- which were actually very cheap for tourists.

He offered to show them all the wildlife: lions, elephants, giraffes, zebras and much, much more. He even had a relative there who ran a lodge for guests. He said he would ensure they got an extra good deal.

Vic could see this man's business brain working out how to get the most from his tourist visitors. He did not mind. After all, Mark was paying for this bit, and they knew he could well afford it. And he had also asked them to do something like this.

Therefore, Limpopo National Park it was. Vic said this to Susan. She had been busy talking to her children and Nathaniel.

She grinned, "To the 'great grey-green greasy Limpopo River, all set about by fever trees,'… Seeing that would be something. Perhaps we could even see the elephant child of Rudyard Kipling's story. Oh, do let's go."

With this statement of agreement, the guide asked the grandmother. She gave a beaming smile which told them of her agreement without any words being needed. They invited the boy, themselves, conversing with him in his well-spoken English. They could tell he was delighted for he was grinning widely. He said it had been a long time since he had left the village. It sounded like a whole new and exciting adventure to him.

They said nothing about his leaving his grandmother and coming to Australia, at this time. They simply talked to him of coming with them to Maputo and Limpopo National Park for the next five days. His eyes told them how desperately he wanted to come.

With everything set, Nathaniel packed his clothes, along with a few other belongings, in a plastic shopping bag and sat in the car. He was sitting between the other children, who thought he was totally wonderful, being a new grown-up, as well as a play friend.

The next morning, the family packed into the car, with their guide, and drove inland until they came to the National Park set on the mighty Limpopo River. The first evening, they stayed in the lodge their guide had recommended. It looked out over the Limpopo River's bank.

On the bookshelf, Susan found a copy of the 'Just So Stories' by Rudyard Kipling. It was much thumbed by many other readers. In the falling dusk, she read the story of the Elephant's Child to her assembled family.

As she spoke of the broad hippopotamus aunt, who smacked the Elephant's Child with her broad, broad hoof, they watched a hippopotamus rise from the water and make a mighty yawn. Soon after, walking along the river bank, came a group of elephants with a baby elephant following close behind its mother. It looked just like they imagined the Elephant's Child. They were full of 'satiable curiosity' to discover this new world. Fortunately, of crocodiles, there was no sign.

The next day, they drove out onto wide grassy plains which were dotted with zebra, giraffe and innumerable antelope. They watched a group of hunting lions as they fanned out in search of prey. Later, they saw a leopard resting in a tree, troupes of baboons and the dark-shadowed bulk of a rhino half-hidden behind thorn trees. None of them wanted their holiday to end.

By the end of the trip, it felt like Nathaniel belonged with them. He was just one more of their family. He asked endless questions of Vic- mostly about how he learned to fly a helicopter. Vic knew Nathaniel really wanted to fly in one and felt a strong desire to show him one. Maybe he could even to teach him to fly as he had been taught. Even though he looked very different from his father, Vic felt the shadow of Mark in Nathaniel. He could see it in his intense and focused interest in various things. Also, he saw it in Nathaniel's ability to concentrate and learn new things.

That night, when they were all back in Maputo sitting on the beach and looking across the vast Indian Ocean towards the continent on the other side, Australia, Vic and Susan asked him if he would like to come and live with them over there.

Now, Nathaniel had a shy and nervous look on his face- as if this fortune was beyond all dreams. He answered, "Yes. I will come if grandmother and the spirits will it," He gave a rapturous smile to his new brothers and sister.

On the final day before they caught the plane, they went and saw his grandmother to seek her permission. She gave it without hesitation, signing a legal paper with the imprint of her thumb, to indicate her agreement.

It was not an official adoption form, but a document proposing this was quickly drawn up by a Maputo lawyer, which declared their wish to adopt this boy, Nathaniel. It included a statement saying they had the agreement of his grandmother to do so. They did not know if it was legally valid, but it was a start. It was a promise of intent that they could build on.

Vic also promised he would come back, as needed, to complete the full process. It would take time for all the formalities to be done in both Australia and Mozambique, but they stated their willingness to give sponsorship and other undertakings, as required. Formal adoption was what they proposed.

In the meantime, they arranged for a payment of $100 Australian dollars a month to come to the grandmother. This payment would also come with an extra $20 month commission to their guide in return for him ensuring the money got to her. He would also make sure that any other needs of both her and her grandson were met. They also promised the guide a bonus of $1000 if he could ensure the legal adoption steps were completed quickly. He would also receive another $1000 paid, as needed, to cover any expenses he had to meet along the way to achieve the adoption.

For their guide, this was a vast sum which he could use to buy a new life for himself and his family. He could even buy his own car for his business. With this, they were confident he would hold up his side of the deal. Even if he did not, it was only money. With more money, they could find someone else to do it if he failed to do so.

The lawyer was also left with a good retainer for the work he needed to undertake in the process. Once again, there was a promise of more money if success was achieved.

They had done all they could for now. They told Nathaniel, "One day, hopefully soon, we want you to join our family in a new home, far away."

Nathaniel nodded, saying, "Yes- if the spirits will it."

Susan hugged him to herself. The children hugged him, too, before they waved goodbye. Vic shook his hand and told him, "Soon, I would teach you how to fly a helicopter." Vic saw Nathaniel's face light up as he turned around to follow the rest of his family onto the plane.

Chapter 45 – Four Weddings and a Funeral

Actually it was three weddings on one day, not four. The fourth wedding had already happened and the funeral came later. But Susan, and her new best friend Cathy, always thought of this day as the day of four weddings and a funeral. Perhaps, it was because of the movie of the same name. The one with the 'oh so dishy Englishman' who they both thought was hot. Maybe it was also because this part of their story really began with the four wedding invitations which had arrived the week before Christmas. The first wedding had happened a month before. Now, it continued with many of the same cast of characters on another remarkable wedding day which followed. Then, the sequence concluded with a funeral, of sorts, a few days later. It was for the remaining parts of a man long gone.

So, Anne had married David. It was something which Susan felt hugely emotional about. It was an emotion of unfettered delight for both David and Anne. On the day of their wedding, with her as a bridesmaid, she had cried many more tears than she had on her own wedding day, the delight she felt on this occasion was almost equal to her delight at her own wedding day.

She knew, from stories others told her about herself, that she had been briefly involved with David and had even been engaged to him. But it was a vanished memory for her. Anne had retold Susan the story of her own first meeting with David. That had been back when he was with Susan and they were almost engaged. Anne took delight in saying how there was a primal spark of attraction between them both, on that first day. Even though they had not acted on it until much later, after Susan had formally broken the engagement and given Anne her blessing, she felt there was an inevitability to all which followed. They were like two attracted magnets which had finally fused. Susan could see their relationship had a rightness to it, in a way which she and David had not had.

She liked David, though. She could feel his charm and could see his good looks. However, he did not melt her insides, the way Vic did, with a single look. She also knew how her own vanishing had torn at David and Anne, forcing them to delay this day. They had been separated over and over, continuing for more than two years, while Anne searched for her.

Now this wedding had a right feeling. It was long overdue for them to formalize their life together. After the ceremony, they were off on a month-long honeymoon, travelling the globe and going to more countries than Susan could count. They returned just in time to celebrate this triple wedding.

On that girl's night out in Darwin, Anne had told her, when Susan had asked about her modest drinking, that she thought she was expecting. It redoubled Susan's delight. Susan then shared her own news that, this time, they would do it together. She told Anne how, only two weeks ago, she had got the positive test result herself. Now that she and Vic had decided to return to Australia to live, it was even possible that they could have their babies together. It would feel almost as if their babies were twins.

Today, both she and Anne wore bridesmaids' dresses. Susan wore one on behalf of Cathy and Anne on behalf of Sandy. It would be lovely to stand side-by-side in the combined bridal party.

It was strange how this event had come about. Three groups of people who had been unknown to each other at the start of last year and two of the couples unknown to each other until after Susan's own marriage last year, had struck up friendships almost overnight. All of them had also decided to get married to their respective partners.

When one couple told the other of wedding plans in Darwin, the second couple admitted they had almost identical plans. Soon after this, all three couples were out for a meeting and drink. It turned out, when they compared notes, all had wedding plans for Darwin in the same week.

Almost as a lark, one person said, "Why don't we just do it all together?"

Five other heads nodded. With this, it was effectively settled.

After that, it was just about figuring out how.

A place of great emotional resonance for all was East Point- the place where Darwin Harbor met the sea. Here, Alan, Sandy, David, Anne, Buck, Julie and Vic had gathered in much sadder times for the opening of a 'Missing Persons' memorial.

The names of Susan Emily MacDonald and Cathy (Fiona) Rodgers, along with others who were also missing, were inscribed on a stone block. Cathy and Susan's names were there still, along with metal plaques which gave the details of when they were last seen before going missing and, now, with a couple lines added about each of their returns. Two other names on the list of over 50 had similar, joyous returns told on their plaques. The fates of the rest remained still unknown.

This was a place of hope- as well as sadness. With the link between all these couples through this story, along with their love of this place with its north-western vista which looked over the vast ocean towards Indonesia, they all had agreed this was the perfect place for their wedding ceremony to be held. Now, on a Saturday in May, they assembled to marry. The late afternoon sun fell towards the sea and made glistening lines on the watery horizon as the ceremony began.

They each had their own individual celebrant marry them, according to their own beliefs. There was a Presbyterian Minister for Cathy, a civil celebrant for Alan and Sandy and a rabbi to mark Beck's Jewish heritage. All assembled there stood as witnesses for the three ceremonies which, together, took an hour. By the end of the third ceremony, the sun was only a hand's breath above where the sea met the sky.

None of them were overly religious. However, all of them felt a sense of destiny and awe at how life had drawn them together. A central figure to all was the aboriginal man, Charlie. He was a friend to all of them. All of them had shared his wife's catfish curry and forged their friendships around his table. Charlie began his speech by welcoming them all to his country, Larrakia land. He spoke first and then a second time, at the end. The second time it was to do a smoking ceremony, wafting clouds of grey into to reddening sky. He began by calling on his rainbow serpent dreamtime ancestor to look kindly on these newly married people and guard their lives together.

When his speaking was done, the sun had fully set. The two hundred guests then moved on to the Fannie Bay Trailer Boat Club for an evening of stories, laughter and celebration.

It was a simple but inspiring ceremony. Susan was so glad to have been a part of it. She looked with equal pride at Vic. He was standing with Buck as a groomsman for Alan. This was something they had both shared in equally.

When the night was done, one ceremony remained for a later time.

It happened a fortnight later. Alan and Sandy were just returned from their honeymoon. It was a much smaller and more somber gathering: just Susan, Vic, Alan, Sandy, Buck, Julie, Charlie and Antonio, an uncle of Mark- his surviving next of kin.

They waited together in the front office of the coroner's building while the only two remaining parts of a man were released from its custody. These had sat there for over three years now while the legal processes around his murder and the inquest about his role in the disappearance of the "Lost Girls" had played out. When all the lawyers were done, this man's mortal remains, only a skull and a forearm, had been forgotten.

Finally, as Sandy tidied up in preparation for her own wedding, taking three months off work to try to have a baby, she had come across these two preserved items resting in a storeroom cabinet. At first, she had not known what to do. There was no obvious family seeking the return of the remains.

She decided to talk to the two best friends of the man, Vic and Buck, about what should be done. While Mark's father was still alive, Mark had explicitly stated in his will that his father was not to have any role in his estate or in any other parts of his affairs. So, they contacted his surviving uncle. This uncle had remembered Mark as a child, with affection. The three of them had agreed on the best plan to put Mark to rest.

What remained of Mark would be cremated, with the ashes divided into three parts. One part would go to his mother's family in Italy. These grandparents were too frail to make the journey, but wanted to bury some part of the grandson they never knew in their family graveyard. The second part of the ashes would be returned to the billabong from whence the body parts came. Vic and Charlie would do this together. It was to return a part to the crocodile spirit which had brought this to pass and whose power they had both experienced.

The third part belonged to Susan. It was for a role given by the man's request. It was something he had asked Susan to do in his farewell note- to take a part of him to a place in the desert he had shown her long ago.

She said she was not ready to do it, yet. She said she would only do this if she had remembrance of who he had been. This memory had not come back. Therefore, she delayed her part in putting his spirit to rest. She waited in hope that, one day, this memory of him would return to her.

Today was the beginning of this. When the small coffin shaped box containing the remains of Mark was brought out, Charlie took his agreed place in the front of the coffin, to lead the man's spirit home. The other four men each took a corner of the little box. Their wives walked with them, each with a hand resting on the box as a mark of respect. They placed the coffin into a waiting hearse and followed it in a funeral parade of two cars behind the vehicle.

They brought it to a private chapel next to the crematorium. Here, a priest of the church of Mark's ancestors would say his Catholic ceremony, to meet the request of his Italian family. Gathered inside the chapel were a handful of other friends. They had come from many places across the outback by personal invitation. They included: Vic's mother, uncle and sister, some miners from leases in unknown places, a store trader from Borroloola, Mick- a fey Irishman from Top Springs, and a few others- mostly with dark skins.

There were no outside observers of this unannounced ceremony. It was not something to advertise for there had been too many hurt by his actions. Yet, in these gathered people's hearts, there was a part which held real affection for the life of this man and good things he had done.

Four photos of the man adorned the chapel. One was from Buck. It showed Mark astride a horse. He had intense concentration on his face as he tamed a wild spirit. Another showed him arm in arm with Vic and Vic's mother- his second family. A third photo showed a small boy going fishing with his uncle, many years ago. The final one was of a mother with a baby in arms: Rosalie holding little Vincent Marco Bassingham. Together, they seemed to make a fitting tribute to the tragic story of the boy's passage into manhood. It was little enough, but it felt as if some good parts of his memory were held and valued by his true friends.

Uncle Antonio, Vic and Buck each told a story of a boy and man, one who was a friend to many in the bush. A few others told their stories, too.

Then, it was done. As the words 'Dust to Dust, Ashes to Ashes' were spoken, what remained of the man they had known passed from sight.

Vic and Buck had tears, as did Mick and some others. Susan remained dry-eyed and wishing for a memory to give her own tribute to this man.

Chapter 46 – Hidden Within Golden Light

Vic felt very nervous. Today, he, Buck, Charlie and Alan planned to take a part of Mark's ashes to the place of the crocodile. It was a billabong on the Mary River, about a hundred miles to the east of Darwin. He had hoped to limit it to just the four of them, but the others from the funeral party said they were coming, too. The only one who didn't come was Mark's uncle. He caught a plane to Italy, taking his own small casket to the family there.

What frightened Vic was not the crocodile or other unnamed terrors. It was bringing his wife to this place of horror. He had been staunchly opposed to her coming from the start.

Vic had discussed it with Charlie who had agreed, saying, "Bad medicine. Best she not come. Bad spirit. Maybe try take her, again."

Vic knew that Susan's mind was held together with 'not much more than' sticky tape. The calm seen from outside belied a place of turmoil within her.

Since the ceremony for Mark, she had begun dreaming again. It seemed the crocodile stone was losing its power. She would push it away from herself in the night. Then, she would dream. At first, Vic tried to push it back into contact with her. However, it was as if it burnt her nighttime skin, for she would flinch and recoil from its touch. During the daytime, she would hold the stone- at least at times. Sometimes, he would discover that she had set it aside. In those times, she would sit there in a semi-dream state and appear unaware of the world around her. Vic felt he was losing Susan all over again. This time, however, it was totally beyond his power to stop it.

Part of Vic felt he should abandon his plan to return to this land and, instead, go back to Scotland. It seemed, as she came closer to the place of the crocodiles, their power to invade her mind grew. He discussed it with Charlie and Ross. Neither had any real solution. Ross suggested either a dream center for night observation or some psychological tests. He said this was the only medicine could offer her. All Charlie could suggest was that he talk to his own medicine man. In turn, this man could then talk to the Baru people, those entrusted with care of the crocodile spirits, to see if there was anyone who knew how to take this possession away from her.

Part of the problem was Susan did not seem to understand what was happening. With this naivety, Susan was determined to go to the place of the crocodiles and take part in the return of Mark's ashes. Along with this return, they hoped the part of his spirit which seemed to belong to the crocodiles of this place would return to it, for good. As her wishes coincided with his plans, there was no keeping her away. It seemed to Vic, despite her saying she could not remember Mark, that some part of the crocodile spirit which connected both Mark and her to this place, was what drove her on.

Despite all the cautionary words spoken by Charlie and the alarm running through his mind, Vic found himself completely unable to stop her from coming.

She said she was sure it was something she was sure she must do. She said believed it may help her regain her memories. She said it with such a hunger of anticipation- it both frightened him and gave him hope.

Perhaps she was actually right. Maybe she had to return to meet the devil in his lair, to know it and leave it there. But Vic knew this was fraught with danger.

Despite knowing this, his fear and caution were to no avail. They were going today, and she was coming- there were no 'ifs,' or 'buts' about it. The one thing which reassured Vic was the fact Sandy was there, too. She still seemed to have a power to see inside Susan's mind. Vic had to trust Sandy to be the watcher and to pull his wife back if danger threatened.

In the early dawn, just when the first traces of light were flushing the eastern sky, they loaded up and got ready to go. The children were staying with Charlie's wife, Rosie, for the day. Rosie would take good care of them. Vic's mother would help as she was there too. Vic had no concerns about his children's safety.

As they were climbing into the car to depart, another car pulled up next to them and the occupants got out. It was Ross and Beck. It turned out Sandy had invited Beck. Ross was determined to go wherever Beck went. Sandy told Vic of the day she and Beck had held the crocodile stone and how their minds had linked through it- like crocodile sisters. Because of this, they had decided to come together. Then, there would be two minds and two bodies watching Susan, which they had both decided was better than one.

They divided themselves between Alan and Charlie's Toyota's and were on their way. In the back of Charlie's vehicle was the body of a small pig. Charlie had bought from a pig hunter friend, only a bite- sized morsel for a large crocodile. They had placed a small slit in its belly and into this opening, inserted the ashes, which were now embedded in a ball of solid glass. They intended for this part of Mark ashes to end up inside the huge crocodile, the one which had watched them before. If it swallowed the pig, it would have a part of Mark within it forever, as its own permanent crocodile stone.

In planning this day, Charlie had advised that, to placate the crocodile spirit, they should return a part of Mark's body to its belly. He wanted to return the forearm. This was not agreed by the others.

Instead, Alan came up with the idea of making the glass crocodile stone. Charlie had the idea of putting it inside a food offering. A glass craftsman had taken the ashes, placed them within a small bottle and melted it into a casing which sealed the contents inside a half-inch of glass. It was now a sort of time capsule.

All too soon, they came to the side of the billabong. At first, Susan stood back. It was as if she were watching it all within a dream. She was holding the flat black crocodile stone, which Charlie had given her, nestled within her hand.

Vic felt relief at her apparent willingness to watch from a distance. On either side of her, each with a hand resting on her shoulder, stood Sandy and Beck, as if they were communing with her, spirit to spirit.

Charlie carried the pig towards the billabong with Buck and Vic flanking him on either side. Alan walked behind the trio and to the side. He carried the Baru crocodile totem in one hand and his police service revolver in the other. The revolver was pointing away from the others, but he had it at the ready- lest some saurian beast emerge from the water.

They reached the side of the water. All was still and nothing was in sight. They placed their pig offering at the water's edge and stepped back a few paces while continuing to watch.

The water remained completely still, not a breath of air moved anywhere. Its surface was like glass.

They stood in a half-ring facing east. It was two hours after dawn. The sun was yet to clear the trees and light the water, so it sat in gloom.

As they stood, watching and waiting, the first shafts of sunlight struck the water. They first hit far out across the billabong and reflected directly into their eyes.

As the sun rose, the water surface turned to dazzling gold, blinding them in reflection. They stood still. They seemed unable to move from the blinding, golden light. A living essence sat at the center of the ball of golden light.

It was the time of the crocodiles. They all knew it in their souls. The crocodiles were coming to claim their own.

Chapter 47 – Crocodile Sprit Dreaming

Susan felt an implacable determination to see this through. Vic had tried to tell her not to come out, in fear of what this place might do to her. She had dismissed this as irrelevant. She knew it could do her harm, Vic was right in that, but not to come was inconceivable. She knew it was required of her.

Even though she could not remember the fateful day when she had been here before, it made no difference. She had been here before. Her hand had ended this man's life. She had a duty to fulfill. She did not know what was required of her, but she knew it would come to her once she returned.

Now, she stood at the back and waited. The stone gave her calm and connected her to other eyes. Through their eyes, she could see all the colors, so she continued to hold the stone in her hands. She found comfort in the hands of her friends which rested on her shoulders. She knew this link let them see through her eyes, as she could see through theirs.

It was a strange sort of linkage. It was as if four sets of images were running together through her mind. One was what her own eyes actually saw, in the here and now. Another two images came from her friends' eyes and minds.

It was what each of them saw, now mixed-up with what they remembered or knew about this place. In this stream of images from Sandy, she could see Sandy's memories of when she first came to this place. She'd been here with Alan. Together, they'd seen the giant crocodile. Sandy had been with Anne when she saw the giant crocodile again, as it called for the return of its own.

In Beck's mind were no images of this place from before. Beck saw it with fresh, curious and unafraid eyes. It gave Susan solidity and a reassuring courage. However, also in Beck's mind, Susan felt her guilt towards herself from when Beck had betrayed them by leaking information. Susan already knew about this since Cathy had told her. Beck did not know that Susan knew what she had done- hence the guilt.

Susan transferred a thought of forgiving acceptance to Beck, *it was done and no harm had come.*

She felt Beck's relief and knew Sandy felt it, too.

However, the strangest part of the mental image flow was the fourth set. They were the images of the hidden part of her mind which was closed to her. She could not see them directly for they were blocked from her. But the block did not hide them from her friends. Because of this, the other two women saw this day, as it happened in her mind from before. Through them, Susan could see it, too, as a reflected image.

This was the place of which she desired knowledge, so she encouraged them to look deeper. Now, it was as if the three of them were there on that fateful day. They were all reliving the awfulness.

She saw herself, lying in bed, in the predawn. Her wrists were handcuffed and chained to the car. She saw the terror of her expected fate bubbling through her mind. She saw herself pick up the knife and hide it in her clothes. She saw Mark squatting at the water's edge, lost in his own contemplation of his fate, making his peace. She saw herself summon her courage and rattle the chain to attract his attention as she formulated her plan of escape. She saw the surprised look on his face. He was not ready for this moment and wanted to stop time.

Susan saw him come and release her. Then, he fixed a bowl of warm water with a washcloth and soap. She saw the kindness and tenderness in his movements which she had never noticed on that day.

Susan saw herself walk away from him, take off her clothes, lay the knife on the ground and begin to wash herself, as his lustful eyes looked on. She saw herself call him over, seeking to create her opportunity and how he trustingly came. She saw and felt his hands as he stroked her breasts and washed her bottom. She saw herself pick up the knife, unseen, and turn towards him. She had the knife in hand and her eyes were seeking the right spot to strike.

At that point, her memory froze in horror. She could look no more. She knew what she'd done to kill him: the knife embedded in his chest, the timber crunching through his skull. She did not want to see this or see how she'd dragged his body to the water's edge. She did not want to see the crocodiles come, take him and tear apart his body. But, as she withdrew, a final image came to her. It was in the moments after the crocodiles had torn him apart, when blood only remained to stain the still water.

It was a miasma, sitting above the water, as if a half-formed cloud. She realized now that her eyes had seen it on this day but had not recognized it for what it was.

Now, she knew it. It was the spirit of a man and crocodile made one. The man had been taken within the body and had exchanged a part of his essence with the beast. However, it had not fully settled into its new home yet. A fragment of this fused crocodile spirit hung in the misty air which covered the water surface.

As Susan drew in a deep, sobbing breath on that fateful day, she had felt this cloud of presence drift over her. She had drawn into herself some part of this other being. Now, it was within her and would continue to be. This being was a thing of pain in its creation. A part of it lived on within her. It was fusing its soul with her own. She did not want it- but could not escape it.

Susan turned her mind away from this image now. She felt the others withdraw, too. They did so in sympathy with her pain.

Instead, she looked towards the golden light, allowing her mind to dwell there. The other eyes followed hers. They were linked to her will and would follow whatever she did. Three sets of eyes and bodies moving as one.

In the center of the light, she saw the three crocodiles come. They were far away and small in her vision, but big in her mind. She realized she was not seeing the physical creatures but seeing their spirits as they came towards her. These were ancient beings, spirits from out of the dreamtime. Today, they were temporarily inhabitants of these physical forms.

Mark faded from her mind. She understood now, because he was of their totem, that when he died, they had taken his spirit within their own and joined it to theirs. With the passage of time, since that day, his fusion with them was complete. They were now one soul, whole and united.

Susan also saw that, in her grief at what she had done on that day, she had taken a part of his leftover spirit within her. In exchange, she had sent part of her spirit with him, as if to provide him with comfort on his soul's passage. Essentially, she had given a part of herself away. It now lived with the beings who approached her. A part of them, also, lived on within her.

It was a fused part of her being now and could not be removed. As Mark belonged to the crocodile totem, so she too belonged. She could no more remove it than tear out her soul. For her to keep living, she must let this spirit inside her keep living, too.

Susan was it, it was her. When it could not find her in her waking hours, it found her in her dreams. When she held the crocodile stone in her hand, its own spirit sat in harmony with hers. This provided easy passage into her soul so this spirit did not have to tear at and overwhelm her mind to gain entry.

In that moment, Susan was at one with these other spirits which came towards her. She sought only to join them. She walked forward to where they came, towards the center of the golden ball of light. The other girls walked with her, hands still on her shoulders, locked together with common purpose.

Susan came to the water's edge and reached down to pick up the pig. She held it in her hands and walked further forward, now knee-deep in the water. She held the pig out in front of her.

Her mind spoke out. *This is a gift, but if you prefer, take me, too. There are three of you and three of us. You can each take one of us, if you want.*

The other girls' minds' spoke alongside her own, "Yes, take us, too."

As if in unison, three crocodiles' mouths opened wide, as if to say, "We accept your gift."

Susan heard a scream from the back of her mind, "NOOOOO!"

A body suddenly hit hers and knocked her sideways. At the same time, the other two were pulled along with her as they were still clasping hands.

The pig fell forward to float on the water. A huge set of jaws closed on it, slowly and with delicacy. It turned and swam away with parts of pig protruding from both sides of its mouth. It turned its head one way and a companion tore off a limb. It turned its head the other way and its other companion took another limb. It opened its mouth, swallowed what was left.

The three creatures disappeared as one. They faded into nothing as the water flowed over them.

Now people were rushing in and pulling her from the water. They were pulling out her friends, too. They remained crocodile spirit sisters.

The stone she had carried had fallen into the water and was somewhere deep below. It had returned to the place of the crocodiles.

Susan sat, as if in a trance, by the water's edge. Faraway, she could hear Vic shouting and screaming at her while he shook her to try to get her to listen. She could not hear the words. There was only her and she was lost in a crocodile spirit dreaming.

Part of her wanted to return to Vic, but another being filled her soul. She was powerless to act against it.

Chapter 48 – Crocodile Man

Vic was shaking with rage. How could she do this? How could she be so stupid and throw away her life, after all they had done together? He screamed at her. He shook her. He even slapped her.

Despite this Susan said not a word. She just sat there, unmoving, staring into another place which only her eyes could see.

The others sat there, too. In contrast, slowly, their minds cleared and their senses returned. They told of what had happened and of where they had been to, the place of the crocodile spirit dreaming.

They had not felt fear and had not perceived any danger. If there had been any danger, they had been incapable of caring in that moment.

They did not know for sure, but thought, the crocodiles were not seeking to harm them. They simply wanted to link with their spirits. Yet, they now acknowledged, what they had done was crazy and the danger was real.

The four men had just stood and watched, too. They had been frozen to the spot and unable to move. It was as if a spell had been cast, rendering all other life immobile, until something had passed. It was only Vic, in desperation, who managed to break free of the spell. He had been able to scream and fling himself at where the women stood, knee deep in water.

Once he moved, the others could move, too. All knew, deep down, that if the crocodiles had sought to really harm them- it would have been too late.

When Vic's anger cooled, he was distraught as he looked at his wife, being lost in a trance. He took her hand and sat beside her. He talked to her and told her he was sorry. He asked her to come back.

Still, Susan said not a word. She just sat there, staring into space.

Alan walked across and lifted her up. Her body was an automaton and did not move itself, but it did not resist him, either. He carried her to the car and placed her on a seat. Then Alan took Vic by the shoulders and walked him to the car. Alan pushed Vic into the car, so he sat beside Susan.

At home, Susan sat in a chair and said nothing. They dressed her, fed her and put her to bed. They woke her up in the morning. She moved when they moved her and did not resist- but it was the moves of reshaping a doll.

Vic wished he had never returned to this God forsaken place.

A week passed, then another. He had to do something. The children wanted their mother back. He wanted his Susan back.

He asked Sandy and Beck if they could better explain what happened at the billabong. He was hoping that together they might figure out how to reach her. However, for them, this memory and knowledge was now gone.

Ross visited each day and tried to hypnotize Susan, to reach her that way. Susan did not respond to anything Ross did. He took her to the hospital to run brain scans and connect her to an EEG machine. Her brain showed no physical damage, but it was working at the most basal level.

Ross said it was operating like a reptilian brain now: breathing, heart, digestion and other the basic functions. There were no signs of arousal in her higher brain centers. The slow, reptilian-like brain waves of her brain stem went on and on, unchanging.

Ross conferred with other specialists who suggested a range of drugs and electro-convulsive therapy which could be tried. Vic, however, would have none of this. He would not let anyone do things to her which may harm her more. Ross had no belief in their likely benefit, either.

After all this had been tried, Vic went and saw Charlie. Vic knew there must be someone to help him.

Charlie had been asking about how Susan had been doing. He felt a share of the blame in what happened to her. He sat silent for a long time, as if seeking guidance, then said, "We must take her to the place of the crocodile spirit totem. There we will seek help from the medicine man of that tribe, the man who talks to the crocodile spirits. Perhaps he can talk to the spirits, ask the spirits to leave her."

With this decided, they caught a flight to Gove: just Charlie, Vic and Susan. An old, grey-haired man, tall and thin with frizzy hair and a wise face, was waiting for them. He took Susan by the hand and she walked with him. He brought her to an old, battered Toyota tray-back and sat her in the cabin. He did not speak and neither did she.

Uninvited, Charlie and Vic got on the back. They drove, no words said, for an unknown passage of time. First, the road was good. Then, it got rougher. It ended in two-wheel tracks which climbed up to a gap in the hills. They crested the rise and saw, open before them, a view of coast and islands. Just behind the coast, at the end of the wheel tracks, lay a round pool of water which was connected by a small creek to the sea.

Still, the man spoke not. He looked towards the water as the car stopped.

He took Susan by the hand and led her to the pool. He brought her to a place where a flat rock was lapped by the water. He sat her down and then sat down beside her.

From his pocket he pulled out a Baru, like the one of Mark had once owned. He started a chant and tapped two sticks together. It was a crooning, pleading sound. It rose in intensity while keeping time with his tapping.

The sound rose to a crescendo and then fell away to a whisper. Then, it was silent. The silence continued. Then, the crocodile came.

It was not so big- not as big as the last one. But it was old, its teeth were worn, its body seemed spare of flesh, as if it were too small for its skin. It placed its jaw on the stone ledge, resting it between their legs. The old man placed his hand on its head, just behind its eyes. Susan did the same.

Then, the old man sang a song. It was a song like no other, for it had no words. It only contained clicks, grunts and barking noises. However, as the sounds came and went, they formed into a melody. As the melody swelled, so did the crocodile. It was growing in size and power. It was glowing with light. It filled the pool and still continued to grow as the melody grew. Now, its tail touched the ocean and its head dwarfed the bodies beside it.

At the crest of the melody, it opened his own mouth. Its teeth were yellow and its jaws were gaping wide. Ever wider went its mouth, as if sucking the whole world into its being. To Vic, it seemed this spirit had flowed out of its mouth and now enveloped Susan and the old grey crocodile man. Their bodies became shimmering outlines within this other presence. For a time, that seemed to last forever, this world stood still.

Then, the crocodile barked. It barked the bark of a male reclaiming his territory. It shook the sky and the water like a thunder clap.

There was silence.

The man started tapping and singing again. He started loud at first, then the volume diminished slowly until it dwindled to nothing. As the music subsided, so did the crocodile. First it grew smaller. Then it slid backwards and down until all that remained was the water.

The man stood and took Susan's hand. She stood beside him. He signaled for her to walk back to the others. She walked on her own, barefoot in the dust. Vic looked at her. Susan looked back at him and smiled. For a long time, he just held her smile in his eyes. She was so precious to him. Then, he reached out and touched her. With this, she was returned to him.

Afterwards, neither she nor Vic could ever properly describe what happened on that day. But some things they did know: how the old man had sung to the supreme crocodile spirit, and how the spirit had come.

Then, as the music rose, the spirit of that crocodile had come into her mind. It joined with the other crocodile spirit which lived there, absorbing it into the greater being. It had filled her ever more completely, until it was all that she knew. When it had captured the whole of her own crocodile spirit, it had barked. In the bark, it had reclaimed its own and a taken back within itself a part of its ancient being.

With that done, it slowly slid out of her mind. Then, it was just her, again, inside her own mind. Part of her felt sadness for the thing she had lost, part of her felt a peace which she had long forgotten. It just was not there anymore. At the same time, there was no longer a place of absence which restlessly searched to be filled. There was no longer a void which required presence. She felt empty, but content. She was Susan or Emily no longer. She was only Jane, again. She had chosen that name, originally, to be free of the spirit. Now that it was gone, she felt this name belonged best to her.

Chapter 49 – The Places of the Lost

Now she was Jane but with more, a part of the Susan of old seemed to have come back, too. She was driven to do things, to achieve and to catch up for her missing years. The memories had not returned, that must have been caused by something else. But, in their place, was a new found will.

Jane applied herself to the adoption of her new son. In three months, they greeted Nathaniel off a plane in Darwin.

She applied herself to getting Vic setup in his helicopter business, employing a lawyer to draw up the contract for the lease of premises at Darwin airport. She sourced and leased two machines: a small one for mustering and a large one for the heavy lifting. She found a second pilot for the business- someone who Vic had told her he could work with.

Vic went along with her in all her endeavors. His heart was overflowing with gladness. Maybe she had become a bit manic and bossy, but she was his Susan of old. She was oozing willpower and determination. She was unstoppable. He loved her so.

Her belly grew bigger with their second child, but still she powered on. She bought a house in Darwin which was big enough for her whole family and all her friends to visit, all at once, if they chose to do so. She assembled and edited Vic's Afghan ancestor's story. It was a story of a man in whose footsteps walked her husband- someone who had abandoned his home for a woman he loved and made a new home across the sea, to which his bride to be promised to come. However, she had never come to him and he had never returned. The bride of his dreams married another. Then, he had found a dark-skinned girl and loved her, instead. One day, she would publish this book. It was a story deserving to be told.

However, most of her time went into winding up her inheritance from Mark. She catalogued and progressively liquidated the properties and assets Mark had acquired. Only the stones remained. She did not touch them.

When it was all done, there was more than ten million dollars sitting in a bank account. All the debts and bequests were paid with enough remaining to meet any needs that she or Vic could foresee.

With this done she asked Anne to call a meeting of the Trustees of the Lost Girls Trust. She asked Vic to come with her to the meeting in Sydney. When they were all assembled, she asked if she could speak.

She said, "The man who caused all this to begin with, was once my friend and lover. I knew him only as Mark Bennet. When he died, he left me all that he owned. My husband was named the executor of his will and, together, we have made all the bequests he asked. Then, we sold all the assets which were unneeded. Their value was a small amount more than ten million dollars.

"Even though I believe Mark was overall a good man, I know he caused great harm to others. So, I have decided to do two things:

"The first is to donate the money left from his estate to this trust.

"The second is to give his diary to the trust- on the condition that it is maintained for anyone who wants to read it, to get to know of this man. I ask it to be kept somewhere safe. A place where anyone who wants to know of the man, can read it. Reading of it may give to some of those he knew, or those who knew them, a greater level of understanding or comfort."

With that, she laid the diary on the desk in front of her, hers no longer.

Vic took it from the place where it rested. There was something teasing at his mind. It was from the time when he had found the will.

He remembered there were other papers in that place, too. There had been another sheaf of several paper sheets. He had forgotten them, with all which had occurred since then.

Vic opened the back cover and looked at the gap from where the will had come. It was still unrepaired. He eased it open and looked within. The sheets were still there. He took them out and laid them on the table before him. The first sheet was in Mark's writing, saying:

In the event this diary becomes the property of another after my death, I have decided that I should record the places where I buried the persons of whose deaths I tell in this diary.

I hope one day to have the courage to meet Elfin and Belle's parents and tell them about their daughters and how and where their lives ended, but each time I have set my mind to do this, my courage has failed me.

Behind this sheet, each other piece of paper had a name and a diagram. Each diagram was a hand drawing with names and numbers. The first was labeled Elfin, the second was labeled Belle, the third was labeled Josie and the fourth, Amanda. The fifth name was George Davis. Vic tried to place the name George Davis. The name had some ring of familiarity, but he could not remember why. Then, as he looked a second time, it came to him. It was the man whom Cathy and Jacob had sought- the missing uncle of Cathy Rodgers.

Vic said to all assembled, "Just for now, we need to keep these sheets of paper. From what I can see, they tell of the places where Mark buried those he killed or who died while with him. This information needs to go, first, to the police and also to their next of kin."

The last sheet he handed to Jane.

He said, "You should ring Cathy, tell her of this."

*

Two weeks later, Alan set off. The district police were happy to do the site visits locally and see what they could find. However, Alan wanted to be there himself and see it with his own eyes. He wanted to record each detail and come to his own point of closure with this man, Mark. He did not know if he hated or pitied him- but, certainly, it was a strong emotion which ran through him each time he thought of this name.

It had become much more personal since the day when Sandy had almost joined the crocodiles. The way he had been rooted to the spot and unable to move had left him feeling powerless. Somehow, Vic had found the willpower to break free of the spell.

Before that moment, Alan had a desire to help the girl, Susan, and not have her blood on his hands. It had been personal, sort of. But when she had drawn Sandy into that crazy space inside her head, a place which was full of crocodiles, it had become fully real for him.

Now, he knew how powerful was the destructive force associated with this man. He had been dead now for three years, but he still shaped events from beyond the grave. Although Alan could not see how, he sensed that there were yet more dangers, both seen and unseen, in following this man's trail to the very end.

Therefore, Alan was determined that he, and only he, of all of them, would go to see these places, first. The others could make their own visits, later, if they wanted. Both Jane and Anne were heavily pregnant now, so he easily had David and Vic on side. Strangely, neither woman protested much. Perhaps it had shocked them all to the core at just how dangerous the last trip had been. Cathy and Jacob had protested the most, but they had their own trip to make to try and find the uncle. He was the one where 'what happened' was most clear- but the location was not. Sandy had remained unexpectedly quiet.

Now, Alan was off on his own. A policeman from each locality was coming with him to help interpret the clues. The first stop was Birdsville, where his chartered plane would land. He would be collected there by the local policeman, Fred Howard. Fred would come with him as they worked their way east, following the directions to the place named for Elfin.

They could have come another way, but Alan wanted to retrace the journey which Mark described he had made from Birdsville to this place. Mark had noted in small writing, alongside the diagram he had drawn:

I followed the directions of the old miner from Coober Pedy, the way he knew from thirty years earlier. He came there from Birdsville, so I came first from Birdsville. His directions were good.

With this information, they began as Mark had begun, those years before, taking the road that ran through Betoota and on towards Quilpie. Before they reached the junction for the next main road, they looked for a sign to Four Mile Tank. Three miles along this road, they took a track which brought them north along the edge of the Beale Range. From there, the roads were little more than goat tracks. But they still existed, although only as roads used by miners and stations.

Eventually, after another tortuous half-day of driving, finding several dead ends they had to backtrack from, they came to a collection of old mine sites spread across some broken and rocky low ranges. The station owners had fenced these parts off, to stop cattle falling down the mine shafts.

They knew this must be it. There was a river channel below, matching the river Mark described. It was not flowing now, but the ground was lush with dense grass. The grass still had green shoots from last summer's rain.

They searched through the knee-high grass, seeking the rocks Mark had carried to make the shape of a boat. The riverbank was a mud channel with rocks being mostly absent. They found an occasional one amongst the grass.

For two hours, they searched, following along the contour of the riverbank and only found the odd solitary rock. The sun was getting low. They had spent a long day driving and searching. They both had a cold beer on their minds and agreed to stop when they got to the next bend in the river. The rest could wait until tomorrow.

Then Freddie, working downslope while Alan covered the upslope, called out, "Two rocks together, make that three. Bloody Hell, I think this is it."

They cleared away the long grass. It really was it- the place they sought. It was quite unmistakable. The boulders were size of footballs. Mark had brought them down from the hillside. They made a boat shape which was ten feet long by five feet wide.

They gazed in awe at the effort it must have cost for a single and solitary man to dig a hole this size, place a boat with a body in it and then fill it again. And then he had the strength to carry the stones to make this rocky memorial.

Mark had simply said in his diary,

"I dug a hole by the river, big enough to take the boat. I carried her cold body in my arms down from the mine above.

I placed her into the boat with the opals she had found. Perhaps they will pay the ferryman to bring her to a happy place. After I filled the hole, I carried rocks from the hill to mark the place in the shape of the boat.

God, I miss my Elfin Queen.

The next day, a team arrived from Brisbane in a helicopter. This team included a pathologist to complete the excavation. To Alan's surprise, Sandy stepped out of the helicopter alongside her Queensland colleague. She had been determined not to argue with Alan. However, once she knew the find had been made, she had caught the night jet to Brisbane. With her powers of persuasion, she was here for it, too.

They dug down. Each spade full of dirt was checked as they went. Two feet down, the spade struck metal. It was the top edge of the boat's side. It was exactly as Mark had described: the tin boat, a backpack, the opals and a crushed body wrapped in a blanket- pelvis fractured in the rock fall. They lifted the bones out with all the care they could, mindful of the loving way she had once been placed there.

The next day, they moved on to the next site. It was only five miles away and was further up the same rocky ridge. Mark had linked them in his drawings. He had said, in so many words, 'the easiest way to find the place of Amanda, is to go to the place of the boat. Then, you follow the track north five miles along the side of the ridge.'

There you will find the site of the mine which I worked on in the days before she died. It is not as rich as Elin's mine but there is still much of value left there, I have not worked it further. I feel it belongs to her and one day it should be her inheritance, as she sat there, at first patiently, while I dug it out, meaning for her to have it all. If she had only waited a little longer and not made me so angry, I would have given its proceeds to her.

With these directions, finding the mine was easy. It was exactly where his drawing showed. Finding her grave was not so easy. There was no diagram for it. Instead, Mark described the way he had walked. It was vague, as if only half remembered. Maybe he was no longer quite sure when he told of it. What he wrote was:

I hit her hard. I knew I had killed her; I could have softened it, but did not. I left her until my anger passed. Then I picked her up in my arms. She acted like a tigress but was only a cub, easy to carry. I walked with her, her pack on my back, taking two sticks of gelignite and a rope.

I went northeast, until my arms grew tired, perhaps a mile. I rested near an old mine shaft. I lay her down and put on her best dress, that of the first night, sweet of memories. I carried her down to the shaft bottom, where I left her, then set off the gelignite. It covered her grave so none will disturb her. I should be sad but am not, it is better the end was kind.

For an hour I talked to an eagle in the sky, asking him to keep watch over her spirit until it crossed safely over. As I talked, I walked. Part way

It sounded more caring, in the diary, than the way he had told Susan. The way he told her made it sound like none was meant to find her. And find her- none could. They searched but nothing matched what he said. They found plenty of abandoned mine shafts, but they were empty. None were collapsed, as if from explosive.

Her pack was easier to find. It was a bare half kilometer from the mine site. Even then, it still took a week of searching. Eventually, they found this place where her pack was, down in a deep shaft and tied to a coil of rope. In the pack were: the rubies he had given her, a few clothes, a notebook, a computer tablet and twenty thousand dollars. All were almost undamaged- despite the years spent in the ground.

So that was it. They had found the one and knew, almost, the resting place of the other. Amanda's things could be returned to her family.

Alan returned to Darwin for a week of completing paperwork. While these cases were now for the Queensland Police and coroner to deal with, he still had to do his reports, based on what he had found.

After this, he was ready to head on. This time, the site was in the Tanami Desert south of the VRD. It was down towards Laja Manu, otherwise known as Hooker Creek. This time, Sandy was clearly part of the team. She was the assigned NT pathologist for the recovery of this body. This time, any suggestion that the others were not welcome was quickly put to bed.

Vic announced he was travelling down in his big heavy lift helicopter. He informed everyone in their group that it was capable of taking a dozen people, and, as of now, only Jane would travel with him. Vic knew the location so Alan could hardly stop this flight. As Vic had read Mark's directions, it was hardly feasible to exclude him from the search. Also, Alan knew that, for this search, a helicopter would be very useful.

So, it was decided they would all travel together. Alan offered for the government to pay for the helicopter.

Vic said, "Don't be silly. I am doing it for my friend, the way he wanted. It is his money which is paying to make this right."

The first day, they ferried to VRD. Alan, Sandy, Anne, David, Cathy, Jacob and, of course, Jane were all onboard. They stayed the night there with Buck and Julie. Each had their own bunk beds with the boys and girls sleeping separate in the stockmen's quarters.

As they sat over dinner, Jane's first new memory came.

She turned to Buck, "I remember Firefly- not just being told his name but riding on him. It was like a magic carpet, the way his body flowed. Another thing I remember is the helicopter dance in the Wickham Gorge. And, I also remember sitting here over dinner with Mark telling stories. I was falling asleep, so I went to my bunk bed. That's all I remember, but it is something.

"Tell me, have I remembered true, Buck?"

Buck winked at her and said, "Yes, it is true. Now, tell me, do you also remember a day when you sat in a cell and I came to see you? I apologized for not bringing Firefly to see you. You laughed and I laughed until we were out of breath and our sides ached."

Jane thought for a minute and then said, "Yes, I remember that, too. But what I most remember from that day was you told me that Vic was missing, vanished with his helicopter. I thought my heart was broken in two. But he is here, now, so that part cannot have been true."

The next morning, they all left early. Buck flew the station fixed wing plane to Laja Manu where he was to meet the local policeman. They would drive from there to the site of Mark's map. This place was easy to find.

It was on a road which turned off the Kulkarni to Laja Manu road. It ran east for thirty kilometers until it came to a small rocky ridge in the desert. At its base was a pool of water. Behind the ridge, to the east, were sand hills where lots of wildflowers grew after it rained. It was such a season now.

Both Buck and Vic knew this place. It had been shown to them by Mark, a place he had found and loved to visit when he had worked at Laja Manu.

Mark's instruction was to walk to the back of the sand hills, about five kilometers into the desert. There, they would find a place where the sand met a small rocky outcrop. This was her grave. He had carved her name, Josie, into the stone above her grave so the desert would hold her memory.

They landed the helicopter at the end of the road, next to the rock pool where the police vehicle waited. Everyone was let off except for Alan, Sandy and the Laja Manu policeman.

Vic flew to the east, keeping low. Now, all four looked for this place which Mark had described. They were all thinking it should be easy to find. After ten minutes of detailed searching, it was not found. Vic found a clear place on a clay pan and set down on the ground.

He said, "This must be about where, but here is a lot of where."

They each took a quarter mile to search from the ground. They agreed to walk two hundred steps forward before turning back to search from there.

Half-way back, Vic saw a place where the flowers grew thicker in front of a small grove of desert trees. As he came up close, the rocky place stood up. It had been hidden from above by trees but was easy to see from a side profile. It was only about his height above the ground.

Vic shouted out. The others came over. On the rock face was chiseled:

HERE LIES JOSIE
MY LOST KID SISTER

Vic went and ferried the others across before they started digging.

It was as Mark had told: the body of a teenage girl, small bones, wrapped in a soft mohair blanket with no other clothes. A small, round hole in the base of her skull told of the killing. As they lifted her out and carried this blanket wrapped package to the helicopter, they all felt unutterably sad.

Her death seemed so senseless. It was a testament to evil.

David said, "Do you think we could leave her here? I think it is what both she and Mark would both have wanted. He buried her, with love, in a place of desert beauty. I think, here, she would be most happy."

However, it could not be so- at least not, for now. They brought the body to Hooker Creek airport. From there, the policeman arranged a vehicle to carry her to Darwin. It was so official procedures could be done. Buck stayed with the policeman, to help with his paperwork, before returning to VRD.

The others flew on to Halls Creek, to stop for the night, before the last leg of the journey. Dinner in the Halls Creek Hotel was a somber occasion.

Alan could see Cathy and Jacob chatting to David, Anne and Sandy. Vic sat with him while Jane was on the phone. She was checking on her family.

Alan said to Vic, "I could have sworn you knew the way today. You seemed to walk almost straight there once you landed the chopper."

Vic said, "When you spent as long with Mark as I did, you start to think the way he does and look through his eyes. When I saw that little sheltered place, half under the cluster of trees, I knew it was the sort of place he would have chosen. It was alive with flowers. I think they caught my eye in the air.

"So, as we walked away, I chose that side. It seemed the most right. I forced myself to walk all the way out before I looked there, not wanting to miss something else. But, as I walked back, I could feel that place calling to me. As I looked, the brightness of the flowers struck me.

Later, I realized it was because a huge pile of flowers was once there, before. All those seeds had germinated as the flowers broke down, year after year. I could picture it as he left it- not a bouquet or two, but armfuls upon armfuls of flowers. Mark never did things by half. The flowers would have been piled as high as himself before he left."

David joined their conversation saying, "I felt today that it was a place of peace. A place where Josie was happy. I could see she was buried with love. It felt like a sacrilege to disturb her grave. I thought we should leave her there. What was it about her death that moved Mark so and brought out a kindness for her in her death that he could not find for her in her life?"

Vic replied, "I think Mark knew, on that day he killed her, he had done a truly, terrible thing and there was no going back from it. The killings before then were done through desperation or need, or to stop evil people.

"On that day, Mark chose to kill his 'kid sister' for no good reason except she took something of his that he cared about. Once it was done, his only reparation was to bury her with all the love and kindness he could find. It is as if, after it was done, her spirit felt his goodness and forgave what he did. Was happy to know his love. But, for himself, he could find no forgiveness for what he did that day.

"That day, he lost the biggest part of his human soul. Amanda was but a consequence of that day. The hatred of himself became hatred of the part of her that was like him- the person where self-interest came first. His killing Josie made Mark despise himself. Then, killing Amanda was like killing that part of himself he despised, so it was something to take pleasure from.

"When he asked Amanda to come with him, he did it as a challenge- his diary clearly says that. But when she came, he never really gave her a chance. He tested her to meet a standard he knew she could not meet. He set her up to fail and cared not. He knew that leaving her sitting in a God forsaken place, with nothing to do, day after day, when she was used to getting her way- would drive her crazy. Yet, he forced her to hold to the bargain she had made, unknowing. Even as he watched what this boredom did to her, he offered her no relief. He could have taken her on a trip to visit a station, or gone somewhere nice, just for a day. He could have done something, anything, to break the monotony and make her life bearable.

"Instead, he kept on digging, collecting more stones for no good purpose. He neither needed them nor the money they would bring. Yet, he kept her waiting until, in the end, she broke. He knew she was like him- but without his strength to fight back. The tigress who was really a cub.

"When she pulled the knife, he could have stepped aside and taken it from her. This man, who was a mercenary and who stared down charging bulls, was not afraid of a slip of a girl with a kitchen knife. So, he did not need to kill her. He was not frightened. It was not self-defense. He chose to hit her hard enough to kill her when a slap would have sufficed.

"It would have cost him nothing to leave a day or two earlier-nothing but kindness and, for her, he had none. That was because she was like him. and he had no kindness left for himself.

"If Belle had asked him to take her somewhere, he would have driven her a thousand miles without seeking a reason why. But, when Belle died, he lost his hope in goodness. Then, when he killed Josie, he lost his soul. So, for him, it was as if Amanda was a test of himself. She was a new proof he was a being without a soul. She was someone who deserved his own fate of always killing what he loved.

"When it was done, he felt more relief than remorse. Glad to have put her aside. Only after her death, was he able to feel enough tenderness towards her to wish kindness to her in another life.

"Even though he tried to find a part of his humanity again, with Cathy and Susan, from then on, there was always a devil on his shoulder. One always waiting to bring him down. I think, after that day with Josie, his guilt was so great he almost wished for it to happen. The flowers were his way of saying 'sorry' by giving something he knew she loved to try and take away his guilt. She felt his love, but he could not accept her forgiveness. So, nothing could undo that day.

"I think, if I had talked to him on the day he died, to ask him if there was one thing from his life he would have chosen to have undone, it would have been that shot that brought Josie down."

Vic paused now for breath, having exhausted his words. He had never spoken as much before as he did now. It was as if his mind had reached out and grasped for reasons to make sense of his friend. He expected to see just Alan and David sitting there. Instead, as he looked up, Vic saw he was ringed by a circle of all of his friends. They were all listening and nodding. Cathy sat beside him and took his hand.

"Thank you, Vic. In him, I saw a good man tormented by his past. Since I left him, I have asked myself those questions you answered. With each new discovery, I ask them again and again. I have asked myself, time and again: Why? Why? Why? Why could not the past stay in the past? Why could he not let his life move on? For a night or two, he had tried when I loved him. But the devil was always there.

"Even though I knew he would not harm me, a damaged person like he was, I knew he would damage others. It was self-hatred that drove him. I tried to give him hope, but he could not let himself believe in it. I was not strong enough to hold him and bring him through the pain. So, I made myself leave him, even though I felt torn in two as I did.

"Until tonight, I never understood why. Now, I do. For that, I thank you. Susan got closer than me in bringing him past the pain because she offered him acceptance with no conditions. But he could not do himself the kindness to accept her offer. Instead, he fled from her to his devil the only way he knew. In that last day, Susan gave him the kindness he gave to Belle: a quick and kind ending. She, since then, has lived with the devil of her own recrimination. She, too, must learn self-forgiveness."

Vic spoke again, "It is not only for Susan, now Jane. I was his friend-yet I chose to be blind to the things he did. I put my hands over my eyes and looked the other way. When it was tearing my wife's mind apart, I chose to hate him for what he had done. Only now, when I see the price he paid, can I begin to look at him in understanding. So, I now must reconcile myself to the ghost of his passing and the harm he has done."

David said, "While I never knew him, today I walked a mile in his shoes. For far too long, he has haunted my life and Anne's life- as with you, Alan, Sandy, Cathy and Jacob, too."

Cathy nodded, "Perhaps, tomorrow, it is Belle who can bring us to the place where we truly forgive Mark for all the evil he has done, while still remembering the goodness of the man who was once my friend.

I would really like it to be so. Despite all the evil things that I know he has done he was consistently kind and good to me, and I remember him fondly.

I would like the good of his life to be remembered alongside the bad."

Chapter 50 – Laying His Ghost to Rest

The next morning, they flew to Kununurra where they fueled up to maximum fuel and took on two more passengers- a local aboriginal policewoman, Jessie, and Isabelle's father. Jessie was coming as a traditional owner of the place to which they were going. Isabelle's father had flown from France to be with them when they searched for his daughter's things. As there was no suggestion they would find a body, there was no need for a pathologist's attendance. Today was about recovering the personal effects of a person the Northern Territory coroner had already declared deceased. It was a finding with which the Western Australian coroner had agreed.

Therefore, they had a full load of extra fuel and ten people aboard as they got airborne. Vic could feel the load in his big machine. The weight would burn off as he burnt fuel on the trip north.

For an hour, the helicopter flew north, north-west over a rough and broken land. It was a place of red and brown mountains which raised their fractured heads to the sky. Between the scarps narrow gorges plunged, giving glimpses of green trees fringing pools of water and places of yellow sand.

As they flew, Cathy thought about her uncle and all which had passed with him. The note told of how Mark had tracked him down in Oman, already in hiding, as the police were looking for him over other child sex charges.

Mark said he had taken him out to Rub al Khali, otherwise known as the Empty Quarter. Mark gave an approximate place but that was all.

Mark's note said he had talked to her uncle there. He had told him what he knew about how the uncle had raped and abused his two nieces and how one of them had killed herself because of him. He said he had since found out this man had done similar things to other girls, as well. Due to this, Mark had deemed his life forfeit, as payment for his deeds.

Mark wrote, "I told him I should use my knife on him for what he done; cut away the parts that had hurt little girls. But I did not. I gave him a choice, to go to the English police while I watched on, and tell of all he had done, or to stay here and take his chances. I told him there was no water here, none for two hundred miles and no one ever came here. He said he preferred to stay here, perhaps he thought he could cheat death. I knew he could not.

"I left him with a bottle of whiskey and a tablet that I told him would end it. And even though I did not tell him so, in the whiskey was a thing which would bring a speedy end. I knew when the thirst came, he would drink this and soon die, unless he took the tablet first. I drove away, not looking back, and came back the next day to confirm he was dead. It was so. It was clear to me that he died in great pain, for which I am pleased. I left his bloated body lying there for the jackals and vultures to feast on.

Once it was done I came back to Australia. His bones are far out in the Empty Quarter of the Arabian Desert. I do not know exactly where, as they will have been scattered by the birds and animals. I am glad it is so."

It was not as Cathy would have done it, but she could feel it was justice. It was better justice than a court could ever have given. At first, she and Jacob had thought of going there, but there was no point. Whatever was done was finished three years past. There was nothing to gain in driving through an empty desert, searching for bone fragments.

She knew that none would ever see him again. She also knew, the way Mark had done it, survival had never been an option. Her uncle's only choice would have been a fast and kinder death from the tablet. That was how Mark saw justice. After all the people her uncle had harmed, she could not disagree. Now, when she balanced it all up, her main feeling was relief.

Cathy left his memory behind and looked up. Half an hour had passed. She glimpsed and then, saw a blue line on a smoky horizon. The line became the place where the sea met the sky. She hoped there was more joy in this place than where her mind had been.

They came to the coast at a place where sheer red cliffs met an azure sparkling sea. Vic matched this place to his GPS and map. Here he turned west, following the turns of the coast as it twisted and plunged. Fifteen minutes later, he saw a headland overlooking a little bay. It was shaped into a half circle. It looked about right. He came in closer to see it better.

Mid-point of the cliff circle, he saw a small waterfall which fell to ocean. Its spray was all a glisten. Behind the waterfall lay a clear pool of water. Rising behind it were other broken rocky hills. Wheel tracks bent their way to near the side of the cliff and then vanished into the green-grey scrub behind it.

He knew this was it, the place of his map. It was the place which the custodians of this land called Wallaby Dove Pool. A place from where the first spirits came out from this water and joined the land. Now, each evening, their descendants came to drink, the place which Mark called Crystal Creek.

Vic brought the helicopter to rest and sat in it, for a minute, while the turbines wound down. He handed the map to Alan, saying, "Perhaps you should go first, with Jessie, to look. Then, the rest of us will come."

Alan and Jessie nodded. Then they walked away.

Five minutes later, Alan waved them all over. Jessie held a small brass object in her fingers. It was a twenty-two rifle shell. It had been found lying near the cliff side- in a place where the rock had broken away.

"This must be this place, just round from the waterfall, from where she fell," Jesse said, pointing to the ground.

They looked for other signs. There was an old blackened fireplace which appeared unused in years. It was a long time since anyone had camped here- perhaps, the last people had been Mark and Belle. They checked the hillside behind to look for caves and rock crevices.

At last, they found it. The entrance was overgrown by shrubs, a crevice in the rock about two meters long and half a meter high. It had been filled with stones so nothing could enter it except, perhaps, a small mouse. As they cleared away stones, they saw the neck of a guitar with a backpack beside it.

Alan lifted the guitar out and passed it to Belle's father. He took it with his hands shaking. He knew it was hers for it had been a present to her by her family when she was fifteen years old.

He handled it, lovingly, and strummed a few chords. Then, he passed it to the others with a wistful sigh. He opened the pack. Its contents were neatly folded inside and were still dry.

He shook out a shirt, "It is from the local market in our home village," he said, with a tear in his eye. Inside the shirt was a diary. It was only a small, notebook sized one. He opened it and read it aloud:

J'ai passé un moment merveilleux. Je suis enchanté avec cette homme. Cette nuit nous somme devenir amants. Aujourd'hui je suis extatique. Il est un bon homme. Même si on ne se revoit jamais, je ne t'oublierai jamais

This morning, I sang him one of my favourite songs – Piaf is perfect for a day when I am in love. I sang it first in English then in French, then the last verse again in English. The French is far more beautiful as befits my beautiful man.

They all stood in a circle with moist eyes.
It was a story beyond beautiful but also heart rending

Her father picked up the guitar and played the song, by ear. He also sang the words, as she might have sung them:

No, nothing at all,
No, I don't regret anything!
Neither the good that's been done to me,
Nor the bad;
It's all the same to me!

Non, rien de rien
Non, je ne regrette rien
Ni le bien qu'on m'a fait
Ni le mal; tout ça m'est bien égal !

Non, rien de rien
Non, je ne regrette rien
C'est payé, balayé, oublié
Je me fous du passé !

Avec mes souvenirs
J'ai allumé le feu
Mes chagrins, mes plaisirs
Je n'ai plus besoin d'eux !

Balayées les amours
Et tous leurs tremolos
Balayés pour toujours
Je repars à zéro

Non, rien de rien
Non, je ne regrette rien
Ni le bien qu'on m'a fait
Ni le mal; tout ça m'est bien égal !

Non, rien de rien
Non, je ne regrette rien
Car ma vie, car mes joies
Aujourd'hui, ça commence avec toi

No, nothing at all,
No, I don't regret anything!
Because my life,
because my joy,
today
begins with you!

When Belle's father had finished, he was too emotional to speak. They all had lots of tears in their eyes. He walked to the edge of the cliff and flung the guitar into the sky. He watched as it slowly fell to the water below, saying,

"It belongs here, with her. May she always hear its sweet music."

Jane walked over to the helicopter and took out a small bottle. It was the last container of Mark's ashes. At first, she thought to fling it to the place where the guitar had gone, but she remembered her charge from Mark.

She unscrewed the lid, took out a pinch and, with all the love she could bring to her mind, tossed this dust of the man into the air. Her mind was hoping that some part of it would mingle together with whatever life essence remained of Belle. She passed it around and the others did the same.

Then, they loaded Belle's pack into the helicopter and flew home.

That night, they stopped at Timber Creek. It was a storytelling night about Mark and Belle. It was the wake Mark had never had and a memorial for Belle. It might have been sad- but it was not. Those who knew Mark, told a story of him. Those who did not know him, told a story of other lives he had touched. Belle's father told of his daughter. Anne read from the diaries.

It was not quite celebratory, but in all the minds and voices, there was joy, forgiveness and some pain. They remembered a man of two parts: the good and the bad. They also remembered the woman he had lost who regretted nothing.

Chapter 51 – Sunlit Shadow Dance

Jane stood on the cliff took looking out over the valley below. The sun was just touching the horizon and, as it did, suddenly the whole world lit up. The lighting was not just of the ordinary world, but of her world, too. It was fully alive with blinding and full color for the first time in her remembered life. The color was even more beautiful than she could ever have imagined.

As the color came back, the memories did, too. The memories included the good and happy ones, but along with them, the pain and horror filled ones as well. All she had been and all she had done came back to her. She cringed with the pain in her soul as it all came rushing back: the awfulness of it and her awful part in it. Slowly, it faded as she looked far out. Her mind moved on past it.

In that last sunlight of the fading day, she could see the shadows dance. She remembered how, all the years ago, Mark had brought her here. He had told her that, in the last fading light, the shadows came out and danced. They were those of the people who had lived here for over fifty thousand years.

He had asked her to bring his remains back to this place and today they had. They scattered his ashes across the hills and sand plains below. Now, he was one of them. Mark was walking amongst them, a shadow dancing amongst other shadows, in that last sunlight.

She could feel his joy: his joy for himself and his joy in seeing her again. Jane heard the spirits singing in that last light, more beautiful than any sound she had heard before. Their music contained all of life's emotions mixed and blended into ten thousand, million voices. His voice sang the loudest.

Mark stood there now: beckoning, waving, signalling and calling "Come to me. We can go together into this other place. Leave the pain of this world behind. It is a good place. I want you there. Come with me, come now."

Now, she was only Susan, again, and loved Mark only. She remembered still, as if from a great distance, Vic. She remembered how she had shared her life with him and loved him, too. They had taken Mark's children, her children and alongside them they had created their own children together. They had given them all a good life. However,

Mark was her first and truest love. She was his Susan and her spirit must go to him. It must answer his call."

As she stood at the clifftop gazing out across the rocks far below, she knew she would now soar from here like an eagle and fly to Mark. She would rejoin his crocodile spirit to that of hers and be complete again. She would leave behind all the pain which she could not bear to remember.

She stepped forward to where there was only air.

Far below, a small cry came. It somehow penetrated through the other world music and the last sunlight- into the place where still, the shadows danced. It was the voice of her child, David, "Mummy, come back!"

It pulled her back. Again, her feet stood on solid ground.

She knew that this boy, the new Mark, needed her more than the other Mark. It was the same with Vic, Anne, little Vic and her still unborn ones. Today, she must learn to live with the pain, accept what she could not change and take joy in life's little things.

She looked back out across the water. Mark was calling out again. Now, however, she knew it was not for her that he called. As she watched, another girl came out of the shadows. She had dark hair. This girl looked like Jane, but was not. She answered him, singing in a beautiful French voice:

"Non, je ne regrette rien."

As Susan watched, this girl was joined by another, then another and, finally, there were four girls. She knew all their names: the one with dark hair, the two with brown hair and the one of a glorious, shimmering blond. They all joined hands and danced towards the other spirit shadows in that last sunlight.

Susan watched as the light faded. They were gone. Now, she was Jane again. The remnants of Susan had passed from this place.

She walked across the flat ground to where they all stood waiting for her. They all enfolded her in their big and little arms. She was glad she was still here. She stood with them all in the now fading twilight as the sun travelled across another sky. She knew these ancestral spirits had gone there, too: Mark's spirit, the crocodile spirit which had tried to take her there and the spirits of the other women Mark had loved and who had gone on before him.

However, it was not her time to go there. She would live and love in the world of men and women. She would watch her children grow and their children, too. She would share in their joys and pains. She would live again in all life's colors. It was enough.

Epilogue

In the months after they returned from the desert, Jane gradually got the rest of her life in order. She also did what more she could to make reparations for the harm Mark had caused.

For Amanda, the police sent her things back to her family. They asked the family what to do with the money and the notebook of her travels. The family asked they be sent to the man who had loved her, for the money had come from him and the notebook was of value to him. The man and they were now agreed that it was okay for him to read it and write her story. The family also sent him one the rubies. He kept it and was glad to hold it in her memory. It was something of beauty to remember her by after all she had suffered.

However, this was not reparation from Mark. It was just a return of what Amanda had owned, along with Mark's gift to her. Jane wanted to do something from Mark's estate for Amanda. She wrote to the family and asked if there was anything more she could do.

A month later, there came a reply, "We would like to erect a memorial for our daughter at the place she died. Something in her likeness that others will know her by."

Therefore, on the hill of the mine, Jane arranged for the erection of a stone cairn. On its side, a likeness of Amanda's face was made from small ceramic tiles and pieces of colored glass as they were things which would not fade in the bright sunlight.

For Elin's family, the police sent them her things from the grave. Alan told Jane that the fabulous opal now sat in a local museum in Sweden where it was donated in Elin's name. The family had brought Elin's mortal remains home and buried them in the boat grave alongside her mother, the warrior queen and her warrior daughter. On her graveside, they put a small plaque to the man who had loved her in his desert kingdom.

Jane knew it was a thing which would have pleased Mark and wrote to tell them so. They sent her a photo they had taken of this place.

One day, Jane was going through the many things of Mark's which had gradually been located and been sent to her. In a box, she found a series of mining leases for this part of Queensland. There were over thirty in all. Two of these leases were for the mines where Elin and Amanda had died. In finding these, the final thing Jane did was to transfer the one to

Elin's family and the other to Amanda's family. If there were yet things of value in this ground, it was their right to discover them. If there wasn't anything of monetary value left, at least these places held valuable memories of the last resting places of their children. A year later, the two families met on these rocky hills in the desert to agree on a small joint mining venture named after their daughters. Any profits of the venture would go into the Lost Girls Trust.

The final piece of the jigsaw was Josie. Jane traced the bank transaction where Mark transferred the money into her name, as he told in his diary. It gave her a real name: Josephine Kelty. Then, they traced her mother but found out her mother was dead. There was no other next of kin. So, Jane arranged for Josie's bones to be placed in a coffin and taken back to the place in the desert where they found her.

It was in the next winter when the wildflowers were in bloom again. Rather than putting a headstone on the grave, they put a small bronze plaque on the cliff below the inscription which Mark had carved. It simply had Josie's name, date of birth and death. Mark's headstone told the rest.

After it was done, they, their children and their friends walked in the desert for the rest of the day gathering all the wildflowers they could find, to pile them above the grave. When they had finished, the pile was as high as their heads and almost obscured the stone. They hoped that, for many more years, the children of these flowers would bloom in Josie's Place.

The months and years rolled on by. It was wonderful for Jane to have all her colors back. Gradually, more pieces of the memory of her former life came back, too. They did not all come back at once. However, like the myriad pieces of a jigsaw, when one was looking the other way, one would suddenly remember a piece and where it fitted. Then, reach for it and place it.

Five years later, the jigsaw of her mind was mostly complete. There was just an occasional space which may or may not be filled in more time. She knew some pieces may never return. Her jigsaw would always resemble one of those much-loved family favourites, rebuilt over and over again, as time rolled on. Those, like hers, had odd empty spaces. These were places left open for imagination to fill. She called these 'life's missing pieces.'

Jane remembered how one morning, when she was Susan, she had killed her lover. It was a sad place inside her mind, but the pain was gone.

His spirit lived on in the lives of his children who she and Vic watched grow: Nathaniel the apprentice air mechanic and soon to be a pilot, David the quiet, studious boy with a magic touch with animals. David could calm a wild horse and he rode like his father. Some days, when he smiled, Vic said Mark had returned to life. At first, Annie seemed to have the least of Mark and to be, mostly, Jane's Susan child. However, one day Uncle Antonio sent a photo of his sister, Mark's mother, from when she was a girl of Annie' age. The resemblance was so strong that Jane felt she was looking at a photograph of her daughter. She now knew another part of Mark lived on in this child- not just a part of her.

Jane also remembered, from within her own mind, how on the morning of killing, the crocodile spirit had sought out and found entry to her soul. In her anguish, as they tore at Mark's body, she sent out a part of her to be with him in the place of crossing. Into the place inside her soul, now left empty, slid a remnant of another. It had been part of the spirit of his devourer. Slowly, its power had grown within her. It had filled her mind and took over her own spirit.

She remembered too, those days of her vanishing. How she had been seeking to escape it. On that early morning, she had climbed into the car with the other 'Mark man' as he drove to the waterhole in the pre-dawn light. She knew he was really just a fisherman, but she thought he had been sent to meet her. A man to escort her back to her first true love.

Susan had wanted to go back to Mark, Emily had not. They had fought inside this car for the control of her body and, with Susan feeling cocky that she had won, Emily had seized her chance. As they came to the red traffic light where the Arnhem Highway began, Emily opened the door as they were stopped and jumped out. She fled, barefooted across the dirt, with her overnight bag grasped in her hand. At the same time, the Susan part was left in the car holding the plastic bag which contained the Baru crocodile spirit and the pink sandals.

Susan had not been able to find her way back to Emily, try as she might. For a brief moment this escaped person stayed as Emily. But this person knew Emily was not in a safe place and she must leave her behind too, if she was to escape from all the evil which had filled the life that was hers before. With this thought, she tore at Emily to expel her. Emily protested but was thrown out from her body and from her mind, too.

There remained for this person only an empty body and empty mind, with no past life spirit living within.

After this, she had chosen a new name- Jane. However, she had to be Jane somebody. She had chosen a remnant of Mark, in the first B name by which she had known him, Bennet. It was a fitting name for her children to hold. She had, after all, made her marriage promises to him, their father, during the last night they were together. Perhaps it was on that night when her children had been conceived. It made sense that the name was rightfully theirs to keep.

At a roadside stop nearby where she had fled from Susan, she had found a marker in her bag and printed 'Jane Bennet' on her bag's label. This was in case she lost even this memory of her past life.

There was a road train parked nearby. Its decks were empty of cattle, but still with the manure and other excrement of where the cattle had been. She climbed to the upper deck where she would be above eye view. She found a clean corner and lay down. There, she slept, strangely finding comfort in the animal smells. She slept for a long day. The truck went on and on. Sometimes it would stop for a short time. The sun rose high and then went down. She was sheltered from wind and most of the sun in her secluded corner. Late in the next night, it stopped at another roadhouse. This one was on the road to Queensland and was at a place called Barkly Homestead- which she remembered from before. She climbed down, had a drink from the tap and climbed back up to sleep again.

The next day, somewhere in Queensland, she left this truck after hunger forced her exit. She found a place to shower and change her clothes. Then, she bought a meal. Having eaten, she found another different truck to ride in. This time it was a goods truck. It was empty except for furniture blankets. She slept, again, for many hours. She revelled in the comfort of her blanket bed.

Once again, she came out at a roadhouse where she got food and washed herself up again. Then she found another empty cattle truck with a resting place on its top deck, too. It did not have the animal leavings of the first truck as it had been washed clean. She found that, without the animal smell, she was less comfortable. Therefore, when the truck pulled up by the side of the road a few hours later in the night, for the driver to relieve himself, she climbed out and watched it depart down an empty road.

A short distance down this road was a shed with a roof. It had an open side and a rough timber seat. She climbed on this and slept until the daybreak of her new life began. That day, she was just an empty shell. The spirits of Susan and Emily had left her, so she took the name Jane- the name on her bag. Now, a new spirit had created a new life within. The old spirit was gone, and she was glad to be only Jane.

It was now more than seven years since the day of the ending of the first Susan and Emily. Jane was what Vic called her, again. They both agreed Susan and Emily had passed on with the crocodile spirit. Each day since then, Vic grew more handsome and told her how she grew ever more beautiful.

On this day, together, they sat in a restaurant at Watson's Bay. They were enjoying the autumn freshness of wind, sun and sky. The restaurant looked down to the beach in the harbor where a small tribe of children played- some of them hers, some of them belonging to others.

In a circle around the table sat her closest friends. There were Anne and David, looking fondly at the children which they and others had created. There were Sandy and Alan with their own brood. Along with these couples were Beck and Ross, Buck and Julie, and Jacob and Cathy. Of course, the closest person to her forever was Vic.

All their lives were good. No new tragedy had befallen any of them. Their children were well, and they were all well, too. It was more than enough.

Vic raised a glass and spoke, "I propose a toast to a long-departed friend of mine. A man of two parts, good and bad, but still my friend despite it all.

"Without this man, we would never have met and so, we would not be here today. This gladness we share would never have come to be. I still miss him, after all this time. He was a man who lived at the far edge of danger.

"He would enjoy us sitting here, good friends enjoying life's good things. But, even if he was here with us today, his spirit would be forever looking out for a new horizon. A place lit by sunshine but where the shadows gather.

"Let's drink to my friend, Mark B. May his restless crocodile spirit know peace in that dreamtime land where sunlit shadows dance forever."

All raised their glasses and exclaimed in unison – "To Mark!"

About the Author

Graham Wilson lives in Sydney Australia. He has completed and published 13 separate books, and also a range of combined novel box sets.

They comprise two series,

1. The Balmain House Series – three novels

2 The Crocodile Spirit Dreaming Series – seven novels.

along with a family memoir, *Children of Arnhem's Kaleidoscope*.

He has also written two standalone novels, The Glitter and The Mysteries.

The *Balmain House Series* starts with the novel, *Old Balmain House*. Its setting is an old weatherboard cottage, in Sydney, where the author lived for seven years. Here a photo was discovered of a small girl who lived and died about 100 years ago. The book imagines the story of her life and family, based in the real Balmain, an early inner Sydney suburb, with its locations and historical events providing part of the story background. The second novel in this series, *Lizzie*, builds on the Balmain house setting, it is the story of a working-class teenage girl who lives in this same house in the 1950s and 1960s, it tells of how, when pregnant, she is determined not to surrender her baby for adoption and of her struggle to survive in this unforgiving society. The third novel in this series, *Amelie*, follows the next generation of the family in *Lizzie*. Lizzie's daughter is faced with the awful choice of whether to seek help of one of her mother's rapists' in trying to save the life of her own daughter who is inflicted with an incurable disease.

The Crocodile Dreaming Series is based in Outback Australia. It starts with the first novel, *'The Visitor'* which tells the story of an English backpacker, Susan, who visits the Northern Territory and becomes captivated and in great danger from a man who loves crocodiles. The second book in the series, *The Victim*, follows the consequences of the first book based around the discovery of this man's remains. The third book, *The Void*, is about Susan's struggle to retain her sanity in jail while her family and friends desperately try to find out what really happened on that fateful day before it is too late. In *The Vanished* Susan vanishes and it tells the story of the search for her and four other lost girls whose passports were found in the possession of the man she killed. This final book in the series, *The inVisible* is the story of a girl who appears in a remote aboriginal community in North Queensland, without any memory except for a name. It tells how she rebuilds her life from an empty shell and how, as fragments of the past return, with them come dark shadows that threaten to overwhelm her.

The book, *Kaleidoscope*, is the story of the author's life in the Northern Territory: his childhood in an aboriginal community in remote Arnhem Land, in Australia's Northern Territory, of the people, danger and beauty of this place, and of its transformation over the last half century with the coming of aboriginal rights and the discovery or uranium. It also tells of his surviving an attack by a large crocodile and of his work over two decades in the outback of the NT.

Graham is planning a memoir about his family's connections with Ireland called *Memories Only Remain* and is compiling information for a book about the early NT cattle industry, its people and its stories.

Graham writes for the creative pleasure it brings him. He is particularly gratified each time an unknown person chooses to download and read something he has written and particularly to write a review - good or bad, as this gives him an insight into what readers enjoy and helps him make ongoing improvements to his writing.

In his other life Graham is a veterinarian who works in wildlife conservation and for rural landholders. He lived a large part of his life in the Northern Territory and his books reflect this experience.

More information about Graham and his books and writing is available from the following sites:

Graham Wilson – Australian Author on Facebook
Graham Wilson Author Profile on Goodreads, and Amazon
Graham Wilson's Publishing Web Page
    www.grahamwilsonbooks.com.au

If you want to contact Graham directly, please use the email:
    grahamwilsonbooks@gmail.com